Petr Kopl presents
a comic book adaptation
of short stories by
Sir Arthur Conan Doyle

**SHERLOCK HOLMES
THE FINAL PROBLEM**

Based on the detective stories
of Sir Arthur Conan Doyle

Illustrated by: Petr Kopl

Translated by: P&J Simpson
www.simpsontrans.com

Graphic design: Petr Kopl
www.petrkopl.cz

No part of this publication may
be reproduced or distributed
in any form or means,
or reproduced in a database or
in recorded form without
the express permission of the
publisher with the exception of
the publication of short
extracts from the text for review
purposes.

SHERLOCK HOLMES

THE ADVENTURE OF

THE FINAL PROBLEM

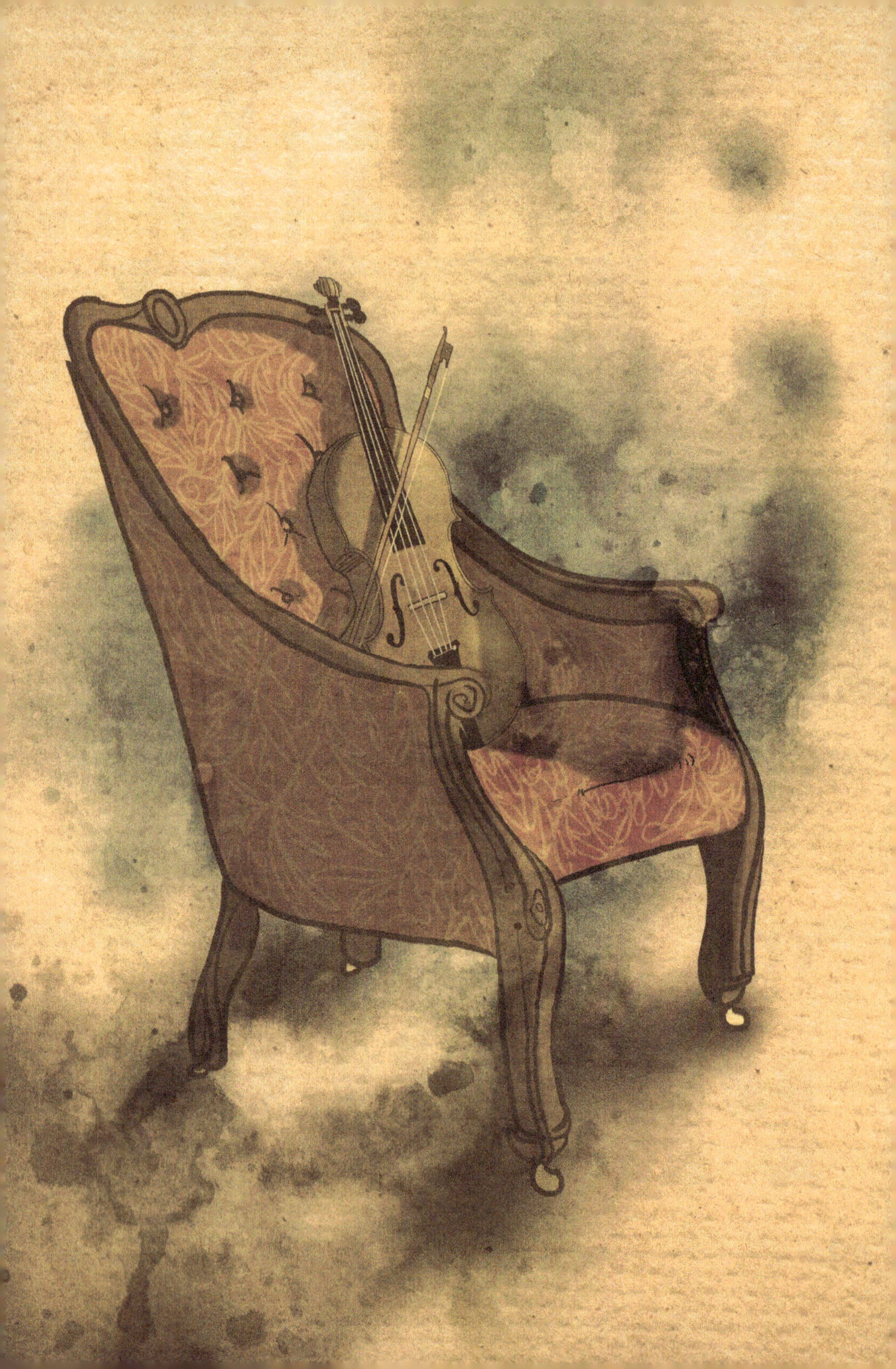

Preface

It has been a number of years since I first encountered comics. I cannot even remember the first one. Among these were Foglar's Fast arrows (Rychlé šípy), which was read with much excitement in old tattered copies of magazines such as Mladý hlasatel or Vpřed. It was much later that the ABC and Čtyřlístek magazines were added to the list. Over time, classic newspaper strips appeared from the USA containing favourite comic book characters such as Peanuts by Charles Schultze, which featured my favourite character, Snoopy. This all happened at some point in the 1970s, by which time I was already deeply engaged with Sherlock Holmes, supported by the various clippings sent to me by fellow Sherlockian and collector from Washington. From then on, my encounters with comics were infrequent, usually only if the genre was of particular interest to me.

However, two years ago, I bought two comics at once—two completely different concepts and adaptations of the same story, probably the best-known detective story in the world today—the Hound of the Baskervilles. In the first case, it was a completely traditional retelling and artistic rendering of the story. Sherlock Holmes himself did not fare too well. However the second comic was a revelation! It was then I discovered Petr Kopl (*1976) and his world of comics. He has already managed to amass an incredible volume of work. These include his excursions into the world of Anglo-Saxon literature, which I am greatly fond of. They have a slightly ironic and typically Czech approach to the topic and demonstrate his knowledge of the settings. Above all, I respect the work involved in transforming the story into a comic book adaptation.

After our first encounter through the Hound of the Baskervilles, I met Petr in person and learned many interesting things about his work. And I learned something new to me—in addition to the comic book adaptations, he also writes and illustrates comic strips. His favourite are the four-window ones, or more precisely in the language of the trade, the four-panel ones.

He has also mastered how to adapt

a literary model and is familiar with the Victorian period.

Unlike many other comic book authors, Petr creates his own script which he breaks down into the bubbles and creates his own drawings. Usually there tends to be two people involved in the creative process. He has fully mastered the art of drawing figures, which is essential for a good result. His approach to the task is highly responsible and he devotes a lot of time to preparation.

He slightly lifts the veil and allows his fans to have a peek at his workshop on his website, and still continues to seek new approaches. His "cartooning" on the following pages uses the watercolour technique, which I personally admire, and I hope that this difficult technique will also be appreciated by his readers.

In the short period of time since our friendship began, I have learned about comics and found that it is considered to be the ninth art; its origins are old–dating back to ancient Egypt.

You are now holding a comic book by Petr Kopl featuring various Sherlock Holmes cases. He artfully weaves several stories and includes many allusions to others—this time Czech literary works; even his Mucky Pup manages to find a way in.

Finally, I would like to wish you pleasant reading. I firmly believe that The Final Problem will not be the last Sherlock Holmes case from Petr's hand. I am looking forward to what he will surprise us with next.

Aleš Kolodrubec
President of the Czech Society of Sherlock Holmes
A member of many foreign Sherlock Holmes societies

Česká společnost Sherlocka Holmese
www.SherlockHolmes.cz

Introduction

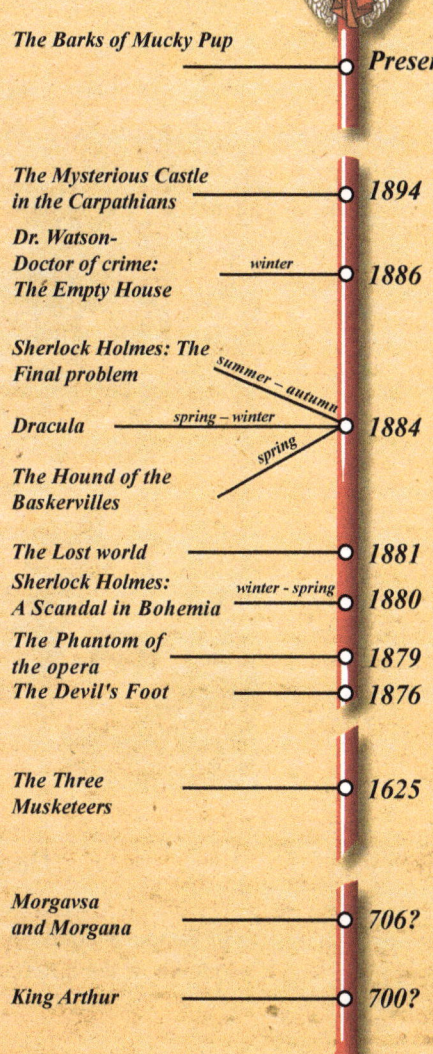

The Victoria Regina series is comprised of eight books:

The Phantom of the Opera
Sherlock Holmes: The Hound of the Baskervilles
Sherlock Holmes: The Final Problem
Sherlock Holmes: A Scandal in Bohemia
Sherlock Holmes: The Devil's Foot
The Lost World
Dracula
The Mysterious Castle in the Carpathians

Although these books can be read as stand-alone, the subtext of the stories intertwine, so it is recommended to read them all for better understanding. The good old Czech practice is that the books are not published in chronological order. Therefore we took the liberty of preparing a chronological timeline which shows the beginning of the plot of each comic book.The timeline also shows other comic books by Petr Kopl: The Barks of Mucky Pup, King Arthur, Morgavsa and Morgana and The Three Musketeers. These stories are not part of the series; however, the artefacts from these stories appear in the Victoria Regina (such as the auction in Dracula, a brief episode with a witch in The Mysterious Castle in the Carpathians, and the stained glass window at the Baskerville estate, etc.)

The Barks of Mucky Pup
Present
The Mysterious Castle in the Carpathians
1894
Dr. Watson- Doctor of crime: The Empty House
winter
1886
Sherlock Holmes: The Final problem
summer – autumn
Dracula
spring – winter
1884
spring
The Hound of the Baskervilles
The Lost world
1881
Sherlock Holmes: A Scandal in Bohemia
winter - spring
1880
The Phantom of the opera
1879
The Devil's Foot
1876
The Three Musketeers
1625
Morgavsa and Morgana
706?
King Arthur
700?

Dedication:

To Bohouš Dvořák and all the people who, as he does, know the difference between real friendship and true love… which is none…

Petr Kopl

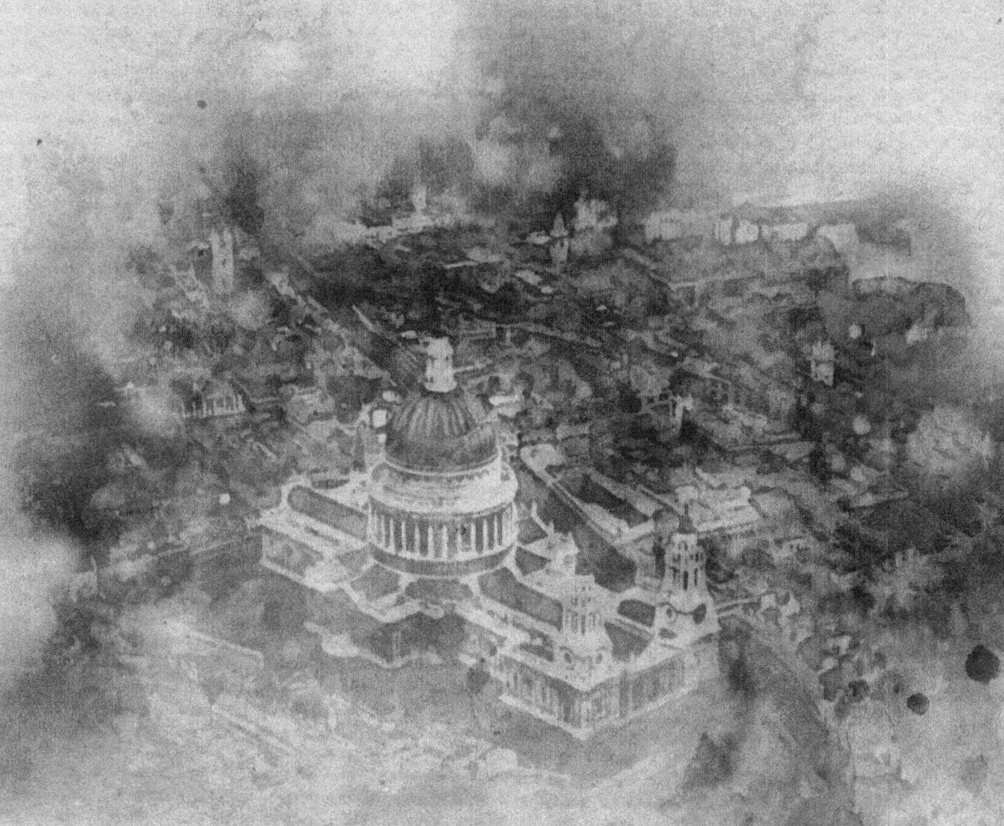

PROLOGUE

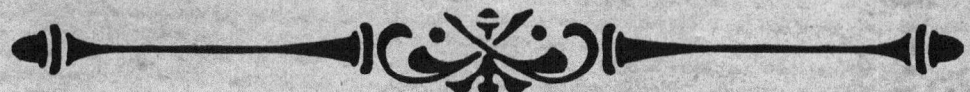

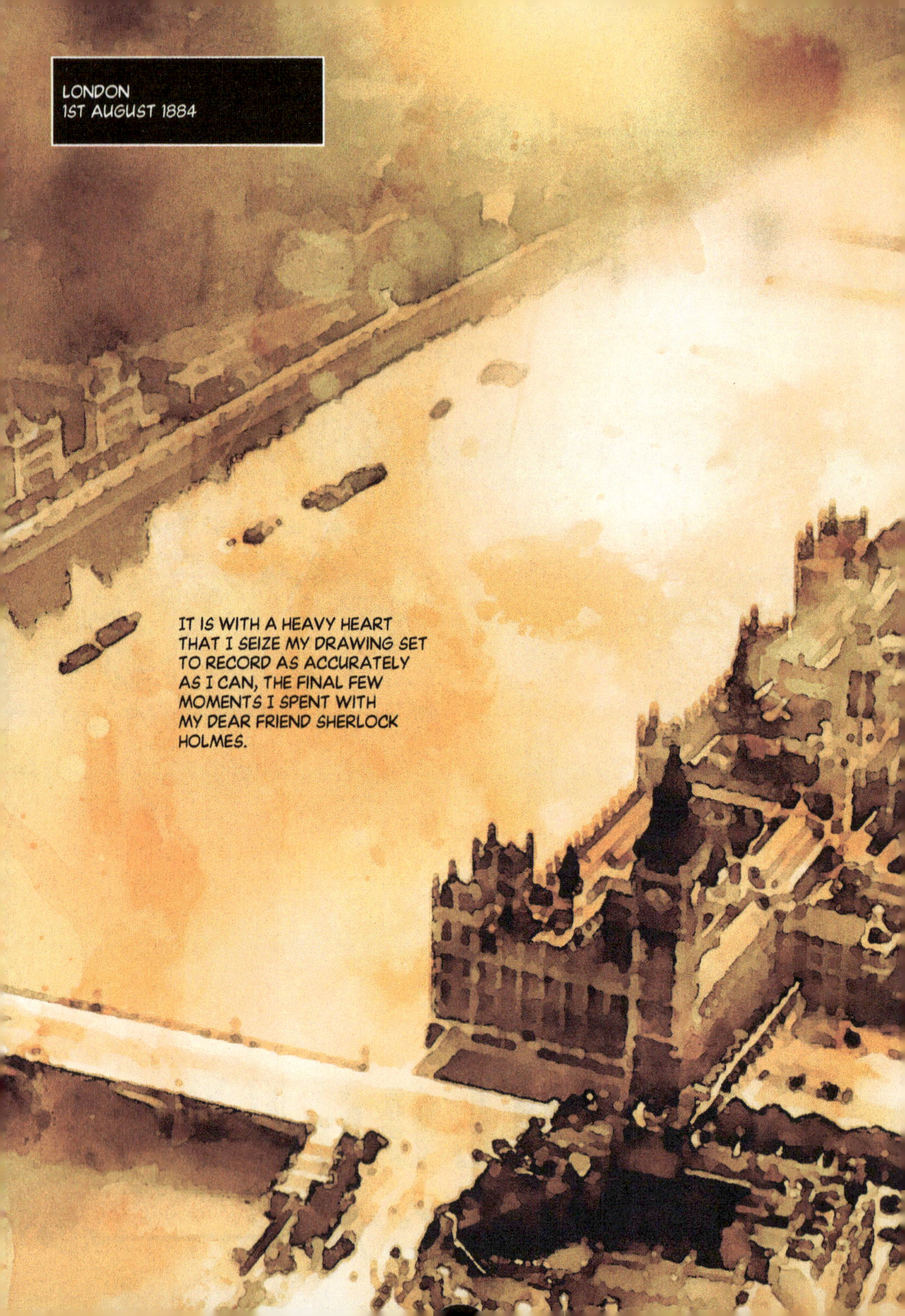
LONDON
1ST AUGUST 1884
IT IS WITH A HEAVY HEART THAT I SEIZE MY DRAWING SET TO RECORD AS ACCURATELY AS I CAN, THE FINAL FEW MOMENTS I SPENT WITH MY DEAR FRIEND SHERLOCK HOLMES.

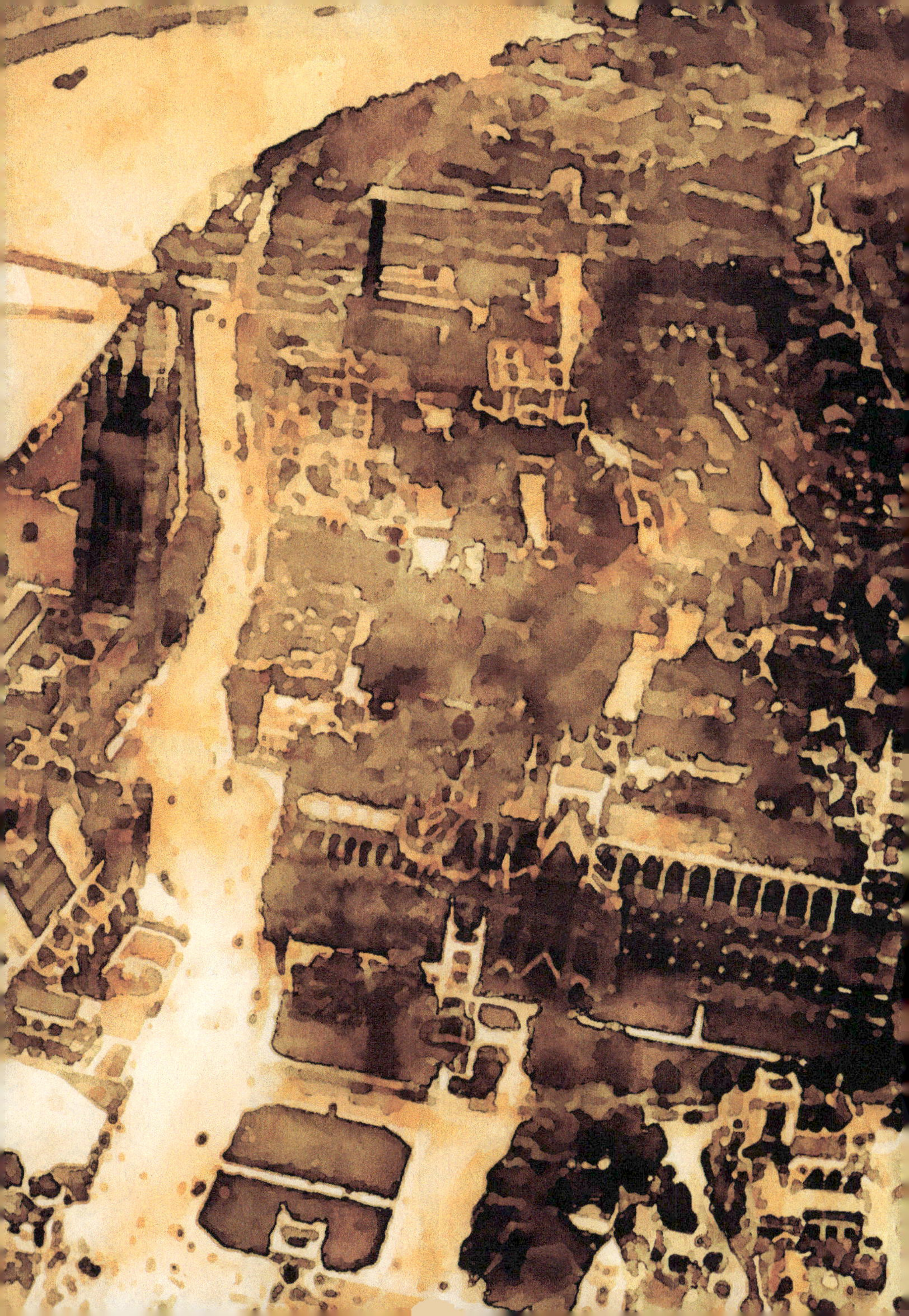

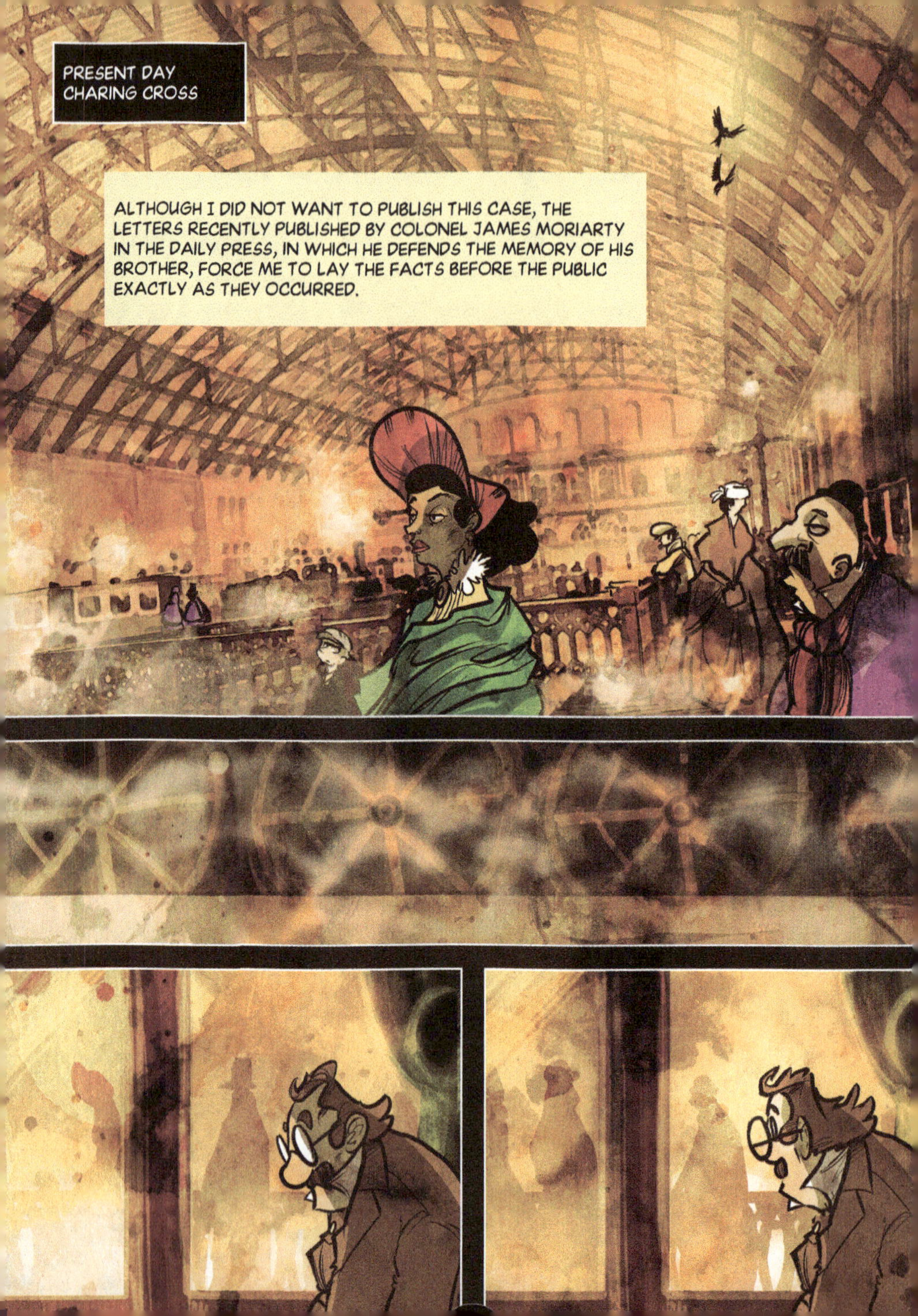
PRESENT DAY
CHARING CROSS
ALTHOUGH I DID NOT WANT TO PUBLISH THIS CASE, THE LETTERS RECENTLY PUBLISHED BY COLONEL JAMES MORIARTY IN THE DAILY PRESS, IN WHICH HE DEFENDS THE MEMORY OF HIS BROTHER, FORCE ME TO LAY THE FACTS BEFORE THE PUBLIC EXACTLY AS THEY OCCURRED.

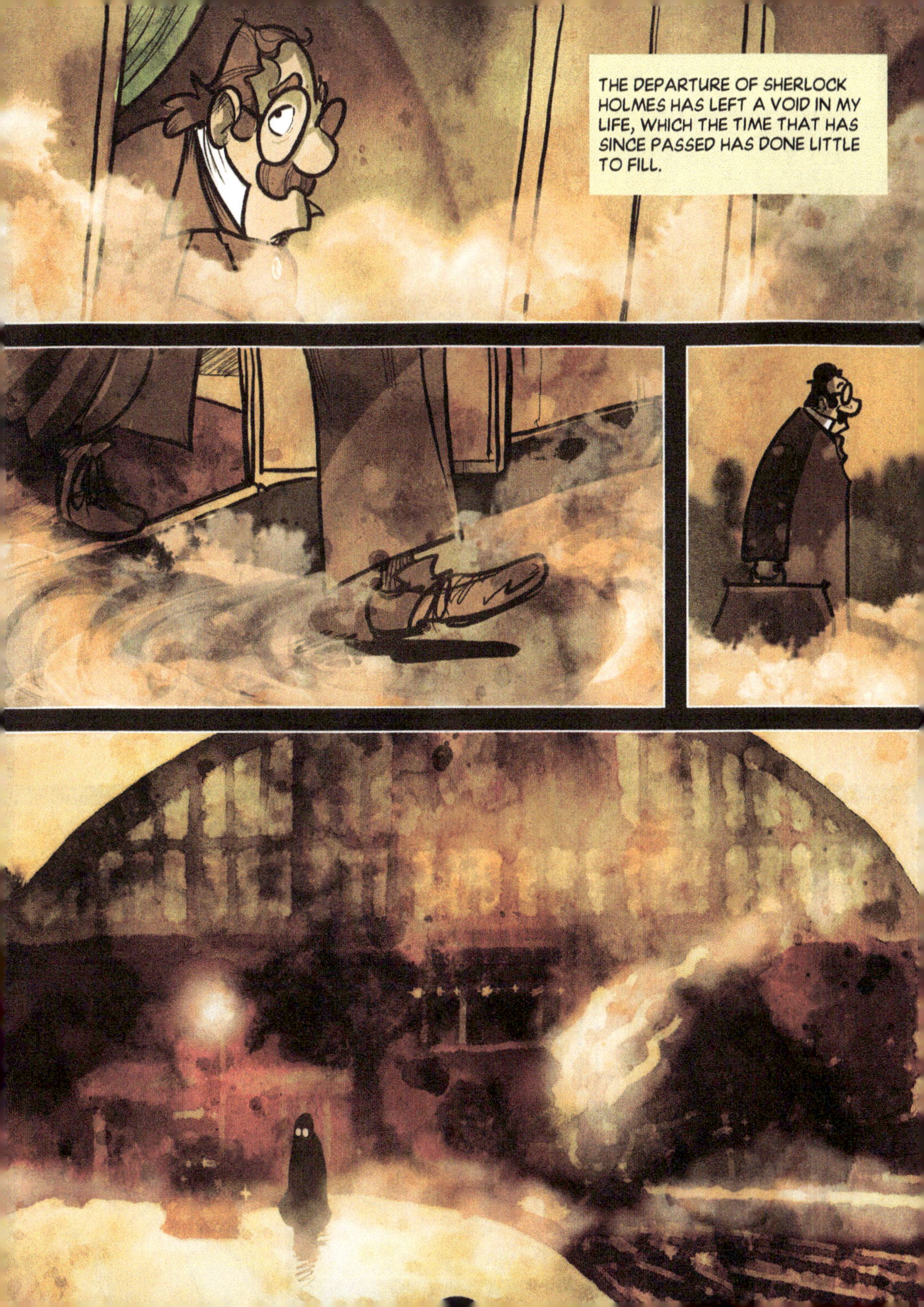
THE DEPARTURE OF SHERLOCK HOLMES HAS LEFT A VOID IN MY LIFE, WHICH THE TIME THAT HAS SINCE PASSED HAS DONE LITTLE TO FILL.

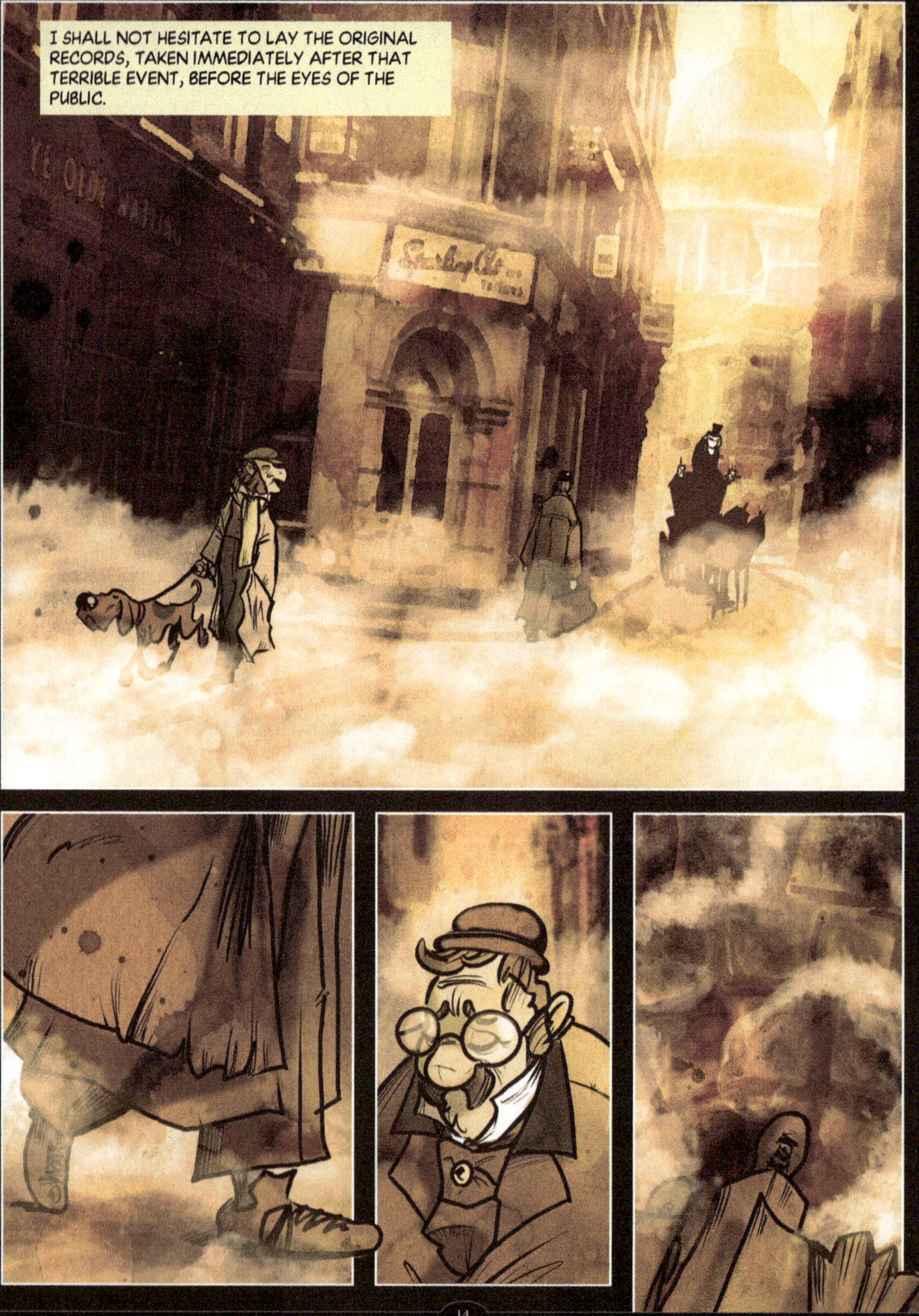
I SHALL NOT HESITATE TO LAY THE ORIGINAL RECORDS, TAKEN IMMEDIATELY AFTER THAT TERRIBLE EVENT, BEFORE THE EYES OF THE PUBLIC.

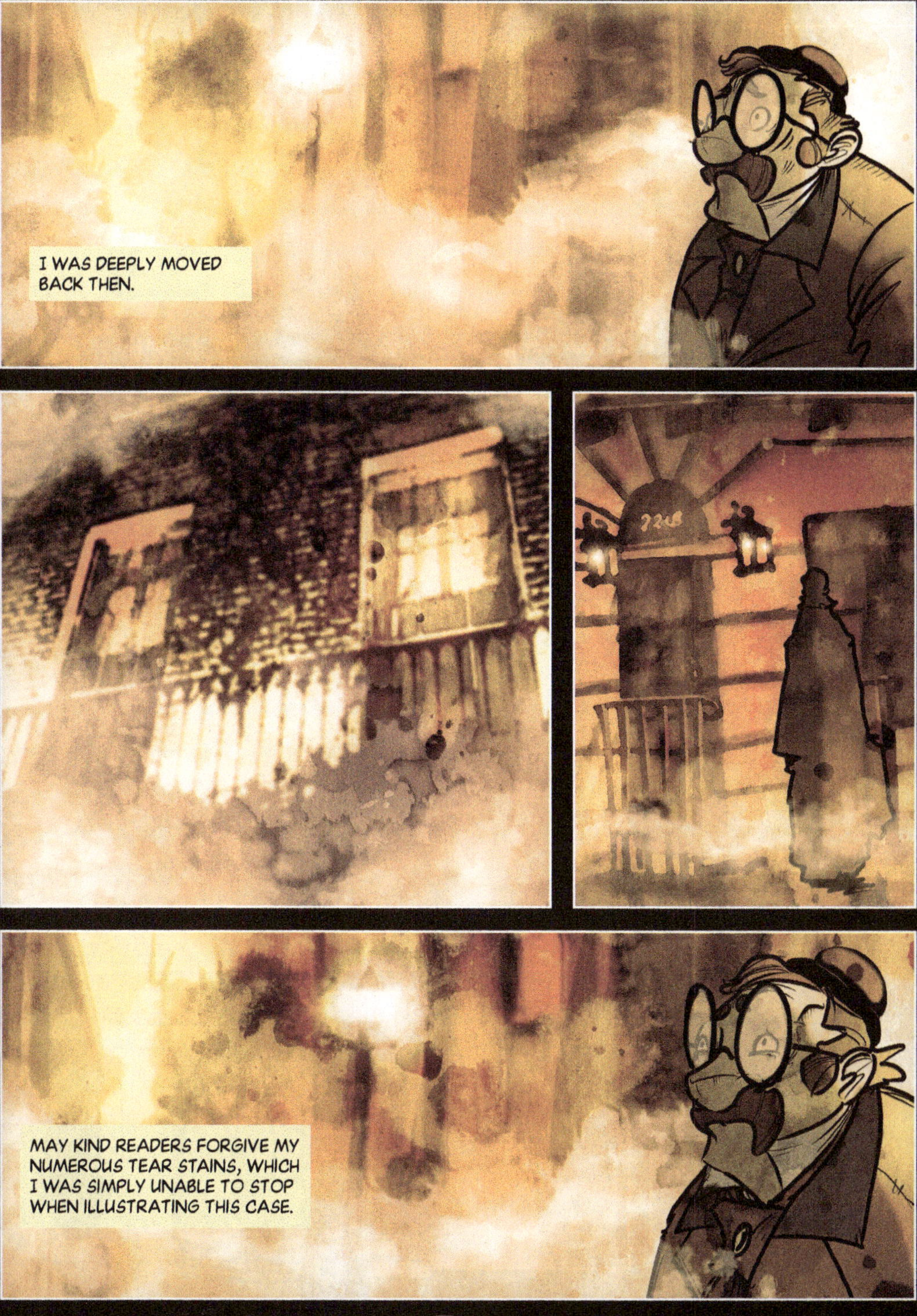
I WAS DEEPLY MOVED BACK THEN.
MAY KIND READERS FORGIVE MY NUMEROUS TEAR STAINS, WHICH I WAS SIMPLY UNABLE TO STOP WHEN ILLUSTRATING THIS CASE.

PRESENT DAY
221B BAKER STREET

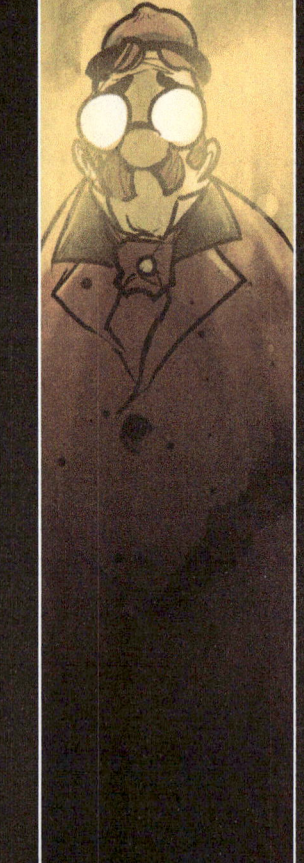

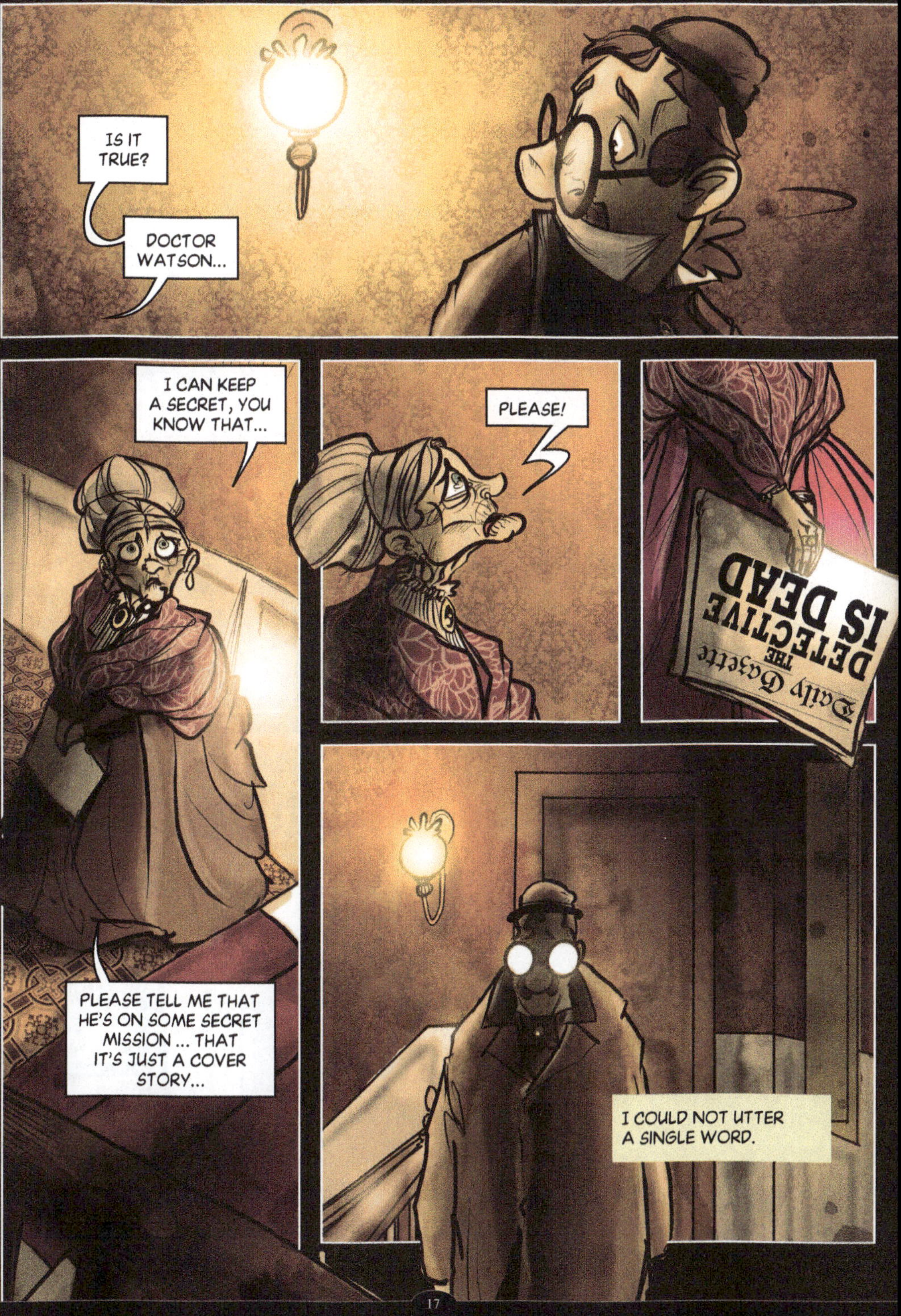
IS IT TRUE?
DOCTOR WATSON...
I CAN KEEP A SECRET, YOU KNOW THAT...
PLEASE TELL ME THAT HE'S ON SOME SECRET MISSION ... THAT IT'S JUST A COVER STORY...
PLEASE!
Daily Gazette
THE DETECTIVE IS DEAD
I COULD NOT UTTER A SINGLE WORD.

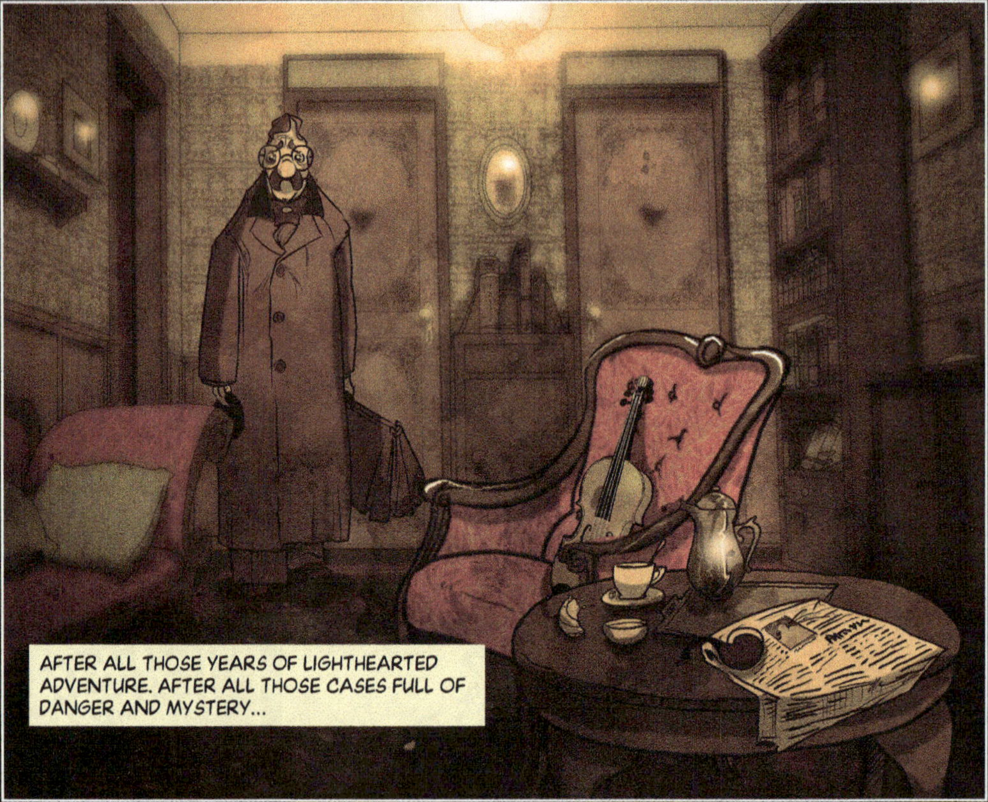
AFTER ALL THOSE YEARS OF LIGHTHEARTED ADVENTURE. AFTER ALL THOSE CASES FULL OF DANGER AND MYSTERY...

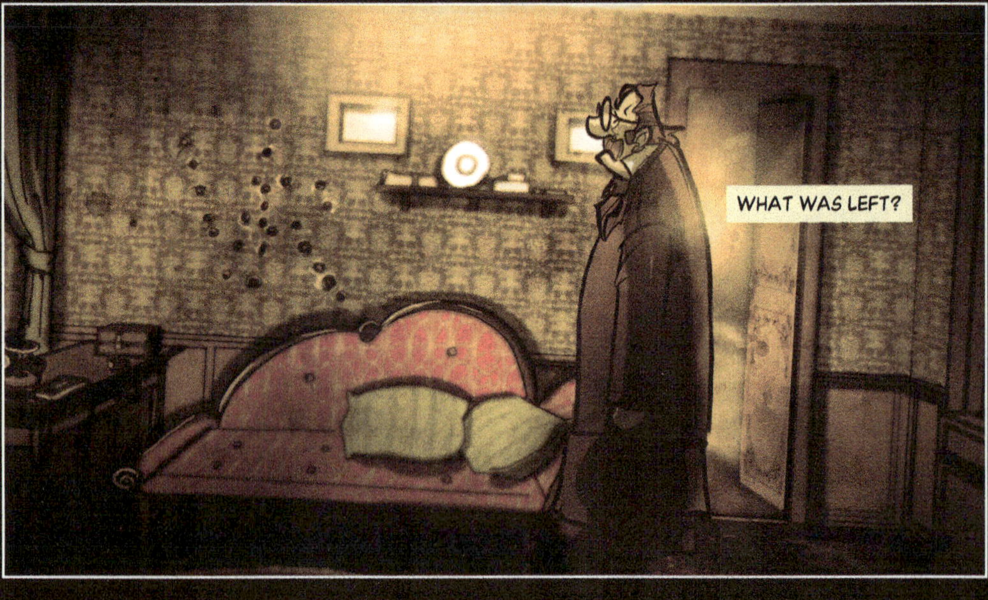
WHAT WAS LEFT?

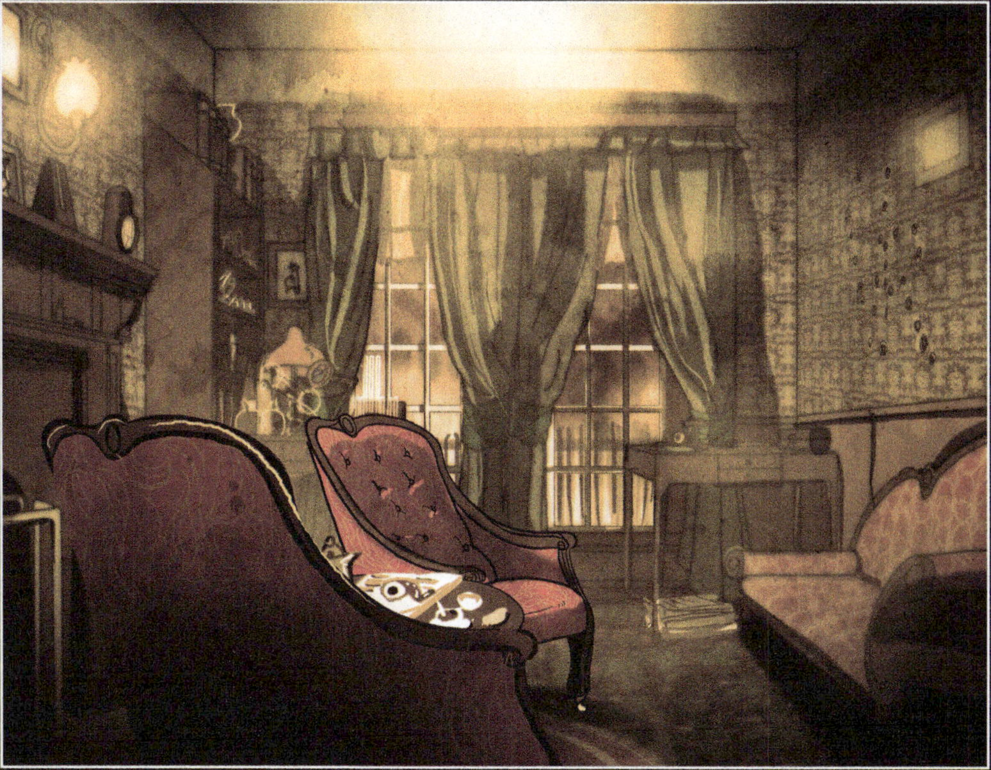

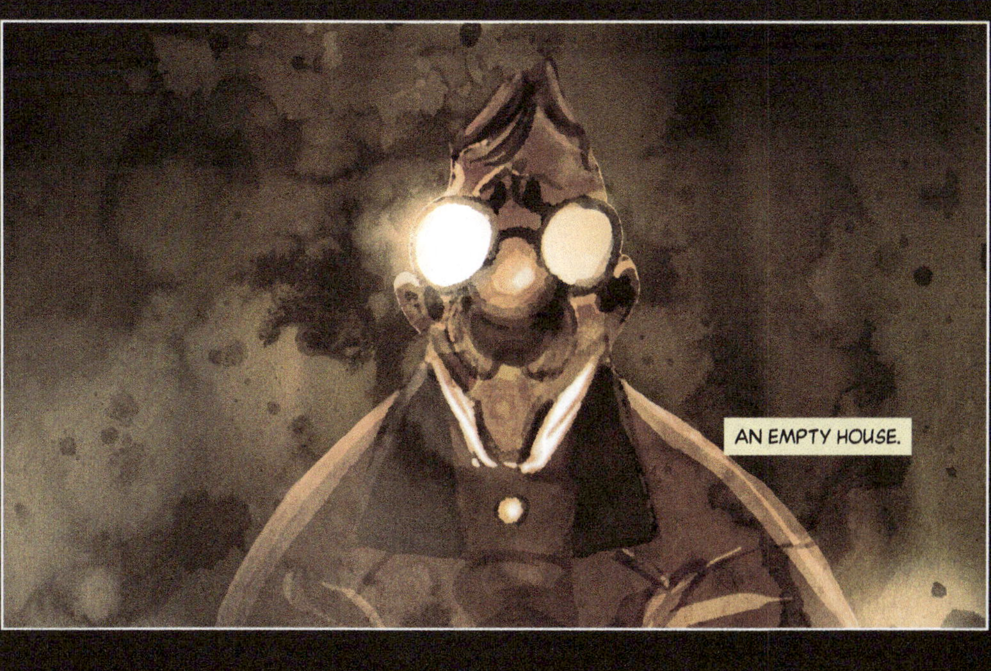
AN EMPTY HOUSE.

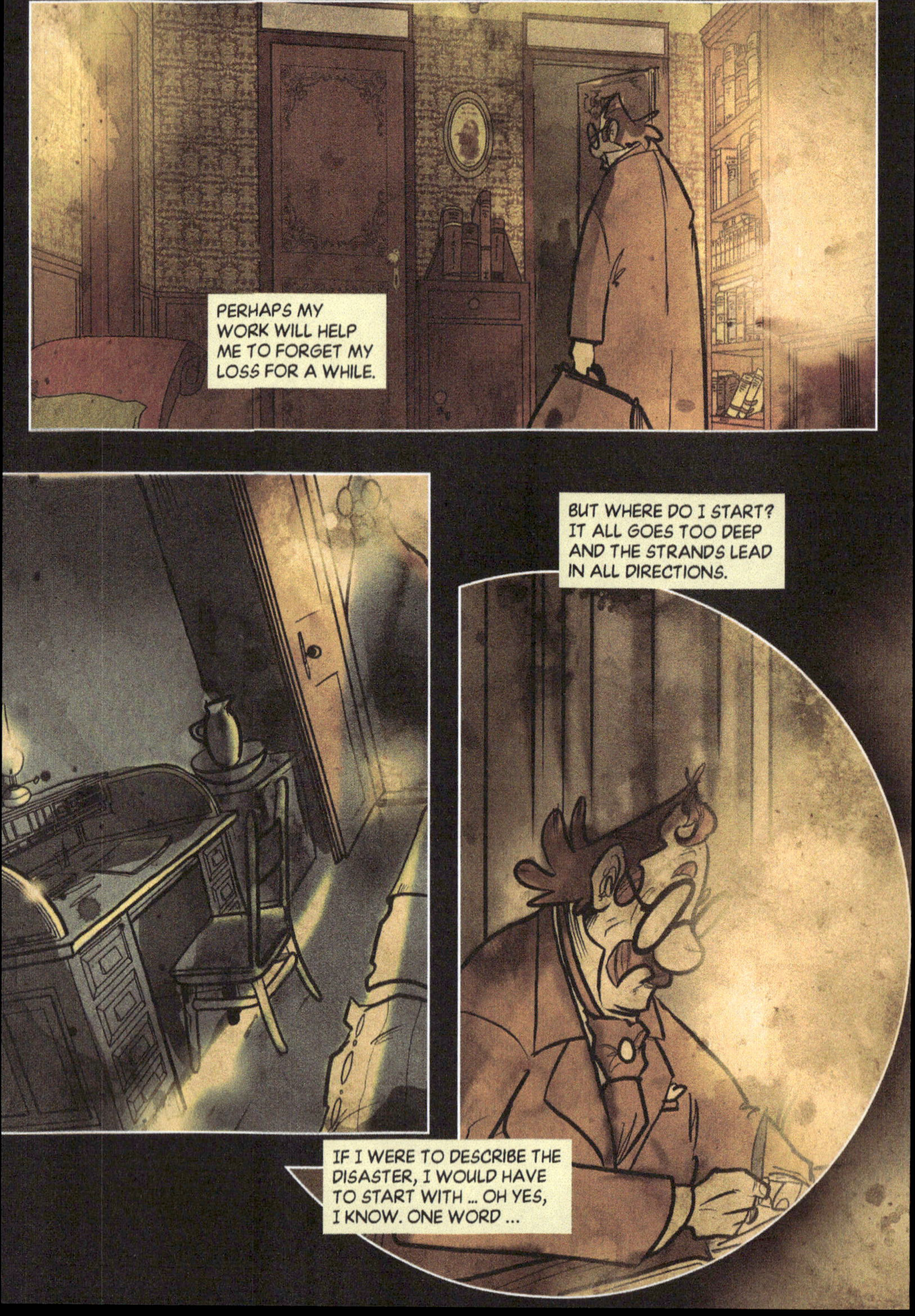
PERHAPS MY WORK WILL HELP ME TO FORGET MY LOSS FOR A WHILE.
BUT WHERE DO I START? IT ALL GOES TOO DEEP AND THE STRANDS LEAD IN ALL DIRECTIONS.
IF I WERE TO DESCRIBE THE DISASTER, I WOULD HAVE TO START WITH ... OH YES, I KNOW. ONE WORD ...

THE MASTER
BLACKMAILER

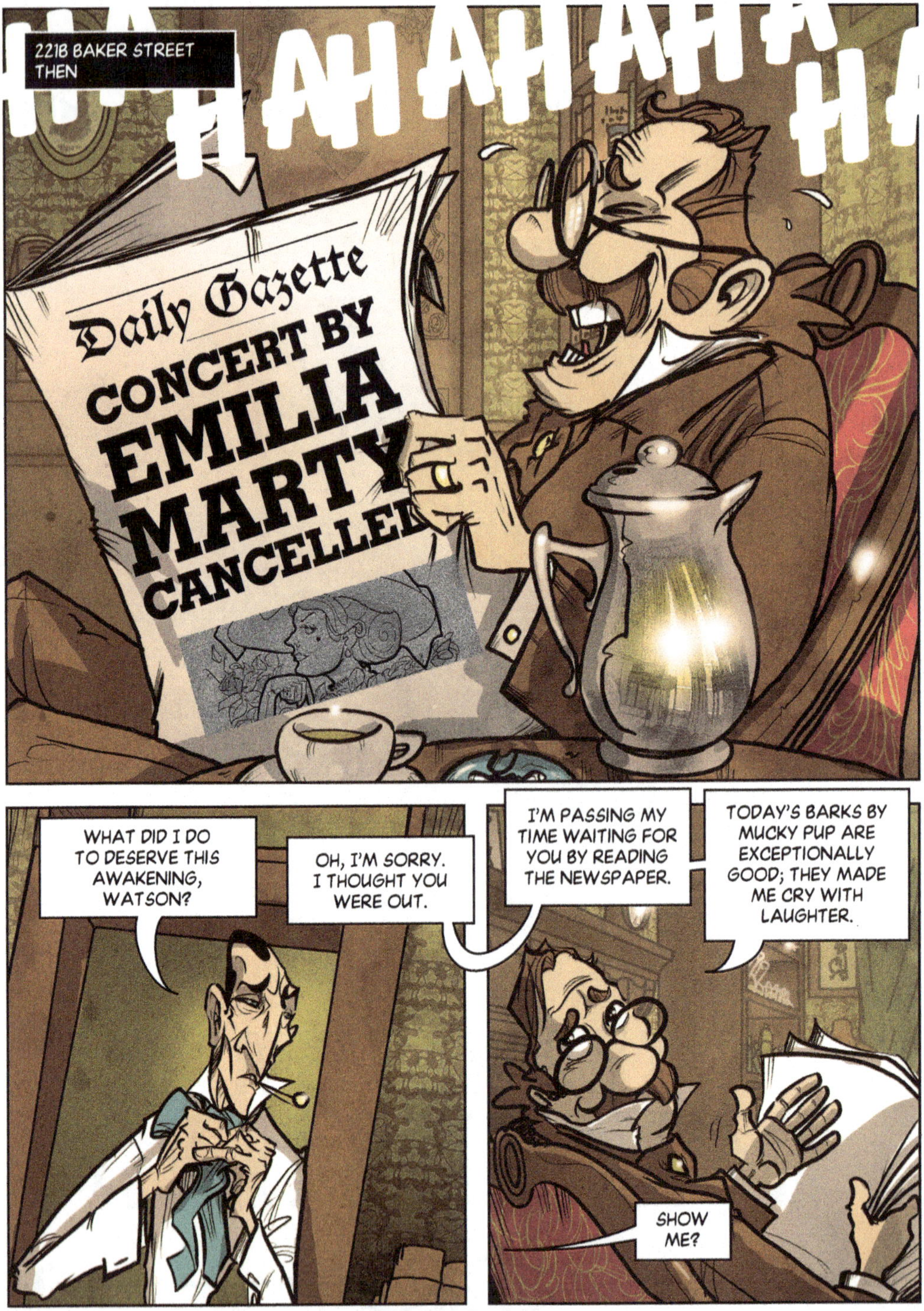
221B BAKER STREET
THEN
HA HA HA HA HA HA HA HA HA
Daily Gazette
CONCERT BY EMILIA MARTY CANCELLED
WHAT DID I DO TO DESERVE THIS AWAKENING, WATSON?
OH, I'M SORRY. I THOUGHT YOU WERE OUT.
I'M PASSING MY TIME WAITING FOR YOU BY READING THE NEWSPAPER.
TODAY'S BARKS BY MUCKY PUP ARE EXCEPTIONALLY GOOD; THEY MADE ME CRY WITH LAUGHTER.
SHOW ME?

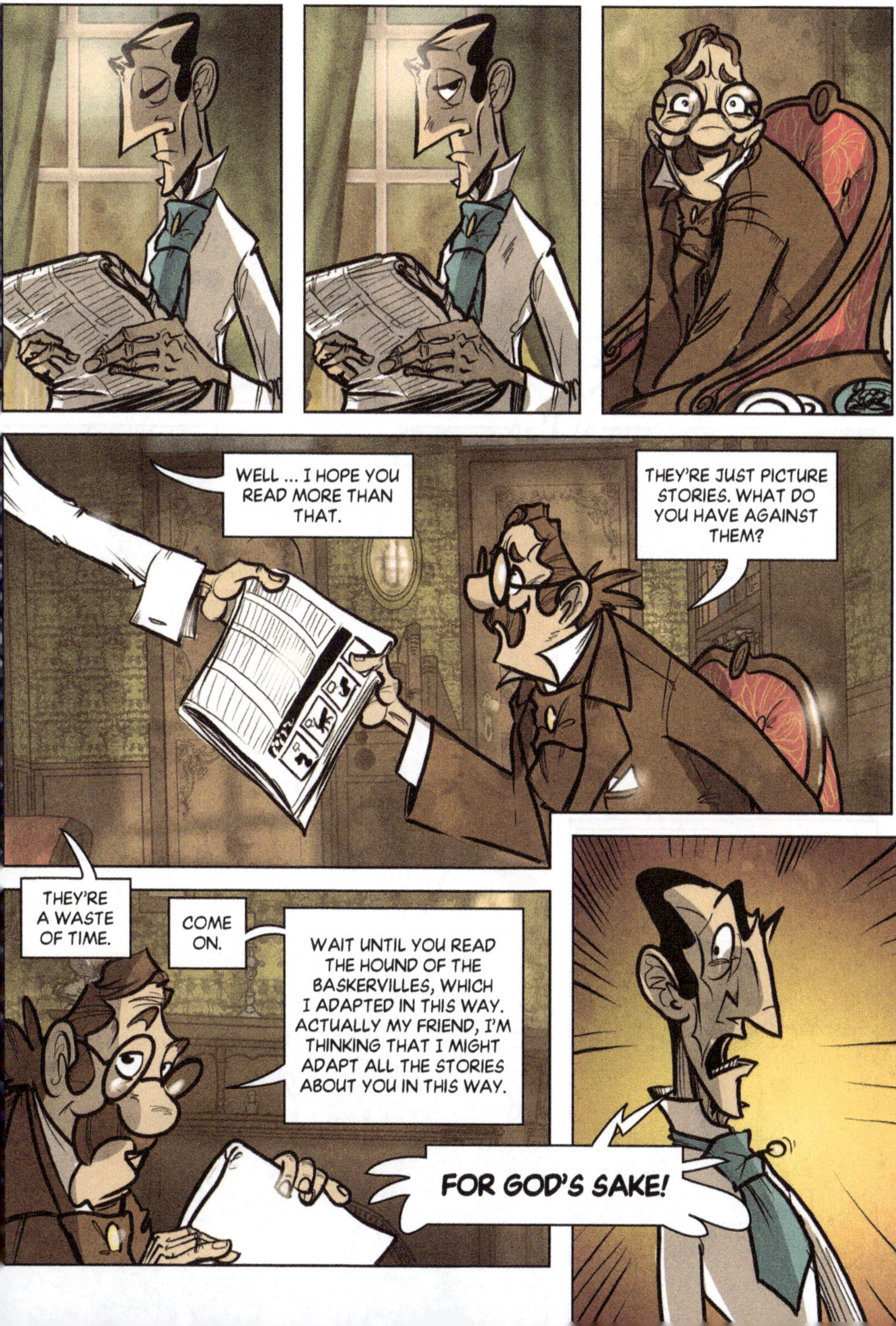
WELL ... I HOPE YOU READ MORE THAN THAT.
THEY'RE JUST PICTURE STORIES. WHAT DO YOU HAVE AGAINST THEM?
THEY'RE A WASTE OF TIME.
COME ON.
WAIT UNTIL YOU READ THE HOUND OF THE BASKERVILLES, WHICH I ADAPTED IN THIS WAY. ACTUALLY MY FRIEND, I'M THINKING THAT I MIGHT ADAPT ALL THE STORIES ABOUT YOU IN THIS WAY.
FOR GOD'S SAKE!

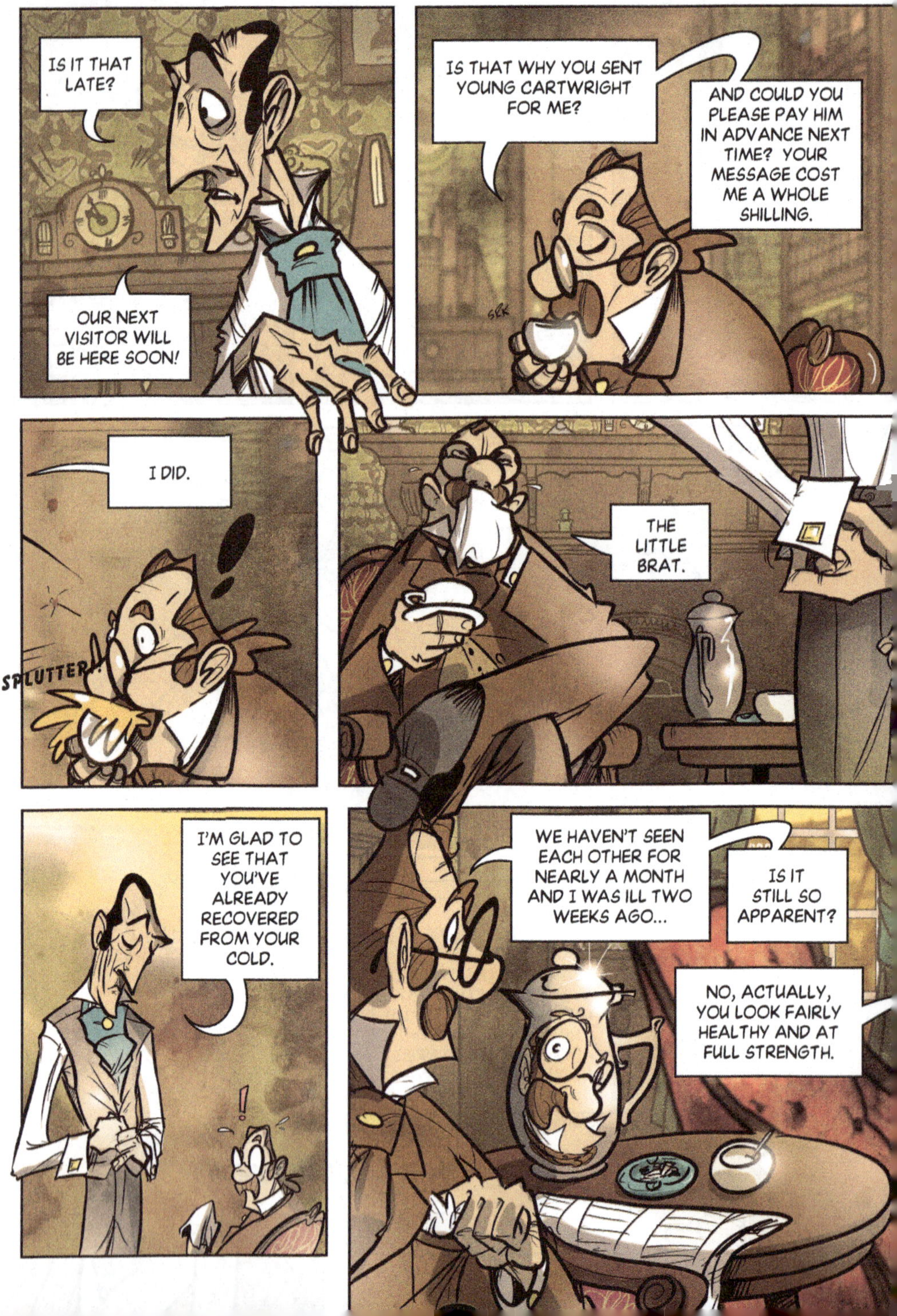
IS IT THAT LATE?
OUR NEXT VISITOR WILL BE HERE SOON!
IS THAT WHY YOU SENT YOUNG CARTWRIGHT FOR ME?
AND COULD YOU PLEASE PAY HIM IN ADVANCE NEXT TIME? YOUR MESSAGE COST ME A WHOLE SHILLING.
I DID.
SPLUTTER!
THE LITTLE BRAT.
I'M GLAD TO SEE THAT YOU'VE ALREADY RECOVERED FROM YOUR COLD.
WE HAVEN'T SEEN EACH OTHER FOR NEARLY A MONTH AND I WAS ILL TWO WEEKS AGO...
IS IT STILL SO APPARENT?
NO, ACTUALLY, YOU LOOK FAIRLY HEALTHY AND AT FULL STRENGTH.

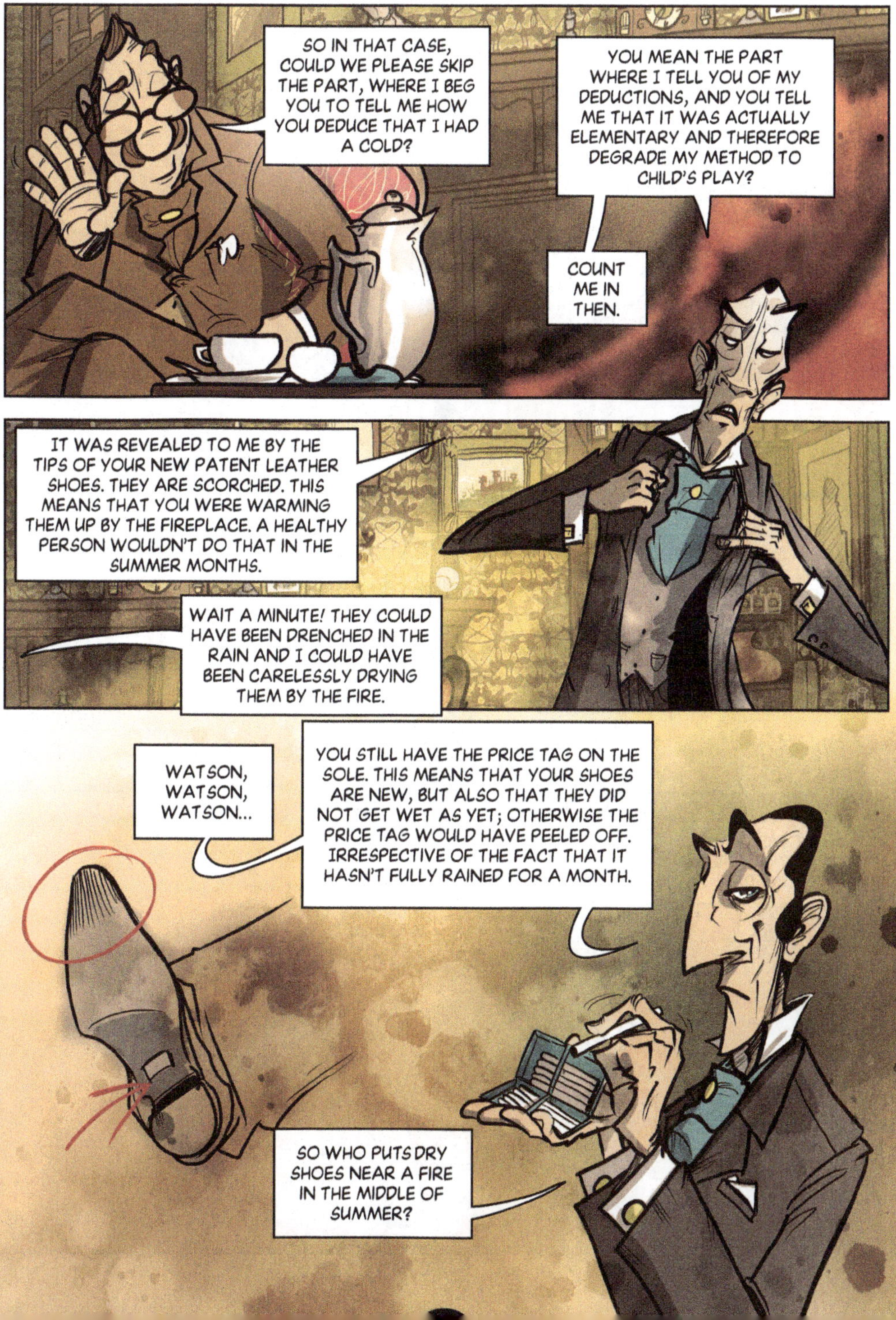
SO IN THAT CASE, COULD WE PLEASE SKIP THE PART, WHERE I BEG YOU TO TELL ME HOW YOU DEDUCE THAT I HAD A COLD?
YOU MEAN THE PART WHERE I TELL YOU OF MY DEDUCTIONS, AND YOU TELL ME THAT IT WAS ACTUALLY ELEMENTARY AND THEREFORE DEGRADE MY METHOD TO CHILD'S PLAY?
COUNT ME IN THEN.
IT WAS REVEALED TO ME BY THE TIPS OF YOUR NEW PATENT LEATHER SHOES. THEY ARE SCORCHED. THIS MEANS THAT YOU WERE WARMING THEM UP BY THE FIREPLACE. A HEALTHY PERSON WOULDN'T DO THAT IN THE SUMMER MONTHS.
WAIT A MINUTE! THEY COULD HAVE BEEN DRENCHED IN THE RAIN AND I COULD HAVE BEEN CARELESSLY DRYING THEM BY THE FIRE.
WATSON, WATSON, WATSON...
YOU STILL HAVE THE PRICE TAG ON THE SOLE. THIS MEANS THAT YOUR SHOES ARE NEW, BUT ALSO THAT THEY DID NOT GET WET AS YET; OTHERWISE THE PRICE TAG WOULD HAVE PEELED OFF. IRRESPECTIVE OF THE FACT THAT IT HASN'T FULLY RAINED FOR A MONTH.
SO WHO PUTS DRY SHOES NEAR A FIRE IN THE MIDDLE OF SUMMER?

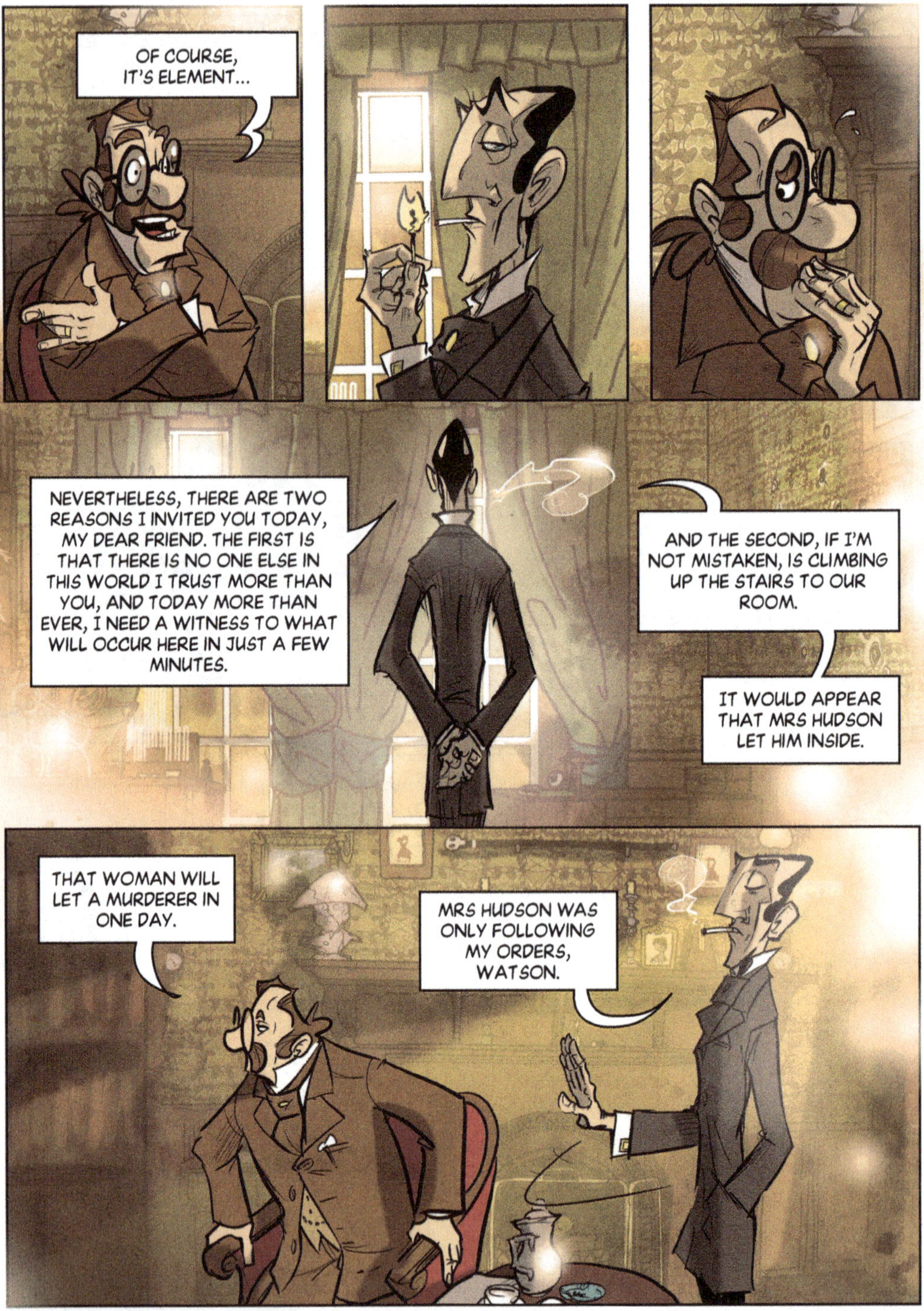
OF COURSE, IT'S ELEMENT...
NEVERTHELESS, THERE ARE TWO REASONS I INVITED YOU TODAY, MY DEAR FRIEND. THE FIRST IS THAT THERE IS NO ONE ELSE IN THIS WORLD I TRUST MORE THAN YOU, AND TODAY MORE THAN EVER, I NEED A WITNESS TO WHAT WILL OCCUR HERE IN JUST A FEW MINUTES.
AND THE SECOND, IF I'M NOT MISTAKEN, IS CLIMBING UP THE STAIRS TO OUR ROOM.
IT WOULD APPEAR THAT MRS HUDSON LET HIM INSIDE.
THAT WOMAN WILL LET A MURDERER IN ONE DAY.
MRS HUDSON WAS ONLY FOLLOWING MY ORDERS, WATSON.

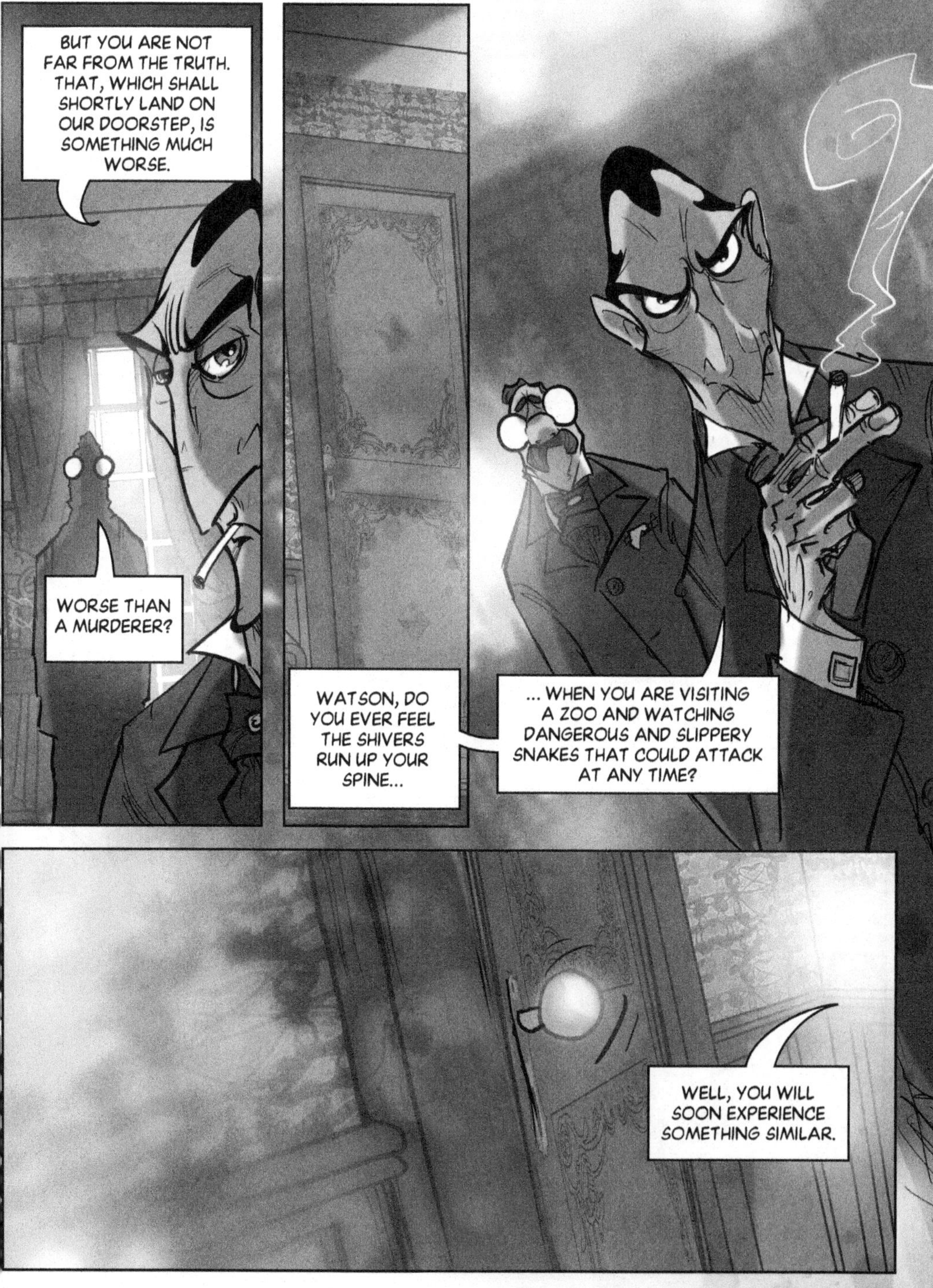
BUT YOU ARE NOT FAR FROM THE TRUTH. THAT, WHICH SHALL SHORTLY LAND ON OUR DOORSTEP, IS SOMETHING MUCH WORSE.
WORSE THAN A MURDERER?
WATSON, DO YOU EVER FEEL THE SHIVERS RUN UP YOUR SPINE...
... WHEN YOU ARE VISITING A ZOO AND WATCHING DANGEROUS AND SLIPPERY SNAKES THAT COULD ATTACK AT ANY TIME?
WELL, YOU WILL SOON EXPERIENCE SOMETHING SIMILAR.

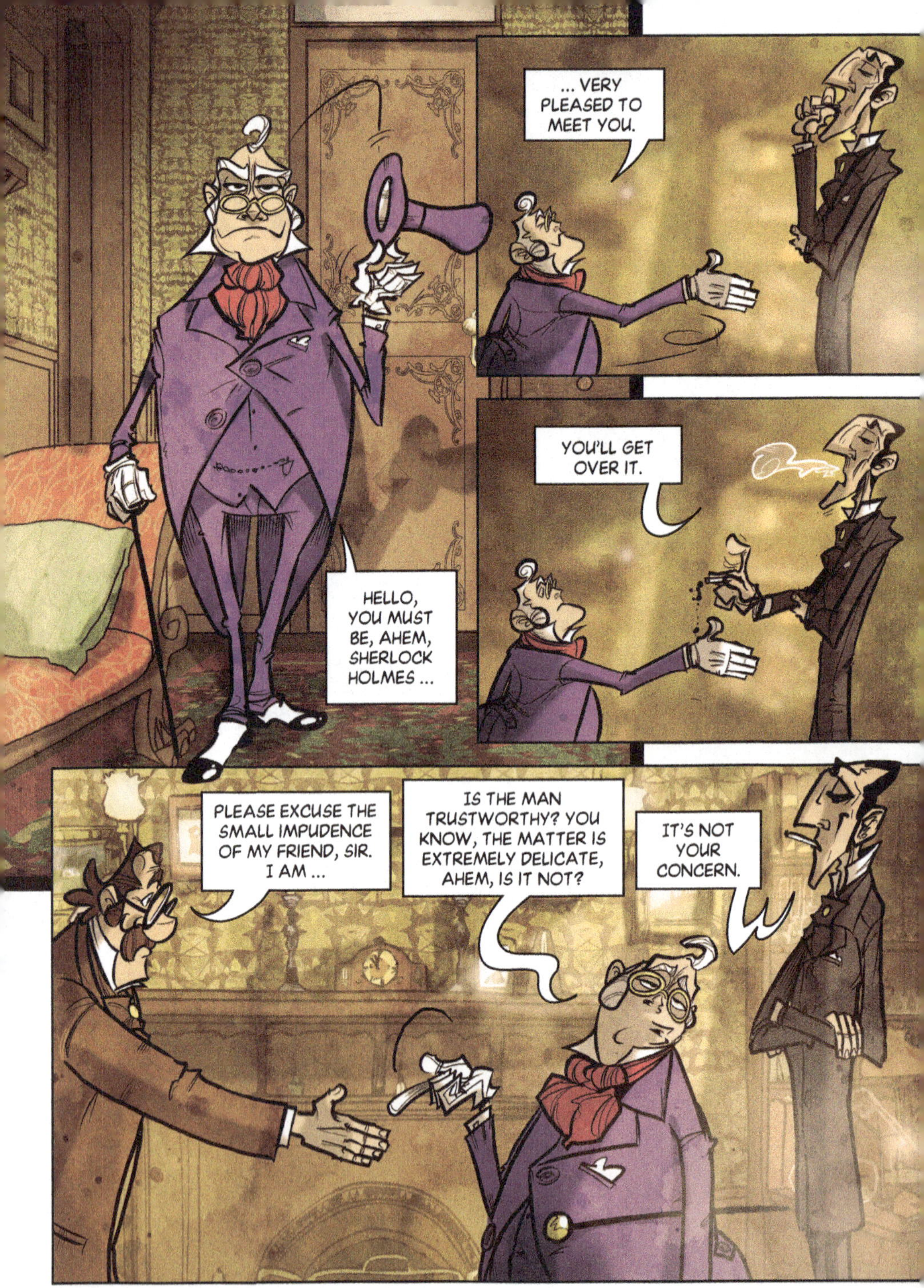
HELLO, YOU MUST BE, AHEM, SHERLOCK HOLMES ...
... VERY PLEASED TO MEET YOU.
YOU'LL GET OVER IT.
PLEASE EXCUSE THE SMALL IMPUDENCE OF MY FRIEND, SIR. I AM ...
IS THE MAN TRUSTWORTHY? YOU KNOW, THE MATTER IS EXTREMELY DELICATE, AHEM, IS IT NOT?
IT'S NOT YOUR CONCERN.

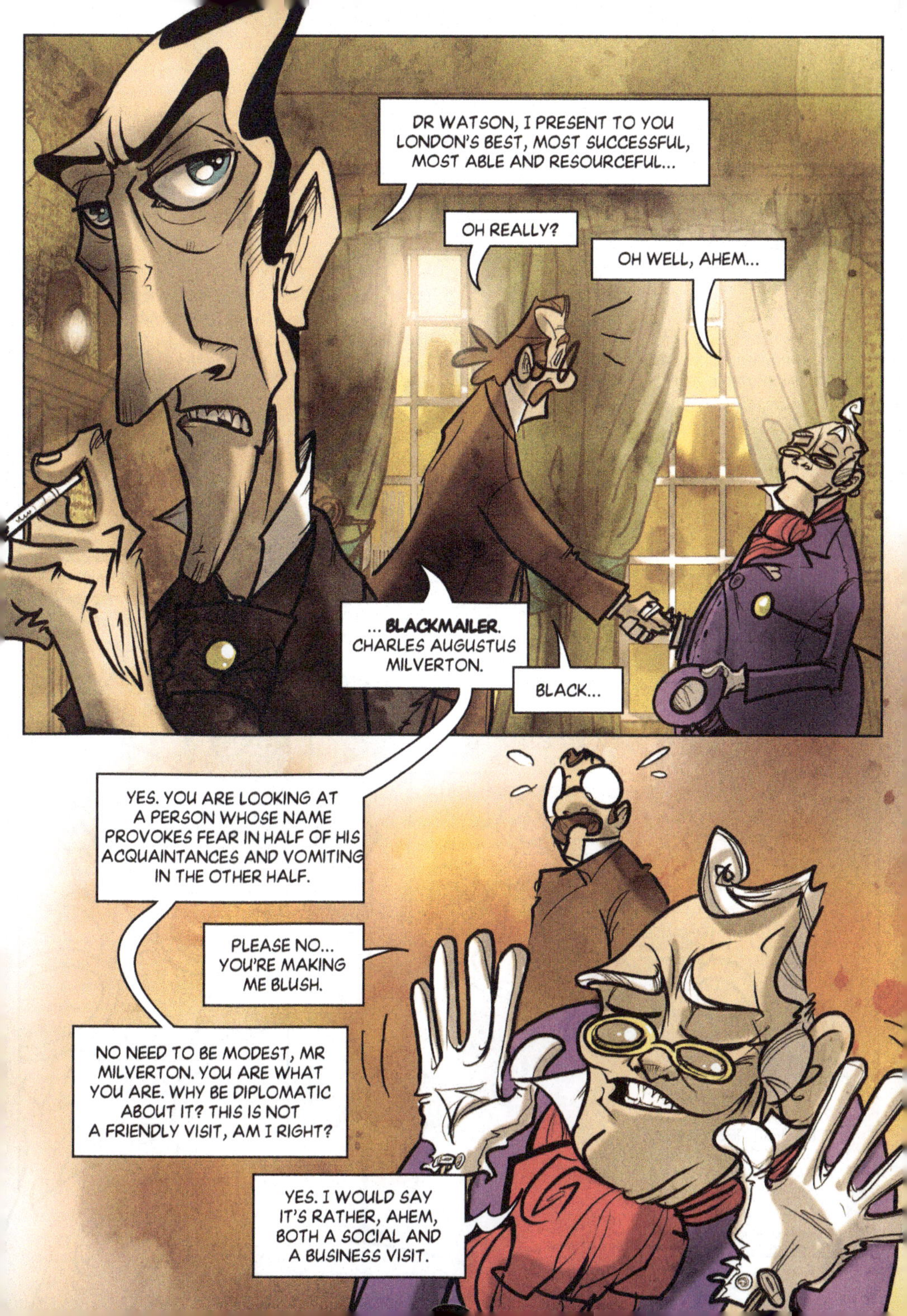
DR WATSON, I PRESENT TO YOU LONDON'S BEST, MOST SUCCESSFUL, MOST ABLE AND RESOURCEFUL...
OH REALLY?
OH WELL, AHEM...
... BLACKMAILER. CHARLES AUGUSTUS MILVERTON.
BLACK...
YES. YOU ARE LOOKING AT A PERSON WHOSE NAME PROVOKES FEAR IN HALF OF HIS ACQUAINTANCES AND VOMITING IN THE OTHER HALF.
PLEASE NO... YOU'RE MAKING ME BLUSH.
NO NEED TO BE MODEST, MR MILVERTON. YOU ARE WHAT YOU ARE. WHY BE DIPLOMATIC ABOUT IT? THIS IS NOT A FRIENDLY VISIT, AM I RIGHT?
YES. I WOULD SAY IT'S RATHER, AHEM, BOTH A SOCIAL AND A BUSINESS VISIT.

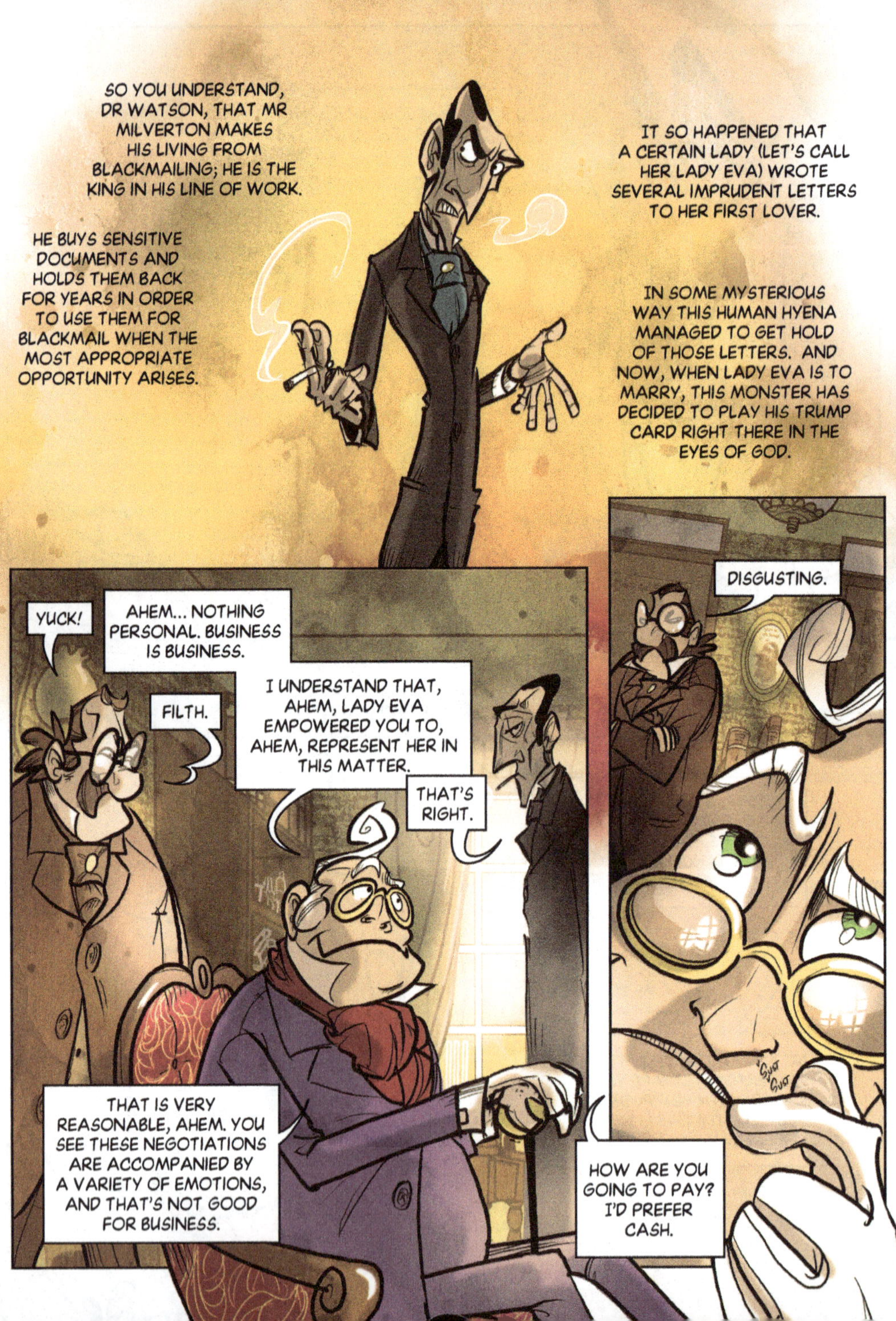
SO YOU UNDERSTAND, DR WATSON, THAT MR MILVERTON MAKES HIS LIVING FROM BLACKMAILING; HE IS THE KING IN HIS LINE OF WORK.
HE BUYS SENSITIVE DOCUMENTS AND HOLDS THEM BACK FOR YEARS IN ORDER TO USE THEM FOR BLACKMAIL WHEN THE MOST APPROPRIATE OPPORTUNITY ARISES.
IT SO HAPPENED THAT A CERTAIN LADY (LET'S CALL HER LADY EVA) WROTE SEVERAL IMPRUDENT LETTERS TO HER FIRST LOVER.
IN SOME MYSTERIOUS WAY THIS HUMAN HYENA MANAGED TO GET HOLD OF THOSE LETTERS. AND NOW, WHEN LADY EVA IS TO MARRY, THIS MONSTER HAS DECIDED TO PLAY HIS TRUMP CARD RIGHT THERE IN THE EYES OF GOD.
YUCK!
AHEM... NOTHING PERSONAL. BUSINESS IS BUSINESS.
FILTH.
I UNDERSTAND THAT, AHEM, LADY EVA EMPOWERED YOU TO, AHEM, REPRESENT HER IN THIS MATTER.
THAT'S RIGHT.
THAT IS VERY REASONABLE, AHEM. YOU SEE THESE NEGOTIATIONS ARE ACCOMPANIED BY A VARIETY OF EMOTIONS, AND THAT'S NOT GOOD FOR BUSINESS.
DISGUSTING.
HOW ARE YOU GOING TO PAY? I'D PREFER CASH.

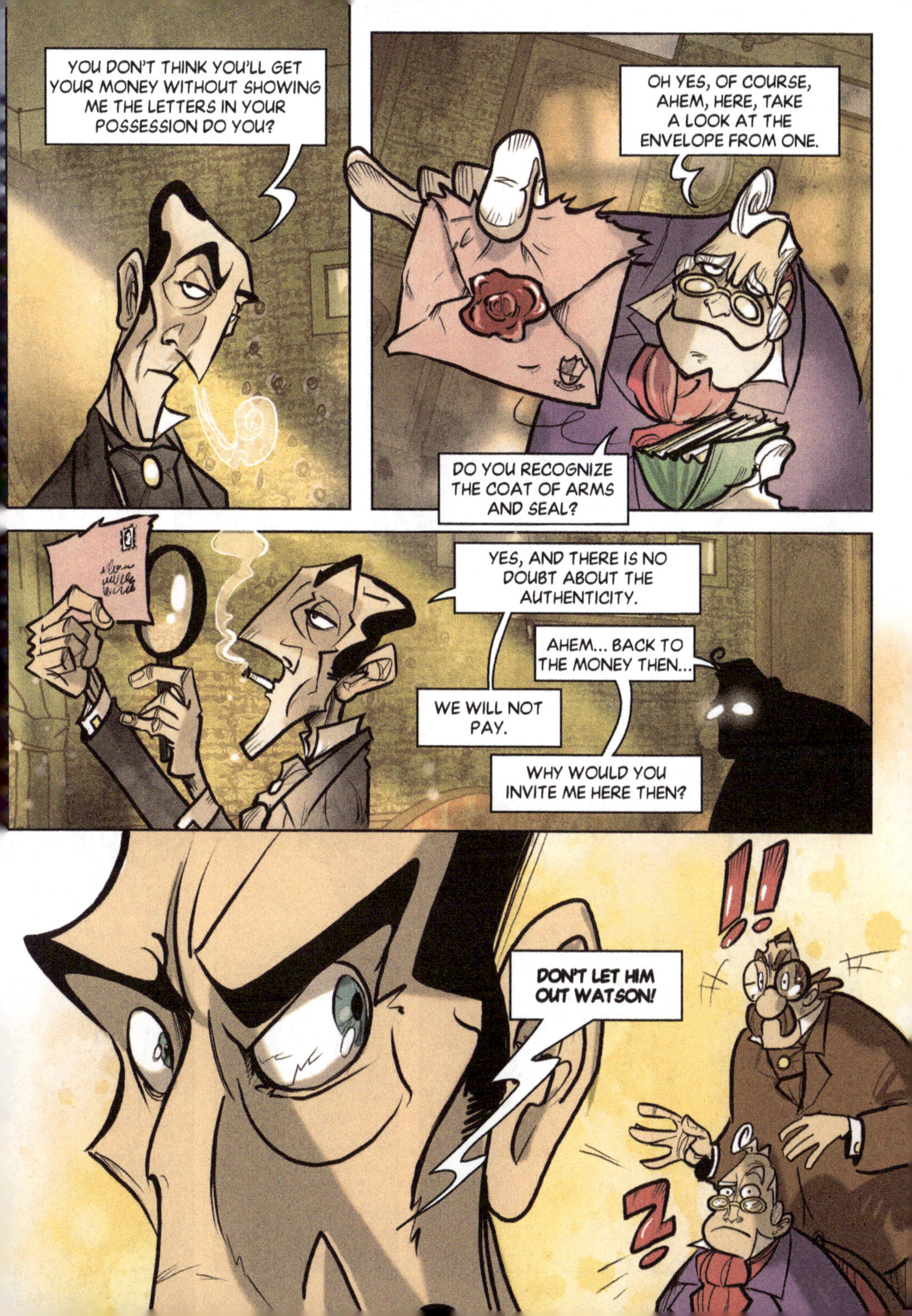
YOU DON'T THINK YOU'LL GET YOUR MONEY WITHOUT SHOWING ME THE LETTERS IN YOUR POSSESSION DO YOU?
OH YES, OF COURSE, AHEM, HERE, TAKE A LOOK AT THE ENVELOPE FROM ONE.
DO YOU RECOGNIZE THE COAT OF ARMS AND SEAL?
YES, AND THERE IS NO DOUBT ABOUT THE AUTHENTICITY.
AHEM... BACK TO THE MONEY THEN...
WE WILL NOT PAY.
WHY WOULD YOU INVITE ME HERE THEN?
!!
DON'T LET HIM OUT WATSON!

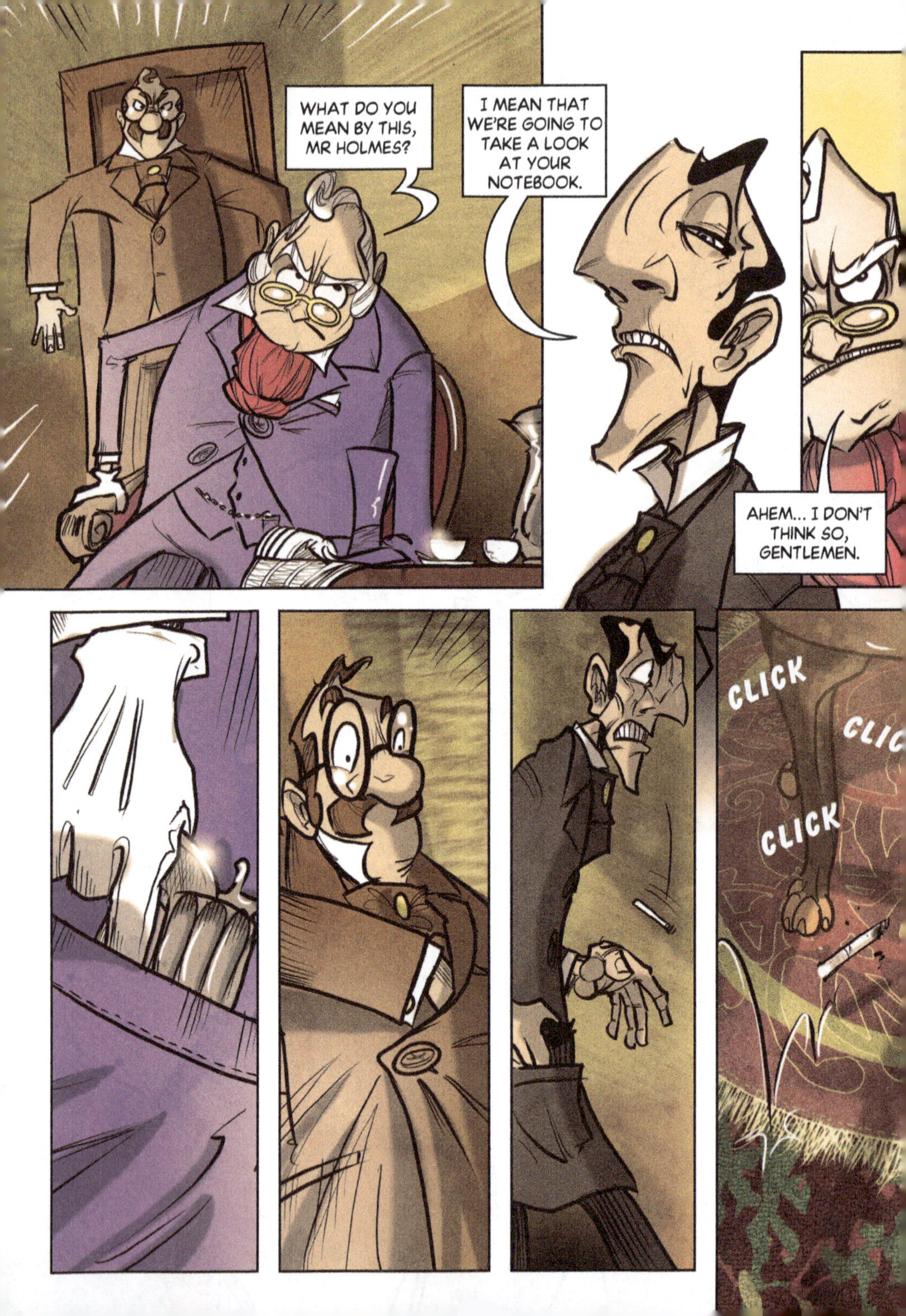
WHAT DO YOU MEAN BY THIS, MR HOLMES?
I MEAN THAT WE'RE GOING TO TAKE A LOOK AT YOUR NOTEBOOK.
AHEM... I DON'T THINK SO, GENTLEMEN.
CLICK
CLIC
CLICK

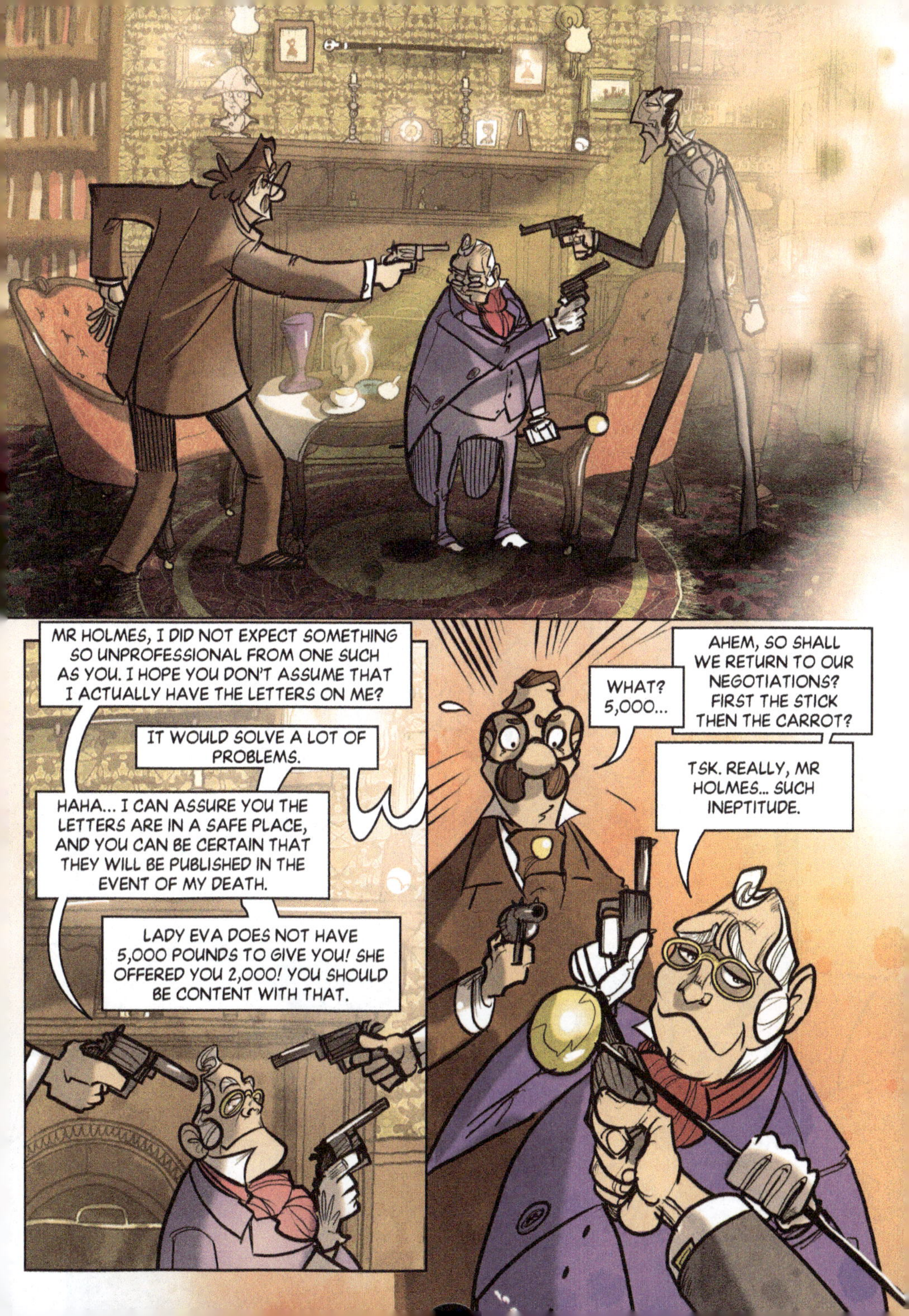
MR HOLMES, I DID NOT EXPECT SOMETHING SO UNPROFESSIONAL FROM ONE SUCH AS YOU. I HOPE YOU DON'T ASSUME THAT I ACTUALLY HAVE THE LETTERS ON ME?
IT WOULD SOLVE A LOT OF PROBLEMS.
HAHA... I CAN ASSURE YOU THE LETTERS ARE IN A SAFE PLACE, AND YOU CAN BE CERTAIN THAT THEY WILL BE PUBLISHED IN THE EVENT OF MY DEATH.
LADY EVA DOES NOT HAVE 5,000 POUNDS TO GIVE YOU! SHE OFFERED YOU 2,000! YOU SHOULD BE CONTENT WITH THAT.
WHAT? 5,000...
AHEM, SO SHALL WE RETURN TO OUR NEGOTIATIONS? FIRST THE STICK THEN THE CARROT?
TSK. REALLY, MR HOLMES... SUCH INEPTITUDE.

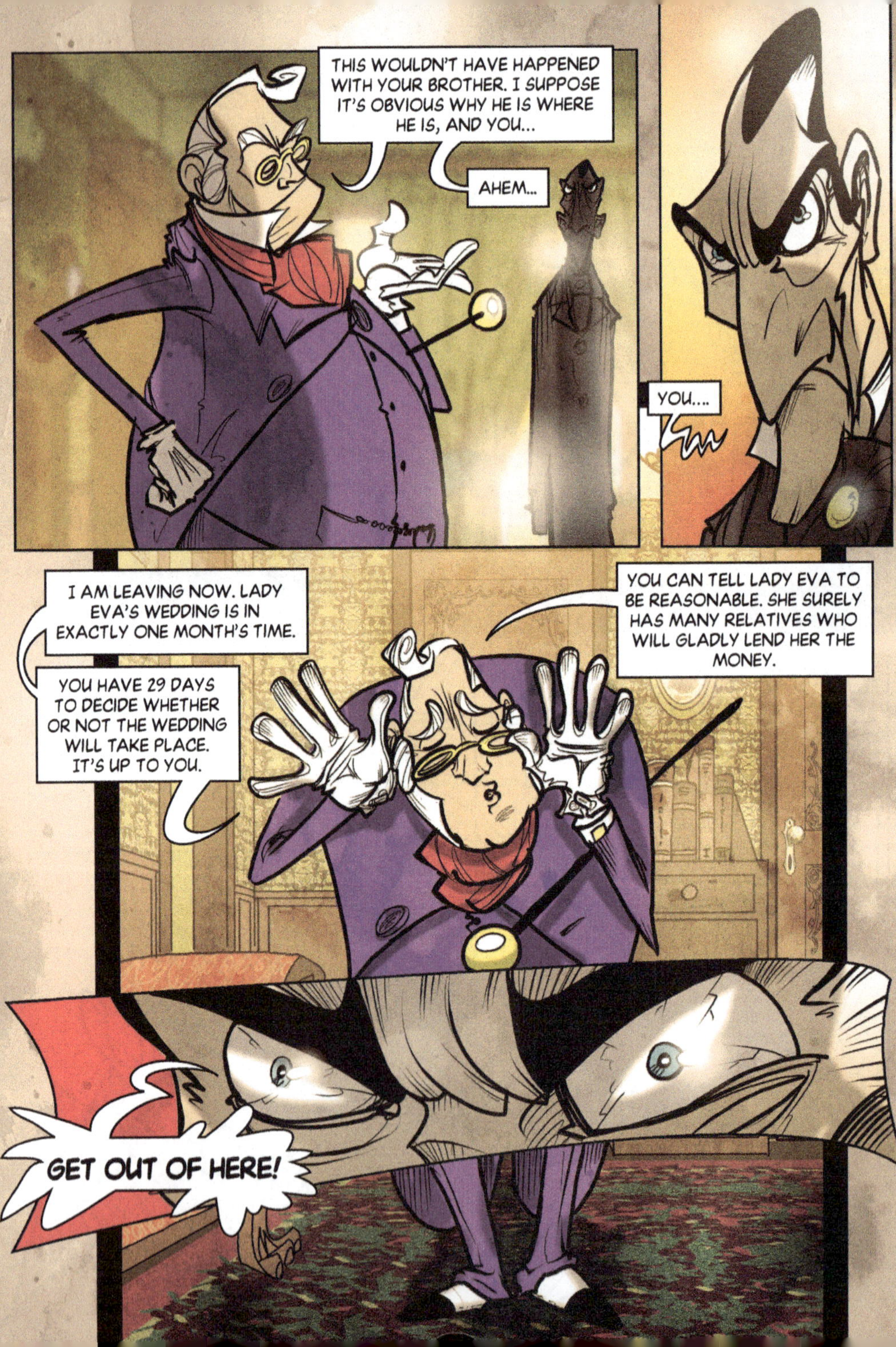
THIS WOULDN'T HAVE HAPPENED WITH YOUR BROTHER. I SUPPOSE IT'S OBVIOUS WHY HE IS WHERE HE IS, AND YOU...
AHEM...
YOU....
I AM LEAVING NOW. LADY EVA'S WEDDING IS IN EXACTLY ONE MONTH'S TIME.
YOU HAVE 29 DAYS TO DECIDE WHETHER OR NOT THE WEDDING WILL TAKE PLACE. IT'S UP TO YOU.
YOU CAN TELL LADY EVA TO BE REASONABLE. SHE SURELY HAS MANY RELATIVES WHO WILL GLADLY LEND HER THE MONEY.
GET OUT OF HERE!

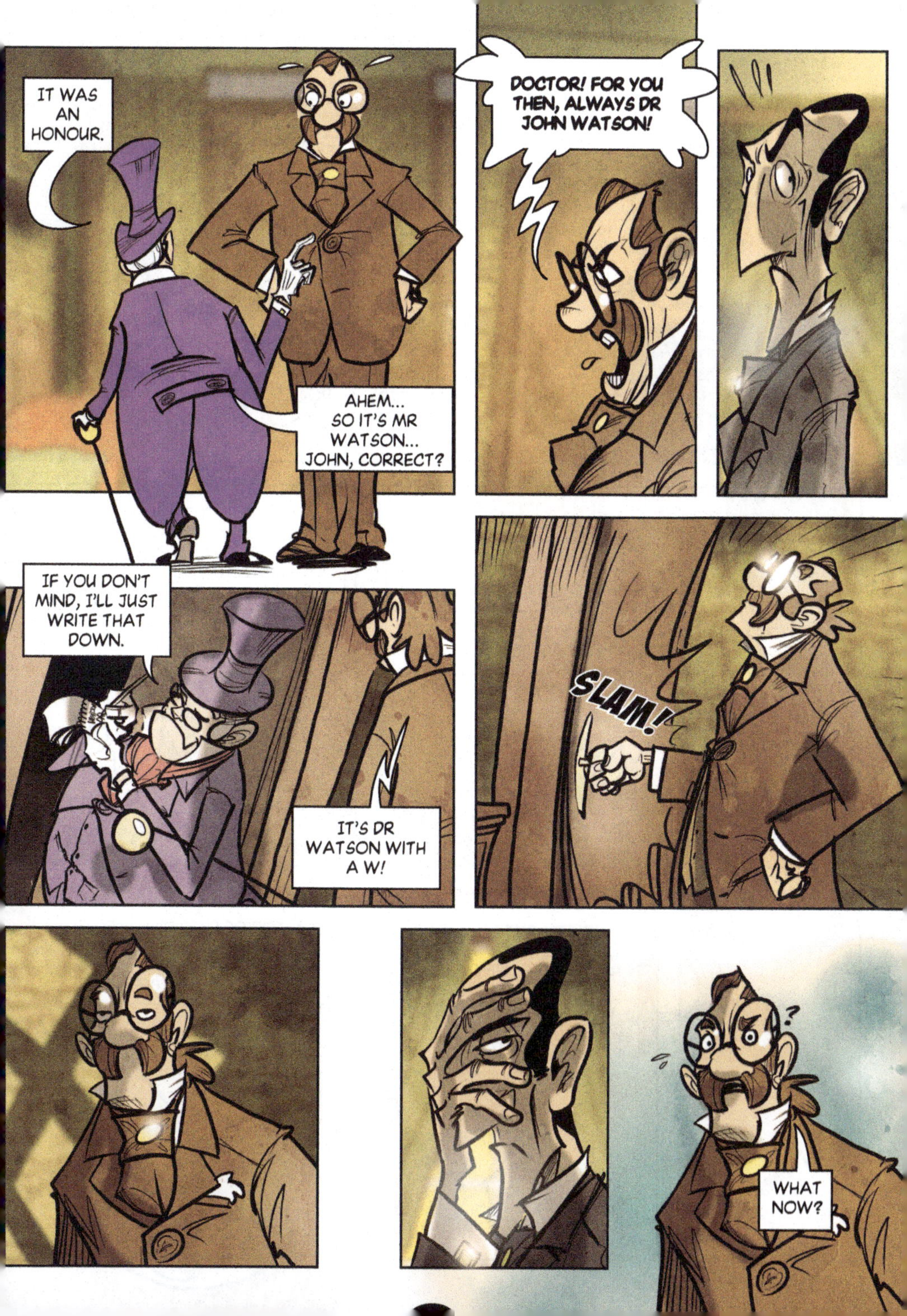
IT WAS AN HONOUR.
AHEM... SO IT'S MR WATSON... JOHN, CORRECT?
DOCTOR! FOR YOU THEN, ALWAYS DR JOHN WATSON!
IF YOU DON'T MIND, I'LL JUST WRITE THAT DOWN.
IT'S DR WATSON WITH A W!
SLAM!
WHAT NOW?

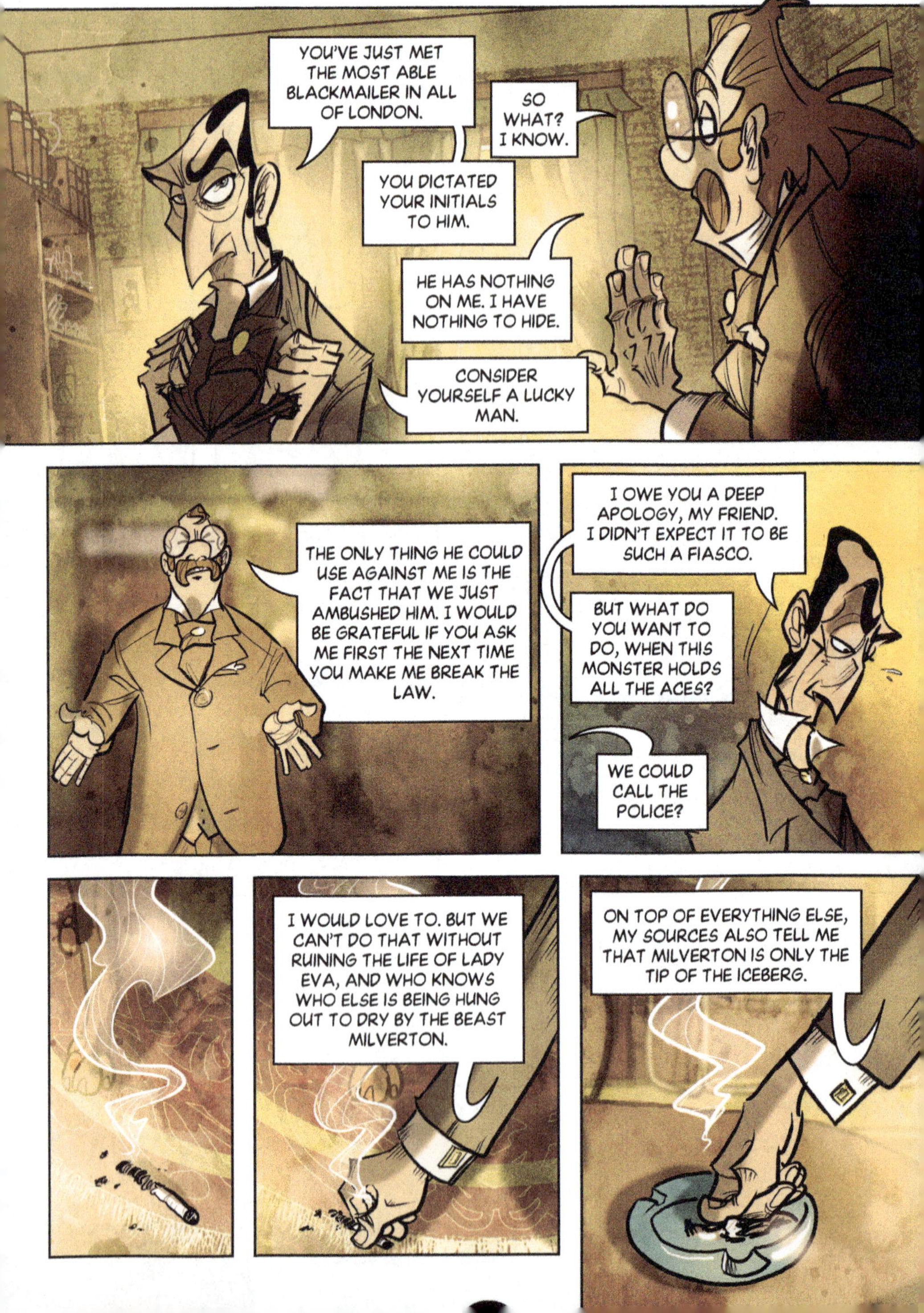
YOU'VE JUST MET THE MOST ABLE BLACKMAILER IN ALL OF LONDON.
SO WHAT? I KNOW.
YOU DICTATED YOUR INITIALS TO HIM.
HE HAS NOTHING ON ME. I HAVE NOTHING TO HIDE.
CONSIDER YOURSELF A LUCKY MAN.
THE ONLY THING HE COULD USE AGAINST ME IS THE FACT THAT WE JUST AMBUSHED HIM. I WOULD BE GRATEFUL IF YOU ASK ME FIRST THE NEXT TIME YOU MAKE ME BREAK THE LAW.
I OWE YOU A DEEP APOLOGY, MY FRIEND. I DIDN'T EXPECT IT TO BE SUCH A FIASCO.
BUT WHAT DO YOU WANT TO DO, WHEN THIS MONSTER HOLDS ALL THE ACES?
WE COULD CALL THE POLICE?
I WOULD LOVE TO. BUT WE CAN'T DO THAT WITHOUT RUINING THE LIFE OF LADY EVA, AND WHO KNOWS WHO ELSE IS BEING HUNG OUT TO DRY BY THE BEAST MILVERTON.
ON TOP OF EVERYTHING ELSE, MY SOURCES ALSO TELL ME THAT MILVERTON IS ONLY THE TIP OF THE ICEBERG.

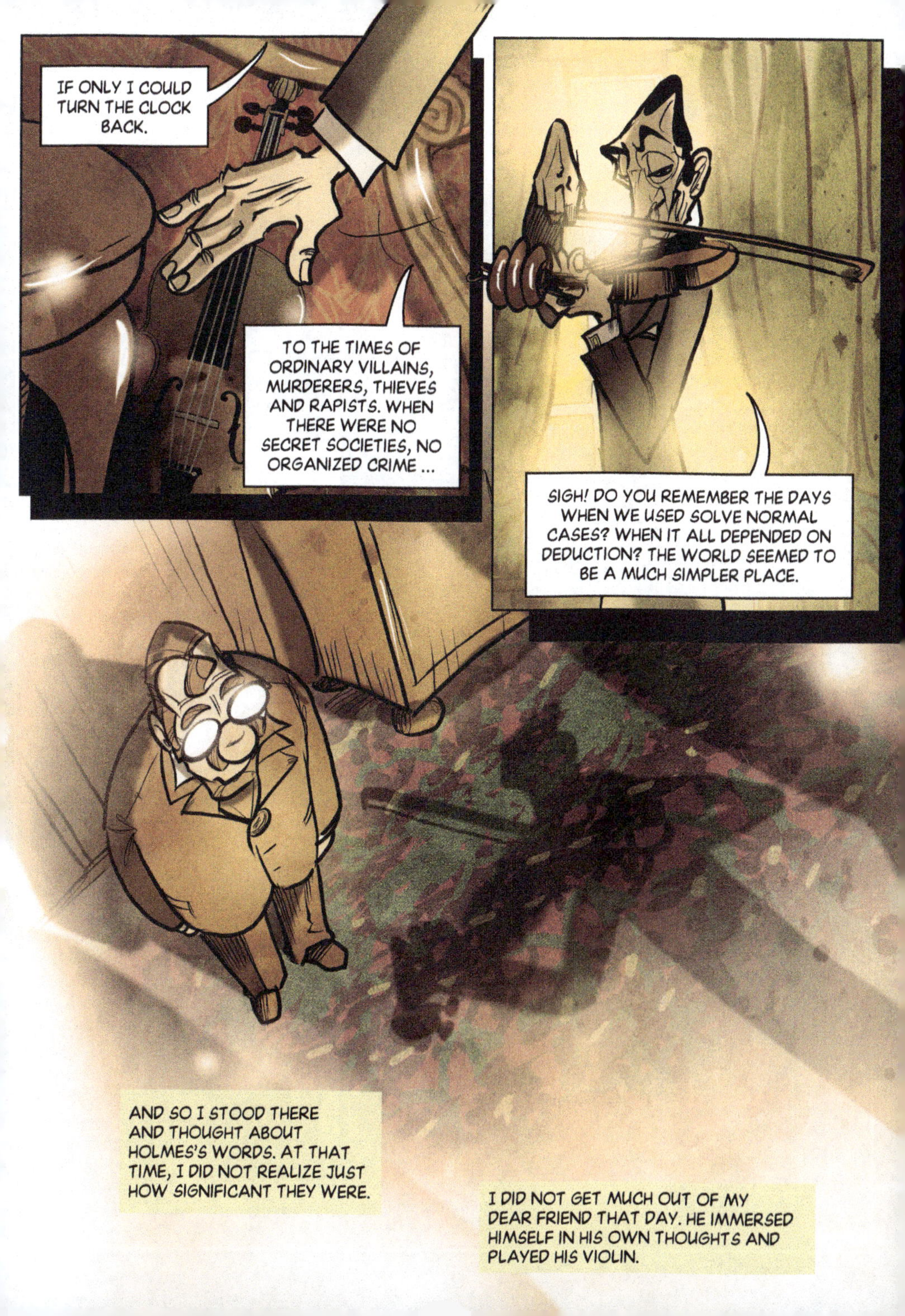
IF ONLY I COULD TURN THE CLOCK BACK.
TO THE TIMES OF ORDINARY VILLAINS, MURDERERS, THIEVES AND RAPISTS. WHEN THERE WERE NO SECRET SOCIETIES, NO ORGANIZED CRIME ...
SIGH! DO YOU REMEMBER THE DAYS WHEN WE USED SOLVE NORMAL CASES? WHEN IT ALL DEPENDED ON DEDUCTION? THE WORLD SEEMED TO BE A MUCH SIMPLER PLACE.
AND SO I STOOD THERE AND THOUGHT ABOUT HOLMES'S WORDS. AT THAT TIME, I DID NOT REALIZE JUST HOW SIGNIFICANT THEY WERE.
I DID NOT GET MUCH OUT OF MY DEAR FRIEND THAT DAY. HE IMMERSED HIMSELF IN HIS OWN THOUGHTS AND PLAYED HIS VIOLIN.

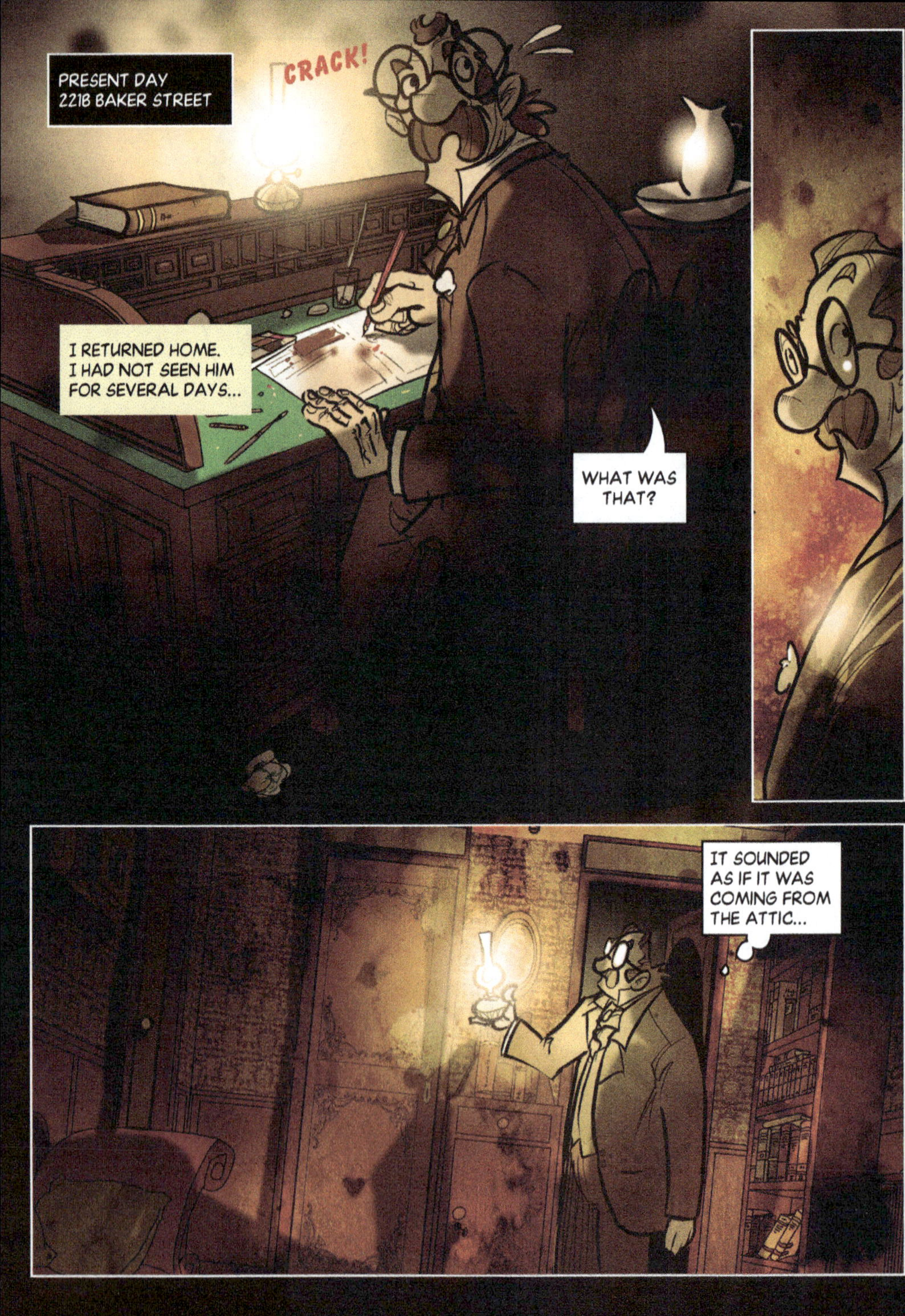
PRESENT DAY
221B BAKER STREET
CRACK!
I RETURNED HOME. I HAD NOT SEEN HIM FOR SEVERAL DAYS...
WHAT WAS THAT?
IT SOUNDED AS IF IT WAS COMING FROM THE ATTIC...

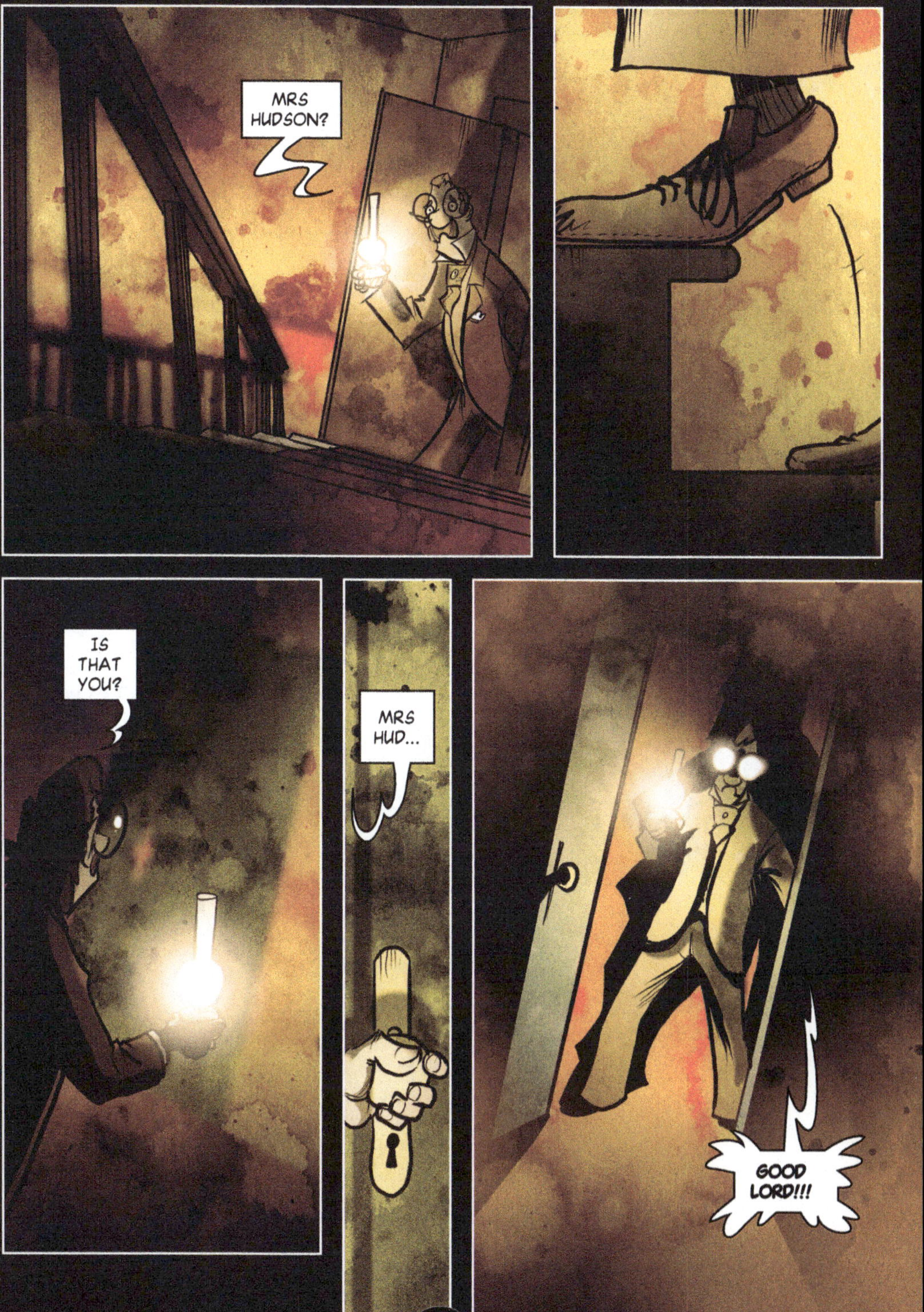
MRS HUDSON?
IS THAT YOU?
MRS HUD...
GOOD LORD!!!

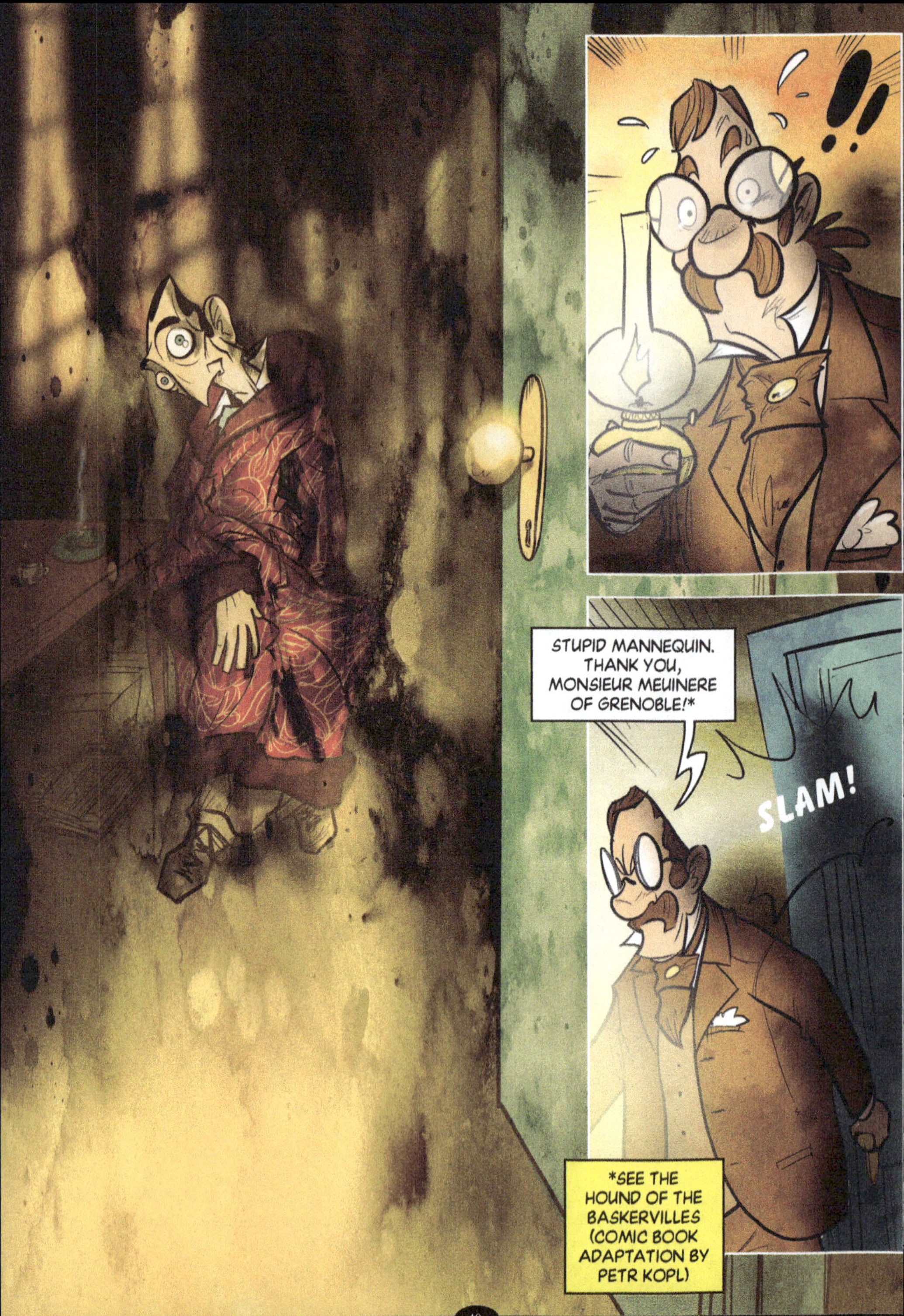
STUPID MANNEQUIN. THANK YOU, MONSIEUR MEUINERE OF GRENOBLE!*
SLAM!
*SEE THE HOUND OF THE BASKERVILLES (COMIC BOOK ADAPTATION BY PETR KOPL)

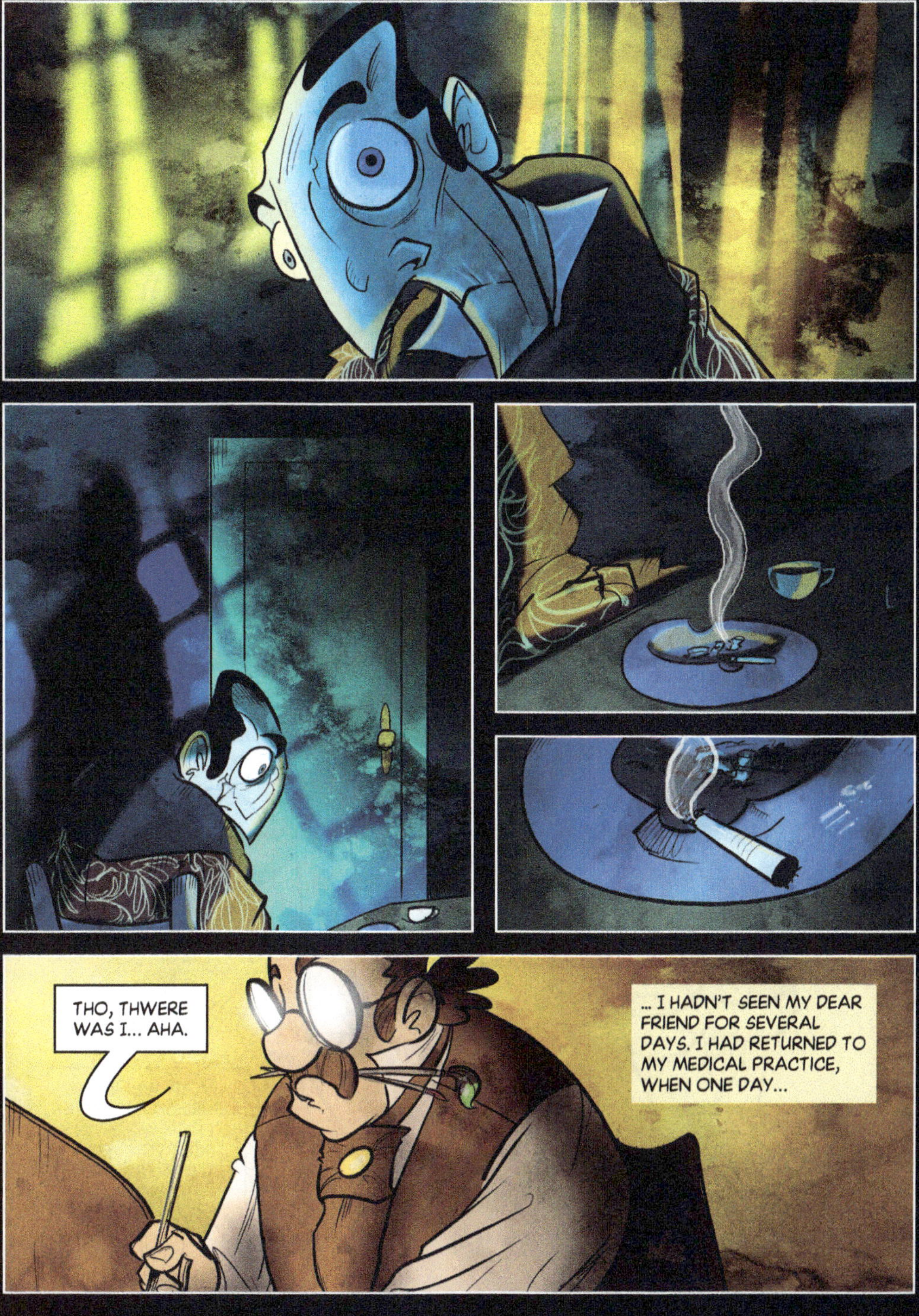
THO, THWERE WAS I... AHA.
... I HADN'T SEEN MY DEAR FRIEND FOR SEVERAL DAYS. I HAD RETURNED TO MY MEDICAL PRACTICE, WHEN ONE DAY...

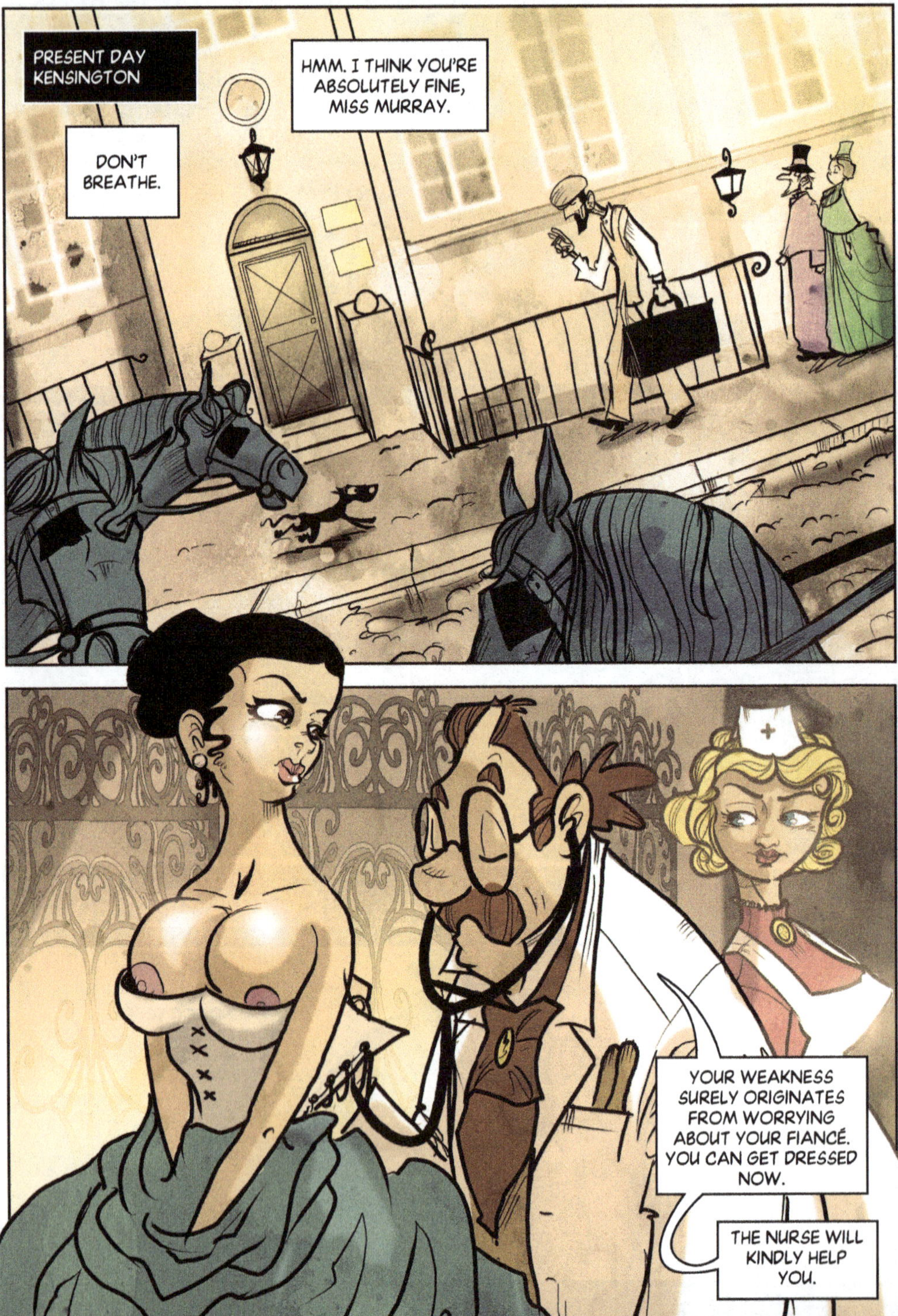
PRESENT DAY KENSINGTON
DON'T BREATHE.
HMM. I THINK YOU'RE ABSOLUTELY FINE, MISS MURRAY.
YOUR WEAKNESS SURELY ORIGINATES FROM WORRYING ABOUT YOUR FIANCÉ. YOU CAN GET DRESSED NOW.
THE NURSE WILL KINDLY HELP YOU.

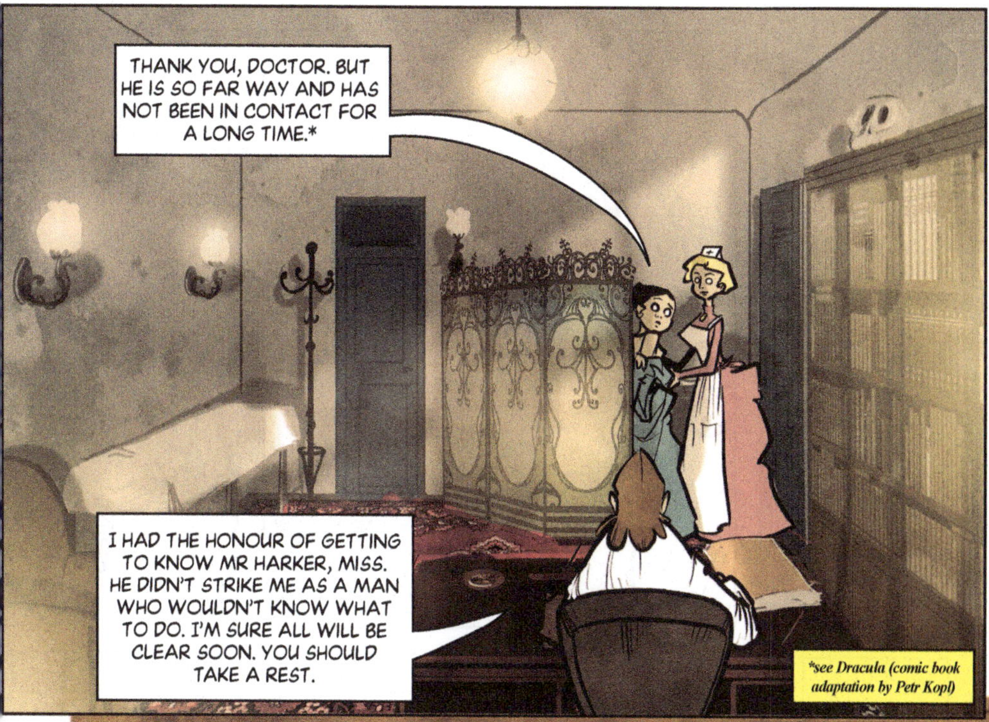
THANK YOU, DOCTOR. BUT HE IS SO FAR WAY AND HAS NOT BEEN IN CONTACT FOR A LONG TIME.*
I HAD THE HONOUR OF GETTING TO KNOW MR HARKER, MISS. HE DIDN'T STRIKE ME AS A MAN WHO WOULDN'T KNOW WHAT TO DO. I'M SURE ALL WILL BE CLEAR SOON. YOU SHOULD TAKE A REST.
*see Dracula (comic book adaptation by Petr Kopl)

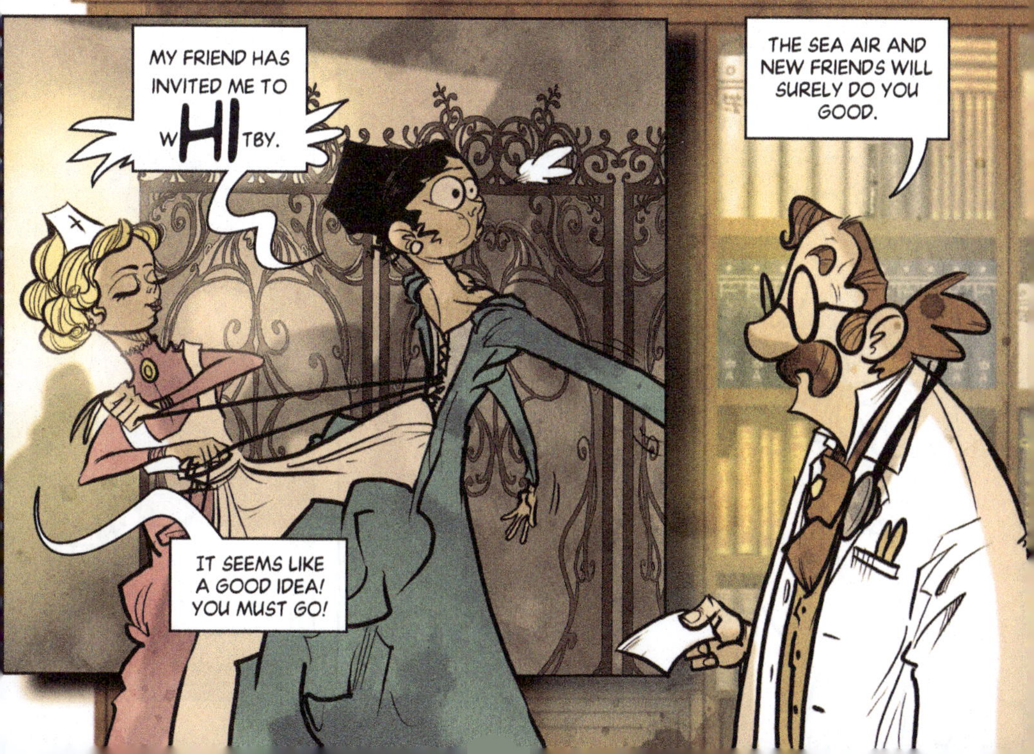
MY FRIEND HAS INVITED ME TO
wHItby.
THE SEA AIR AND NEW FRIENDS WILL SURELY DO YOU GOOD.
IT SEEMS LIKE A GOOD IDEA! YOU MUST GO!

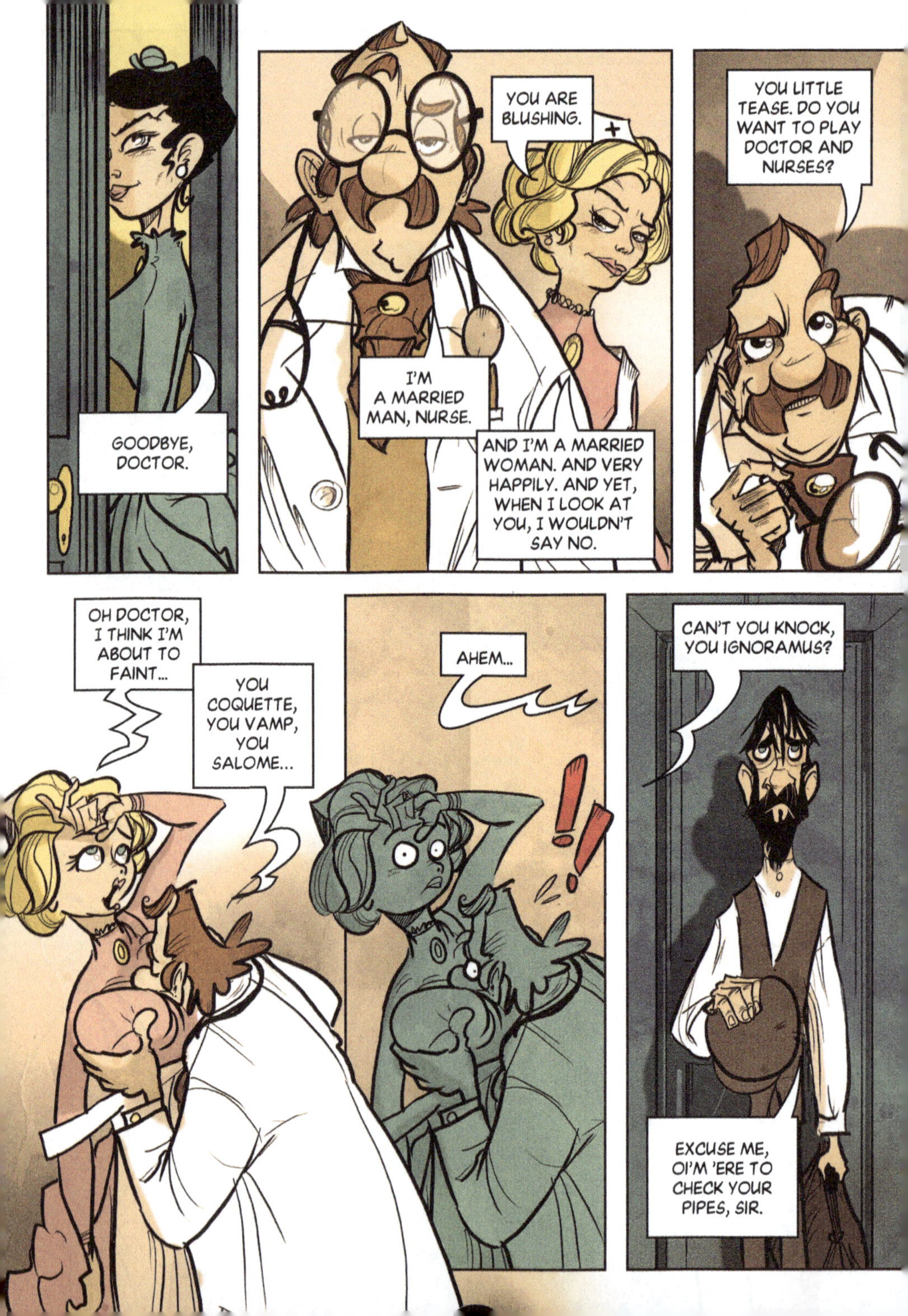
GOODBYE, DOCTOR.
YOU ARE BLUSHING.
I'M A MARRIED MAN, NURSE.
AND I'M A MARRIED WOMAN. AND VERY HAPPILY. AND YET, WHEN I LOOK AT YOU, I WOULDN'T SAY NO.
YOU LITTLE TEASE. DO YOU WANT TO PLAY DOCTOR AND NURSES?
OH DOCTOR, I THINK I'M ABOUT TO FAINT...
YOU COQUETTE, YOU VAMP, YOU SALOME...
AHEM...
!!
CAN'T YOU KNOCK, YOU IGNORAMUS?
EXCUSE ME, OI'M 'ERE TO CHECK YOUR PIPES, SIR.

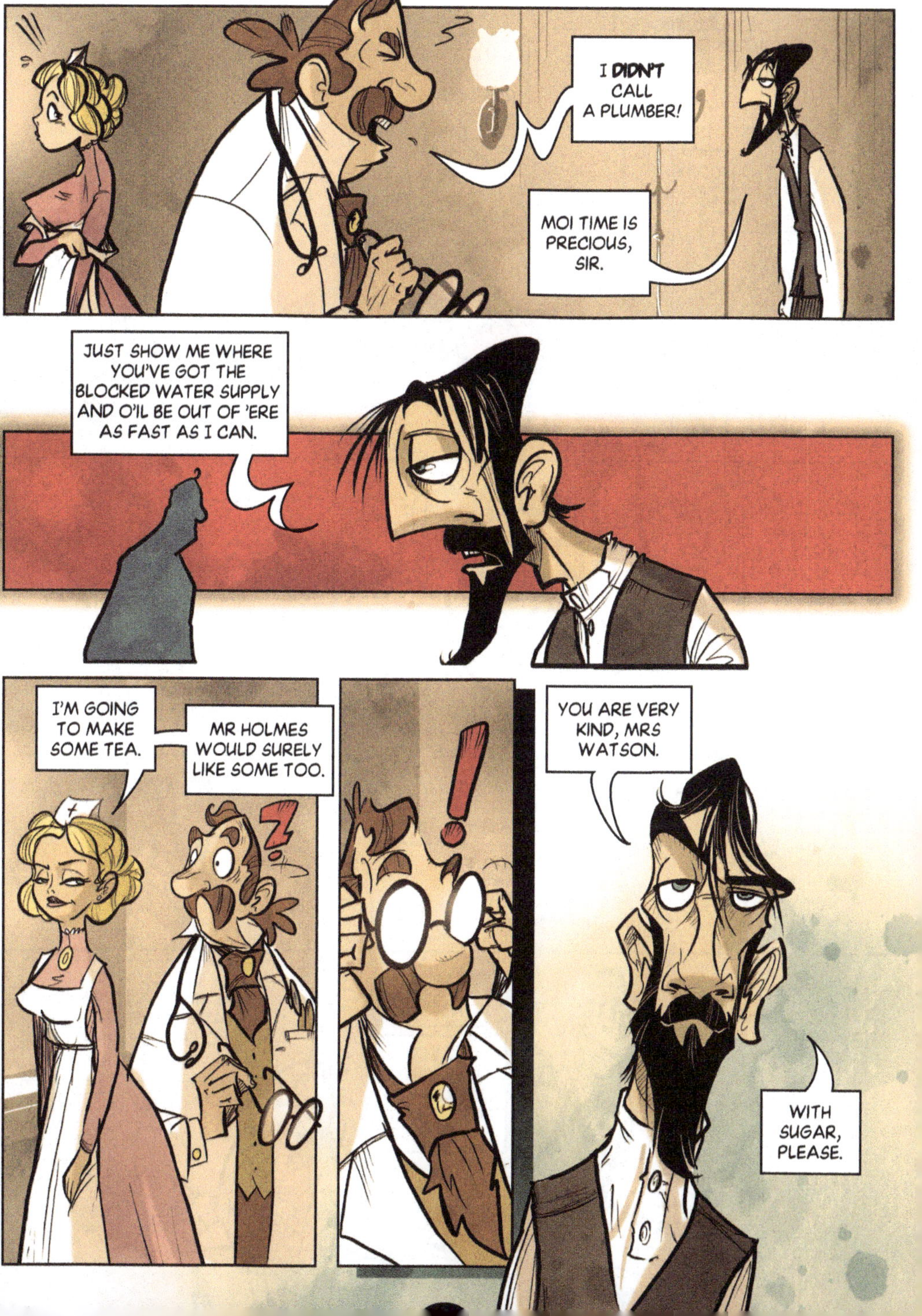
I DIDN'T CALL A PLUMBER!
MOI TIME IS PRECIOUS, SIR.
JUST SHOW ME WHERE YOU'VE GOT THE BLOCKED WATER SUPPLY AND O'IL BE OUT OF 'ERE AS FAST AS I CAN.
I'M GOING TO MAKE SOME TEA.
MR HOLMES WOULD SURELY LIKE SOME TOO.
YOU ARE VERY KIND, MRS WATSON.
WITH SUGAR, PLEASE.

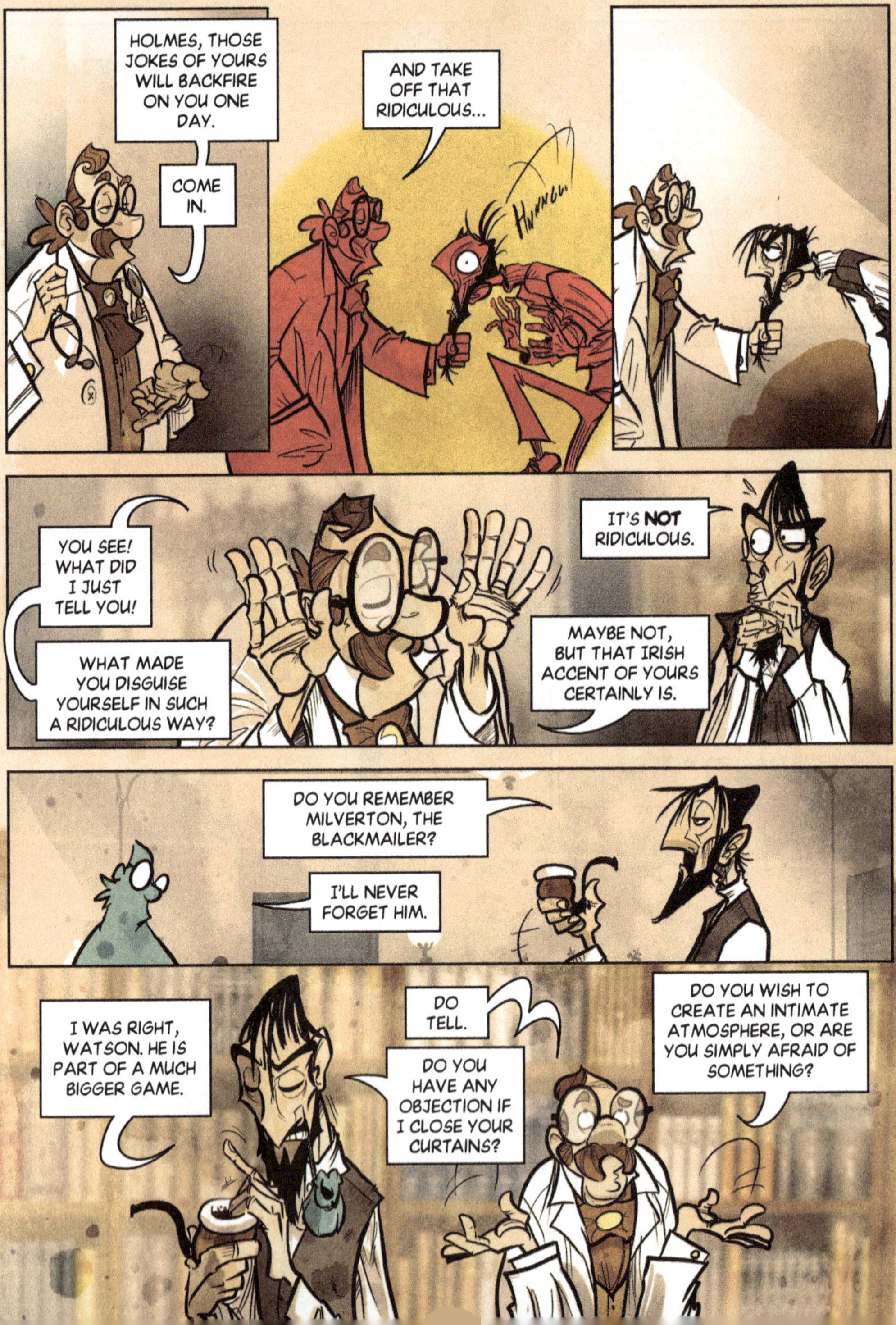

HOLMES, THOSE JOKES OF YOURS WILL BACKFIRE ON YOU ONE DAY.
COME IN.
AND TAKE OFF THAT RIDICULOUS...
HNNNGU!
YOU SEE! WHAT DID I JUST TELL YOU!
WHAT MADE YOU DISGUISE YOURSELF IN SUCH A RIDICULOUS WAY?
IT'S **NOT** RIDICULOUS.
MAYBE NOT, BUT THAT IRISH ACCENT OF YOURS CERTAINLY IS.
DO YOU REMEMBER MILVERTON, THE BLACKMAILER?
I'LL NEVER FORGET HIM.
I WAS RIGHT, WATSON. HE IS PART OF A MUCH BIGGER GAME.
DO TELL.
DO YOU HAVE ANY OBJECTION IF I CLOSE YOUR CURTAINS?
DO YOU WISH TO CREATE AN INTIMATE ATMOSPHERE, OR ARE YOU SIMPLY AFRAID OF SOMETHING?

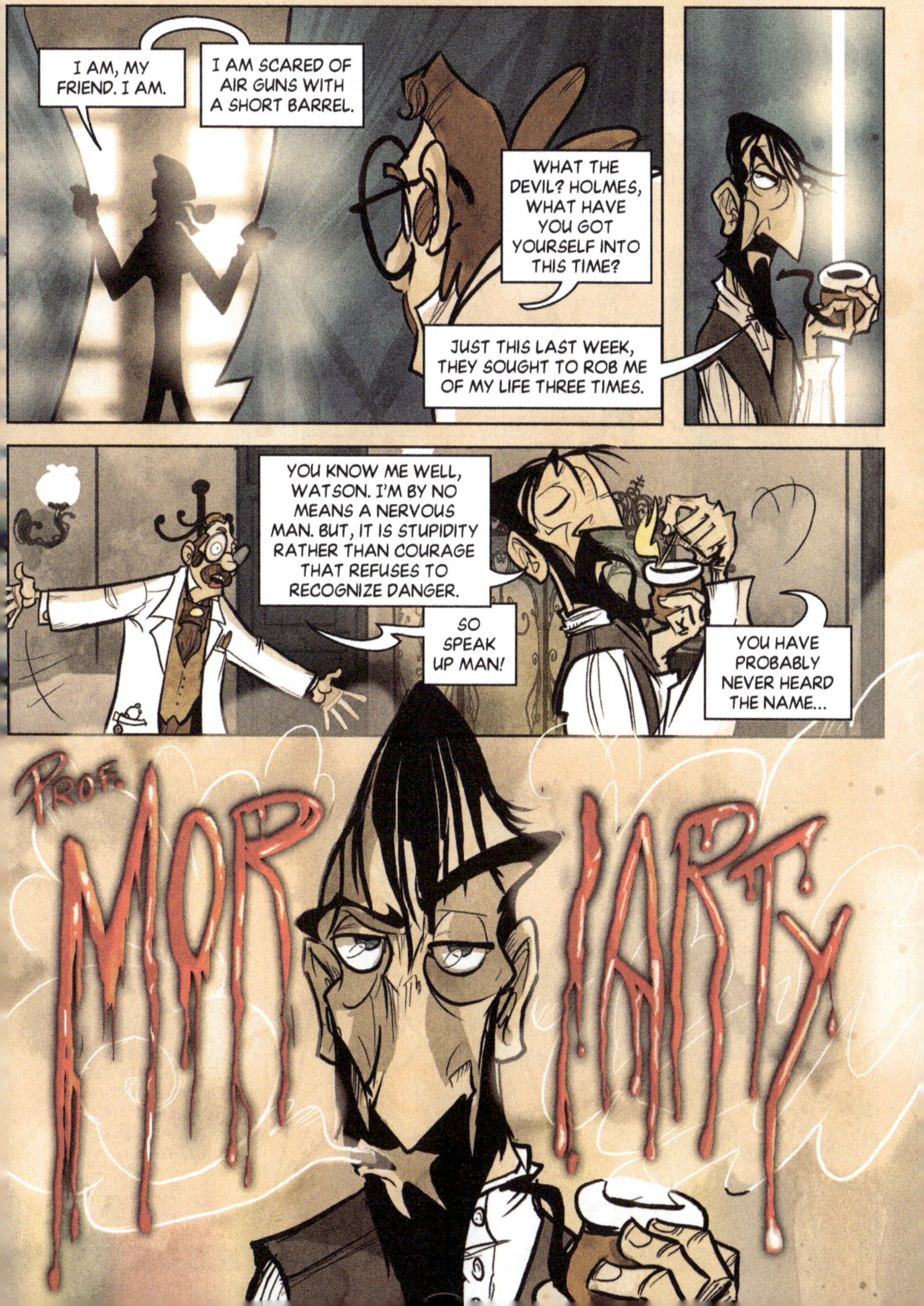
I AM SCARED OF AIR GUNS WITH A SHORT BARREL.
I AM, MY FRIEND. I AM.
WHAT THE DEVIL? HOLMES, WHAT HAVE YOU GOT YOURSELF INTO THIS TIME?
JUST THIS LAST WEEK, THEY SOUGHT TO ROB ME OF MY LIFE THREE TIMES.
YOU KNOW ME WELL, WATSON. I'M BY NO MEANS A NERVOUS MAN. BUT, IT IS STUPIDITY RATHER THAN COURAGE THAT REFUSES TO RECOGNIZE DANGER.
SO SPEAK UP MAN!
YOU HAVE PROBABLY NEVER HEARD THE NAME...
PROF. MORIARTY

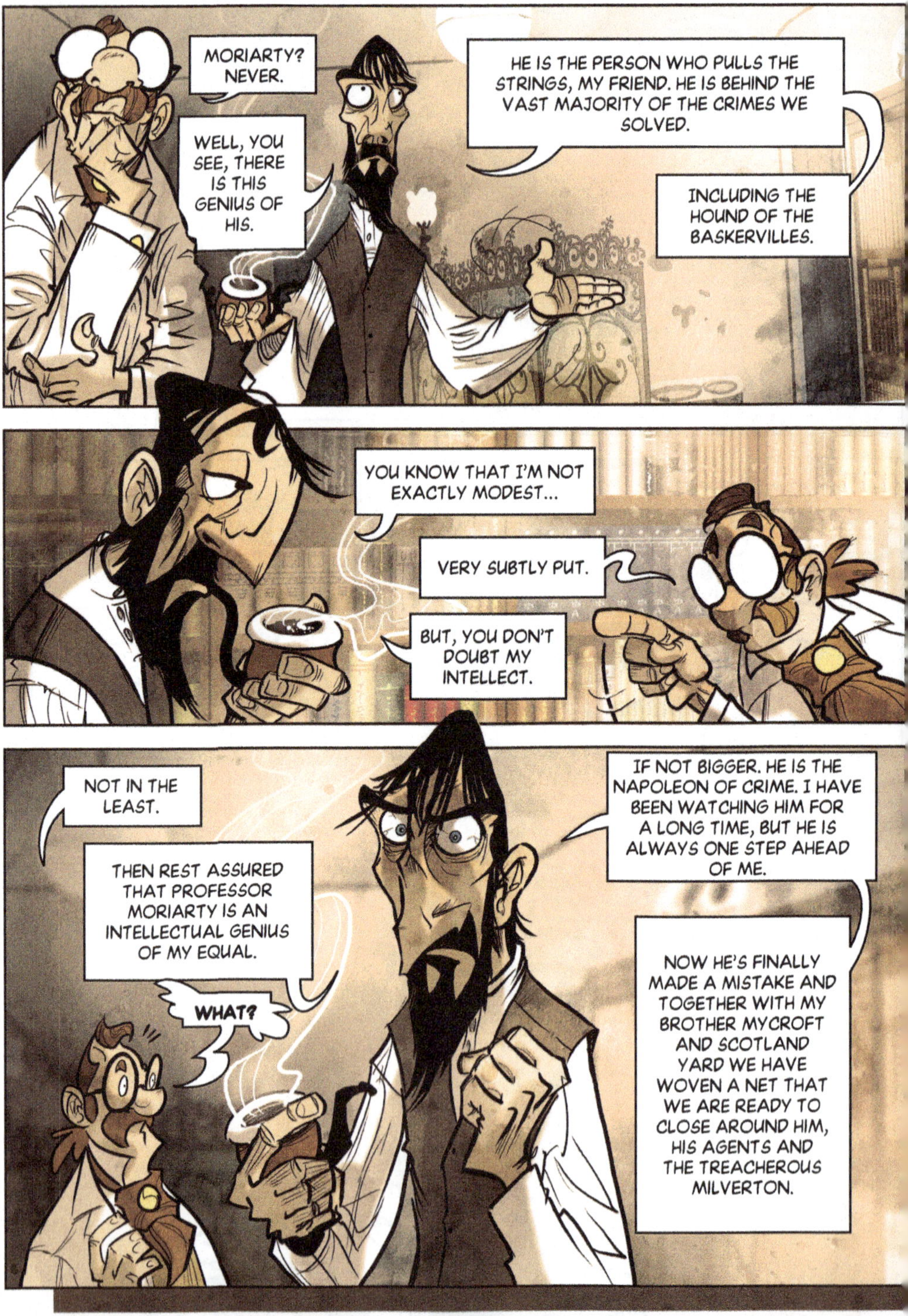
MORIARTY? NEVER.
WELL, YOU SEE, THERE IS THIS GENIUS OF HIS.
HE IS THE PERSON WHO PULLS THE STRINGS, MY FRIEND. HE IS BEHIND THE VAST MAJORITY OF THE CRIMES WE SOLVED.
INCLUDING THE HOUND OF THE BASKERVILLES.
YOU KNOW THAT I'M NOT EXACTLY MODEST...
VERY SUBTLY PUT.
BUT, YOU DON'T DOUBT MY INTELLECT.
NOT IN THE LEAST.
THEN REST ASSURED THAT PROFESSOR MORIARTY IS AN INTELLECTUAL GENIUS OF MY EQUAL.
WHAT?
IF NOT BIGGER. HE IS THE NAPOLEON OF CRIME. I HAVE BEEN WATCHING HIM FOR A LONG TIME, BUT HE IS ALWAYS ONE STEP AHEAD OF ME.
NOW HE'S FINALLY MADE A MISTAKE AND TOGETHER WITH MY BROTHER MYCROFT AND SCOTLAND YARD WE HAVE WOVEN A NET THAT WE ARE READY TO CLOSE AROUND HIM, HIS AGENTS AND THE TREACHEROUS MILVERTON.

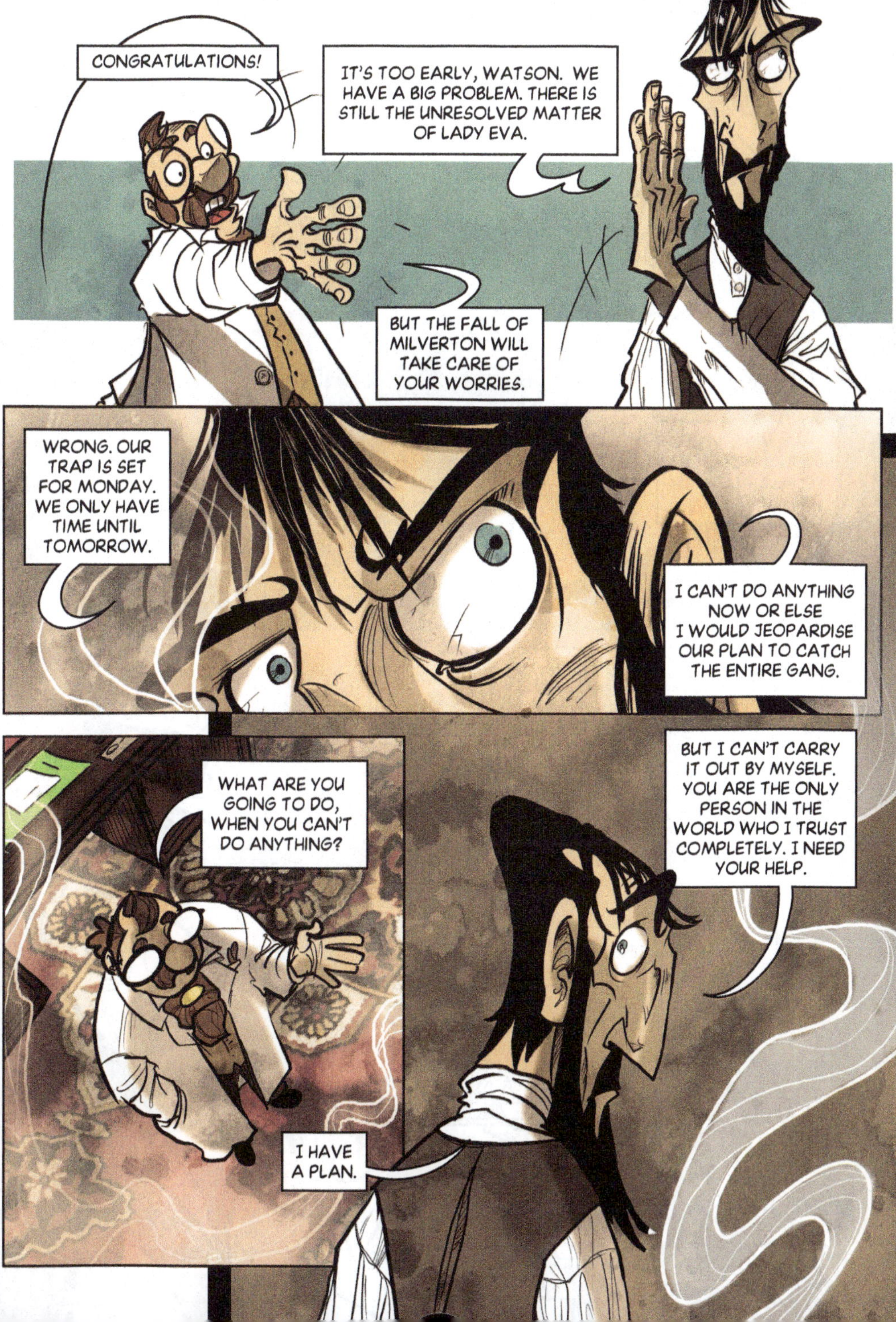
CONGRATULATIONS!
IT'S TOO EARLY, WATSON. WE HAVE A BIG PROBLEM. THERE IS STILL THE UNRESOLVED MATTER OF LADY EVA.
BUT THE FALL OF MILVERTON WILL TAKE CARE OF YOUR WORRIES.
WRONG. OUR TRAP IS SET FOR MONDAY. WE ONLY HAVE TIME UNTIL TOMORROW.
I CAN'T DO ANYTHING NOW OR ELSE I WOULD JEOPARDISE OUR PLAN TO CATCH THE ENTIRE GANG.
WHAT ARE YOU GOING TO DO, WHEN YOU CAN'T DO ANYTHING?
BUT I CAN'T CARRY IT OUT BY MYSELF. YOU ARE THE ONLY PERSON IN THE WORLD WHO I TRUST COMPLETELY. I NEED YOUR HELP.
I HAVE A PLAN.

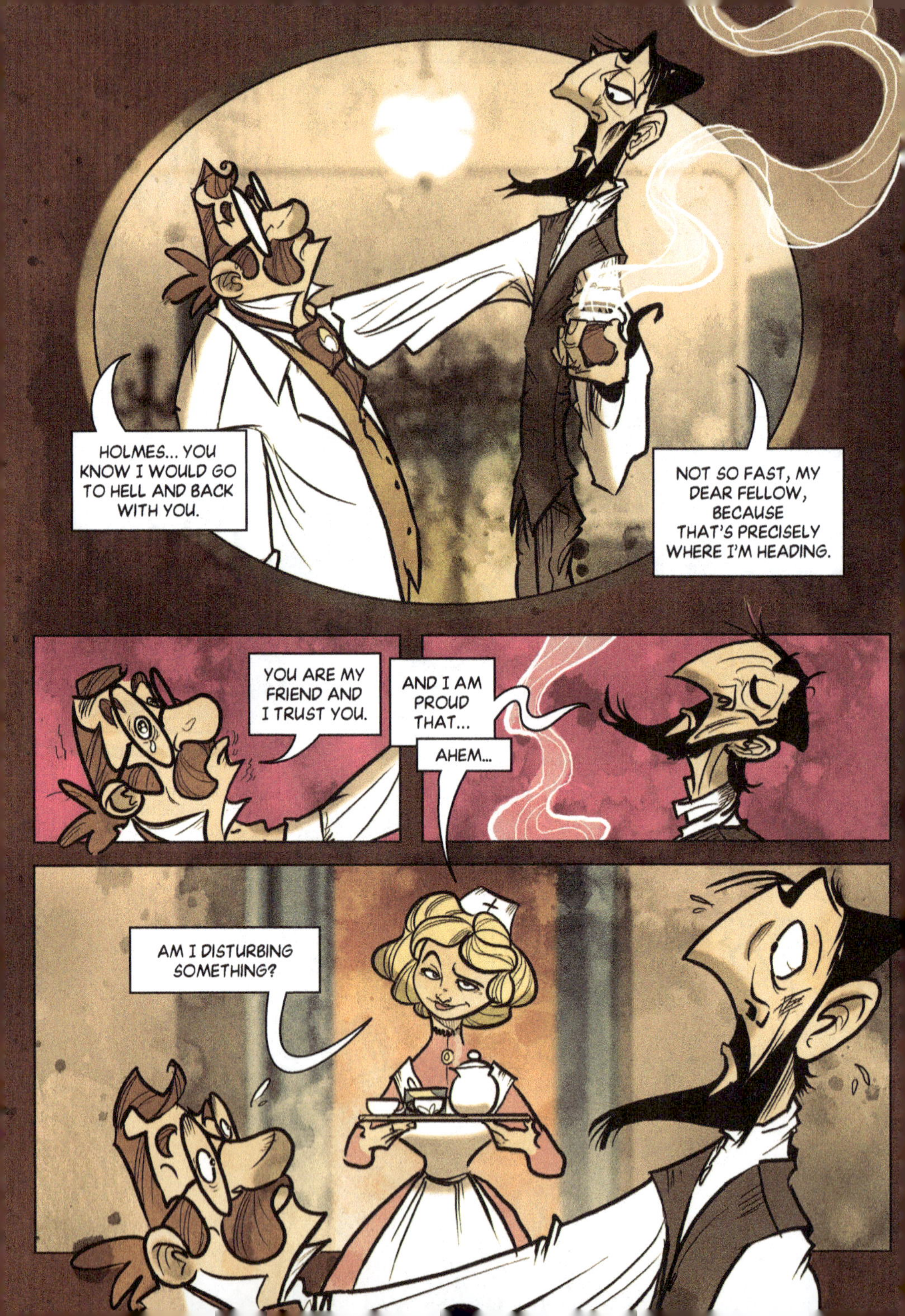
HOLMES... YOU KNOW I WOULD GO TO HELL AND BACK WITH YOU.
NOT SO FAST, MY DEAR FELLOW, BECAUSE THAT'S PRECISELY WHERE I'M HEADING.
YOU ARE MY FRIEND AND I TRUST YOU.
AND I AM PROUD THAT...
AHEM...
AM I DISTURBING SOMETHING?

NOT AT ALL... SO,...

... THANK YOU, MRS WATSON...

... I KNEW I WOULD NEVER GET LADY EVA'S LETTERS OFF MILVERTON.

THEREFORE I TRIED TO GET INTO THE VILLAIN'S HOUSE IN DISGUISE AS A PLUMBER, IN WHICH I SUCCEEDED WITH A LITTLE HELP FROM THE HOUSEMAID.

I'M AFRAID THAT THE POOR SOUL IS IN LOVE WITH ME.

I BETTER RETREAT BEFORE THE SAME FATE BEFALLS ME.

SO, I'M TO BE MARRIED NEXT WEEK.

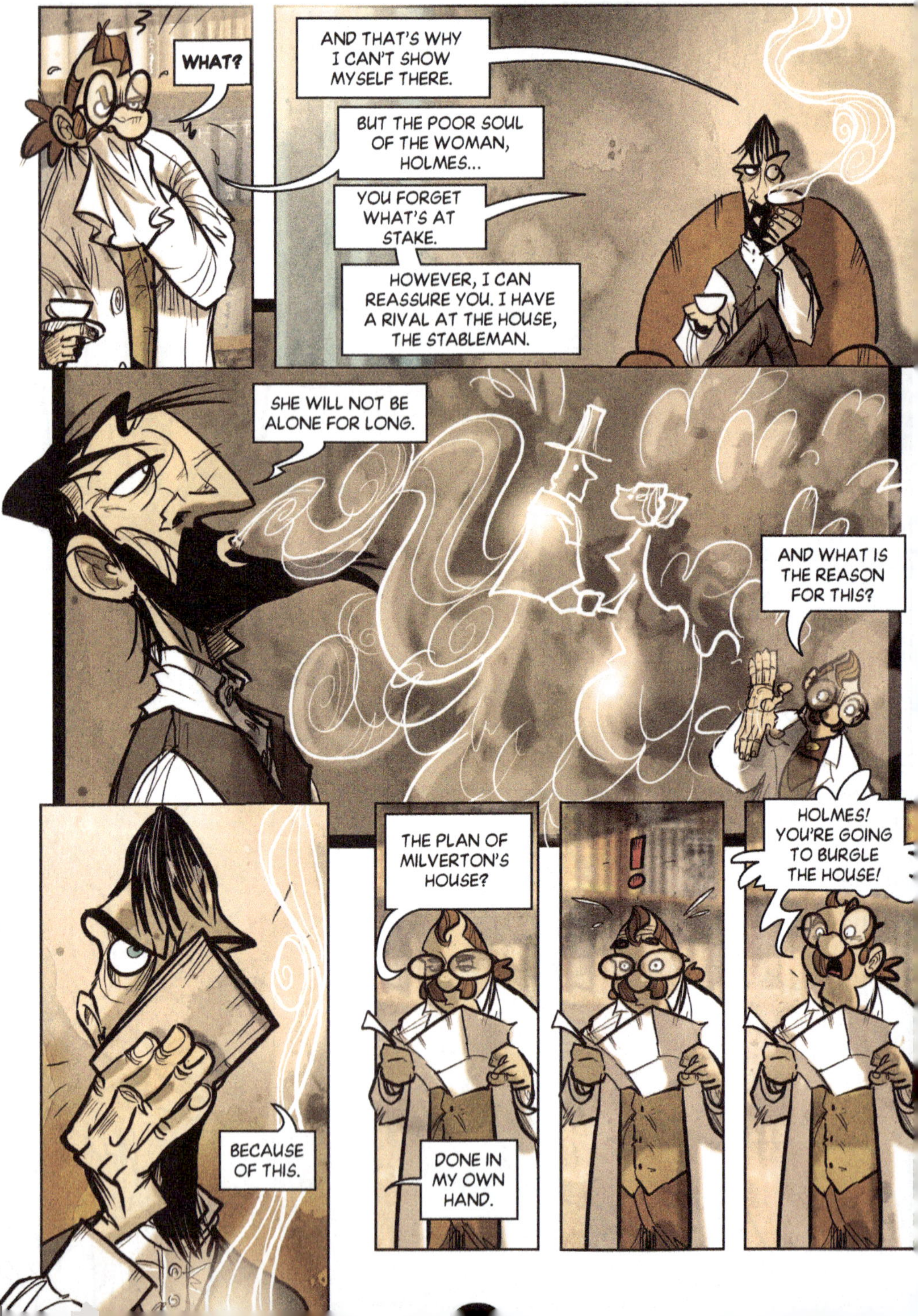
WHAT?
AND THAT'S WHY I CAN'T SHOW MYSELF THERE.
BUT THE POOR SOUL OF THE WOMAN, HOLMES...
YOU FORGET WHAT'S AT STAKE.
HOWEVER, I CAN REASSURE YOU. I HAVE A RIVAL AT THE HOUSE, THE STABLEMAN.
SHE WILL NOT BE ALONE FOR LONG.
AND WHAT IS THE REASON FOR THIS?
BECAUSE OF THIS.
THE PLAN OF MILVERTON'S HOUSE?
DONE IN MY OWN HAND.
!
HOLMES! YOU'RE GOING TO BURGLE THE HOUSE!

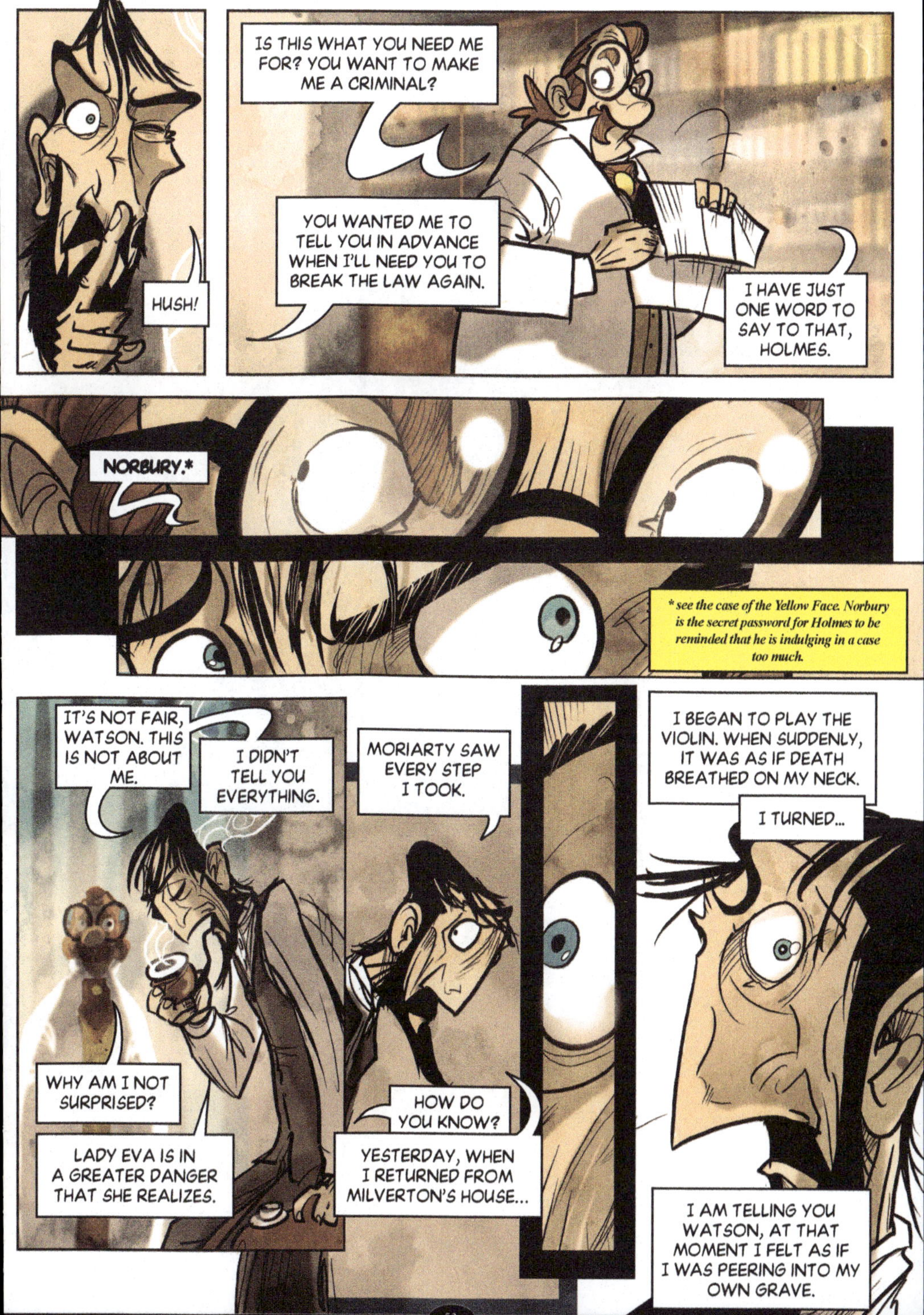
HUSH!
IS THIS WHAT YOU NEED ME FOR? YOU WANT TO MAKE ME A CRIMINAL?
YOU WANTED ME TO TELL YOU IN ADVANCE WHEN I'LL NEED YOU TO BREAK THE LAW AGAIN.
I HAVE JUST ONE WORD TO SAY TO THAT, HOLMES.
NORBURY.*
* see the case of the Yellow Face. Norbury is the secret password for Holmes to be reminded that he is indulging in a case too much.
IT'S NOT FAIR, WATSON. THIS IS NOT ABOUT ME.
I DIDN'T TELL YOU EVERYTHING.
WHY AM I NOT SURPRISED?
LADY EVA IS IN A GREATER DANGER THAT SHE REALIZES.
MORIARTY SAW EVERY STEP I TOOK.
HOW DO YOU KNOW?
YESTERDAY, WHEN I RETURNED FROM MILVERTON'S HOUSE...
I BEGAN TO PLAY THE VIOLIN. WHEN SUDDENLY, IT WAS AS IF DEATH BREATHED ON MY NECK.
I TURNED...
I AM TELLING YOU WATSON, AT THAT MOMENT I FELT AS IF I WAS PEERING INTO MY OWN GRAVE.

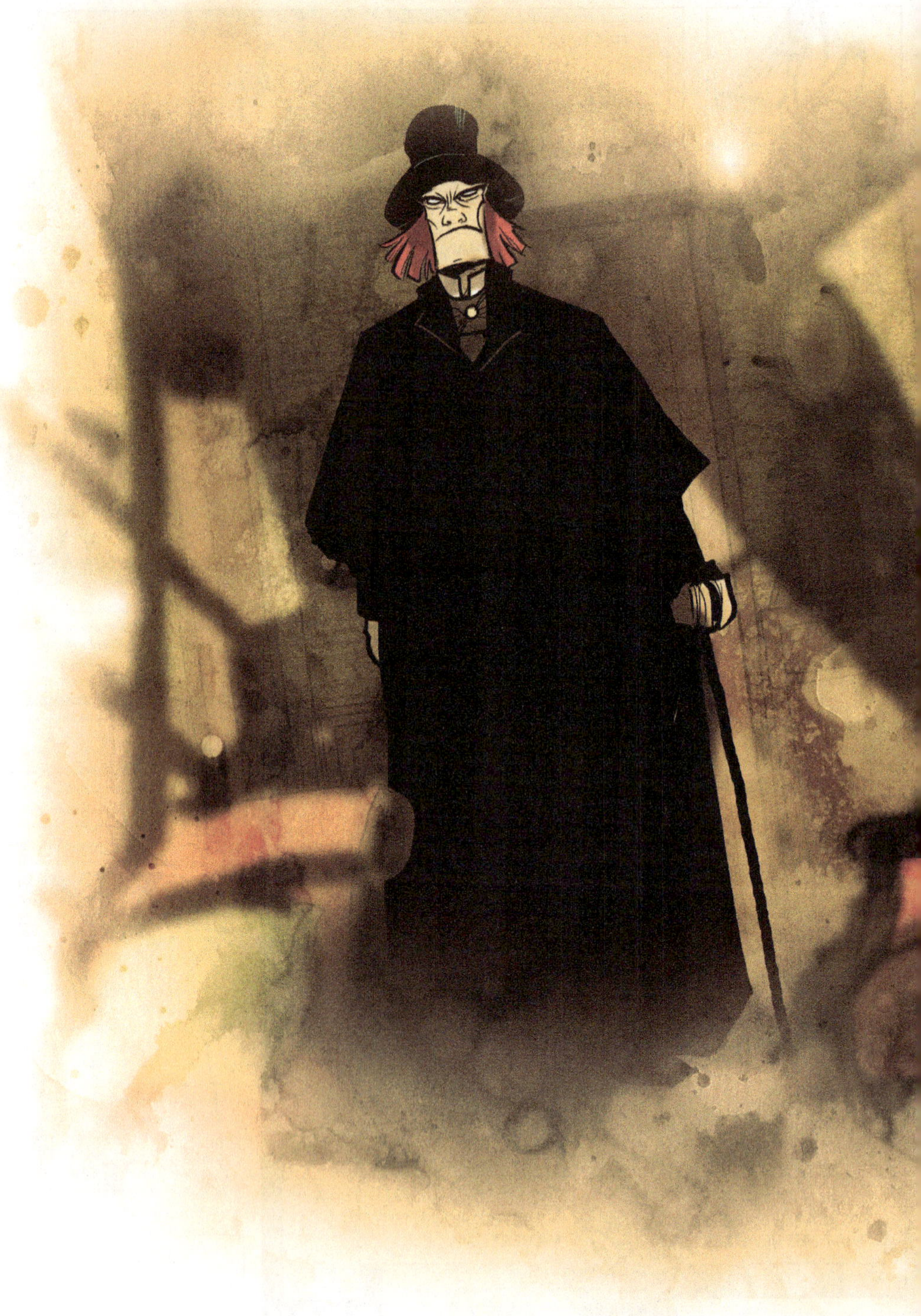

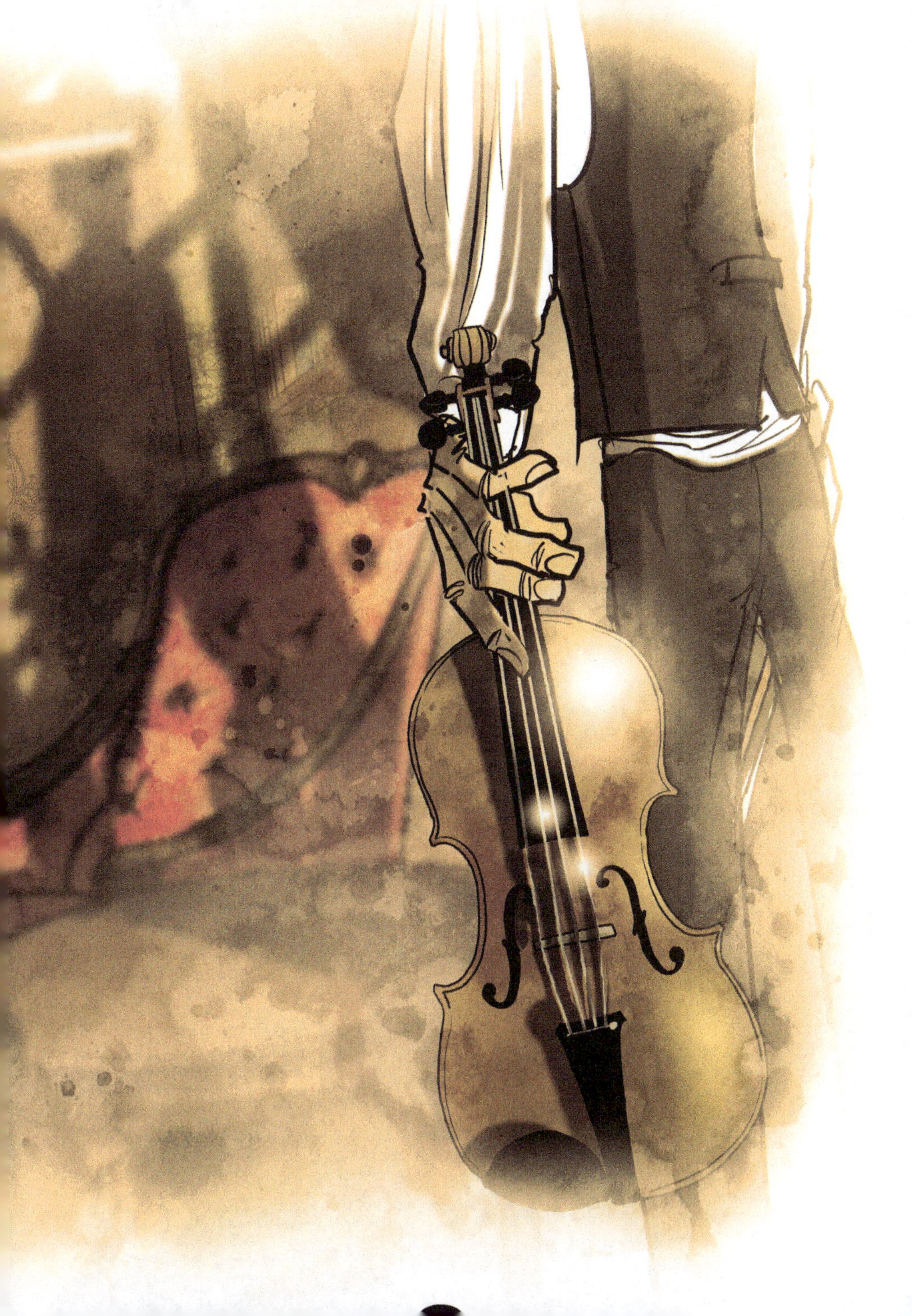

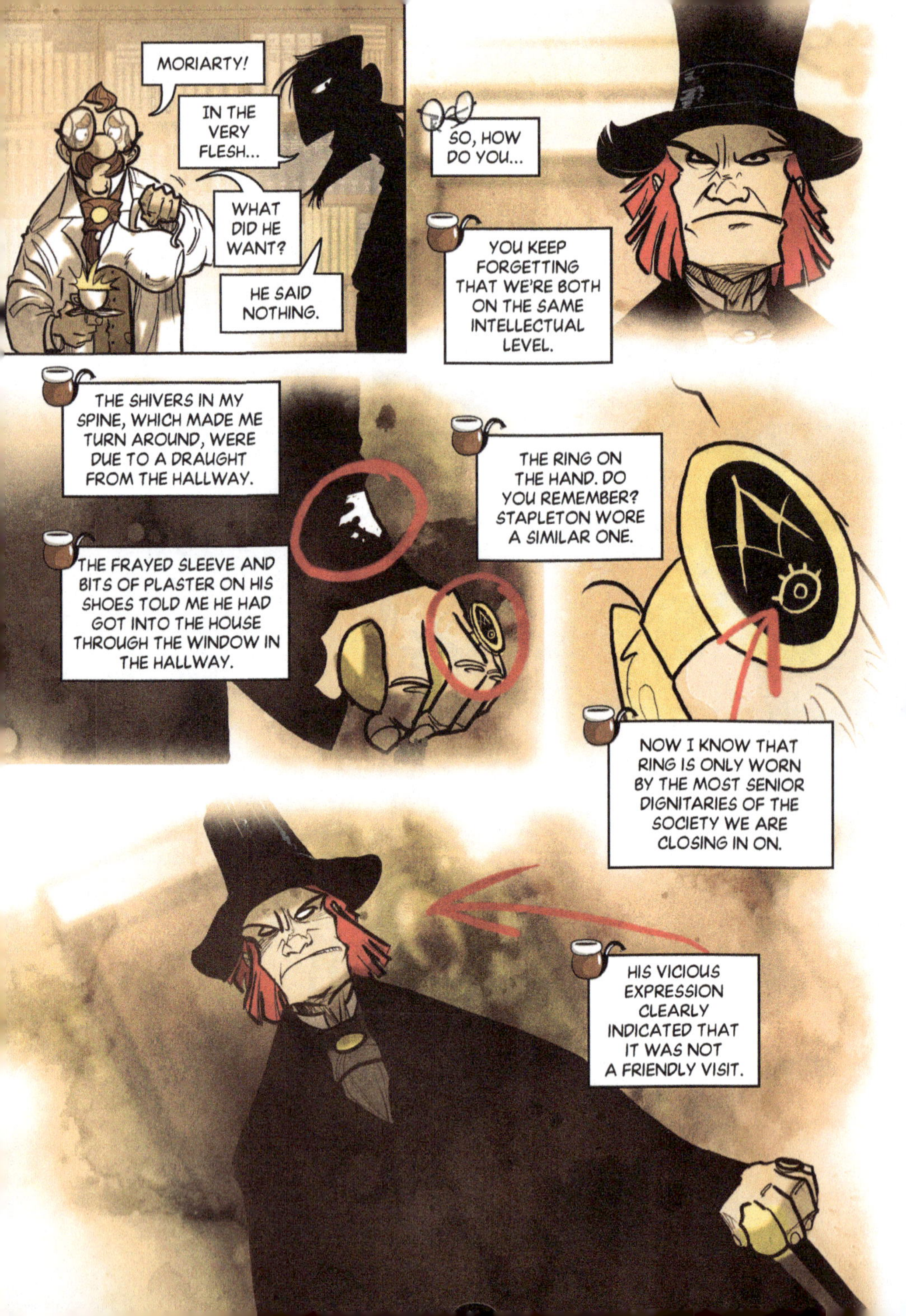
MORIARTY!
IN THE VERY FLESH...
WHAT DID HE WANT?
HE SAID NOTHING.
SO, HOW DO YOU...
YOU KEEP FORGETTING THAT WE'RE BOTH ON THE SAME INTELLECTUAL LEVEL.
THE SHIVERS IN MY SPINE, WHICH MADE ME TURN AROUND, WERE DUE TO A DRAUGHT FROM THE HALLWAY.
THE FRAYED SLEEVE AND BITS OF PLASTER ON HIS SHOES TOLD ME HE HAD GOT INTO THE HOUSE THROUGH THE WINDOW IN THE HALLWAY.
THE RING ON THE HAND. DO YOU REMEMBER? STAPLETON WORE A SIMILAR ONE.
NOW I KNOW THAT RING IS ONLY WORN BY THE MOST SENIOR DIGNITARIES OF THE SOCIETY WE ARE CLOSING IN ON.
HIS VICIOUS EXPRESSION CLEARLY INDICATED THAT IT WAS NOT A FRIENDLY VISIT.

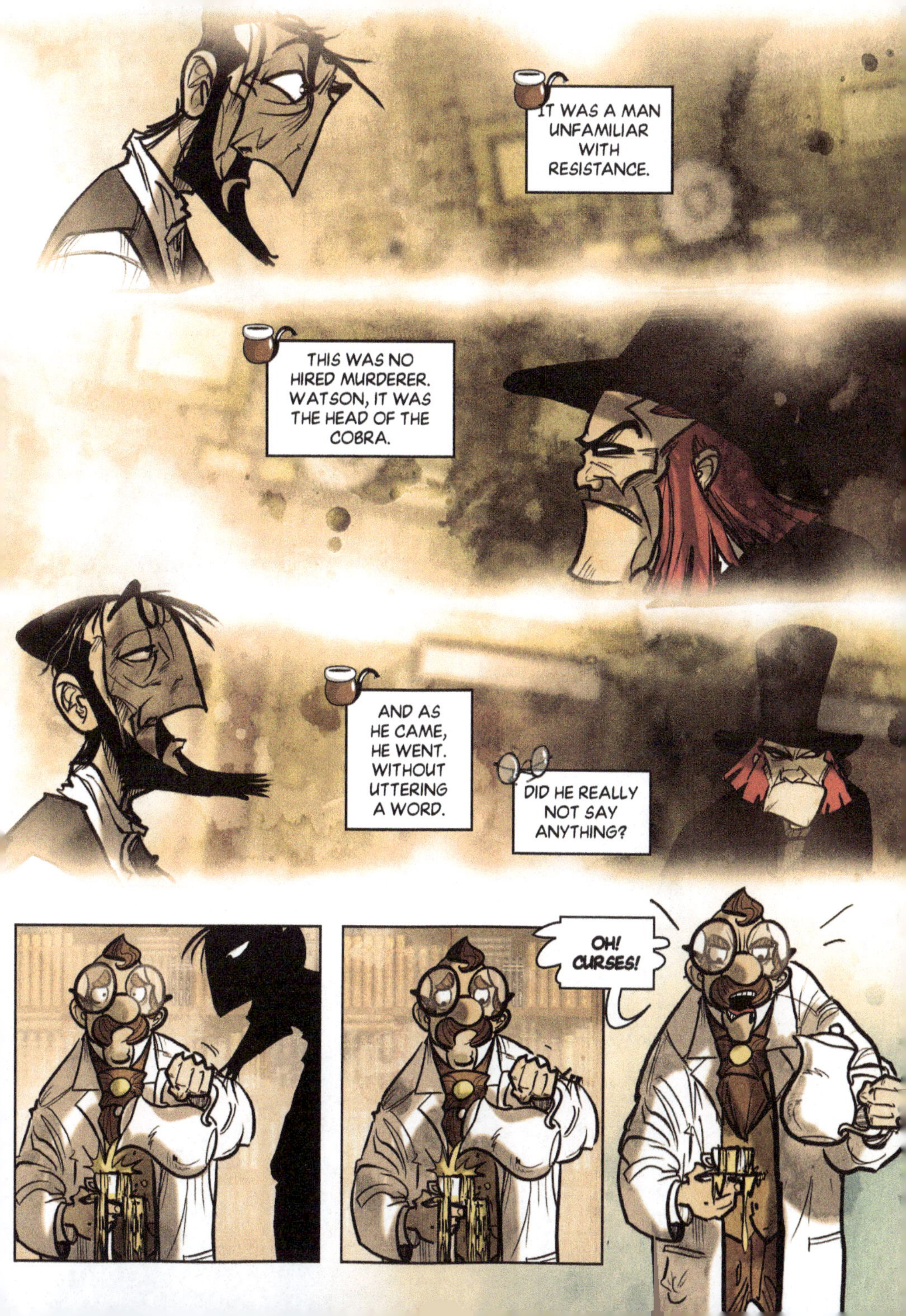
IT WAS A MAN UNFAMILIAR WITH RESISTANCE.
THIS WAS NO HIRED MURDERER. WATSON, IT WAS THE HEAD OF THE COBRA.
AND AS HE CAME, HE WENT. WITHOUT UTTERING A WORD.
DID HE REALLY NOT SAY ANYTHING?
OH! CURSES!

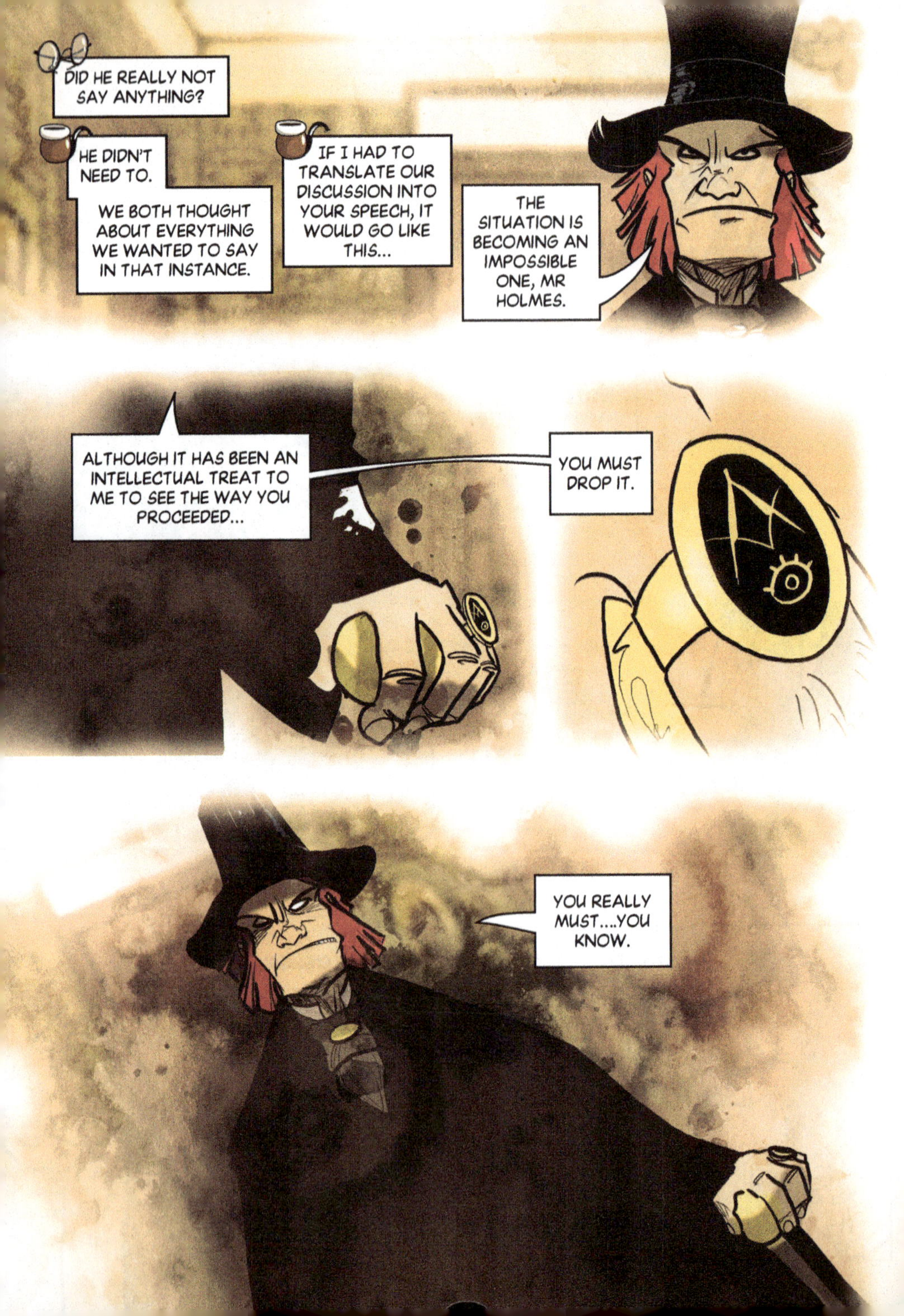
DID HE REALLY NOT SAY ANYTHING?
HE DIDN'T NEED TO.
WE BOTH THOUGHT ABOUT EVERYTHING WE WANTED TO SAY IN THAT INSTANCE.
IF I HAD TO TRANSLATE OUR DISCUSSION INTO YOUR SPEECH, IT WOULD GO LIKE THIS...
THE SITUATION IS BECOMING AN IMPOSSIBLE ONE, MR HOLMES.
ALTHOUGH IT HAS BEEN AN INTELLECTUAL TREAT TO ME TO SEE THE WAY YOU PROCEEDED...
YOU MUST DROP IT.
YOU REALLY MUST....YOU KNOW.

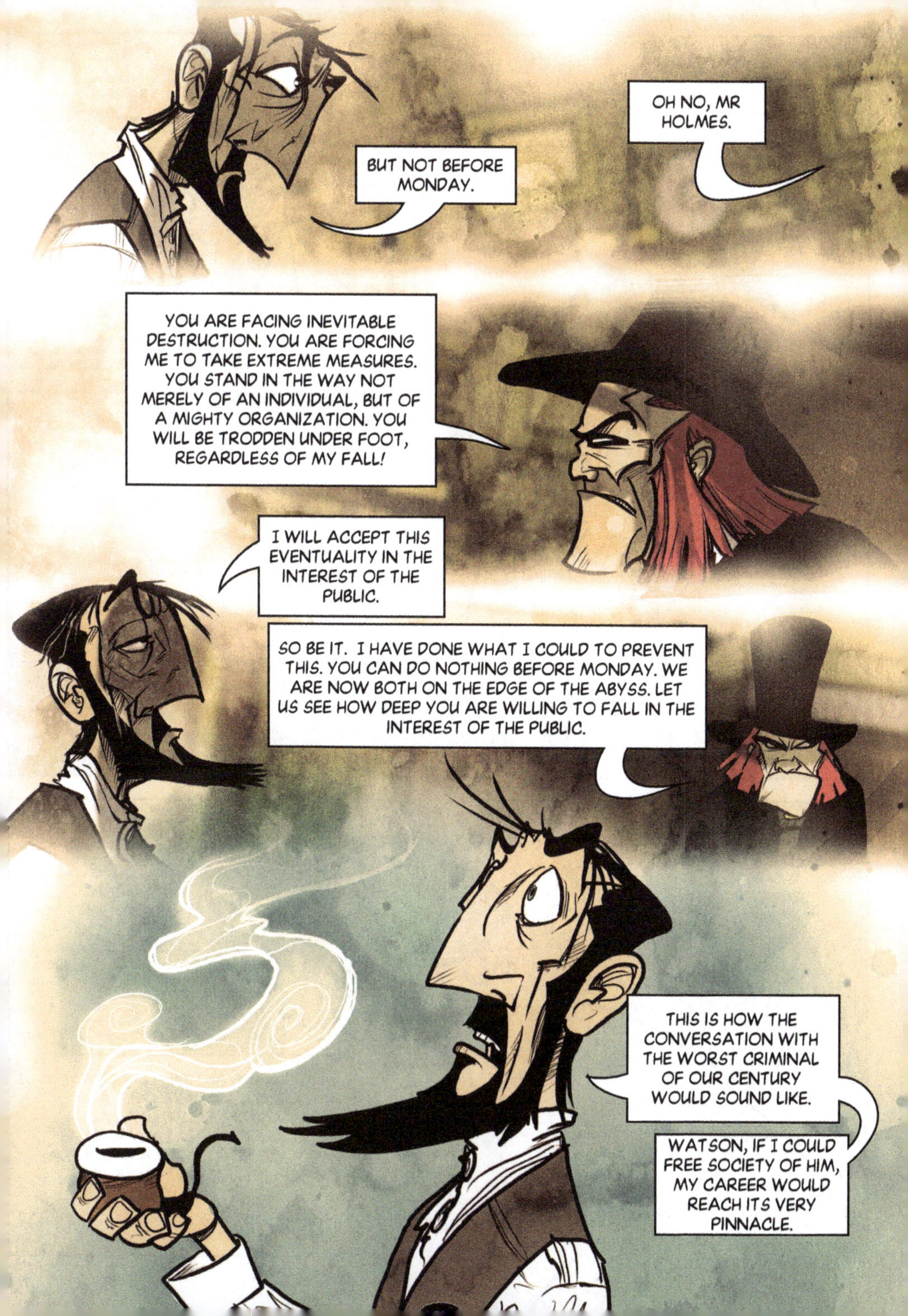
BUT NOT BEFORE MONDAY.
OH NO, MR HOLMES.
YOU ARE FACING INEVITABLE DESTRUCTION. YOU ARE FORCING ME TO TAKE EXTREME MEASURES. YOU STAND IN THE WAY NOT MERELY OF AN INDIVIDUAL, BUT OF A MIGHTY ORGANIZATION. YOU WILL BE TRODDEN UNDER FOOT, REGARDLESS OF MY FALL!
I WILL ACCEPT THIS EVENTUALITY IN THE INTEREST OF THE PUBLIC.
SO BE IT. I HAVE DONE WHAT I COULD TO PREVENT THIS. YOU CAN DO NOTHING BEFORE MONDAY. WE ARE NOW BOTH ON THE EDGE OF THE ABYSS. LET US SEE HOW DEEP YOU ARE WILLING TO FALL IN THE INTEREST OF THE PUBLIC.
THIS IS HOW THE CONVERSATION WITH THE WORST CRIMINAL OF OUR CENTURY WOULD SOUND LIKE.
WATSON, IF I COULD FREE SOCIETY OF HIM, MY CAREER WOULD REACH ITS VERY PINNACLE.

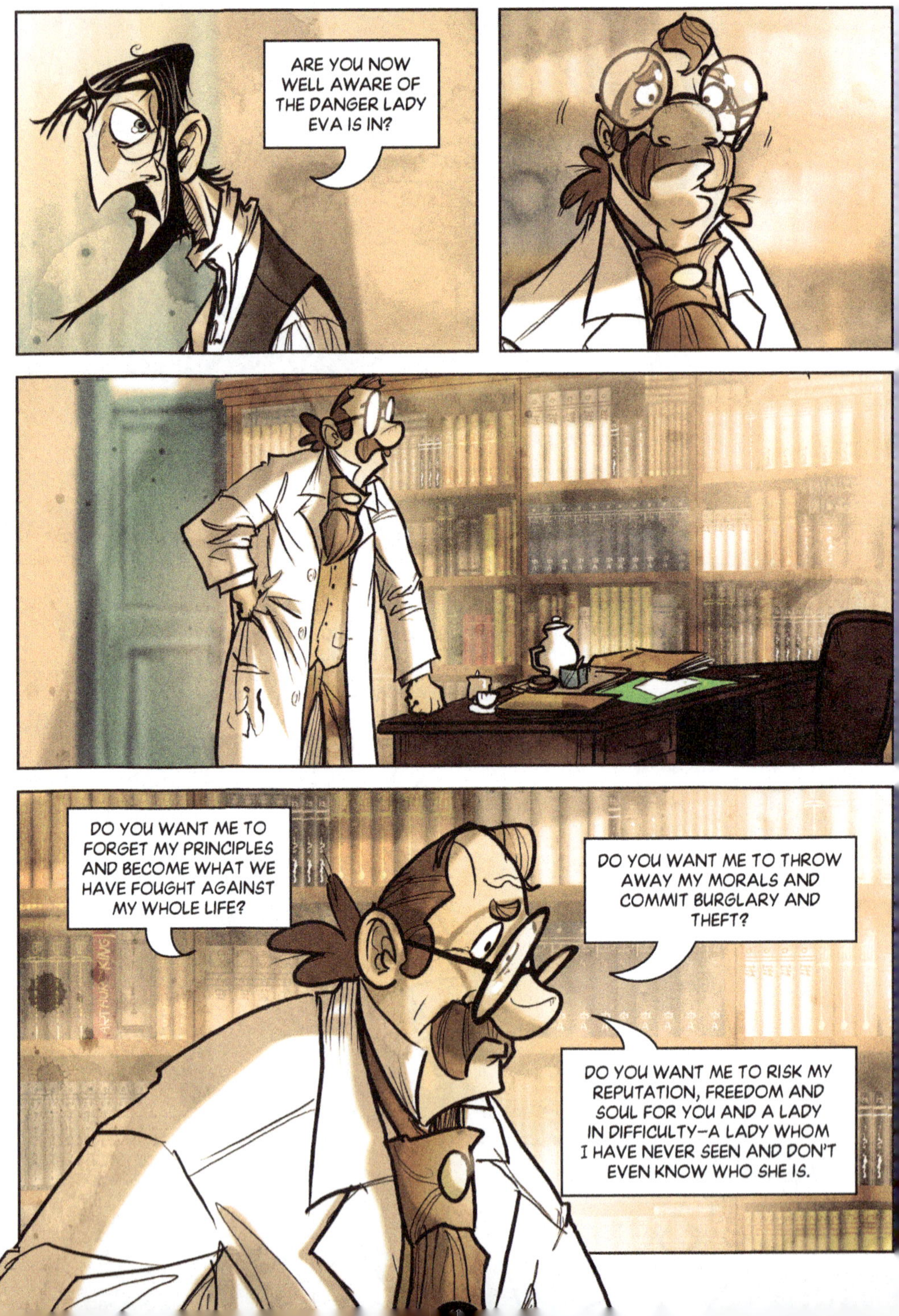
ARE YOU NOW WELL AWARE OF THE DANGER LADY EVA IS IN?
DO YOU WANT ME TO FORGET MY PRINCIPLES AND BECOME WHAT WE HAVE FOUGHT AGAINST MY WHOLE LIFE?
DO YOU WANT ME TO THROW AWAY MY MORALS AND COMMIT BURGLARY AND THEFT?
DO YOU WANT ME TO RISK MY REPUTATION, FREEDOM AND SOUL FOR YOU AND A LADY IN DIFFICULTY—A LADY WHOM I HAVE NEVER SEEN AND DON'T EVEN KNOW WHO SHE IS.

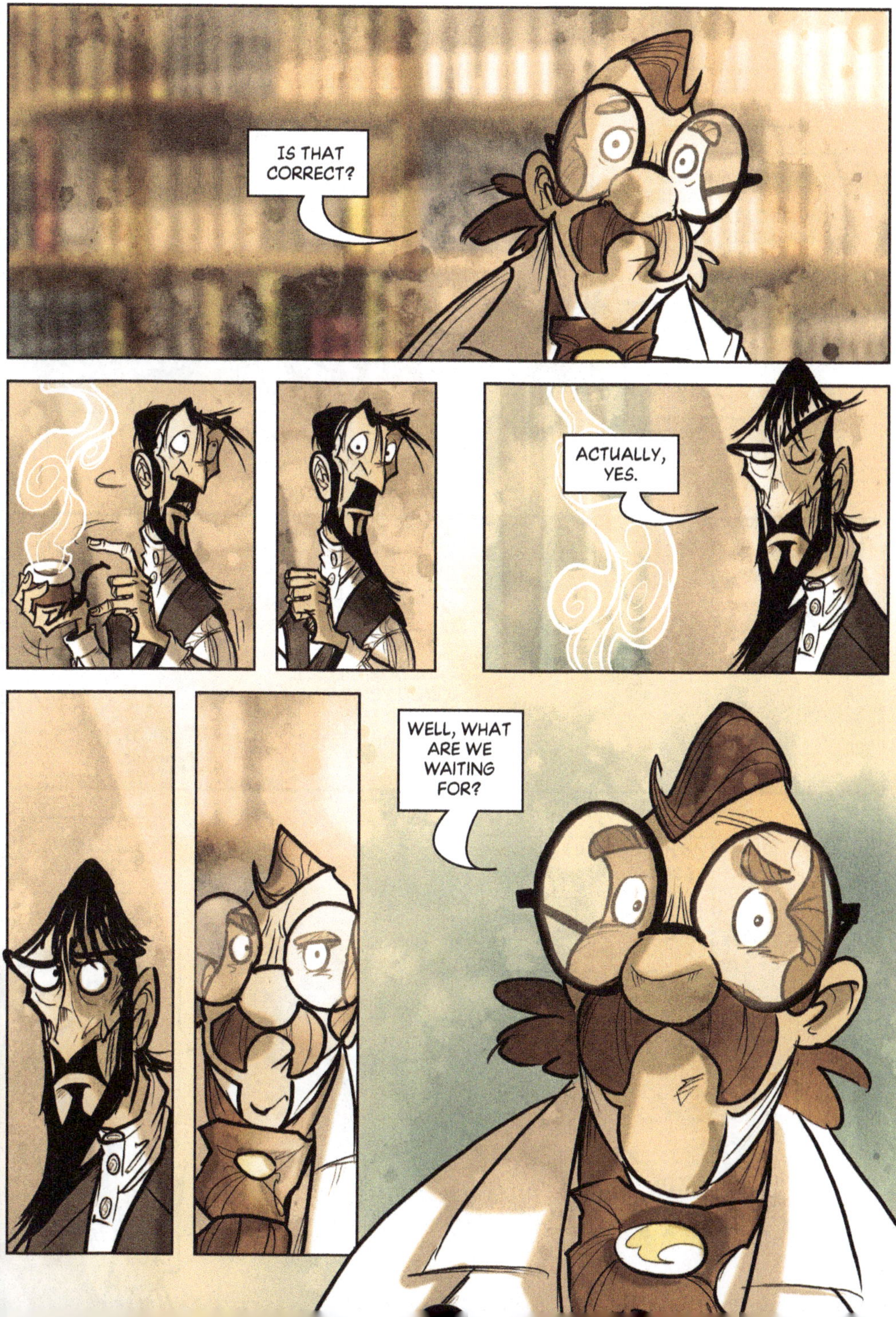
IS THAT CORRECT?
ACTUALLY, YES.
WELL, WHAT ARE WE WAITING FOR?

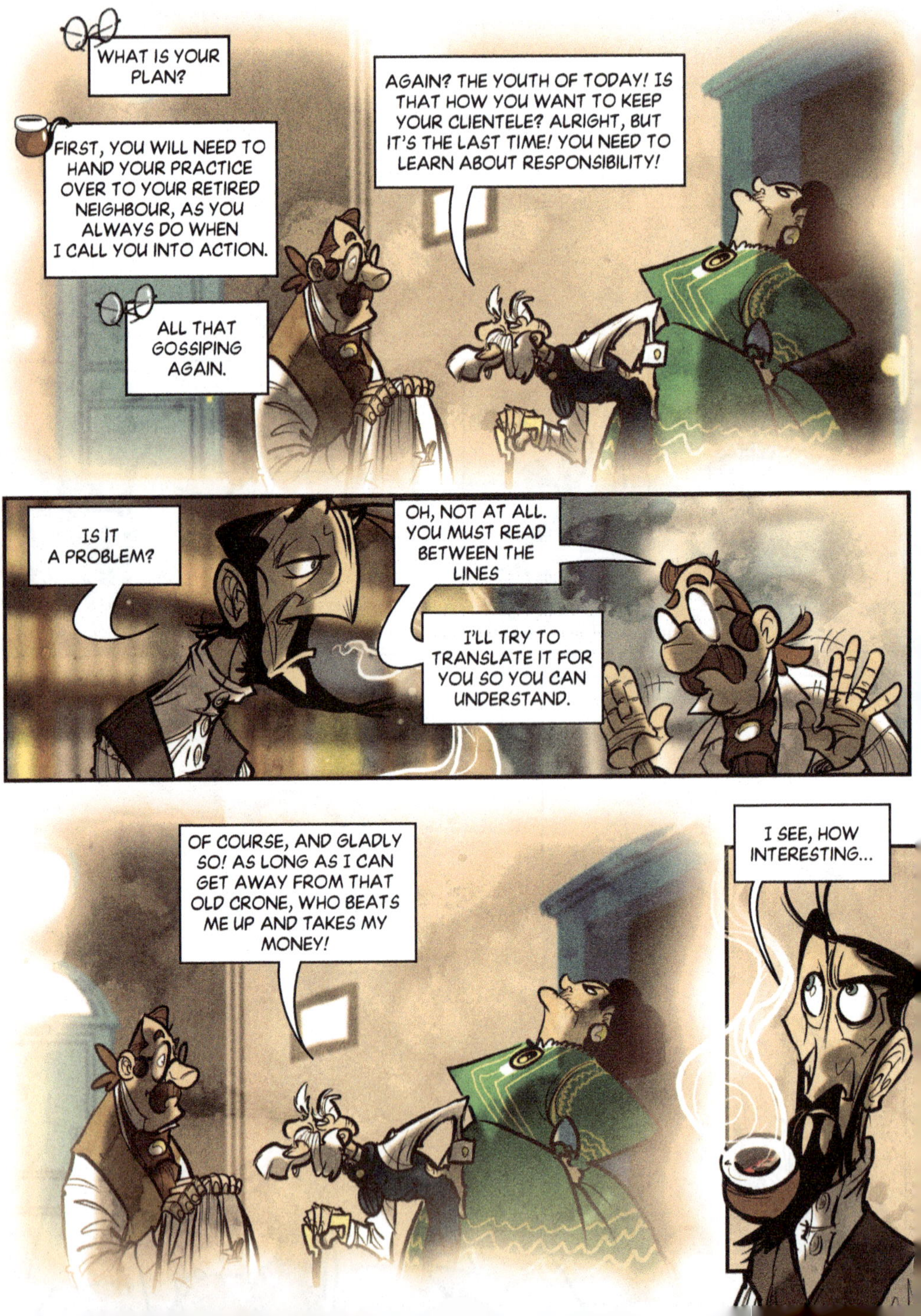
WHAT IS YOUR PLAN?
FIRST, YOU WILL NEED TO HAND YOUR PRACTICE OVER TO YOUR RETIRED NEIGHBOUR, AS YOU ALWAYS DO WHEN I CALL YOU INTO ACTION.
ALL THAT GOSSIPING AGAIN.
AGAIN? THE YOUTH OF TODAY! IS THAT HOW YOU WANT TO KEEP YOUR CLIENTELE? ALRIGHT, BUT IT'S THE LAST TIME! YOU NEED TO LEARN ABOUT RESPONSIBILITY!
IS IT A PROBLEM?
OH, NOT AT ALL. YOU MUST READ BETWEEN THE LINES
I'LL TRY TO TRANSLATE IT FOR YOU SO YOU CAN UNDERSTAND.
OF COURSE, AND GLADLY SO! AS LONG AS I CAN GET AWAY FROM THAT OLD CRONE, WHO BEATS ME UP AND TAKES MY MONEY!
I SEE, HOW INTERESTING...

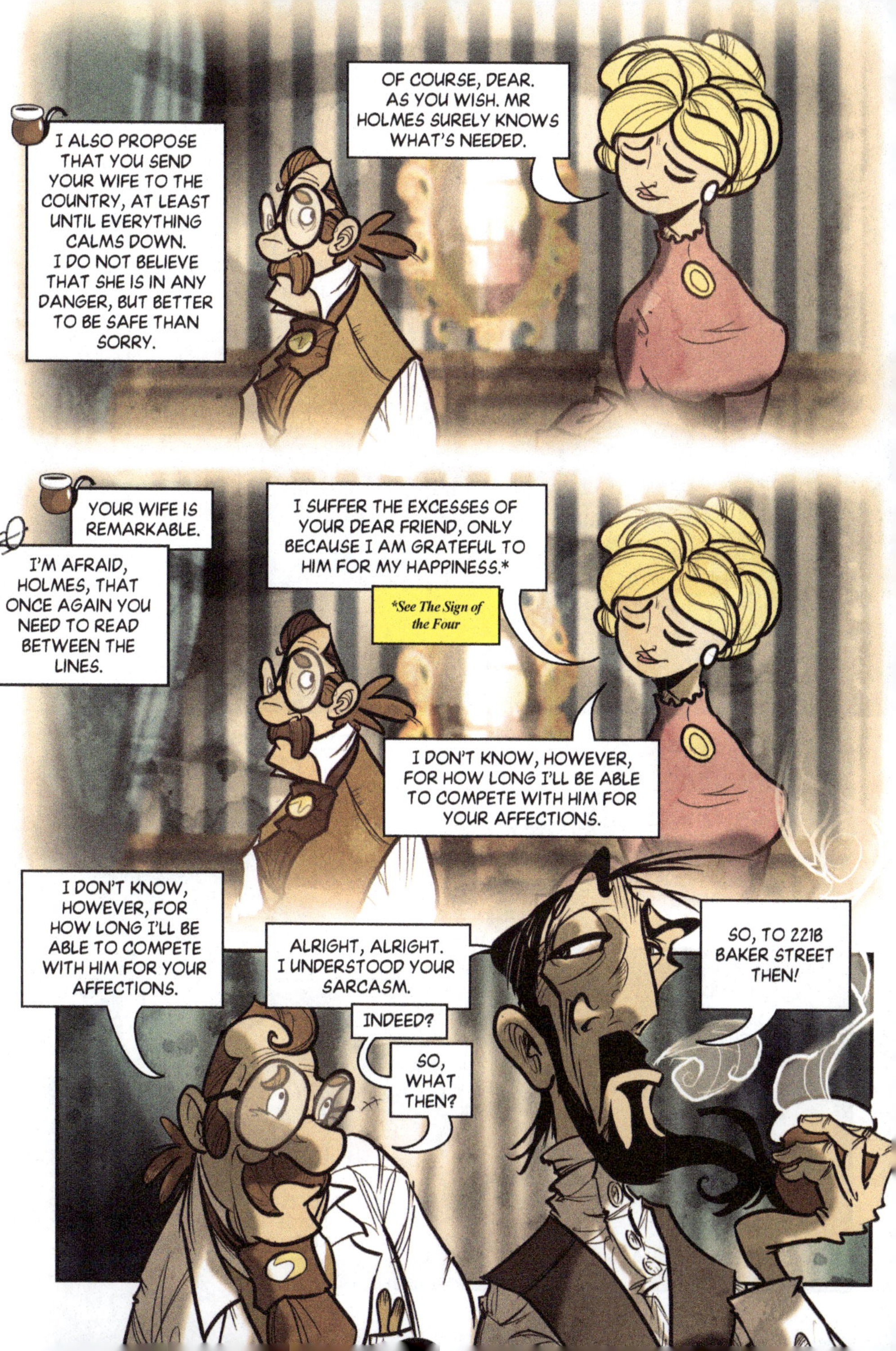
I ALSO PROPOSE THAT YOU SEND YOUR WIFE TO THE COUNTRY, AT LEAST UNTIL EVERYTHING CALMS DOWN. I DO NOT BELIEVE THAT SHE IS IN ANY DANGER, BUT BETTER TO BE SAFE THAN SORRY.
OF COURSE, DEAR. AS YOU WISH. MR HOLMES SURELY KNOWS WHAT'S NEEDED.
YOUR WIFE IS REMARKABLE.
I SUFFER THE EXCESSES OF YOUR DEAR FRIEND, ONLY BECAUSE I AM GRATEFUL TO HIM FOR MY HAPPINESS.*
*See The Sign of the Four
I'M AFRAID, HOLMES, THAT ONCE AGAIN YOU NEED TO READ BETWEEN THE LINES.
I DON'T KNOW, HOWEVER, FOR HOW LONG I'LL BE ABLE TO COMPETE WITH HIM FOR YOUR AFFECTIONS.
I DON'T KNOW, HOWEVER, FOR HOW LONG I'LL BE ABLE TO COMPETE WITH HIM FOR YOUR AFFECTIONS.
ALRIGHT, ALRIGHT. I UNDERSTOOD YOUR SARCASM.
INDEED?
SO, WHAT THEN?
SO, TO 221B BAKER STREET THEN!

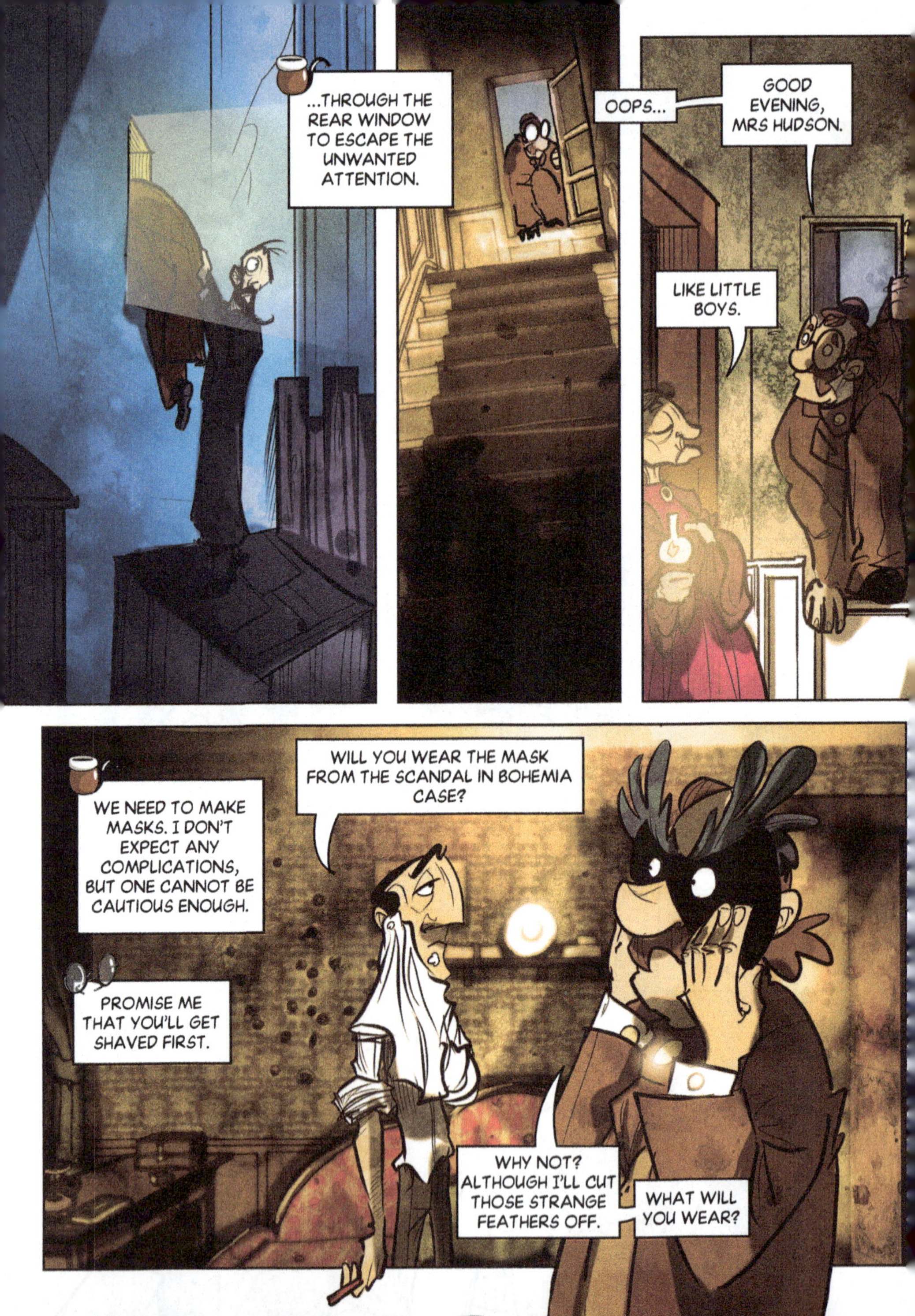
...THROUGH THE REAR WINDOW TO ESCAPE THE UNWANTED ATTENTION.
OOPS...
GOOD EVENING, MRS HUDSON.
LIKE LITTLE BOYS.
WE NEED TO MAKE MASKS. I DON'T EXPECT ANY COMPLICATIONS, BUT ONE CANNOT BE CAUTIOUS ENOUGH.
WILL YOU WEAR THE MASK FROM THE SCANDAL IN BOHEMIA CASE?
PROMISE ME THAT YOU'LL GET SHAVED FIRST.
WHY NOT? ALTHOUGH I'LL CUT THOSE STRANGE FEATHERS OFF.
WHAT WILL YOU WEAR?

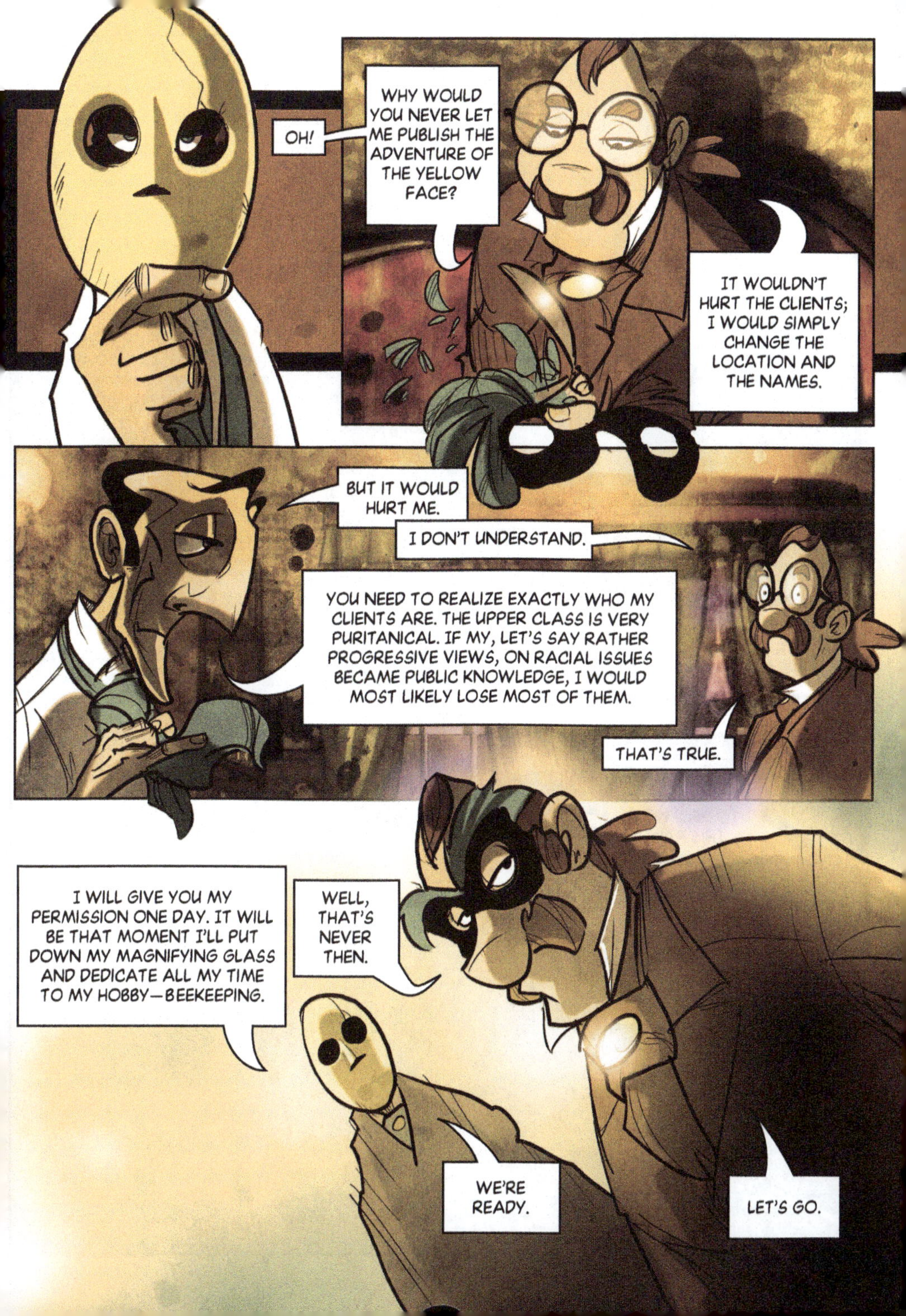
WHY WOULD YOU NEVER LET ME PUBLISH THE ADVENTURE OF THE YELLOW FACE?
OH!
IT WOULDN'T HURT THE CLIENTS; I WOULD SIMPLY CHANGE THE LOCATION AND THE NAMES.
BUT IT WOULD HURT ME.
I DON'T UNDERSTAND.
YOU NEED TO REALIZE EXACTLY WHO MY CLIENTS ARE. THE UPPER CLASS IS VERY PURITANICAL. IF MY, LET'S SAY RATHER PROGRESSIVE VIEWS, ON RACIAL ISSUES BECAME PUBLIC KNOWLEDGE, I WOULD MOST LIKELY LOSE MOST OF THEM.
THAT'S TRUE.
I WILL GIVE YOU MY PERMISSION ONE DAY. IT WILL BE THAT MOMENT I'LL PUT DOWN MY MAGNIFYING GLASS AND DEDICATE ALL MY TIME TO MY HOBBY—BEEKEEPING.
WELL, THAT'S NEVER THEN.
WE'RE READY.
LET'S GO.

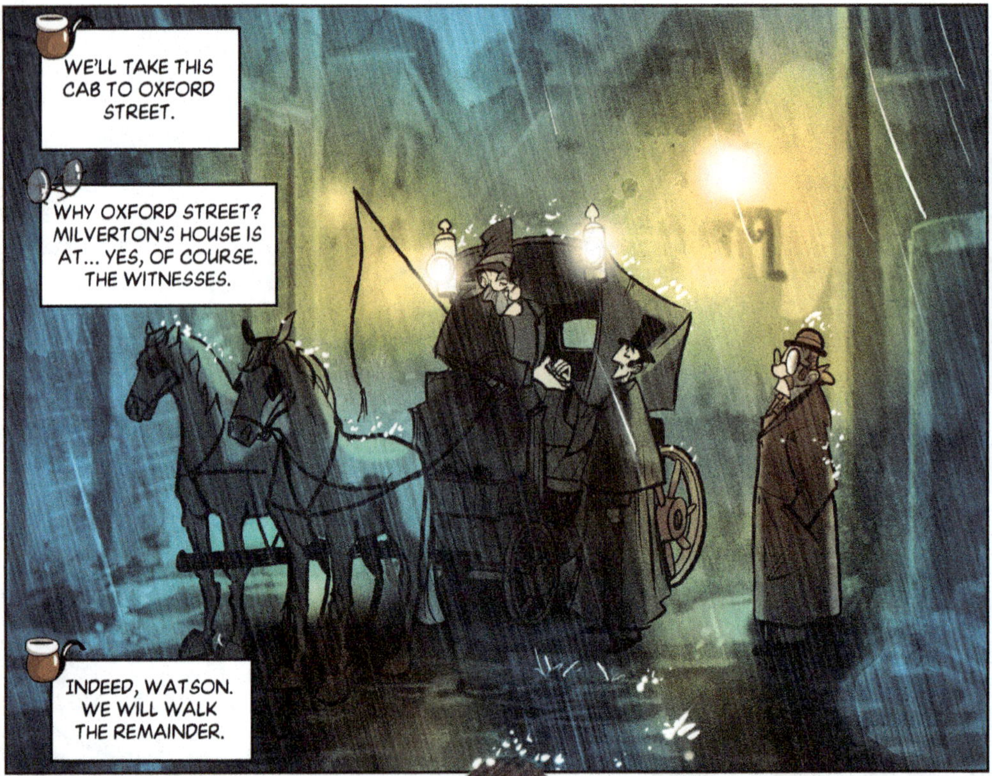
WE'LL TAKE THIS CAB TO OXFORD STREET.
WHY OXFORD STREET? MILVERTON'S HOUSE IS AT... YES, OF COURSE. THE WITNESSES.
INDEED, WATSON. WE WILL WALK THE REMAINDER.

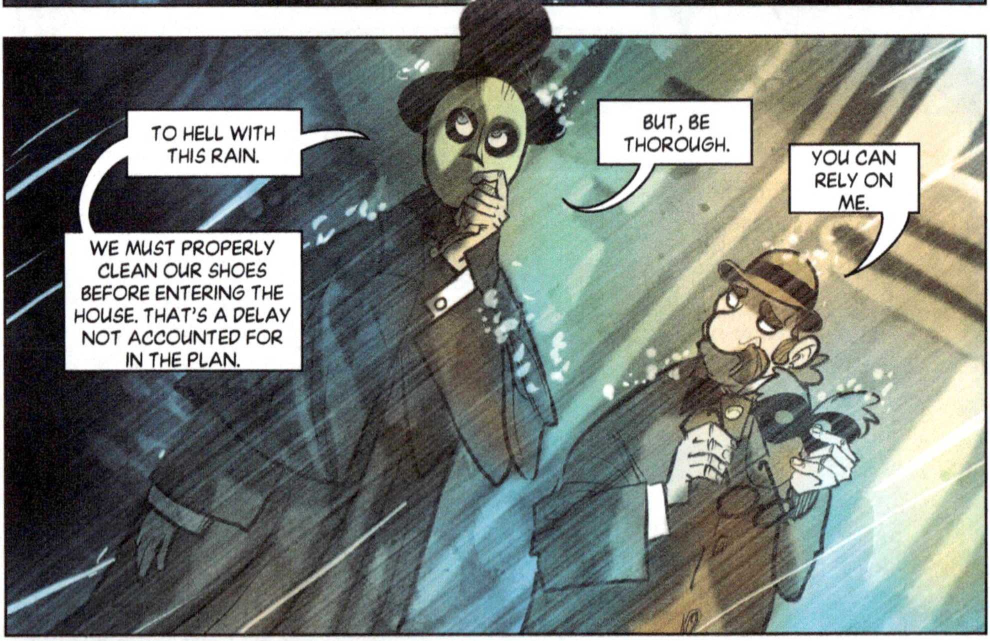
TO HELL WITH THIS RAIN.
WE MUST PROPERLY CLEAN OUR SHOES BEFORE ENTERING THE HOUSE. THAT'S A DELAY NOT ACCOUNTED FOR IN THE PLAN.
BUT, BE THOROUGH.
YOU CAN RELY ON ME.

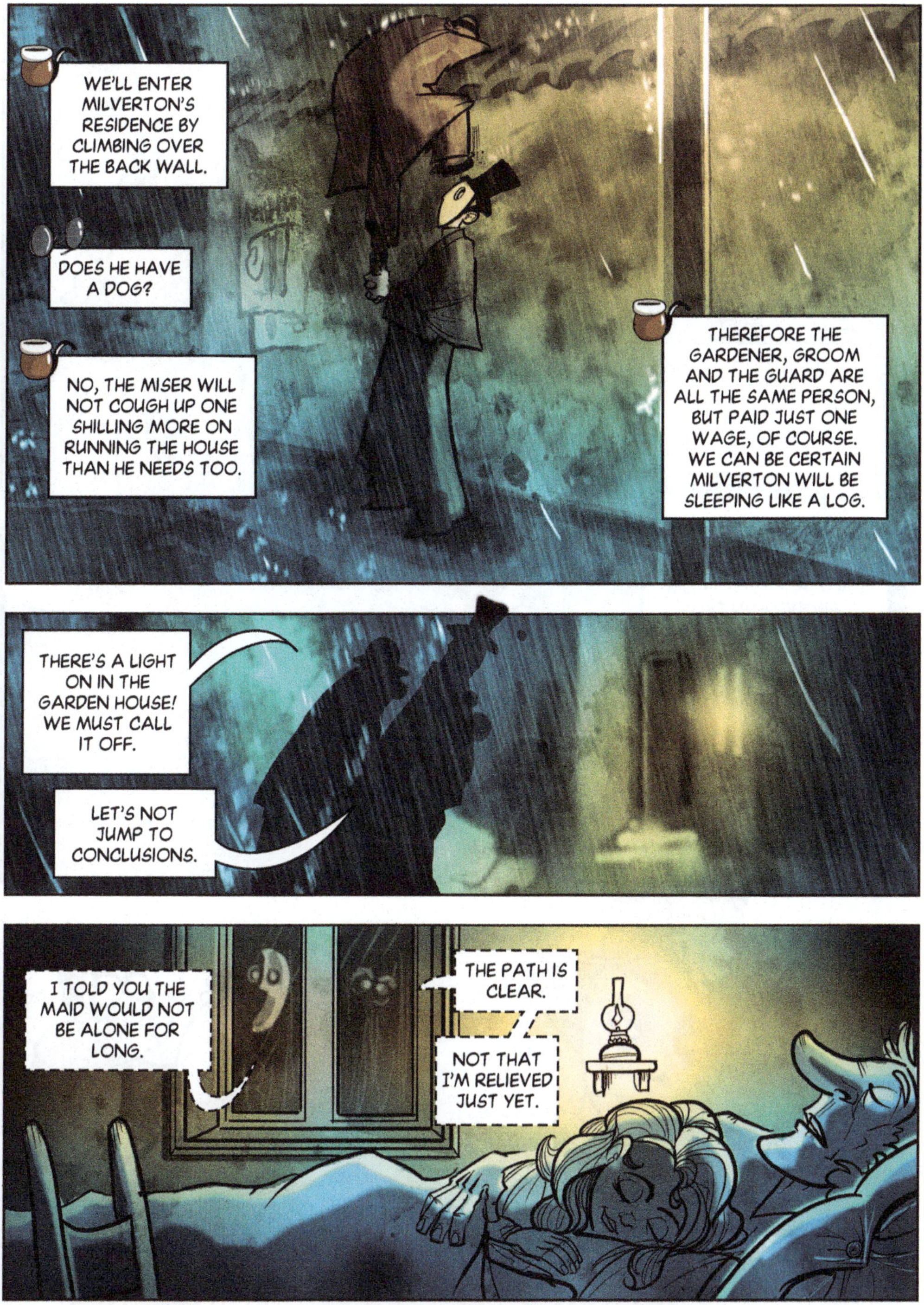
WE'LL ENTER MILVERTON'S RESIDENCE BY CLIMBING OVER THE BACK WALL.
DOES HE HAVE A DOG?
NO, THE MISER WILL NOT COUGH UP ONE SHILLING MORE ON RUNNING THE HOUSE THAN HE NEEDS TOO.
THEREFORE THE GARDENER, GROOM AND THE GUARD ARE ALL THE SAME PERSON, BUT PAID JUST ONE WAGE, OF COURSE. WE CAN BE CERTAIN MILVERTON WILL BE SLEEPING LIKE A LOG.
THERE'S A LIGHT ON IN THE GARDEN HOUSE! WE MUST CALL IT OFF.
LET'S NOT JUMP TO CONCLUSIONS.
I TOLD YOU THE MAID WOULD NOT BE ALONE FOR LONG.
THE PATH IS CLEAR.
NOT THAT I'M RELIEVED JUST YET.

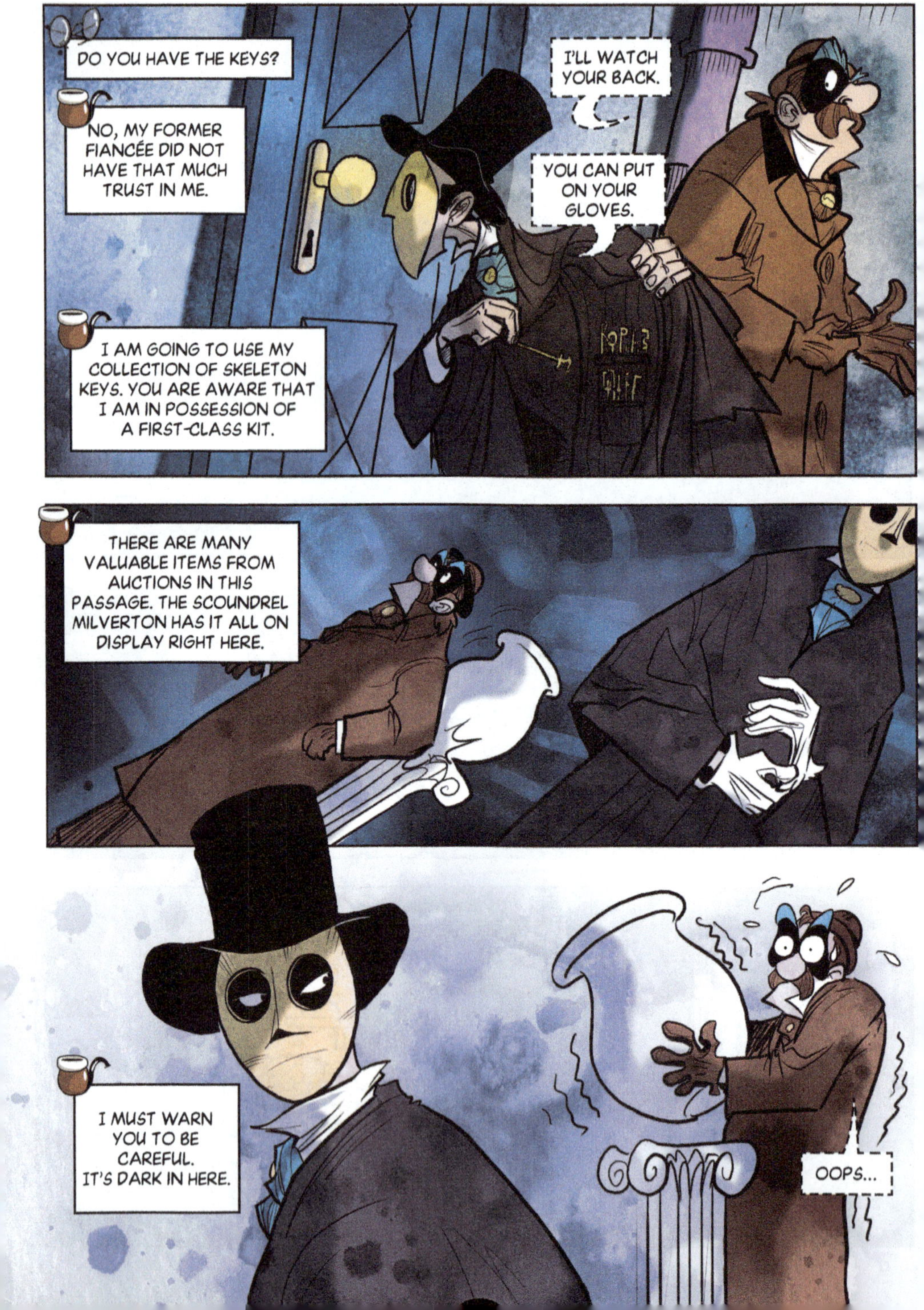
DO YOU HAVE THE KEYS?
NO, MY FORMER FIANCÉE DID NOT HAVE THAT MUCH TRUST IN ME.
I'LL WATCH YOUR BACK.
YOU CAN PUT ON YOUR GLOVES.
I AM GOING TO USE MY COLLECTION OF SKELETON KEYS. YOU ARE AWARE THAT I AM IN POSSESSION OF A FIRST-CLASS KIT.
THERE ARE MANY VALUABLE ITEMS FROM AUCTIONS IN THIS PASSAGE. THE SCOUNDREL MILVERTON HAS IT ALL ON DISPLAY RIGHT HERE.
I MUST WARN YOU TO BE CAREFUL. IT'S DARK IN HERE.
OOPS...

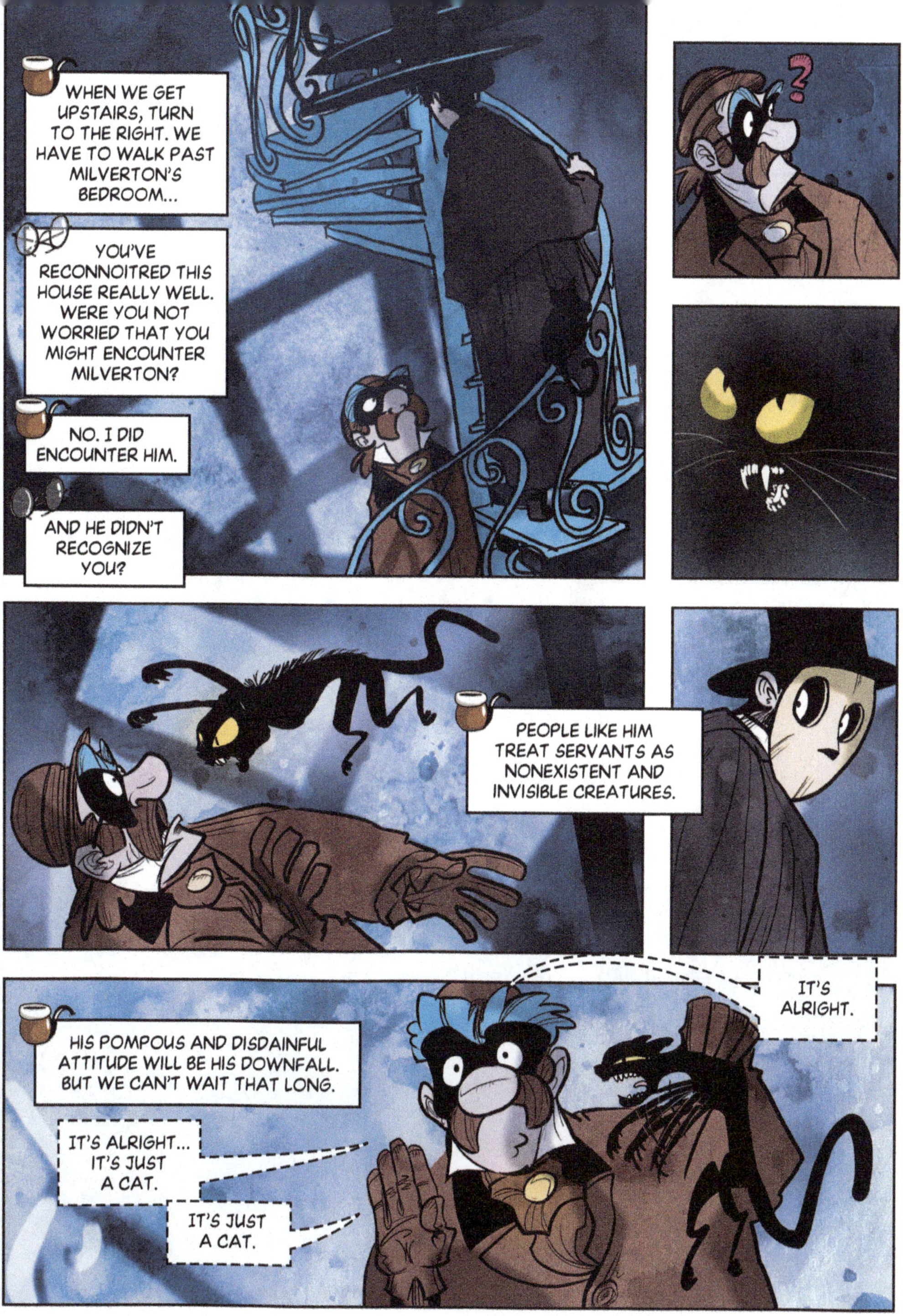
WHEN WE GET UPSTAIRS, TURN TO THE RIGHT. WE HAVE TO WALK PAST MILVERTON'S BEDROOM...
YOU'VE RECONNOITRED THIS HOUSE REALLY WELL. WERE YOU NOT WORRIED THAT YOU MIGHT ENCOUNTER MILVERTON?
NO. I DID ENCOUNTER HIM.
AND HE DIDN'T RECOGNIZE YOU?
?
PEOPLE LIKE HIM TREAT SERVANTS AS NONEXISTENT AND INVISIBLE CREATURES.
HIS POMPOUS AND DISDAINFUL ATTITUDE WILL BE HIS DOWNFALL. BUT WE CAN'T WAIT THAT LONG.
IT'S ALRIGHT.
IT'S ALRIGHT... IT'S JUST A CAT.
IT'S JUST A CAT.

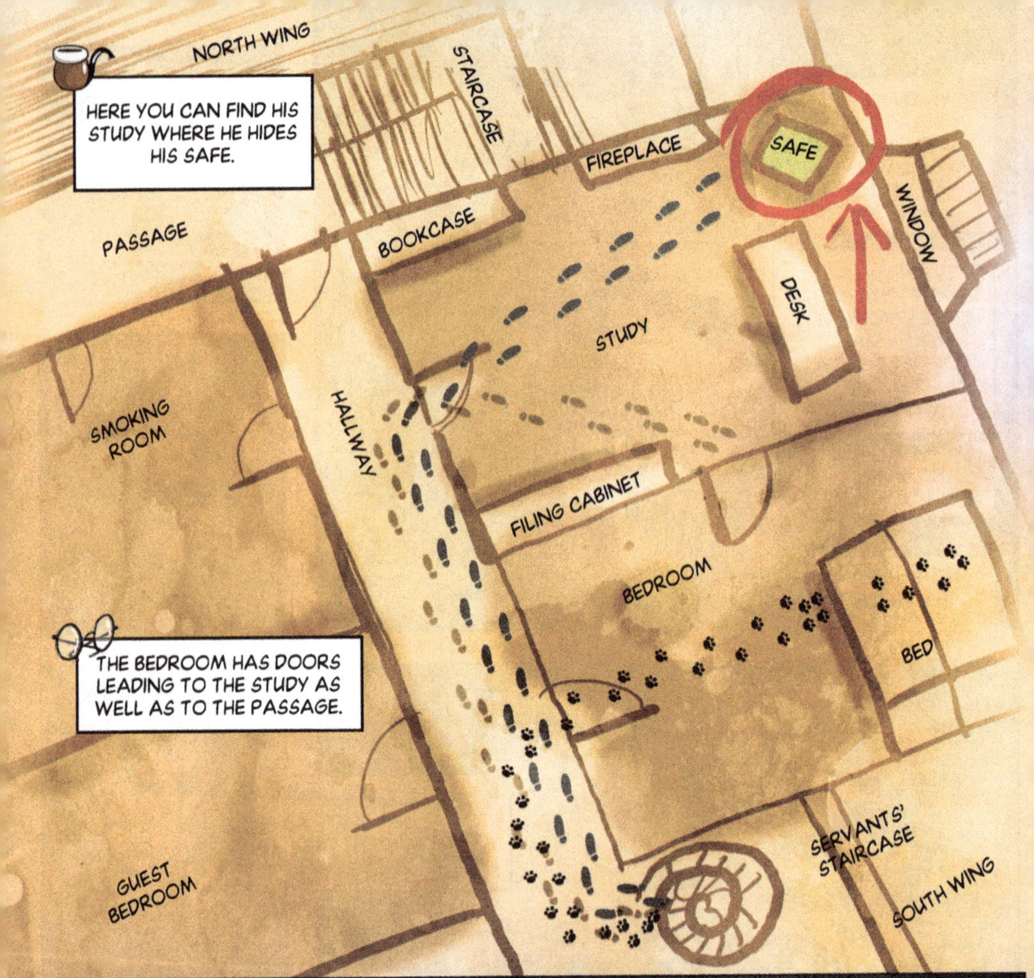
HERE YOU CAN FIND HIS STUDY WHERE HE HIDES HIS SAFE.
NORTH WING
STAIRCASE
FIREPLACE
SAFE
WINDOW
PASSAGE
BOOKCASE
DESK
STUDY
SMOKING ROOM
HALLWAY
FILING CABINET
BEDROOM
BED
THE BEDROOM HAS DOORS LEADING TO THE STUDY AS WELL AS TO THE PASSAGE.
GUEST BEDROOM
SERVANTS' STAIRCASE
SOUTH WING

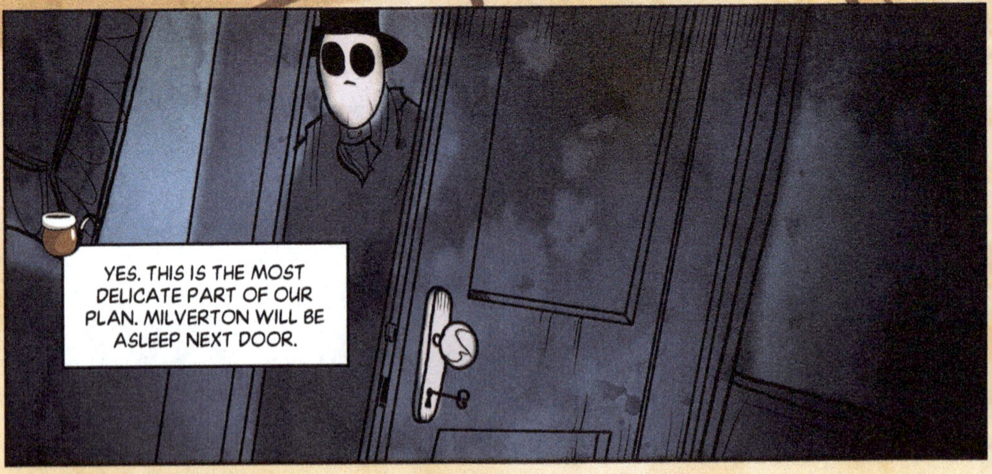
YES. THIS IS THE MOST DELICATE PART OF OUR PLAN. MILVERTON WILL BE ASLEEP NEXT DOOR.

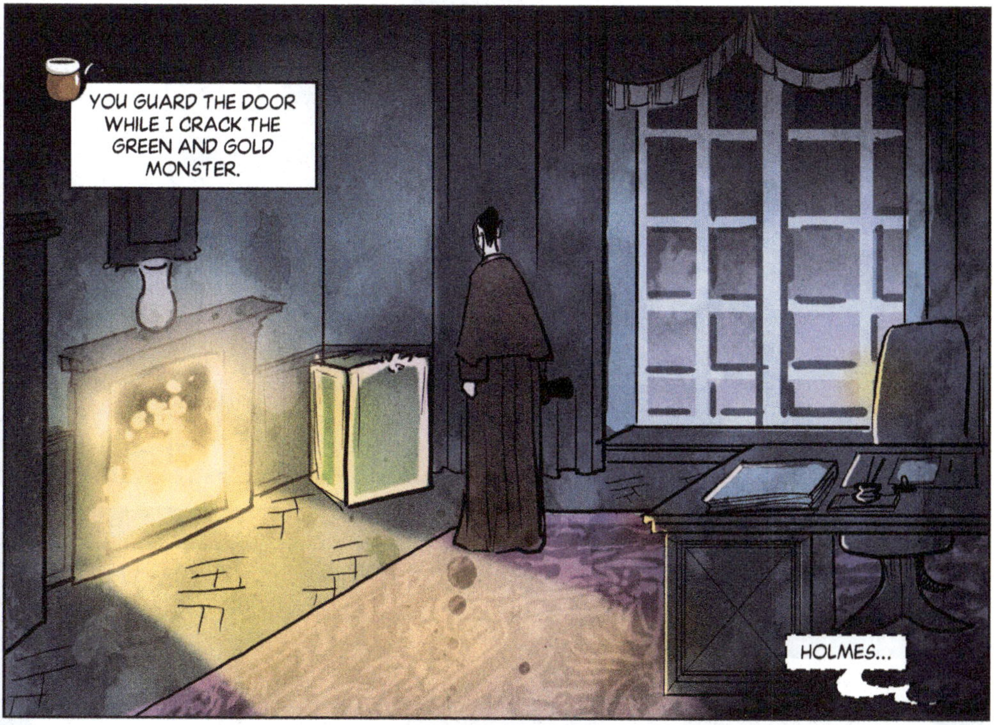
YOU GUARD THE DOOR WHILE I CRACK THE GREEN AND GOLD MONSTER.
HOLMES...

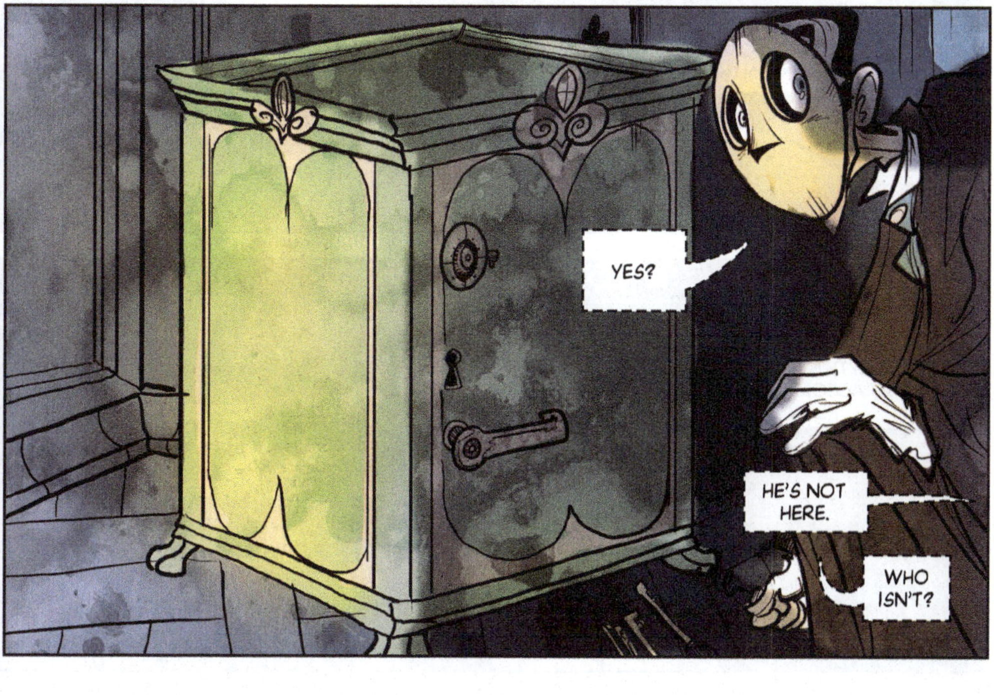
YES?
HE'S NOT HERE.
WHO ISN'T?

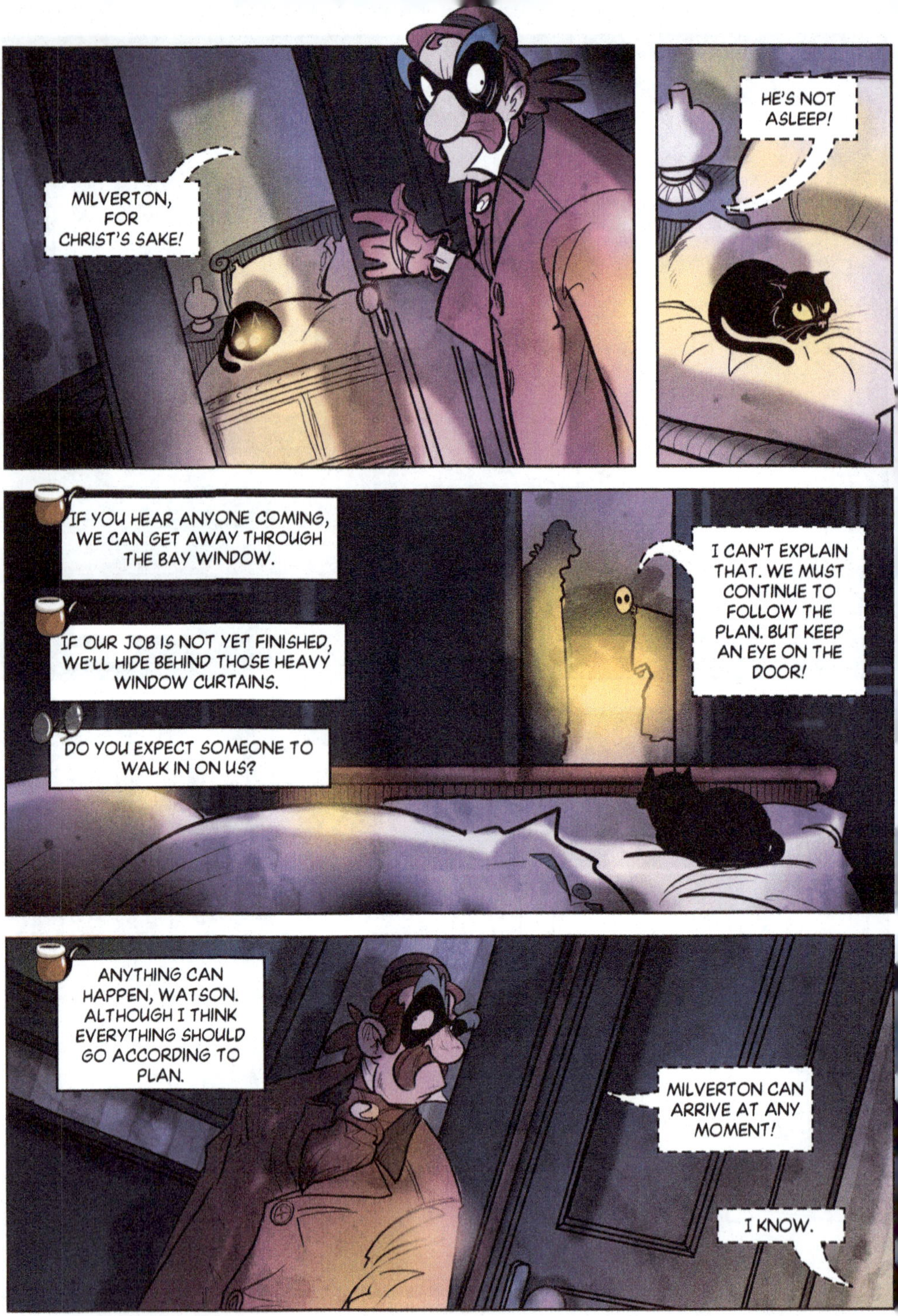
MILVERTON, FOR CHRIST'S SAKE!
HE'S NOT ASLEEP!
IF YOU HEAR ANYONE COMING, WE CAN GET AWAY THROUGH THE BAY WINDOW.
IF OUR JOB IS NOT YET FINISHED, WE'LL HIDE BEHIND THOSE HEAVY WINDOW CURTAINS.
DO YOU EXPECT SOMEONE TO WALK IN ON US?
I CAN'T EXPLAIN THAT. WE MUST CONTINUE TO FOLLOW THE PLAN. BUT KEEP AN EYE ON THE DOOR!
ANYTHING CAN HAPPEN, WATSON. ALTHOUGH I THINK EVERYTHING SHOULD GO ACCORDING TO PLAN.
MILVERTON CAN ARRIVE AT ANY MOMENT!
I KNOW.

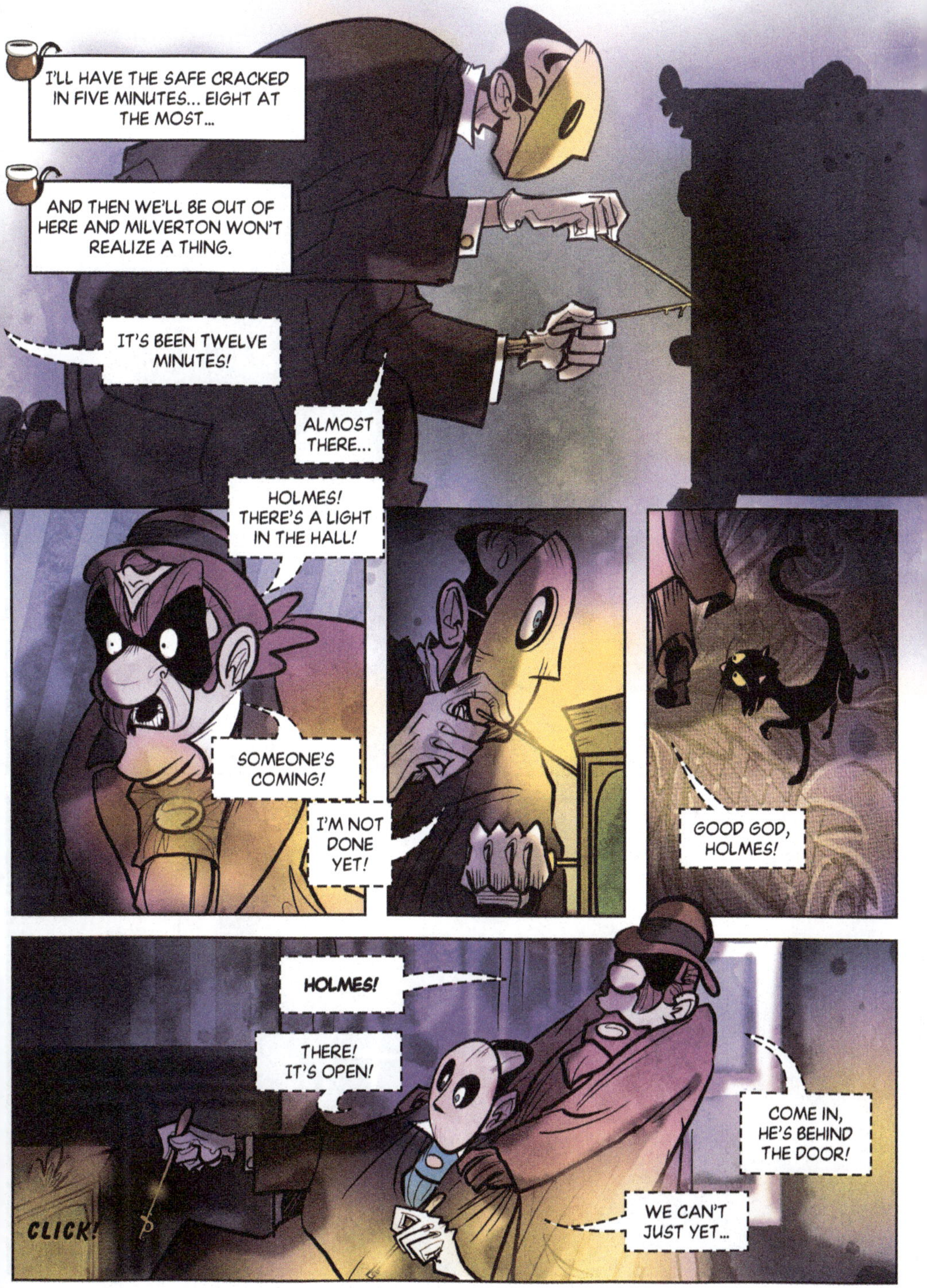
I'LL HAVE THE SAFE CRACKED IN FIVE MINUTES... EIGHT AT THE MOST...
AND THEN WE'LL BE OUT OF HERE AND MILVERTON WON'T REALIZE A THING.
IT'S BEEN TWELVE MINUTES!
ALMOST THERE...
HOLMES! THERE'S A LIGHT IN THE HALL!
SOMEONE'S COMING!
I'M NOT DONE YET!
GOOD GOD, HOLMES!
HOLMES!
THERE! IT'S OPEN!
CLICK!
COME IN, HE'S BEHIND THE DOOR!
WE CAN'T JUST YET...

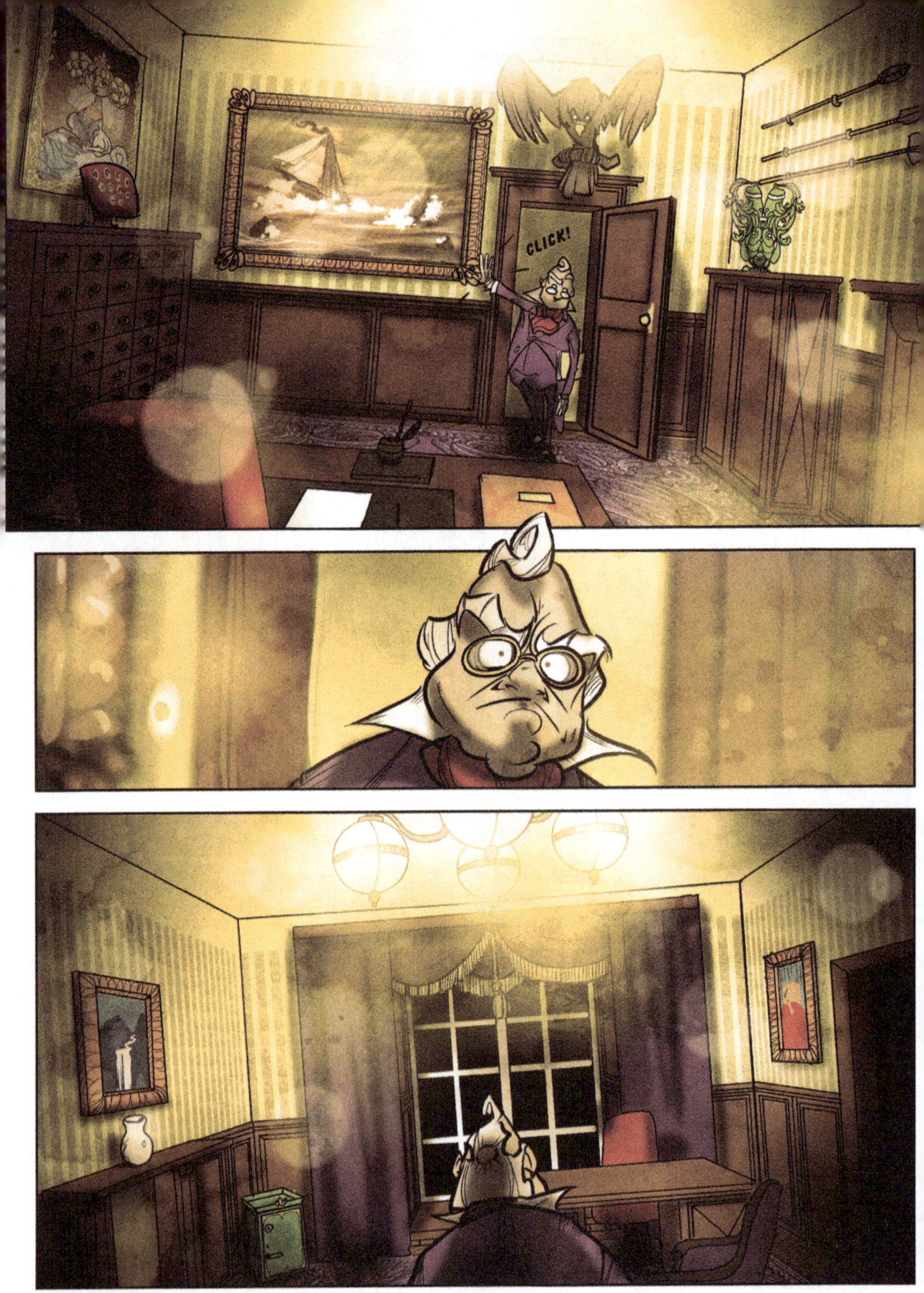
CLICK!

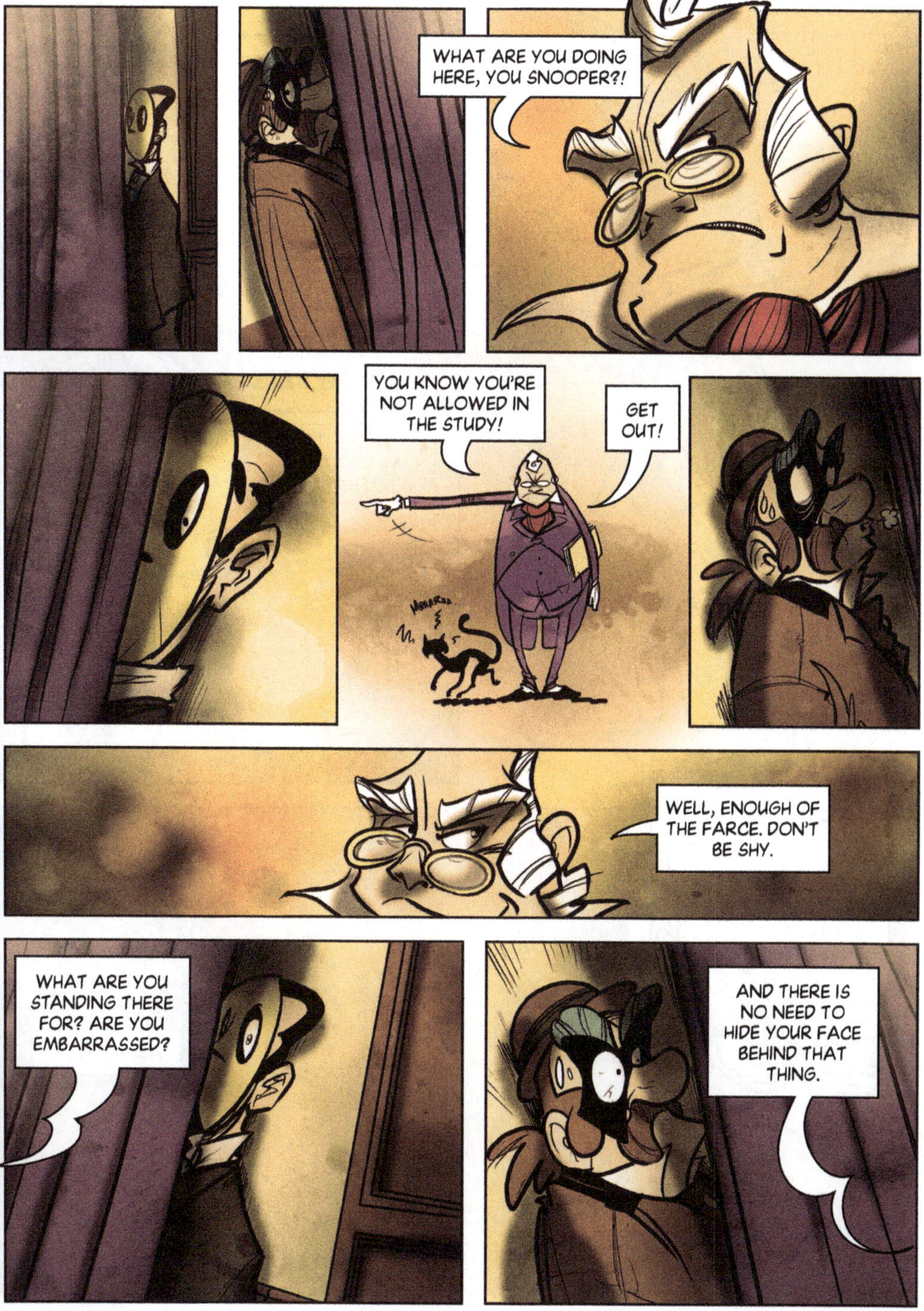
WHAT ARE YOU DOING HERE, YOU SNOOPER?!
YOU KNOW YOU'RE NOT ALLOWED IN THE STUDY!
GET OUT!
WELL, ENOUGH OF THE FARCE. DON'T BE SHY.
WHAT ARE YOU STANDING THERE FOR? ARE YOU EMBARRASSED?
AND THERE IS NO NEED TO HIDE YOUR FACE BEHIND THAT THING.

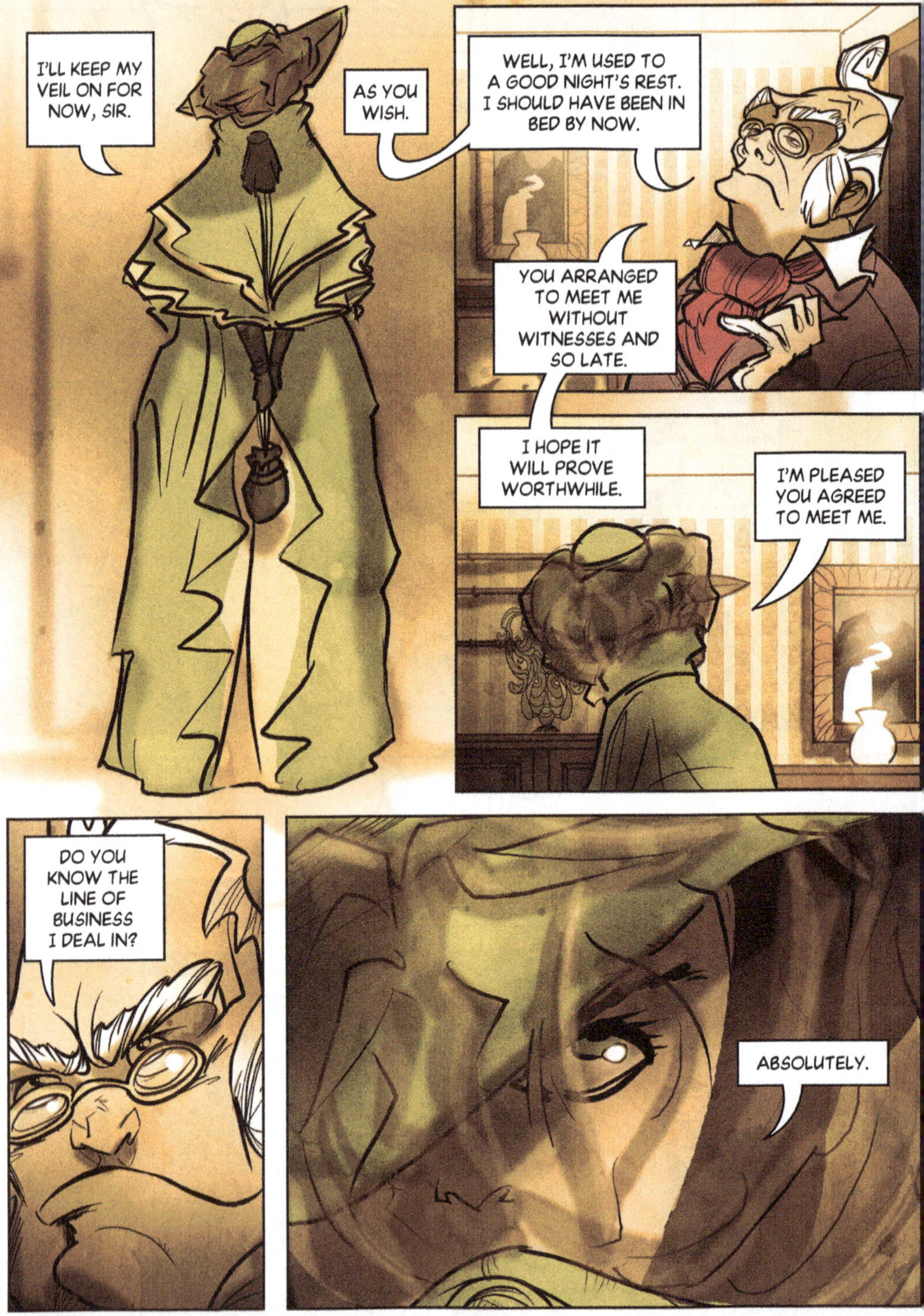
I'LL KEEP MY VEIL ON FOR NOW, SIR.
AS YOU WISH.
WELL, I'M USED TO A GOOD NIGHT'S REST. I SHOULD HAVE BEEN IN BED BY NOW.
YOU ARRANGED TO MEET ME WITHOUT WITNESSES AND SO LATE.
I HOPE IT WILL PROVE WORTHWHILE.
I'M PLEASED YOU AGREED TO MEET ME.
DO YOU KNOW THE LINE OF BUSINESS I DEAL IN?
ABSOLUTELY.

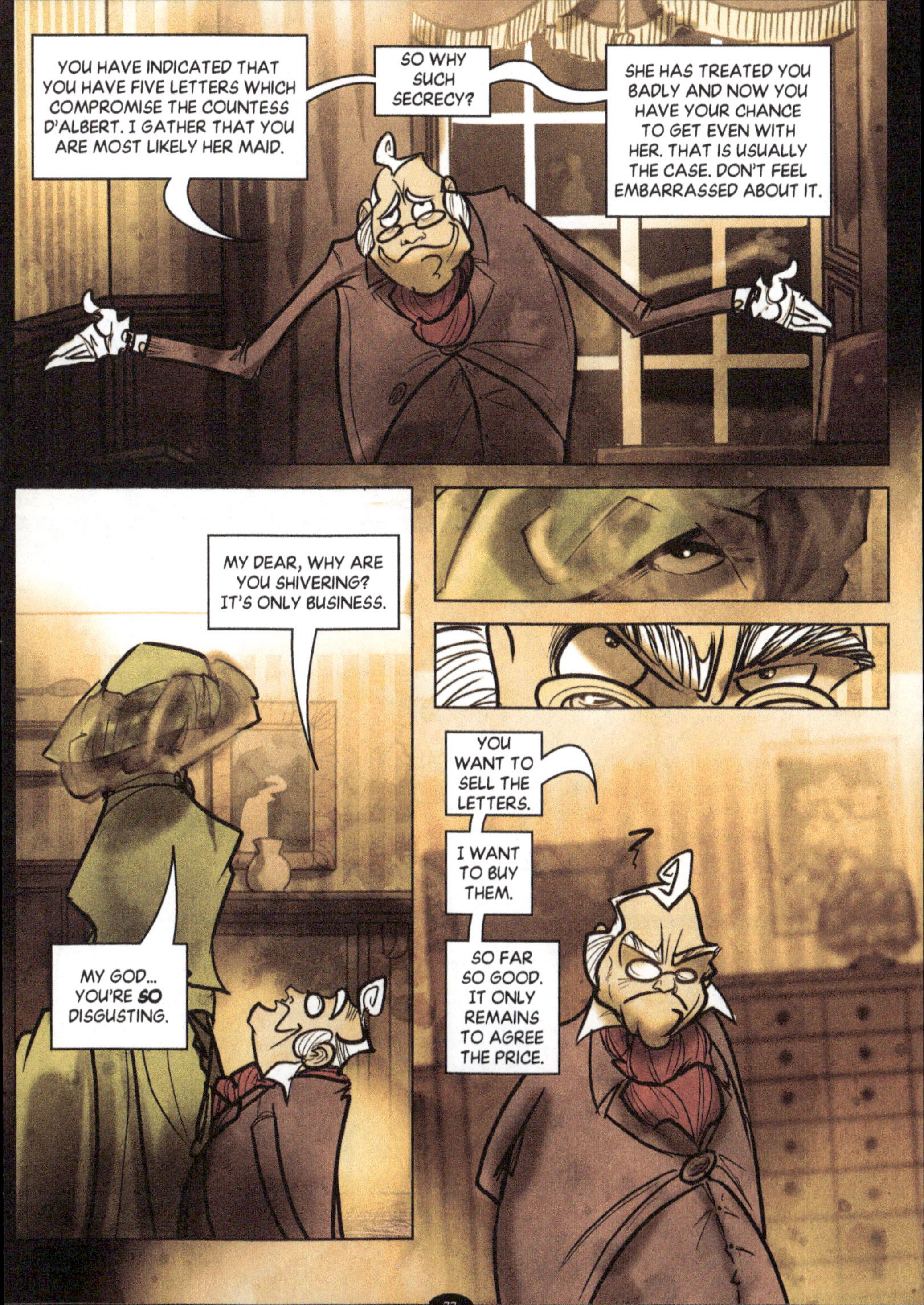
YOU HAVE INDICATED THAT YOU HAVE FIVE LETTERS WHICH COMPROMISE THE COUNTESS D'ALBERT. I GATHER THAT YOU ARE MOST LIKELY HER MAID.
SO WHY SUCH SECRECY?
SHE HAS TREATED YOU BADLY AND NOW YOU HAVE YOUR CHANCE TO GET EVEN WITH HER. THAT IS USUALLY THE CASE. DON'T FEEL EMBARRASSED ABOUT IT.
MY DEAR, WHY ARE YOU SHIVERING? IT'S ONLY BUSINESS.
MY GOD... YOU'RE **SO** DISGUSTING.
YOU WANT TO SELL THE LETTERS.
I WANT TO BUY THEM.
SO FAR SO GOOD. IT ONLY REMAINS TO AGREE THE PRICE.

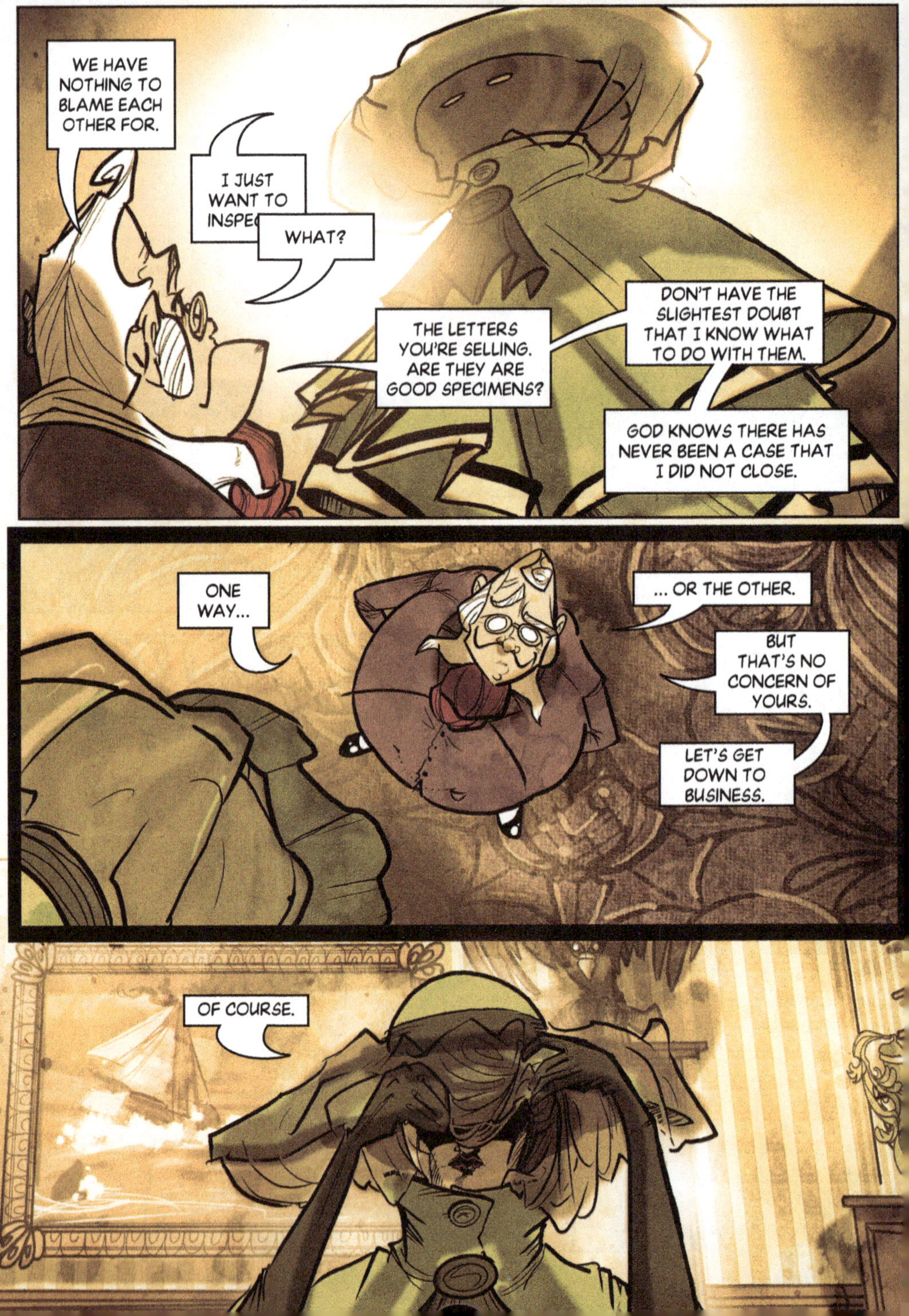
WE HAVE NOTHING TO BLAME EACH OTHER FOR.
I JUST WANT TO INSPE
WHAT?
THE LETTERS YOU'RE SELLING. ARE THEY ARE GOOD SPECIMENS?
DON'T HAVE THE SLIGHTEST DOUBT THAT I KNOW WHAT TO DO WITH THEM.
GOD KNOWS THERE HAS NEVER BEEN A CASE THAT I DID NOT CLOSE.
ONE WAY...
... OR THE OTHER.
BUT THAT'S NO CONCERN OF YOURS.
LET'S GET DOWN TO BUSINESS.
OF COURSE.

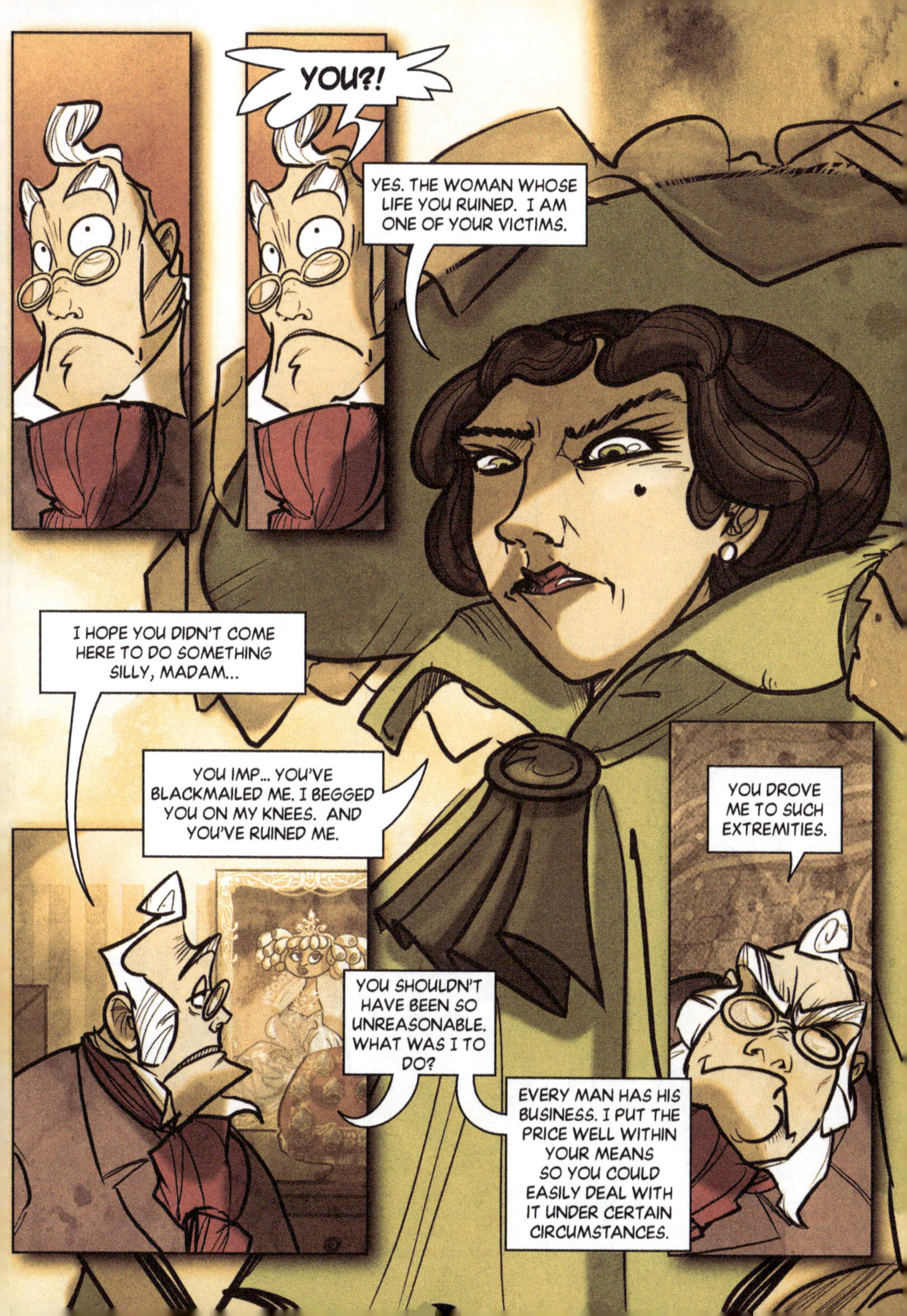
YOU?!
YES. THE WOMAN WHOSE LIFE YOU RUINED. I AM ONE OF YOUR VICTIMS.
I HOPE YOU DIDN'T COME HERE TO DO SOMETHING SILLY, MADAM...
YOU IMP... YOU'VE BLACKMAILED ME. I BEGGED YOU ON MY KNEES. AND YOU'VE RUINED ME.
YOU DROVE ME TO SUCH EXTREMITIES.
YOU SHOULDN'T HAVE BEEN SO UNREASONABLE. WHAT WAS I TO DO?
EVERY MAN HAS HIS BUSINESS. I PUT THE PRICE WELL WITHIN YOUR MEANS SO YOU COULD EASILY DEAL WITH IT UNDER CERTAIN CIRCUMSTANCES.

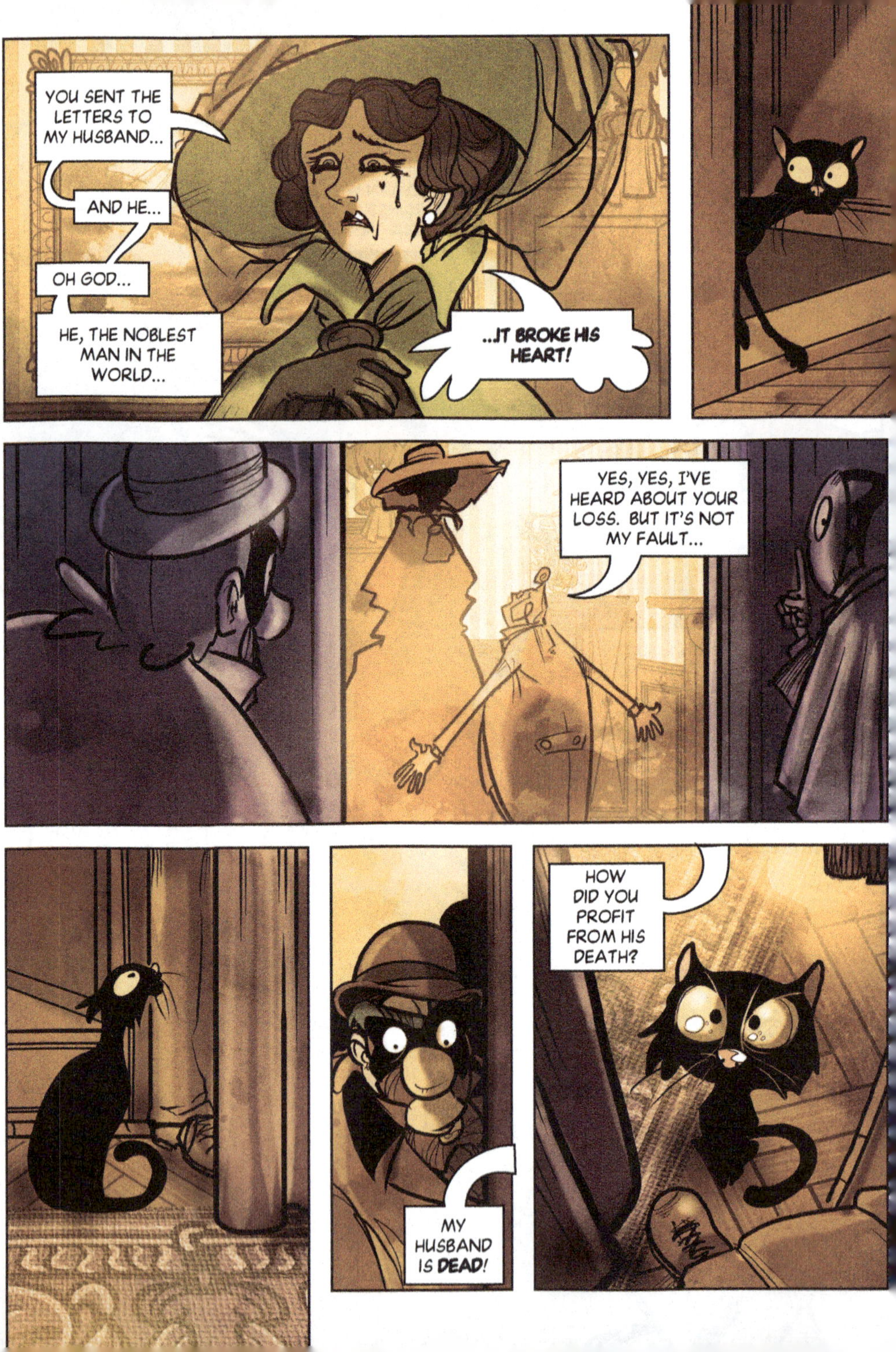
YOU SENT THE LETTERS TO MY HUSBAND...
AND HE...
OH GOD...
HE, THE NOBLEST MAN IN THE WORLD...
...IT BROKE HIS HEART!
YES, YES, I'VE HEARD ABOUT YOUR LOSS. BUT IT'S NOT MY FAULT...
MY HUSBAND IS **DEAD**!
HOW DID YOU PROFIT FROM HIS DEATH?

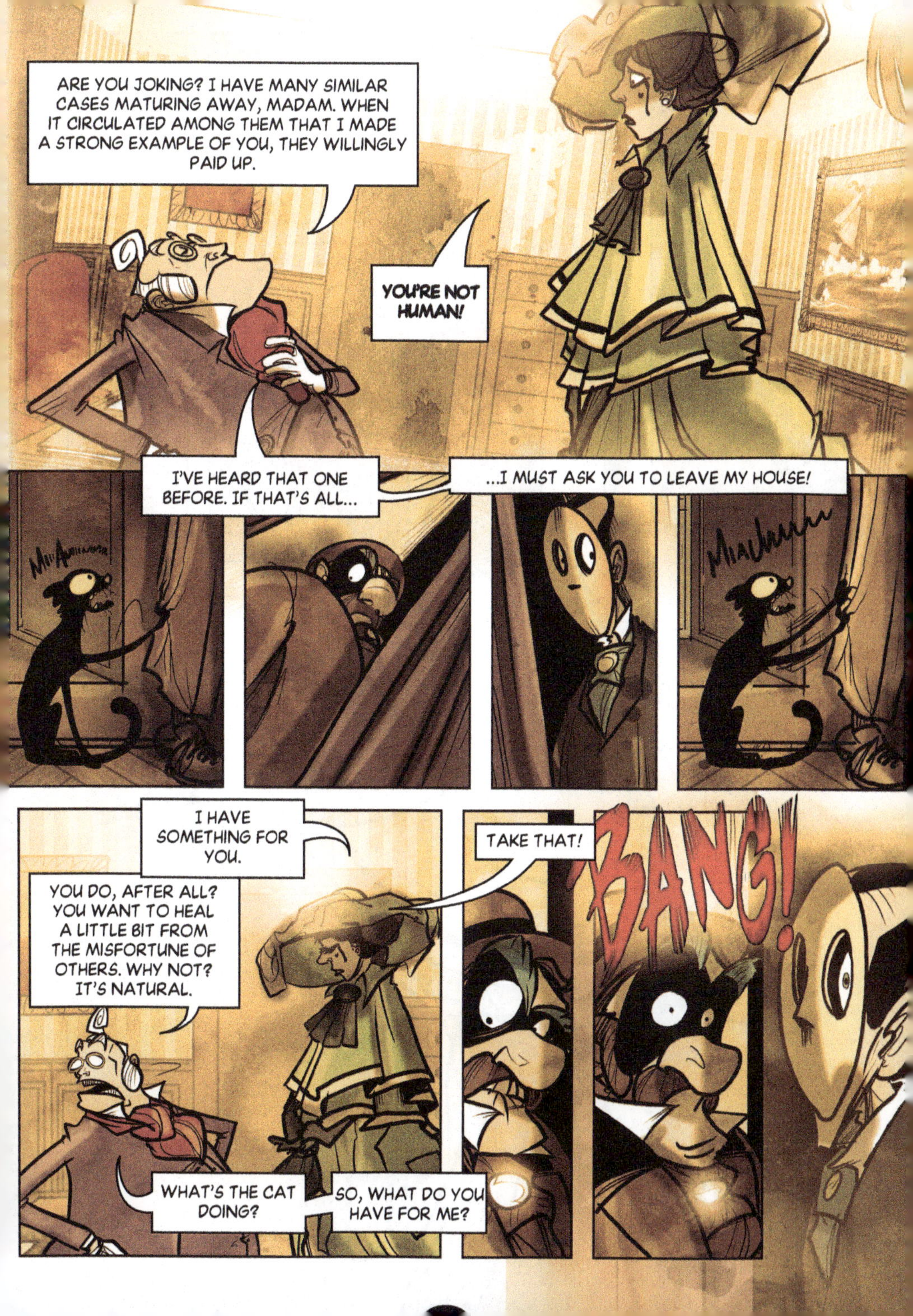
ARE YOU JOKING? I HAVE MANY SIMILAR CASES MATURING AWAY, MADAM. WHEN IT CIRCULATED AMONG THEM THAT I MADE A STRONG EXAMPLE OF YOU, THEY WILLINGLY PAID UP.
YOU'RE NOT HUMAN!
I'VE HEARD THAT ONE BEFORE. IF THAT'S ALL...
...I MUST ASK YOU TO LEAVE MY HOUSE!
I HAVE SOMETHING FOR YOU.
YOU DO, AFTER ALL? YOU WANT TO HEAL A LITTLE BIT FROM THE MISFORTUNE OF OTHERS. WHY NOT? IT'S NATURAL.
WHAT'S THE CAT DOING?
SO, WHAT DO YOU HAVE FOR ME?
TAKE THAT!
BANG!

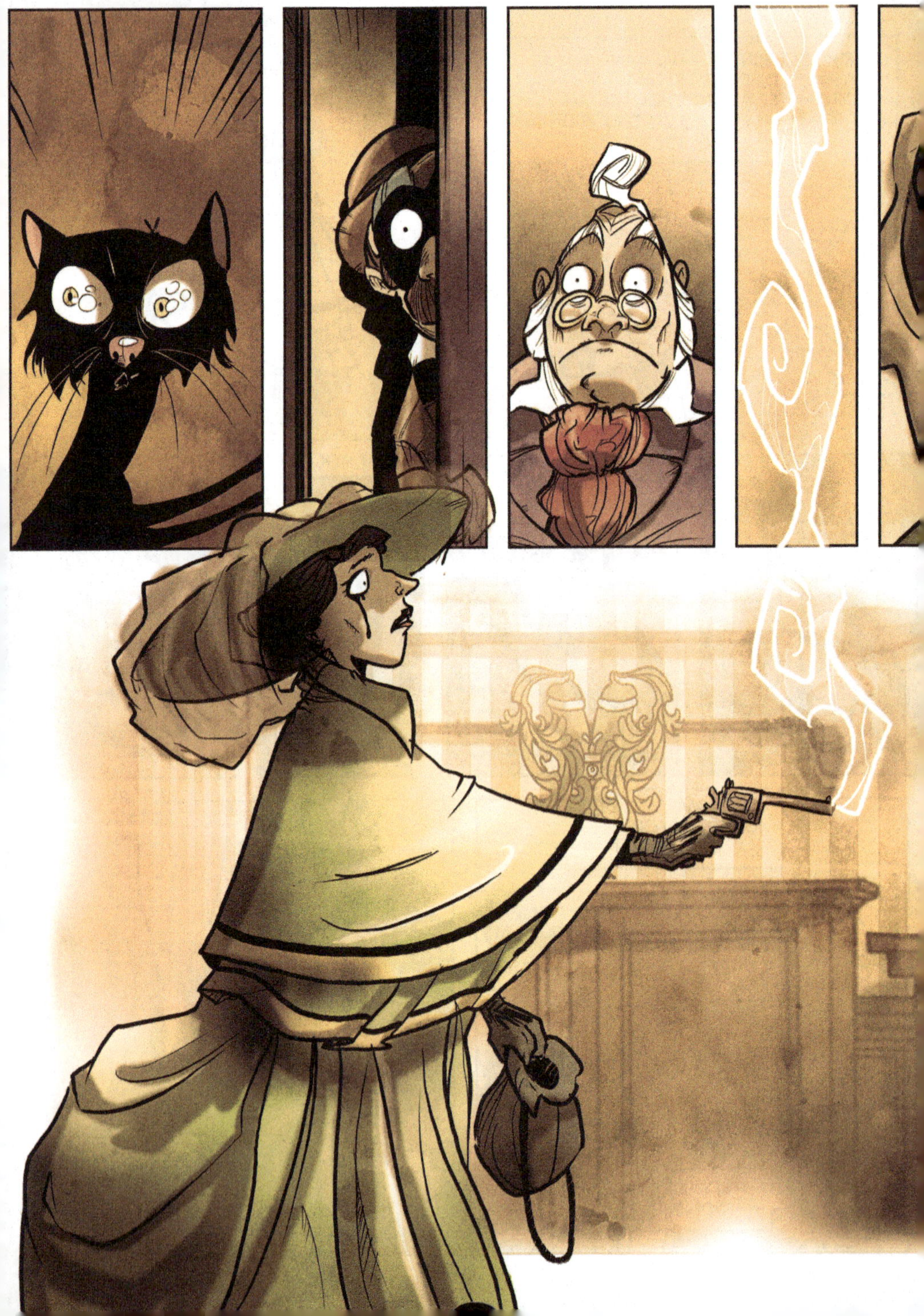

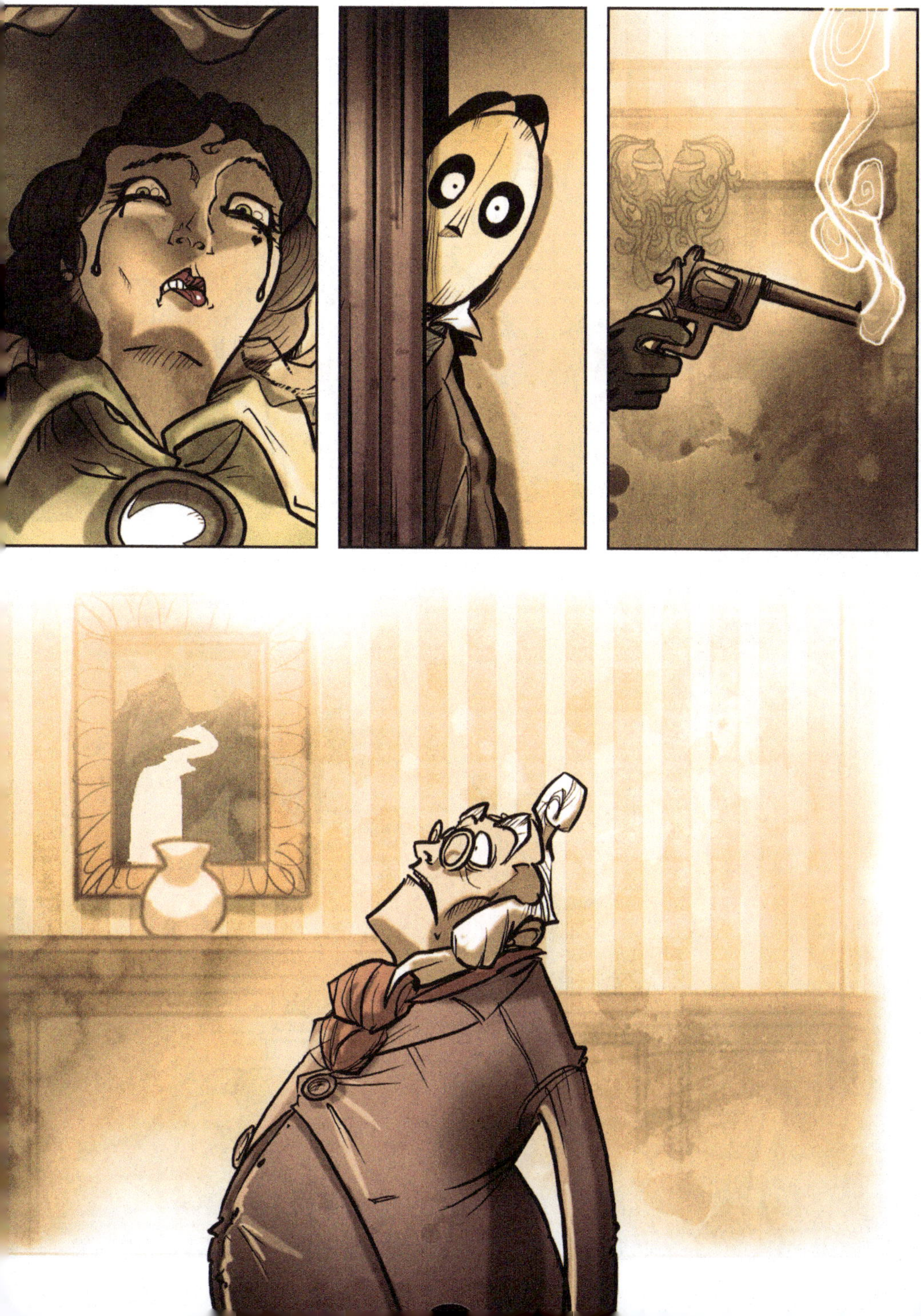

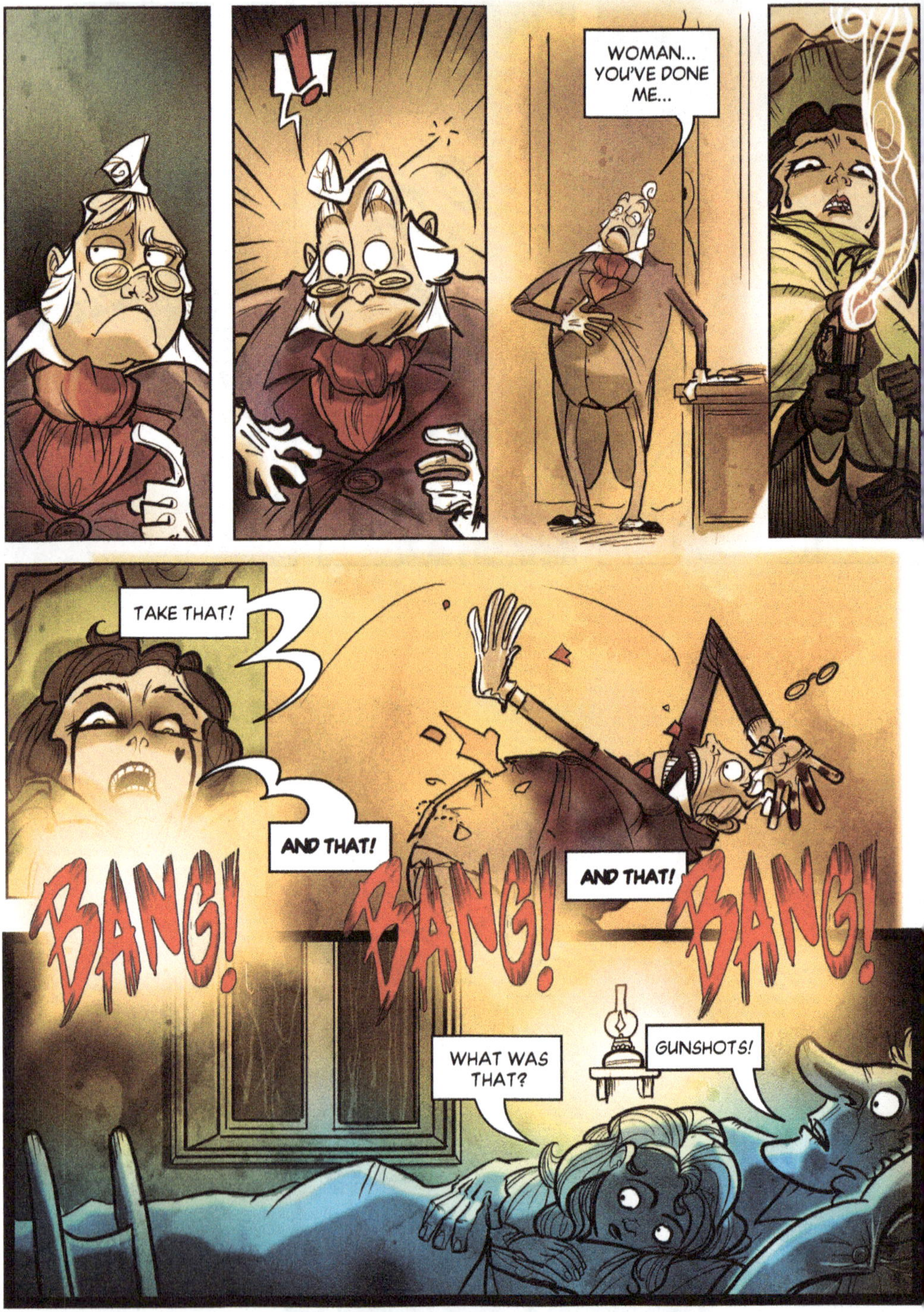
WOMAN... YOU'VE DONE ME...
TAKE THAT!
AND THAT!
BANG!
BANG!
AND THAT!
BANG!
WHAT WAS THAT?
GUNSHOTS!

I WANTED TO INTERFERE...

I WANTED TO STOP THE MADNESS...

HOWEVER THE LOOK THAT SHERLOCK HOLMES GAVE ME STOPPED ME.

MILVERTON IS GETTING HIS JUST DESERTS.

AND THAT!

BANG!

BANG!

HRG!!

CLICK
CLICK
CLICK
CLICK
CLICK

CLICK
CLICK
CLICK

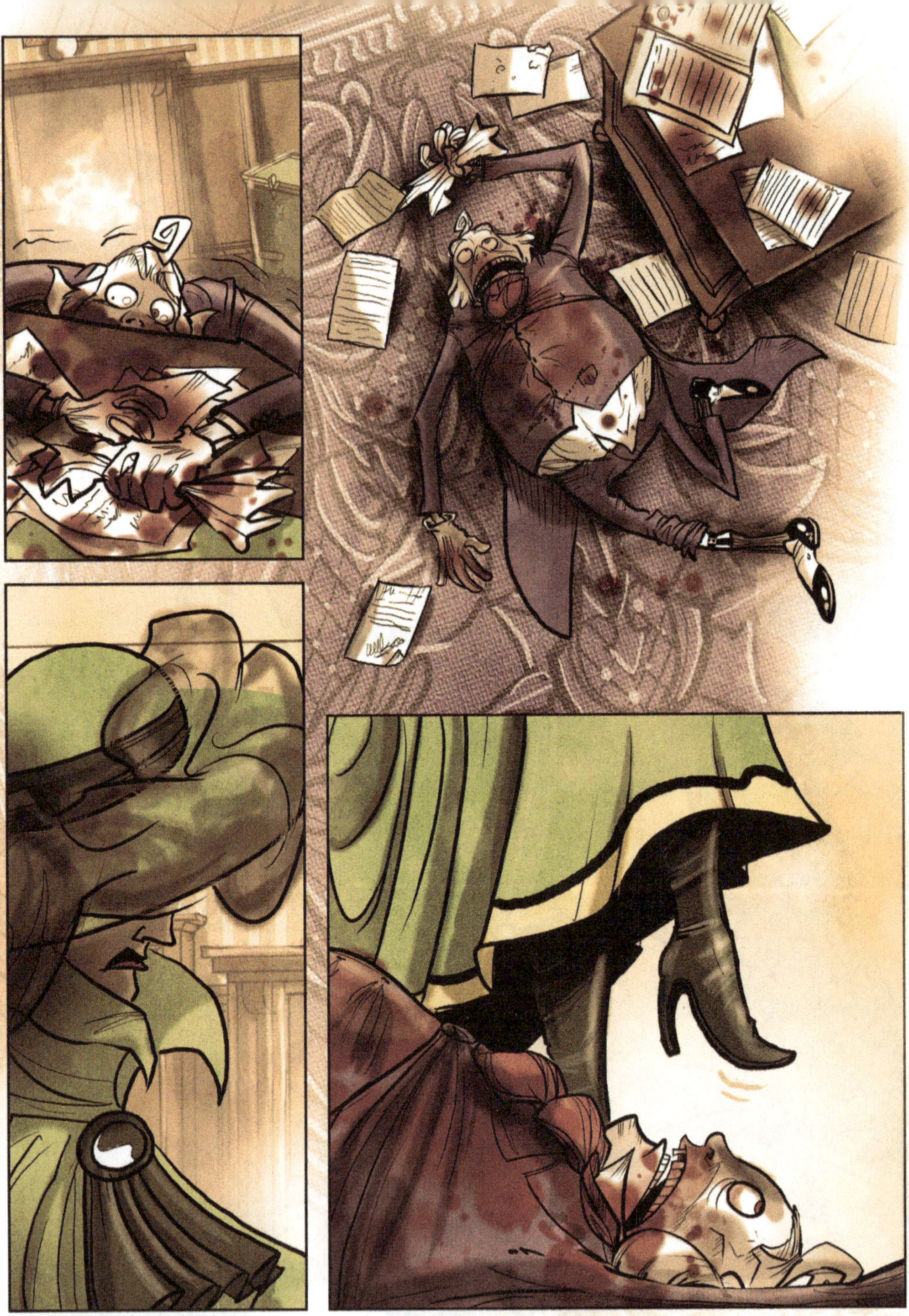

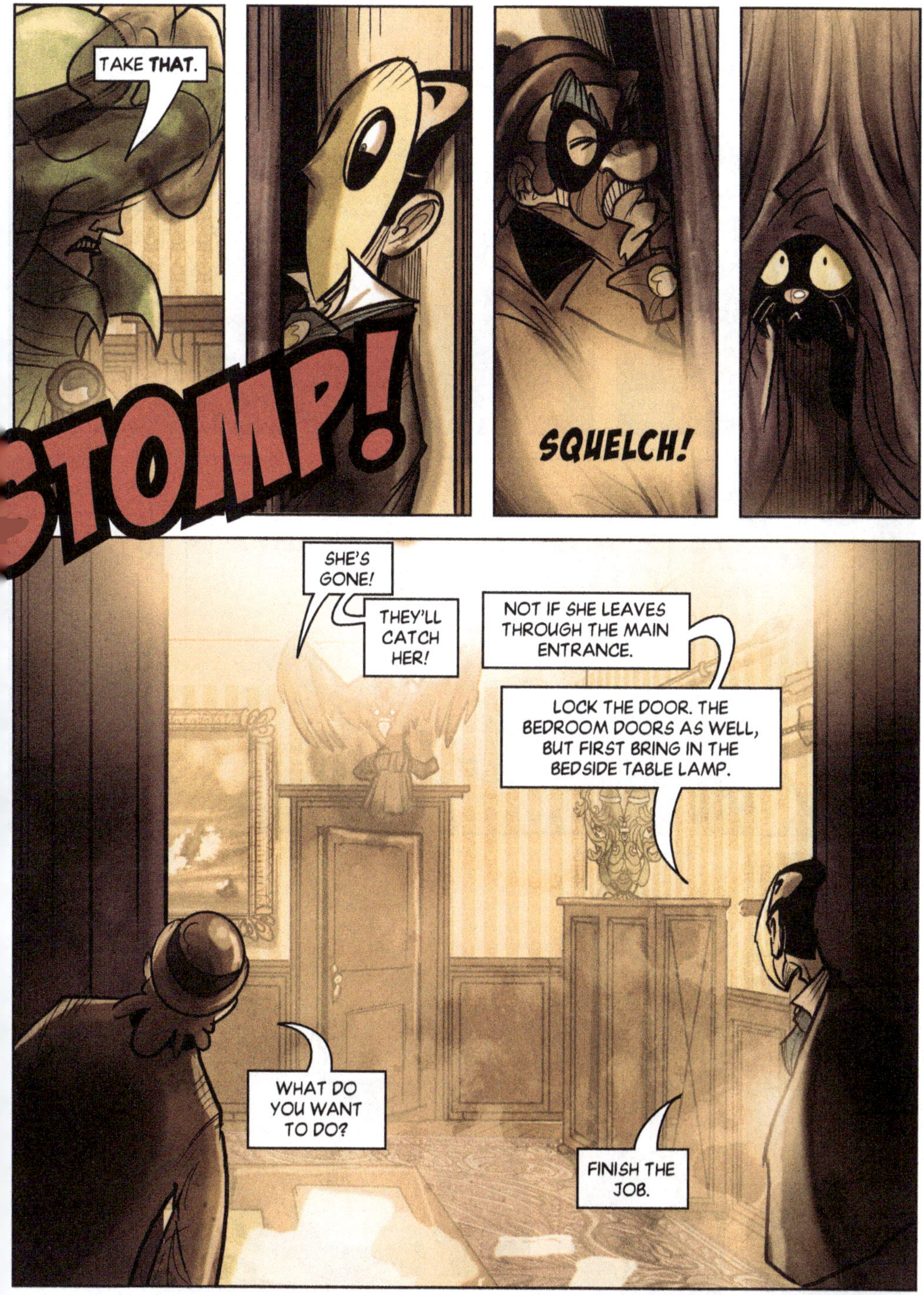
TAKE THAT.
STOMP!
SQUELCH!
SHE'S GONE!
THEY'LL CATCH HER!
NOT IF SHE LEAVES THROUGH THE MAIN ENTRANCE.
LOCK THE DOOR. THE BEDROOM DOORS AS WELL, BUT FIRST BRING IN THE BEDSIDE TABLE LAMP.
WHAT DO YOU WANT TO DO?
FINISH THE JOB.

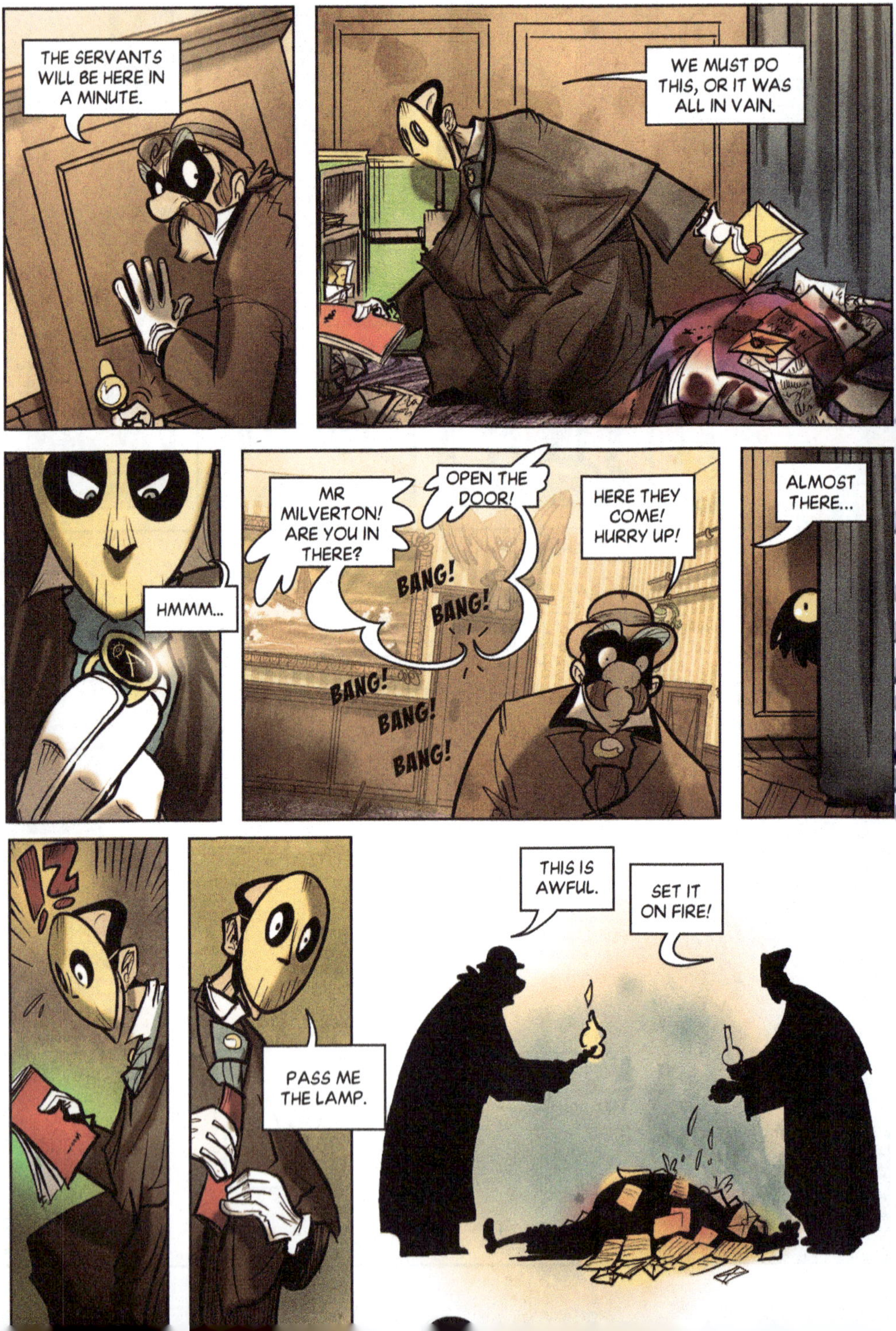
THE SERVANTS WILL BE HERE IN A MINUTE.
WE MUST DO THIS, OR IT WAS ALL IN VAIN.
HMMM...
MR MILVERTON! ARE YOU IN THERE?
OPEN THE DOOR!
BANG! BANG! BANG! BANG! BANG!
HERE THEY COME! HURRY UP!
ALMOST THERE...
!Z
PASS ME THE LAMP.
THIS IS AWFUL.
SET IT ON FIRE!

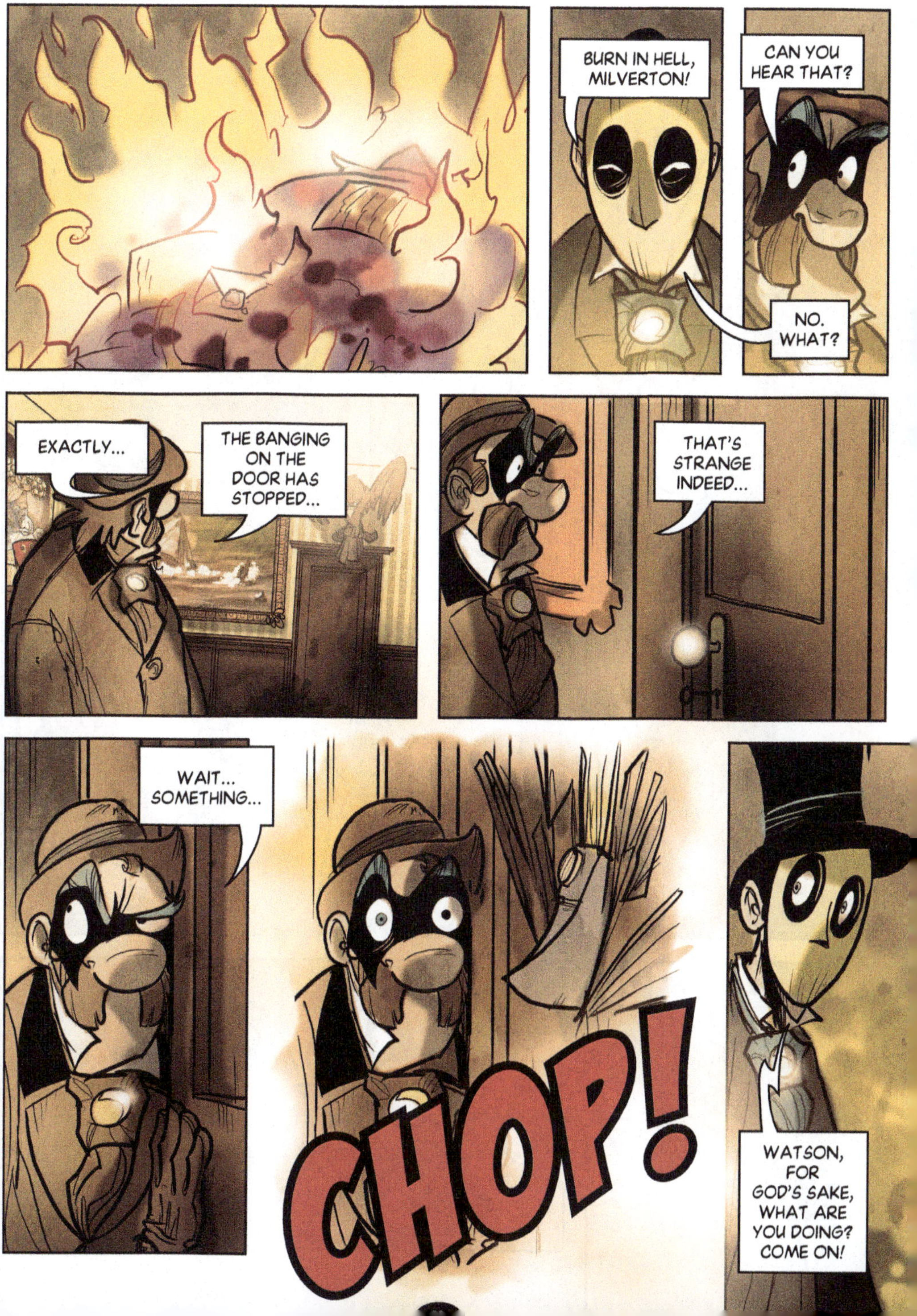
BURN IN HELL, MILVERTON!
CAN YOU HEAR THAT?
NO. WHAT?
EXACTLY...
THE BANGING ON THE DOOR HAS STOPPED...
THAT'S STRANGE INDEED...
WAIT... SOMETHING...
CHOP!
WATSON, FOR GOD'S SAKE, WHAT ARE YOU DOING? COME ON!

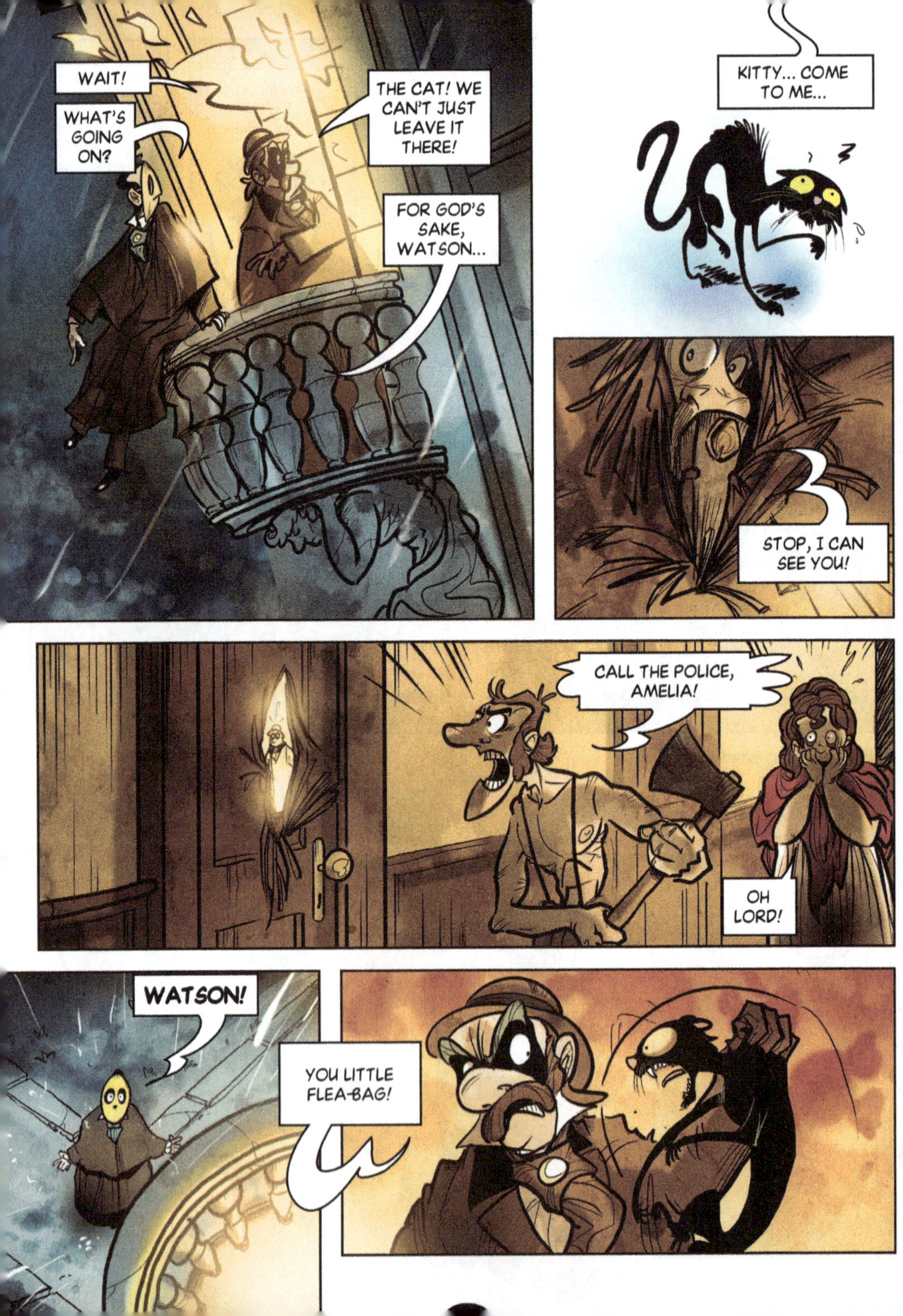
WAIT!
WHAT'S GOING ON?
THE CAT! WE CAN'T JUST LEAVE IT THERE!
FOR GOD'S SAKE, WATSON...
KITTY... COME TO ME...
STOP, I CAN SEE YOU!
CALL THE POLICE, AMELIA!
OH LORD!
WATSON!
YOU LITTLE FLEA-BAG!

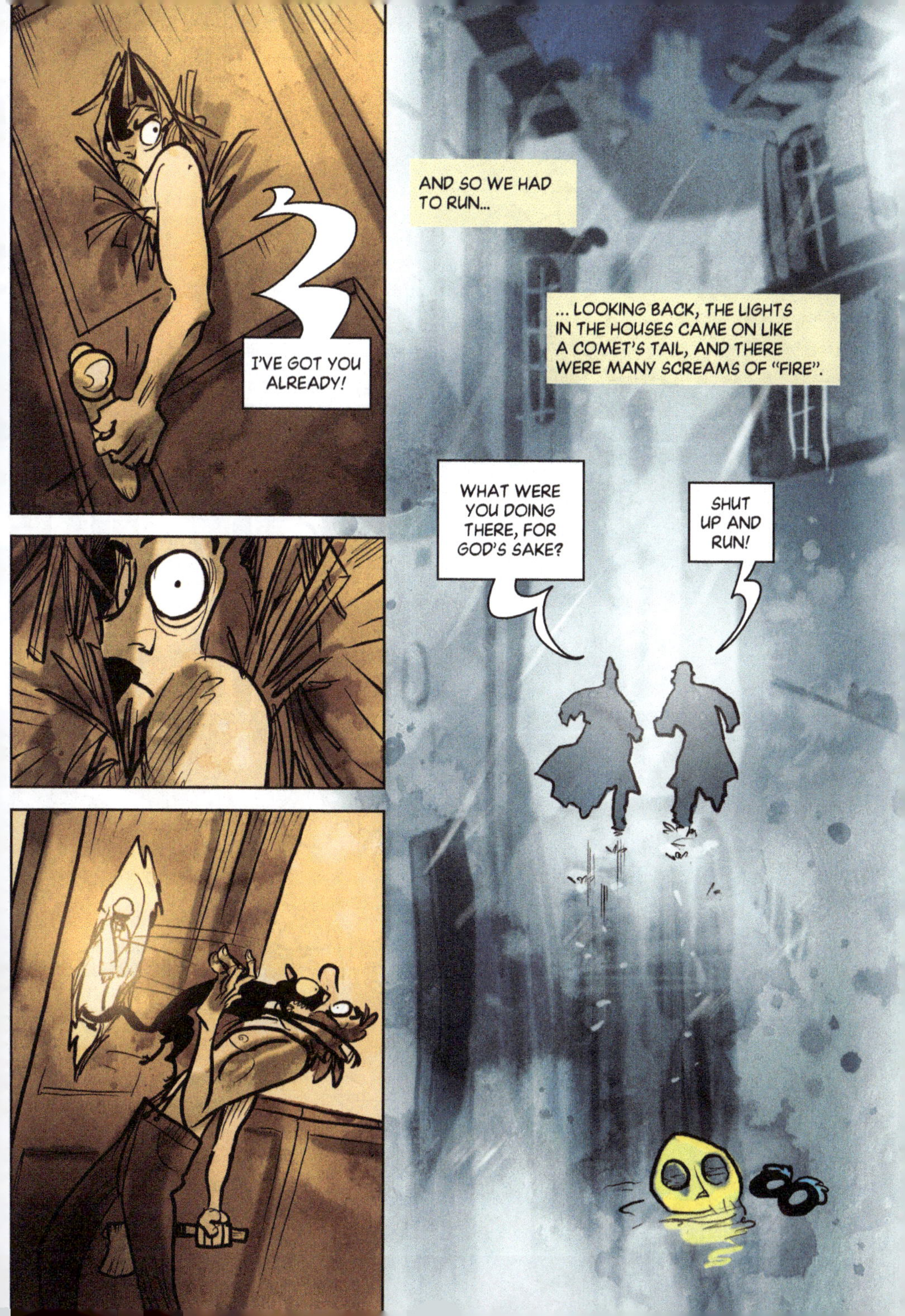
I'VE GOT YOU ALREADY!
AND SO WE HAD TO RUN...
... LOOKING BACK, THE LIGHTS IN THE HOUSES CAME ON LIKE A COMET'S TAIL, AND THERE WERE MANY SCREAMS OF "FIRE".
WHAT WERE YOU DOING THERE, FOR GOD'S SAKE?
SHUT UP AND RUN!

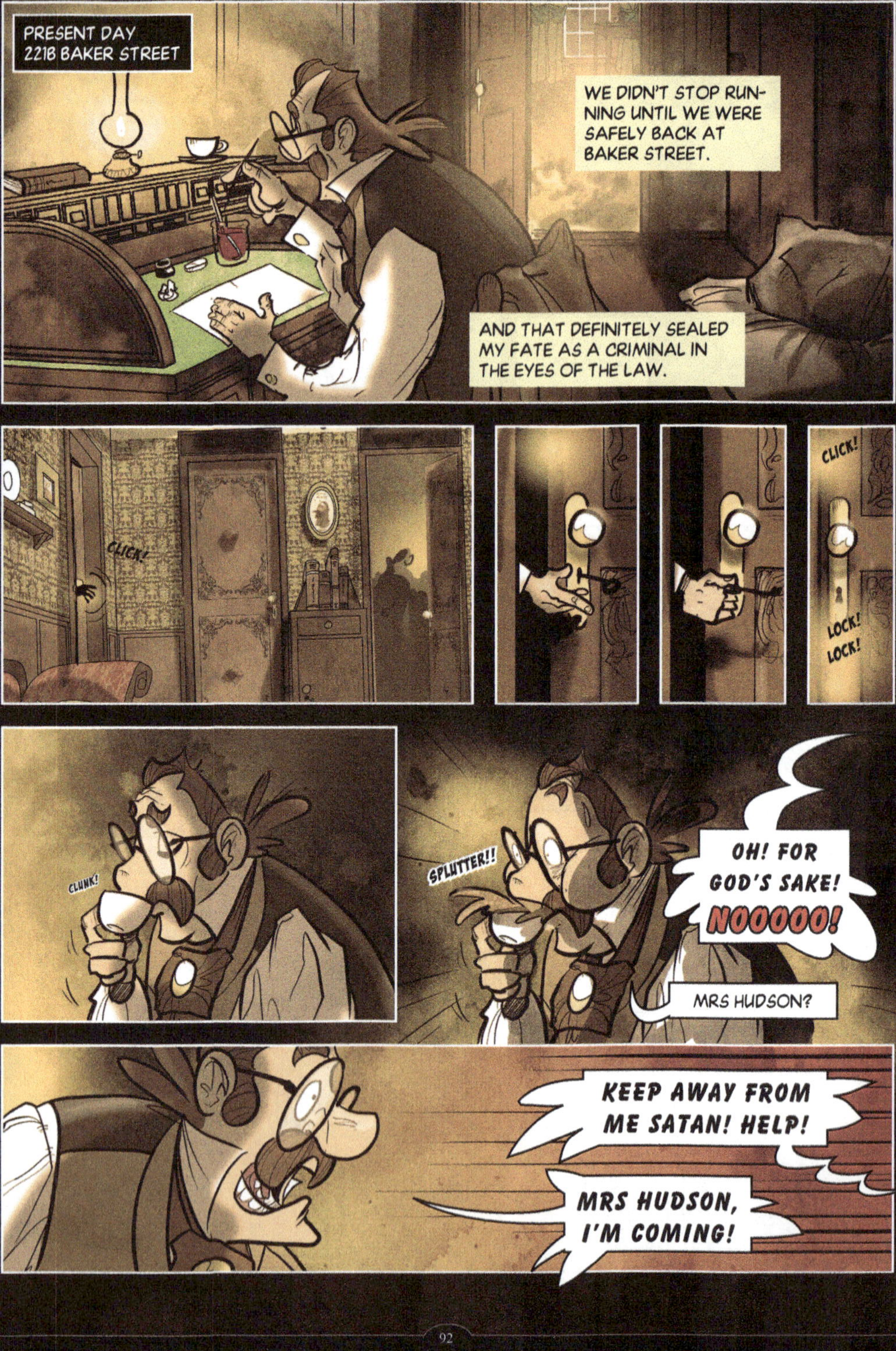
PRESENT DAY
221B BAKER STREET
WE DIDN'T STOP RUNNING UNTIL WE WERE SAFELY BACK AT BAKER STREET.
AND THAT DEFINITELY SEALED MY FATE AS A CRIMINAL IN THE EYES OF THE LAW.
CLICK!
CLICK!
LOCK! LOCK!
CLUNK!
SPLUTTER!!
OH! FOR GOD'S SAKE! NOOOOO!
MRS HUDSON?
KEEP AWAY FROM ME SATAN! HELP!
MRS HUDSON, I'M COMING!

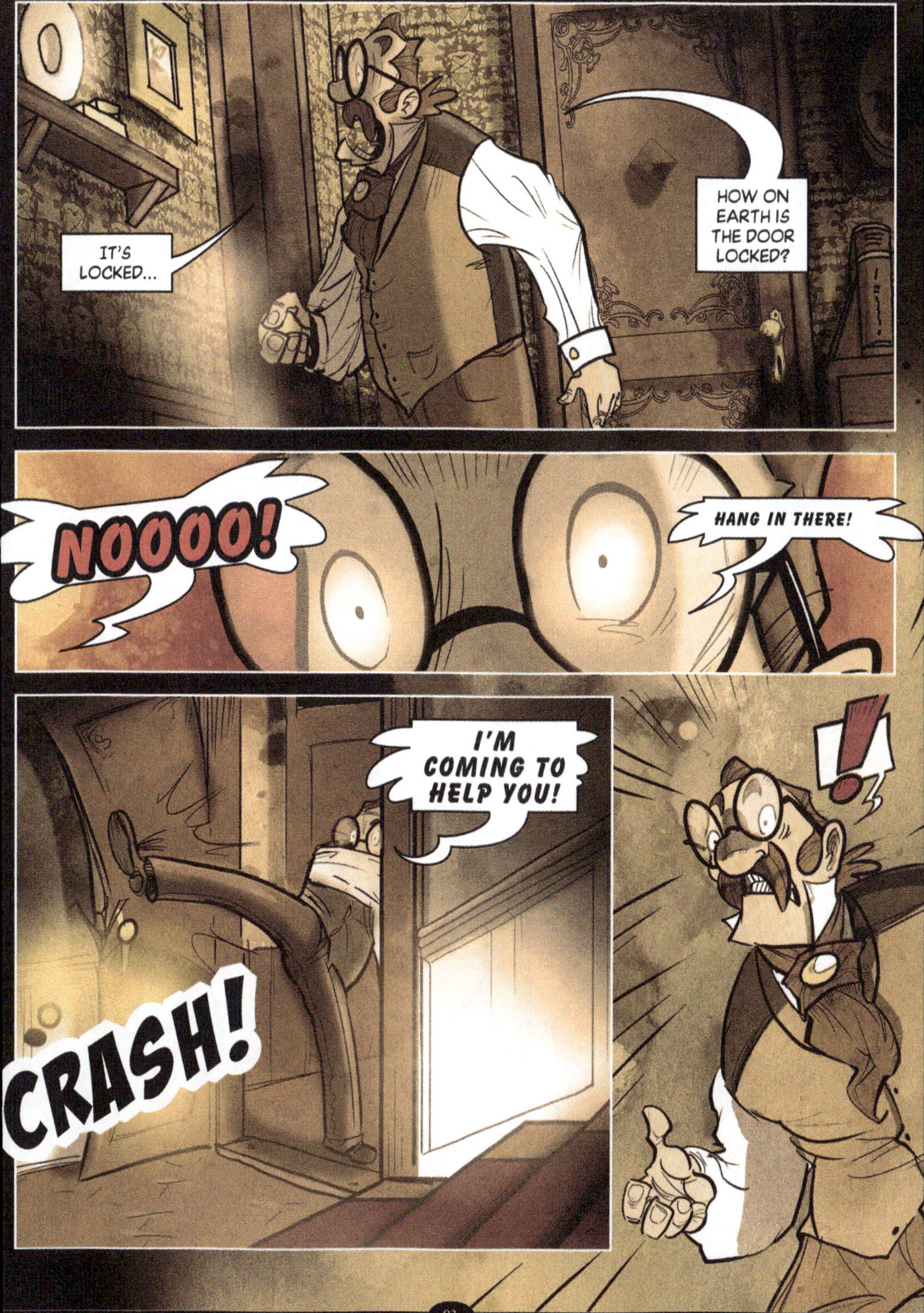
IT'S LOCKED...
HOW ON EARTH IS THE DOOR LOCKED?
NOOOO!
HANG IN THERE!
I'M COMING TO HELP YOU!
!
CRASH!

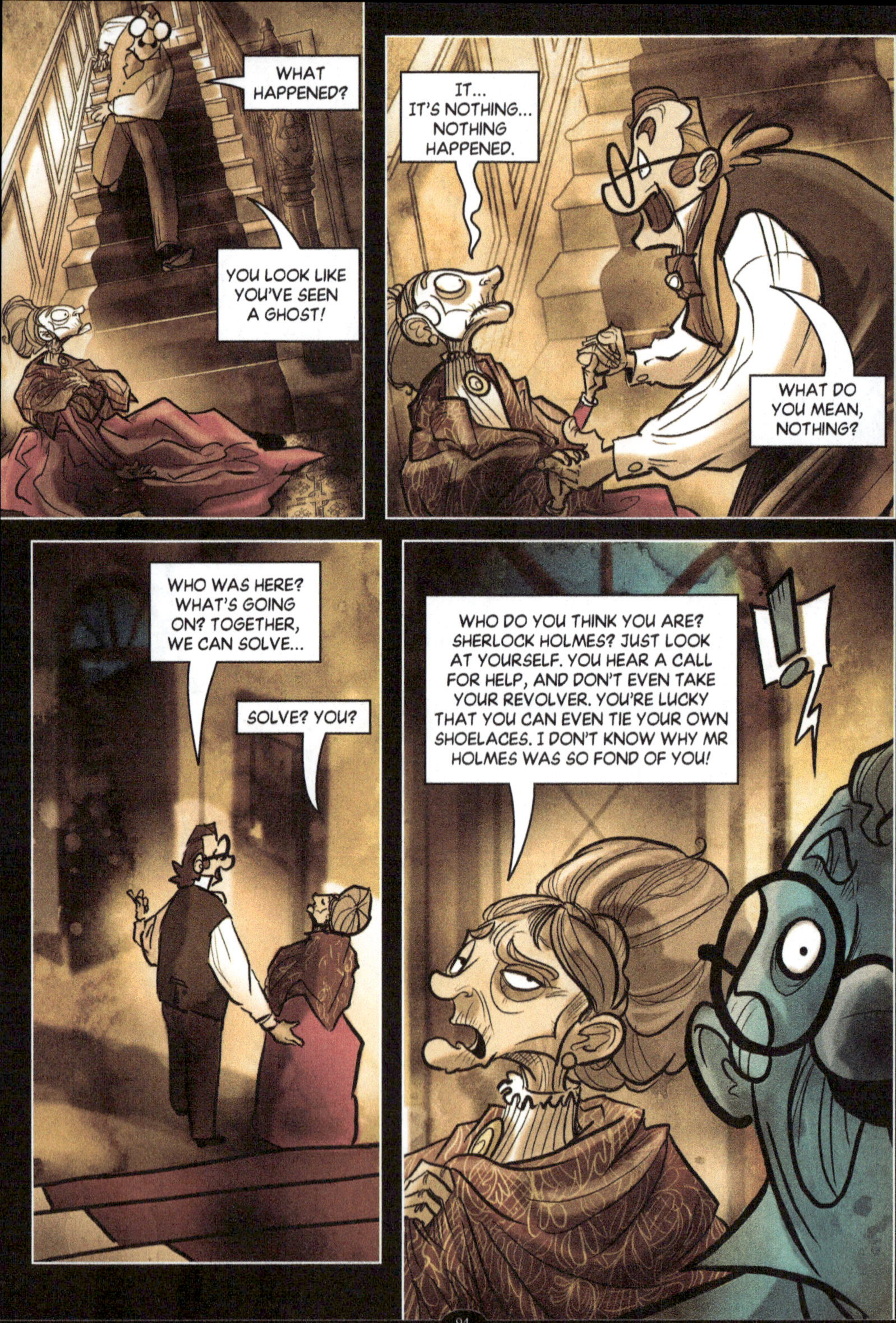
WHAT HAPPENED?
YOU LOOK LIKE YOU'VE SEEN A GHOST!
IT... IT'S NOTHING... NOTHING HAPPENED.
WHAT DO YOU MEAN, NOTHING?
WHO WAS HERE? WHAT'S GOING ON? TOGETHER, WE CAN SOLVE...
SOLVE? YOU?
WHO DO YOU THINK YOU ARE? SHERLOCK HOLMES? JUST LOOK AT YOURSELF. YOU HEAR A CALL FOR HELP, AND DON'T EVEN TAKE YOUR REVOLVER. YOU'RE LUCKY THAT YOU CAN EVEN TIE YOUR OWN SHOELACES. I DON'T KNOW WHY MR HOLMES WAS SO FOND OF YOU!
!

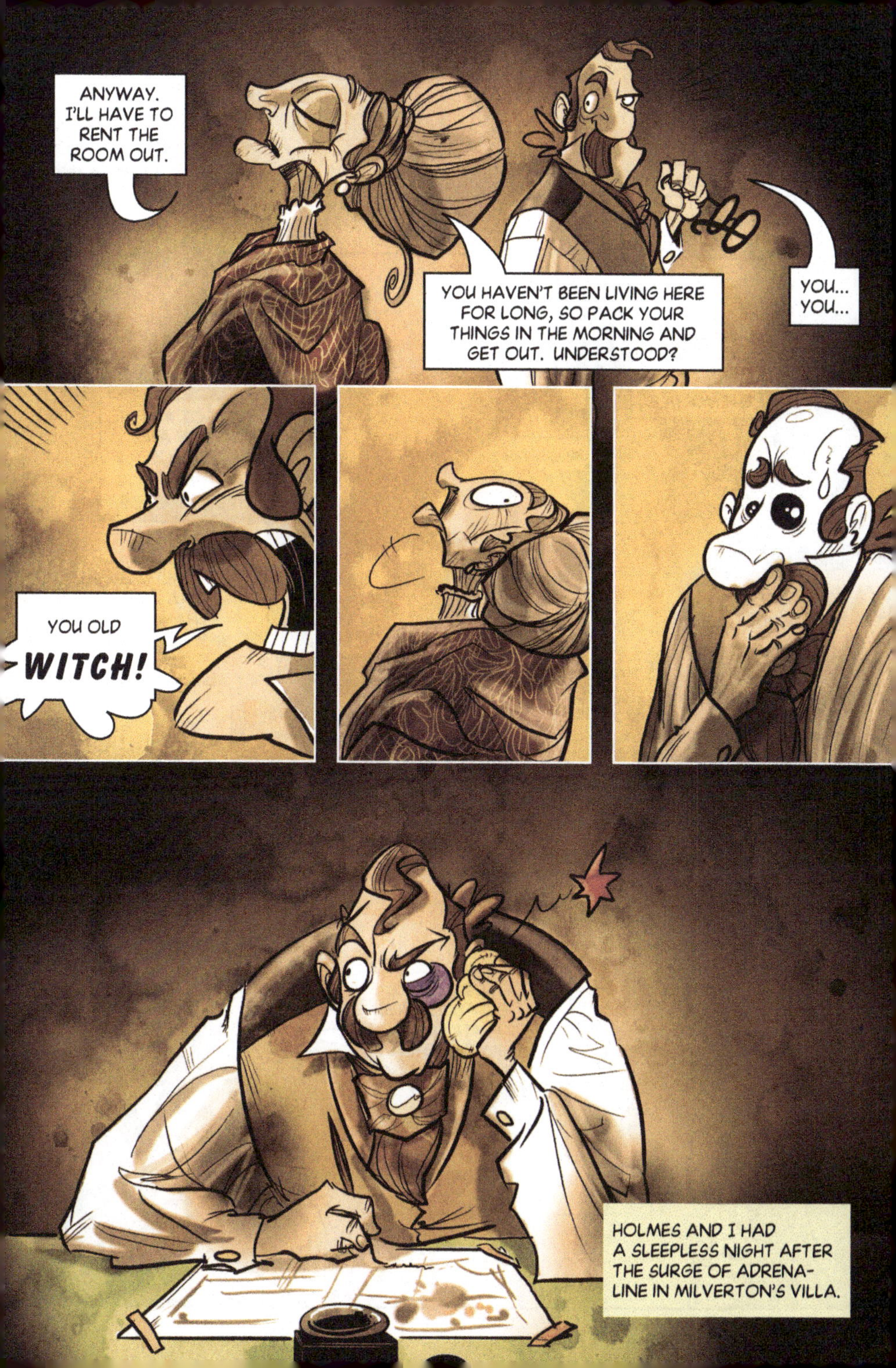
ANYWAY. I'LL HAVE TO RENT THE ROOM OUT.
YOU HAVEN'T BEEN LIVING HERE FOR LONG, SO PACK YOUR THINGS IN THE MORNING AND GET OUT. UNDERSTOOD?
YOU... YOU...
YOU OLD WITCH!
HOLMES AND I HAD A SLEEPLESS NIGHT AFTER THE SURGE OF ADRENA-LINE IN MILVERTON'S VILLA.

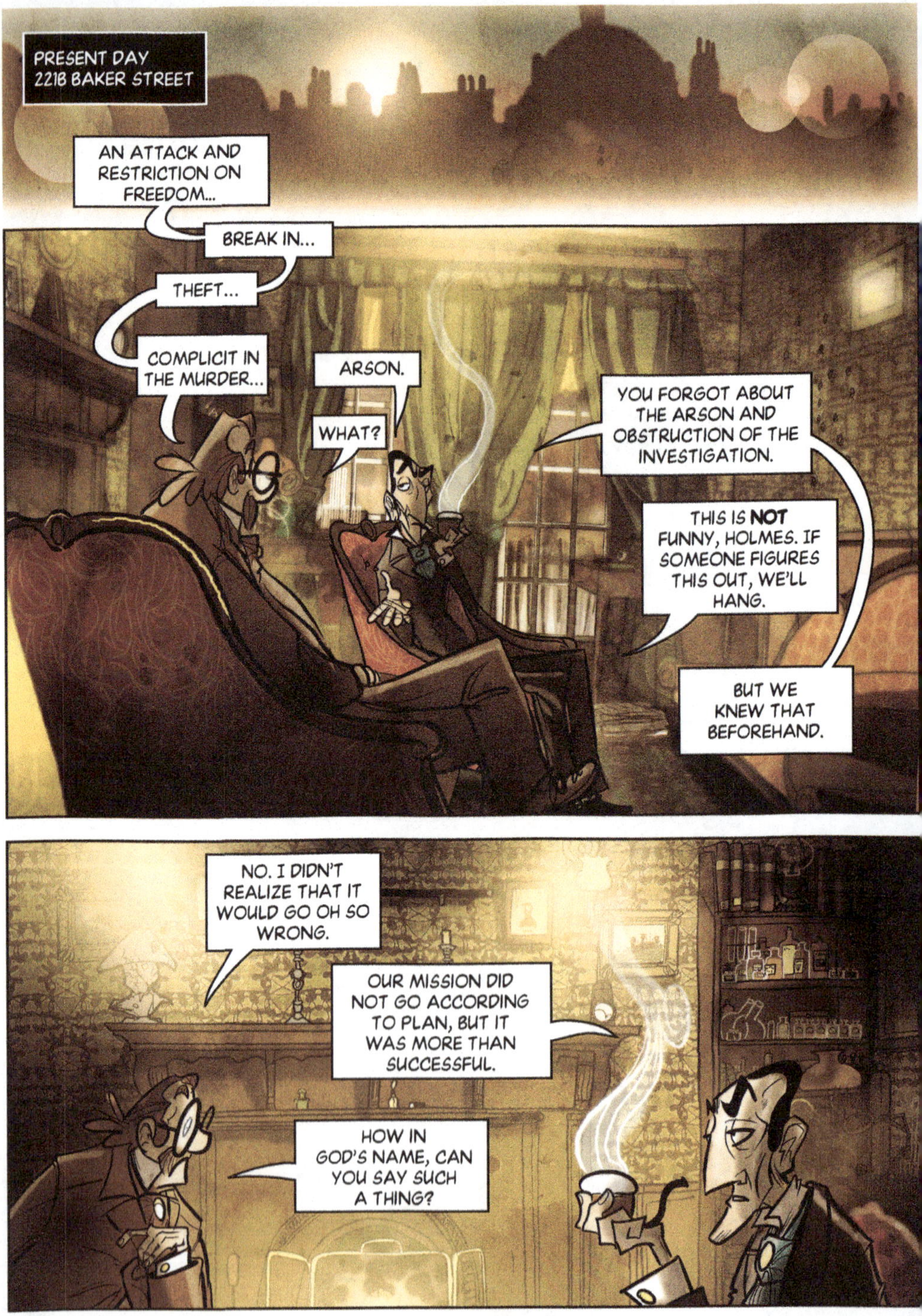
PRESENT DAY
221B BAKER STREET
AN ATTACK AND RESTRICTION ON FREEDOM...
BREAK IN...
THEFT...
COMPLICIT IN THE MURDER...
ARSON.
WHAT?
YOU FORGOT ABOUT THE ARSON AND OBSTRUCTION OF THE INVESTIGATION.
THIS IS **NOT** FUNNY, HOLMES. IF SOMEONE FIGURES THIS OUT, WE'LL HANG.
BUT WE KNEW THAT BEFOREHAND.
NO. I DIDN'T REALIZE THAT IT WOULD GO OH SO WRONG.
OUR MISSION DID NOT GO ACCORDING TO PLAN, BUT IT WAS MORE THAN SUCCESSFUL.
HOW IN GOD'S NAME, CAN YOU SAY SUCH A THING?

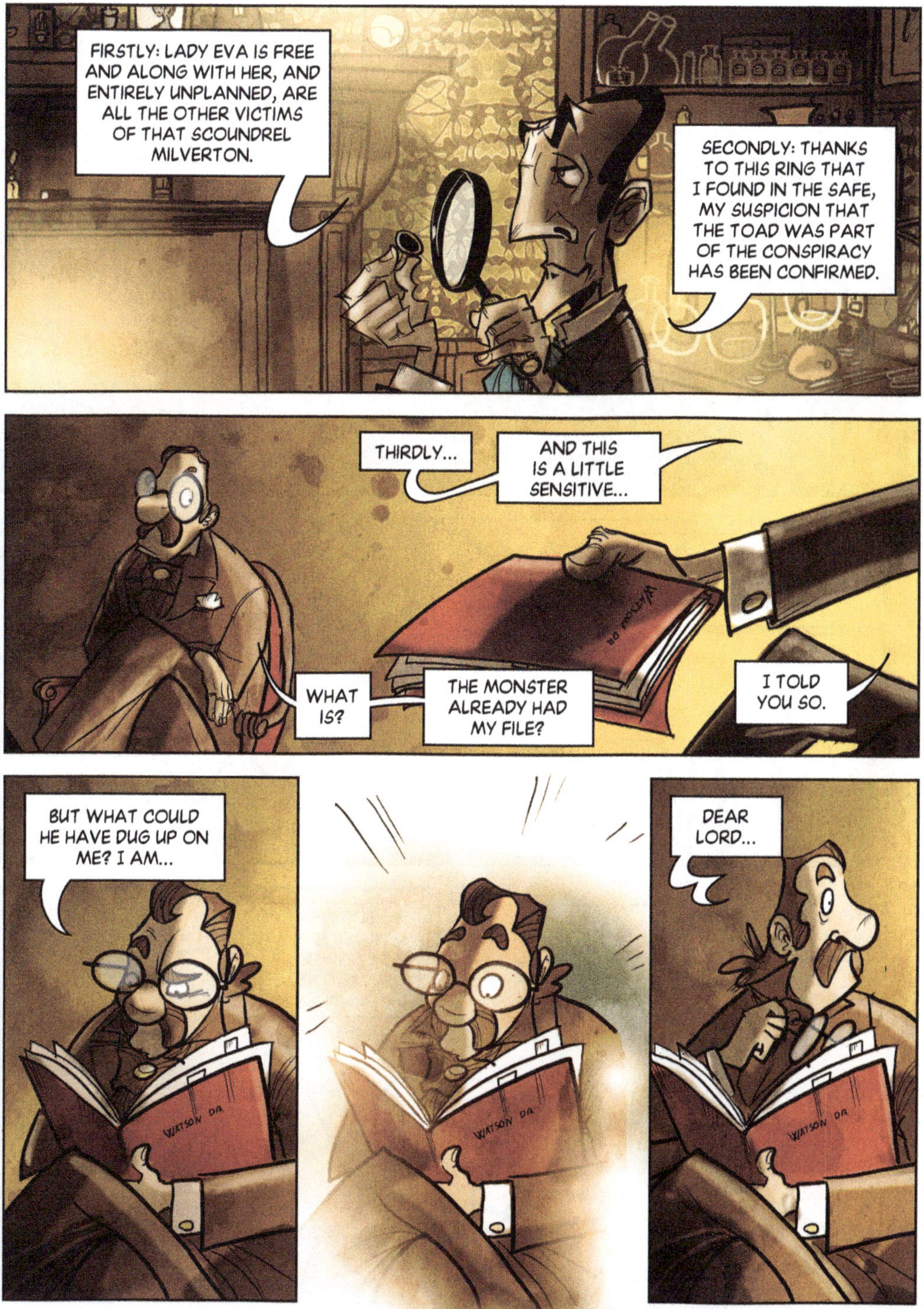

FIRSTLY: LADY EVA IS FREE AND ALONG WITH HER, AND ENTIRELY UNPLANNED, ARE ALL THE OTHER VICTIMS OF THAT SCOUNDREL MILVERTON.
SECONDLY: THANKS TO THIS RING THAT I FOUND IN THE SAFE, MY SUSPICION THAT THE TOAD WAS PART OF THE CONSPIRACY HAS BEEN CONFIRMED.
THIRDLY...
AND THIS IS A LITTLE SENSITIVE...
WHAT IS?
THE MONSTER ALREADY HAD MY FILE?
I TOLD YOU SO.
BUT WHAT COULD HE HAVE DUG UP ON ME? I AM...
WATSON DR
WATSON DR
WATSON DR
DEAR LORD...

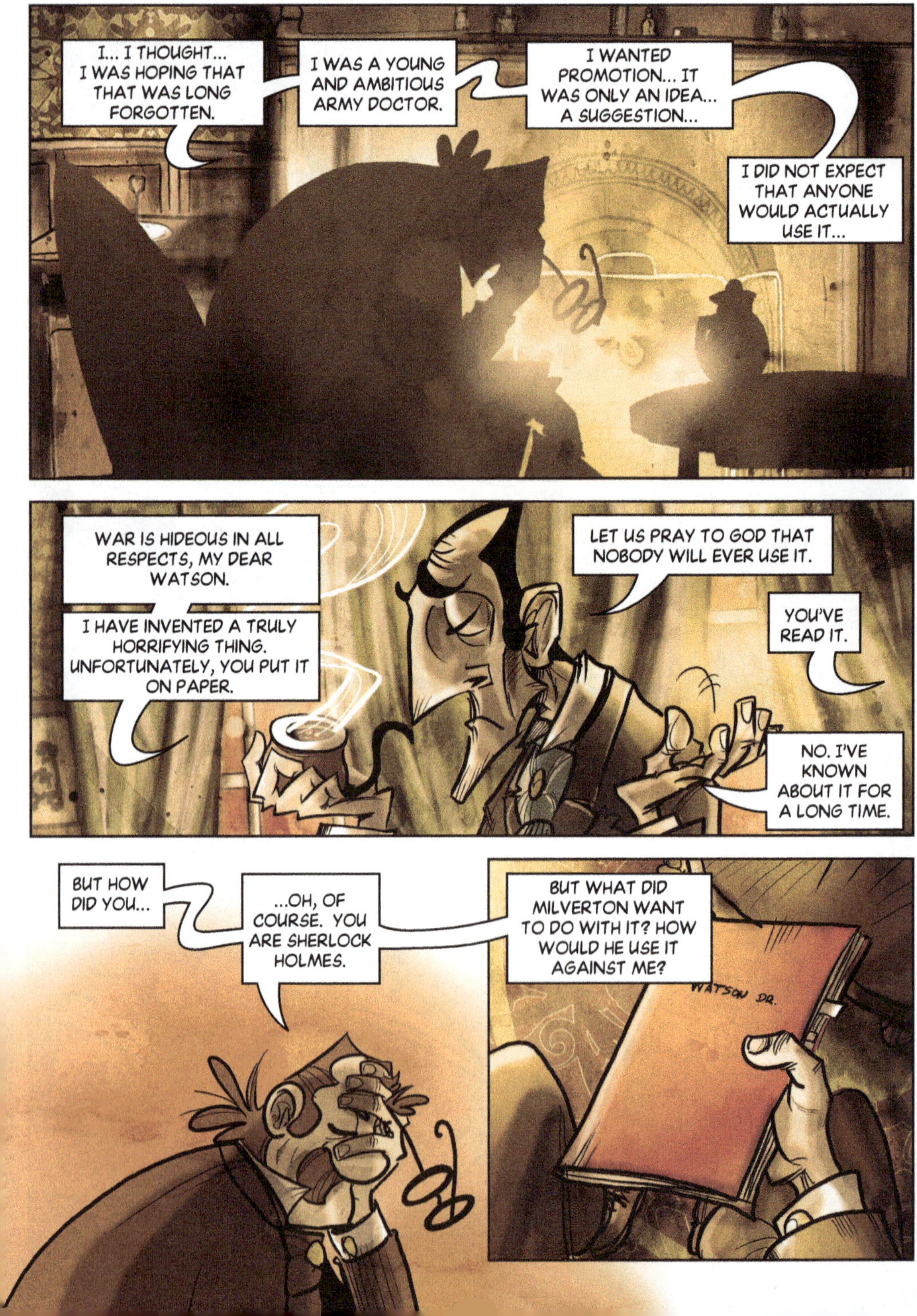
I... I THOUGHT... I WAS HOPING THAT THAT WAS LONG FORGOTTEN.
I WAS A YOUNG AND AMBITIOUS ARMY DOCTOR.
I WANTED PROMOTION... IT WAS ONLY AN IDEA... A SUGGESTION...
I DID NOT EXPECT THAT ANYONE WOULD ACTUALLY USE IT...
WAR IS HIDEOUS IN ALL RESPECTS, MY DEAR WATSON.
I HAVE INVENTED A TRULY HORRIFYING THING. UNFORTUNATELY, YOU PUT IT ON PAPER.
LET US PRAY TO GOD THAT NOBODY WILL EVER USE IT.
YOU'VE READ IT.
NO. I'VE KNOWN ABOUT IT FOR A LONG TIME.
BUT HOW DID YOU...
...OH, OF COURSE. YOU ARE SHERLOCK HOLMES.
BUT WHAT DID MILVERTON WANT TO DO WITH IT? HOW WOULD HE USE IT AGAINST ME?
WATSON DR.

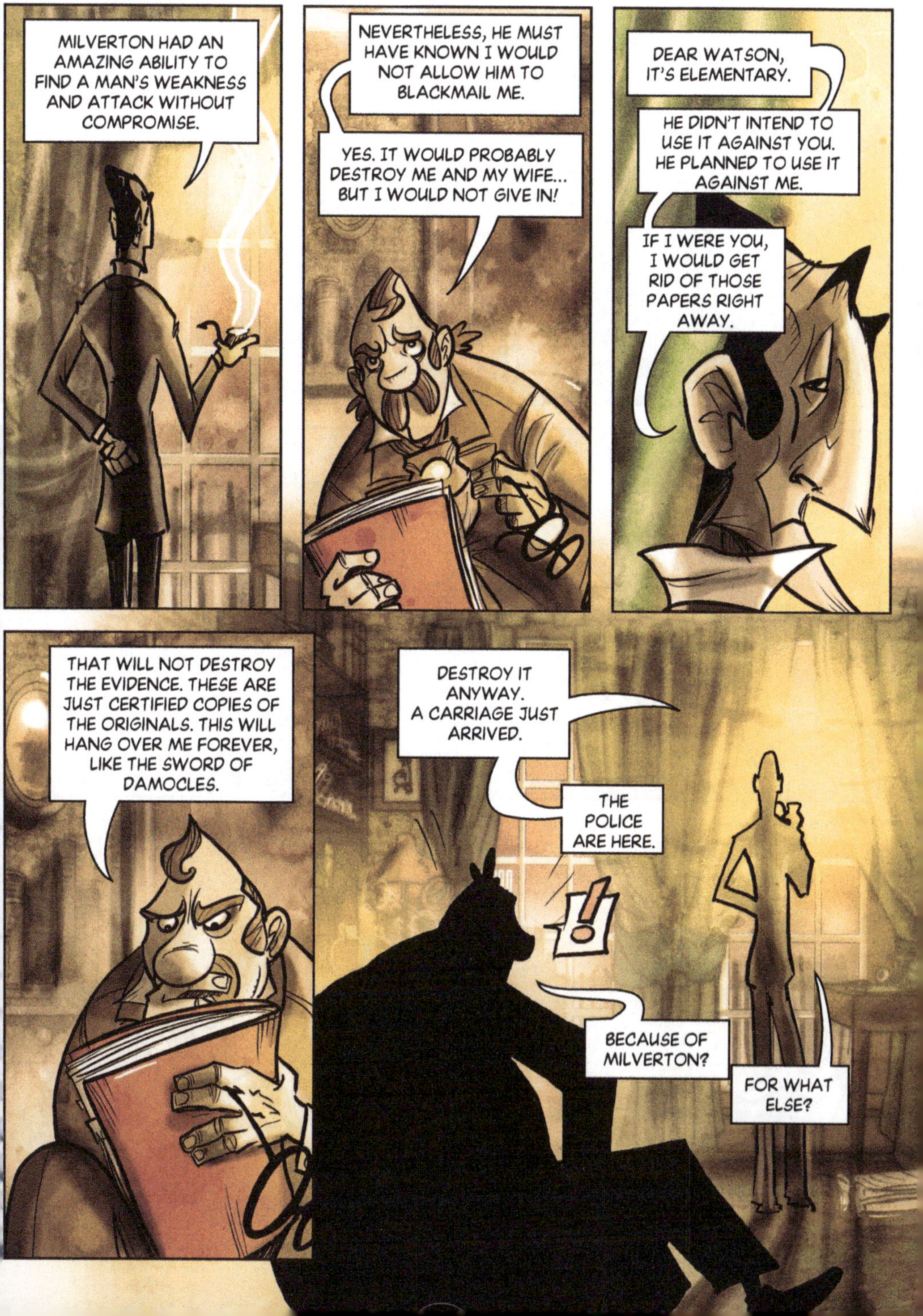
MILVERTON HAD AN AMAZING ABILITY TO FIND A MAN'S WEAKNESS AND ATTACK WITHOUT COMPROMISE.
NEVERTHELESS, HE MUST HAVE KNOWN I WOULD NOT ALLOW HIM TO BLACKMAIL ME.
YES. IT WOULD PROBABLY DESTROY ME AND MY WIFE... BUT I WOULD NOT GIVE IN!
DEAR WATSON, IT'S ELEMENTARY.
HE DIDN'T INTEND TO USE IT AGAINST YOU. HE PLANNED TO USE IT AGAINST ME.
IF I WERE YOU, I WOULD GET RID OF THOSE PAPERS RIGHT AWAY.
THAT WILL NOT DESTROY THE EVIDENCE. THESE ARE JUST CERTIFIED COPIES OF THE ORIGINALS. THIS WILL HANG OVER ME FOREVER, LIKE THE SWORD OF DAMOCLES.
DESTROY IT ANYWAY. A CARRIAGE JUST ARRIVED.
THE POLICE ARE HERE.
!
BECAUSE OF MILVERTON?
FOR WHAT ELSE?

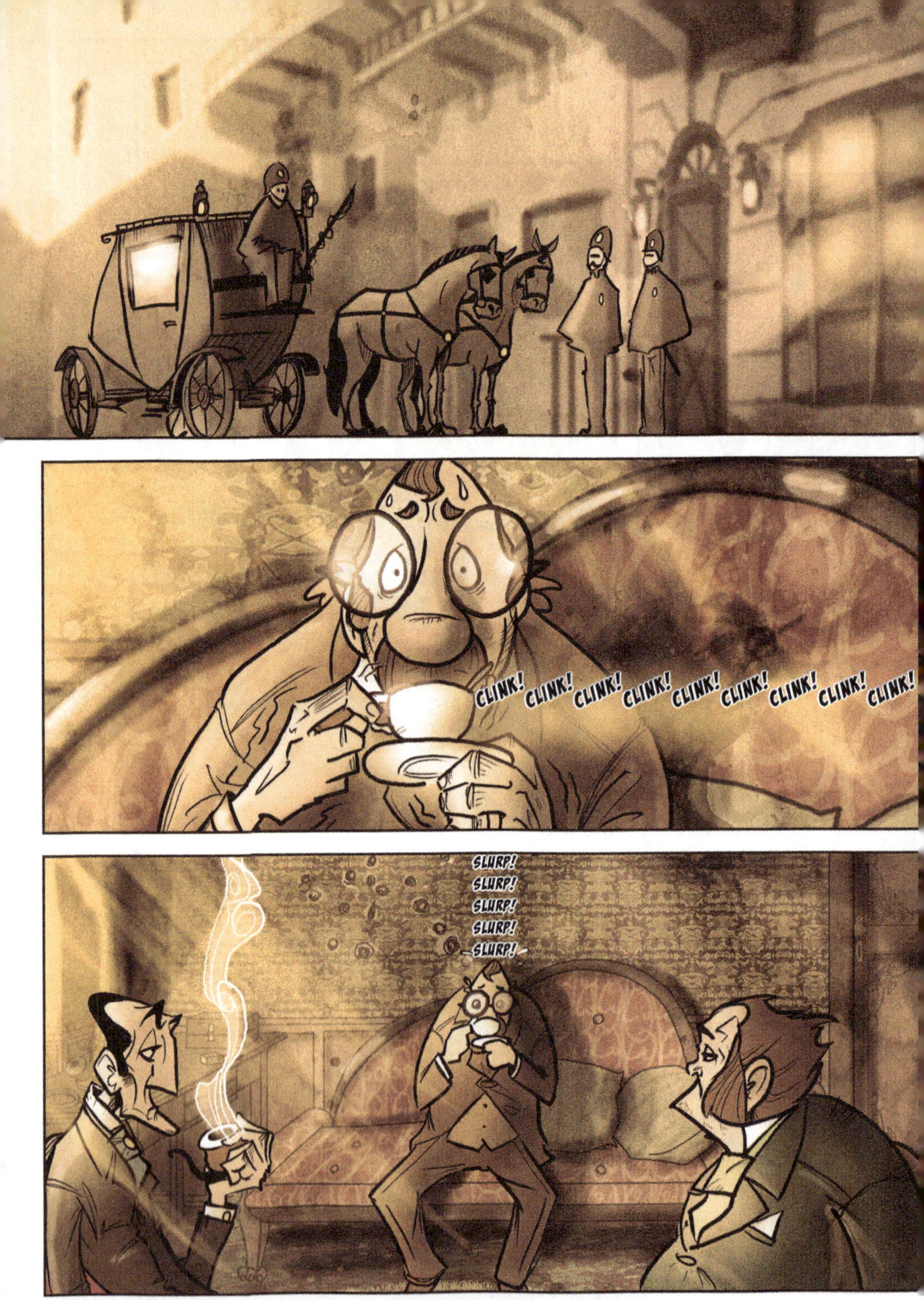
CLINK! CLINK! CLINK! CLINK! CLINK! CLINK! CLINK! CLINK! CLINK!
SLURP!
SLURP!
SLURP!
SLURP!
SLURP!

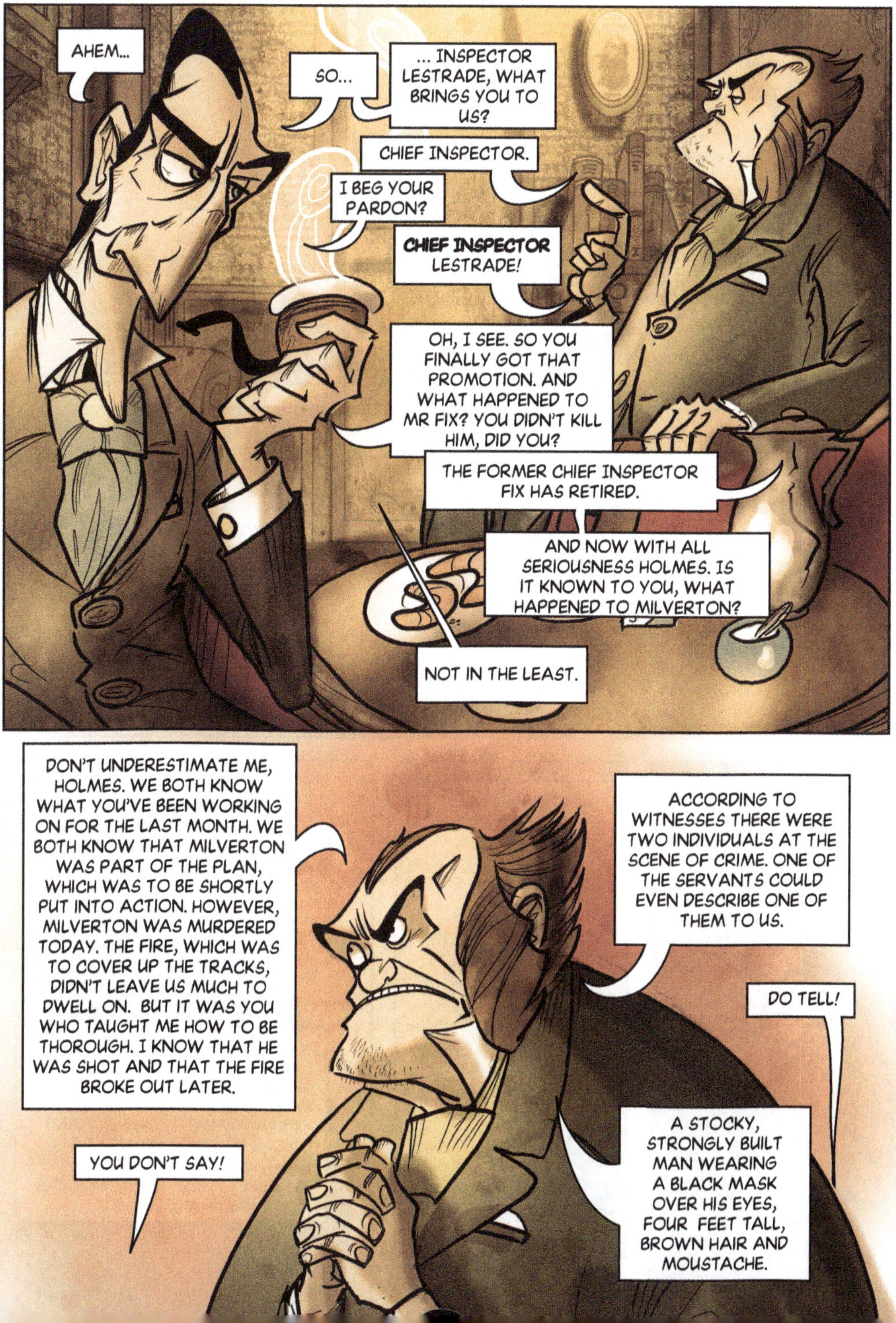
AHEM...
SO...
... INSPECTOR LESTRADE, WHAT BRINGS YOU TO US?
CHIEF INSPECTOR.
I BEG YOUR PARDON?
CHIEF INSPECTOR LESTRADE!
OH, I SEE. SO YOU FINALLY GOT THAT PROMOTION. AND WHAT HAPPENED TO MR FIX? YOU DIDN'T KILL HIM, DID YOU?
THE FORMER CHIEF INSPECTOR FIX HAS RETIRED.
AND NOW WITH ALL SERIOUSNESS HOLMES. IS IT KNOWN TO YOU, WHAT HAPPENED TO MILVERTON?
NOT IN THE LEAST.
DON'T UNDERESTIMATE ME, HOLMES. WE BOTH KNOW WHAT YOU'VE BEEN WORKING ON FOR THE LAST MONTH. WE BOTH KNOW THAT MILVERTON WAS PART OF THE PLAN, WHICH WAS TO BE SHORTLY PUT INTO ACTION. HOWEVER, MILVERTON WAS MURDERED TODAY. THE FIRE, WHICH WAS TO COVER UP THE TRACKS, DIDN'T LEAVE US MUCH TO DWELL ON. BUT IT WAS YOU WHO TAUGHT ME HOW TO BE THOROUGH. I KNOW THAT HE WAS SHOT AND THAT THE FIRE BROKE OUT LATER.
YOU DON'T SAY!
ACCORDING TO WITNESSES THERE WERE TWO INDIVIDUALS AT THE SCENE OF CRIME. ONE OF THE SERVANTS COULD EVEN DESCRIBE ONE OF THEM TO US.
DO TELL!
A STOCKY, STRONGLY BUILT MAN WEARING A BLACK MASK OVER HIS EYES, FOUR FEET TALL, BROWN HAIR AND MOUSTACHE.

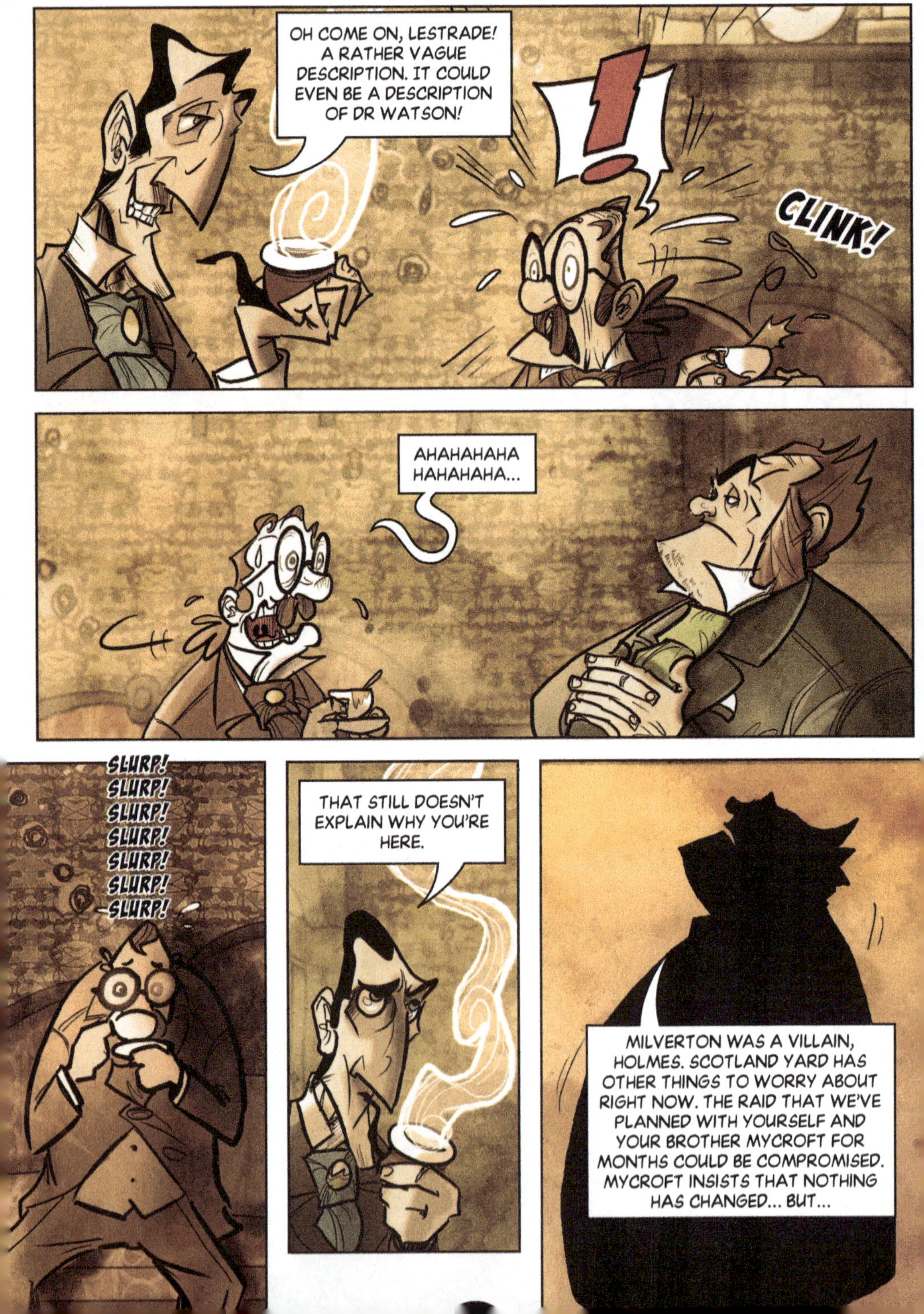
OH COME ON, LESTRADE! A RATHER VAGUE DESCRIPTION. IT COULD EVEN BE A DESCRIPTION OF DR WATSON!
!
CLINK!
AHAHAHAHA HAHAHAHA...
SLURP! SLURP! SLURP! SLURP! SLURP! SLURP! SLURP!
THAT STILL DOESN'T EXPLAIN WHY YOU'RE HERE.
MILVERTON WAS A VILLAIN, HOLMES. SCOTLAND YARD HAS OTHER THINGS TO WORRY ABOUT RIGHT NOW. THE RAID THAT WE'VE PLANNED WITH YOURSELF AND YOUR BROTHER MYCROFT FOR MONTHS COULD BE COMPROMISED. MYCROFT INSISTS THAT NOTHING HAS CHANGED... BUT...

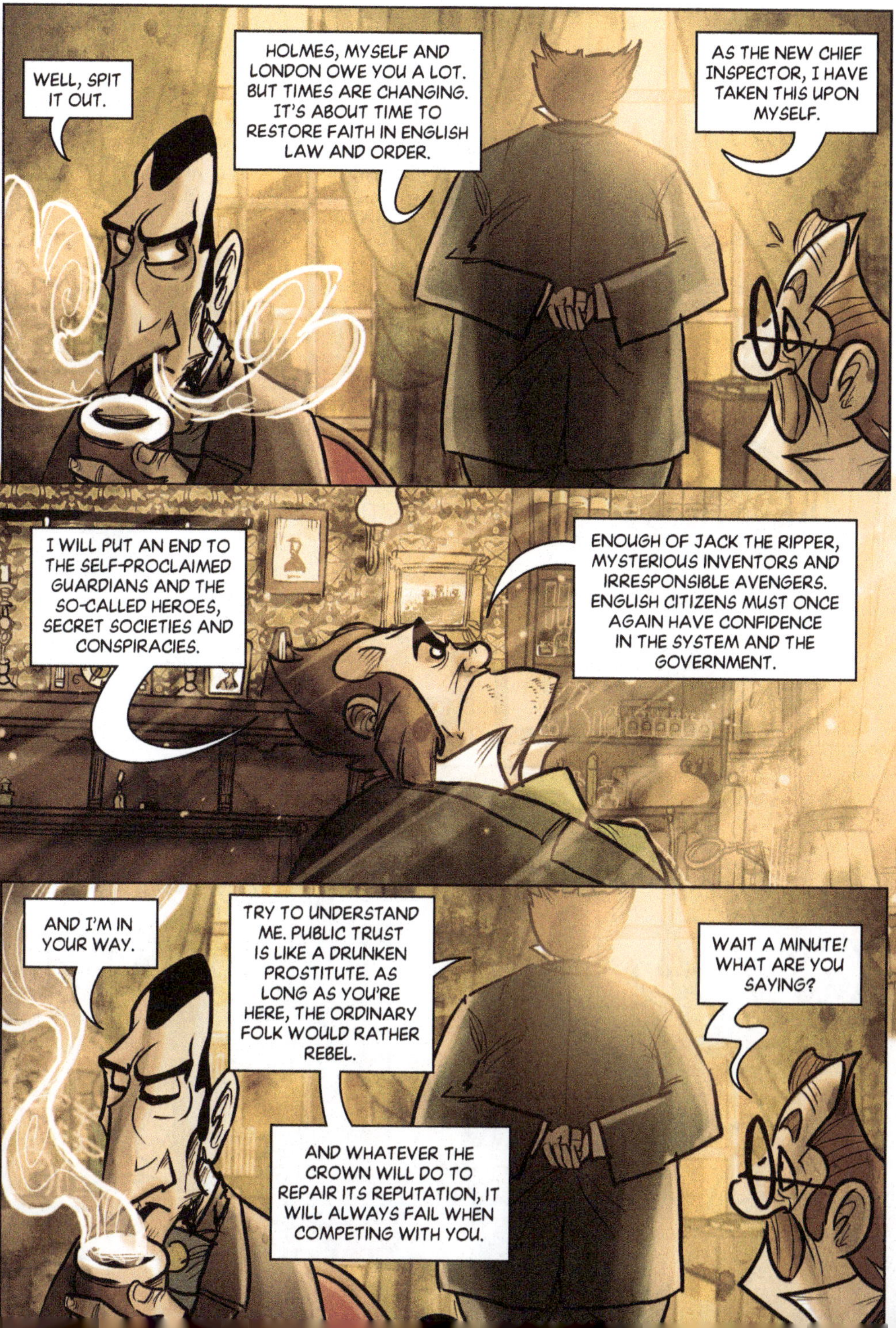
WELL, SPIT IT OUT.
HOLMES, MYSELF AND LONDON OWE YOU A LOT. BUT TIMES ARE CHANGING. IT'S ABOUT TIME TO RESTORE FAITH IN ENGLISH LAW AND ORDER.
AS THE NEW CHIEF INSPECTOR, I HAVE TAKEN THIS UPON MYSELF.
I WILL PUT AN END TO THE SELF-PROCLAIMED GUARDIANS AND THE SO-CALLED HEROES, SECRET SOCIETIES AND CONSPIRACIES.
ENOUGH OF JACK THE RIPPER, MYSTERIOUS INVENTORS AND IRRESPONSIBLE AVENGERS. ENGLISH CITIZENS MUST ONCE AGAIN HAVE CONFIDENCE IN THE SYSTEM AND THE GOVERNMENT.
AND I'M IN YOUR WAY.
TRY TO UNDERSTAND ME. PUBLIC TRUST IS LIKE A DRUNKEN PROSTITUTE. AS LONG AS YOU'RE HERE, THE ORDINARY FOLK WOULD RATHER REBEL.
AND WHATEVER THE CROWN WILL DO TO REPAIR ITS REPUTATION, IT WILL ALWAYS FAIL WHEN COMPETING WITH YOU.
WAIT A MINUTE! WHAT ARE YOU SAYING?

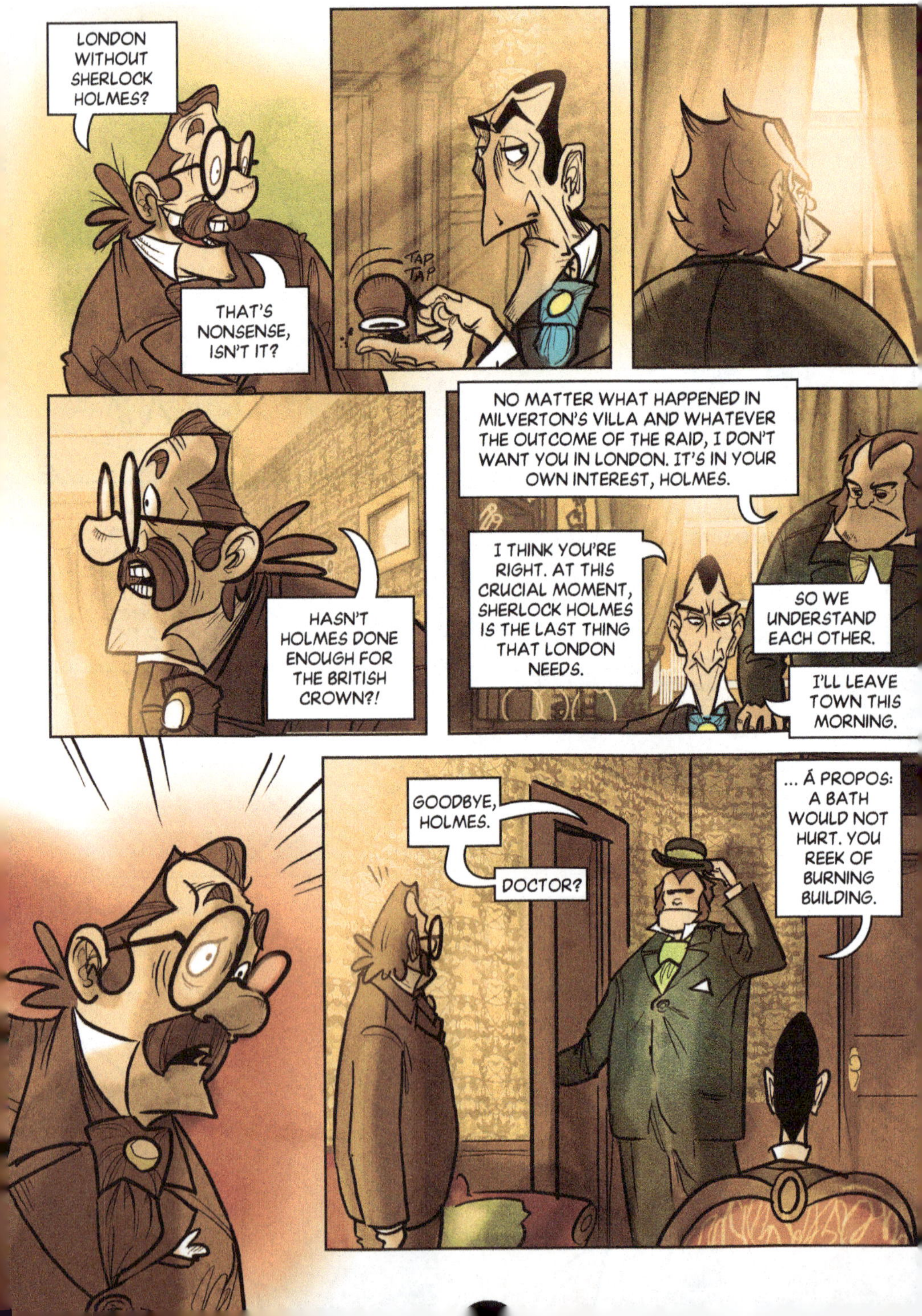
LONDON WITHOUT SHERLOCK HOLMES?
THAT'S NONSENSE, ISN'T IT?
TAP TAP
HASN'T HOLMES DONE ENOUGH FOR THE BRITISH CROWN?!
NO MATTER WHAT HAPPENED IN MILVERTON'S VILLA AND WHATEVER THE OUTCOME OF THE RAID, I DON'T WANT YOU IN LONDON. IT'S IN YOUR OWN INTEREST, HOLMES.
I THINK YOU'RE RIGHT. AT THIS CRUCIAL MOMENT, SHERLOCK HOLMES IS THE LAST THING THAT LONDON NEEDS.
SO WE UNDERSTAND EACH OTHER.
I'LL LEAVE TOWN THIS MORNING.
GOODBYE, HOLMES.
DOCTOR?
... Á PROPOS: A BATH WOULD NOT HURT. YOU REEK OF BURNING BUILDING.

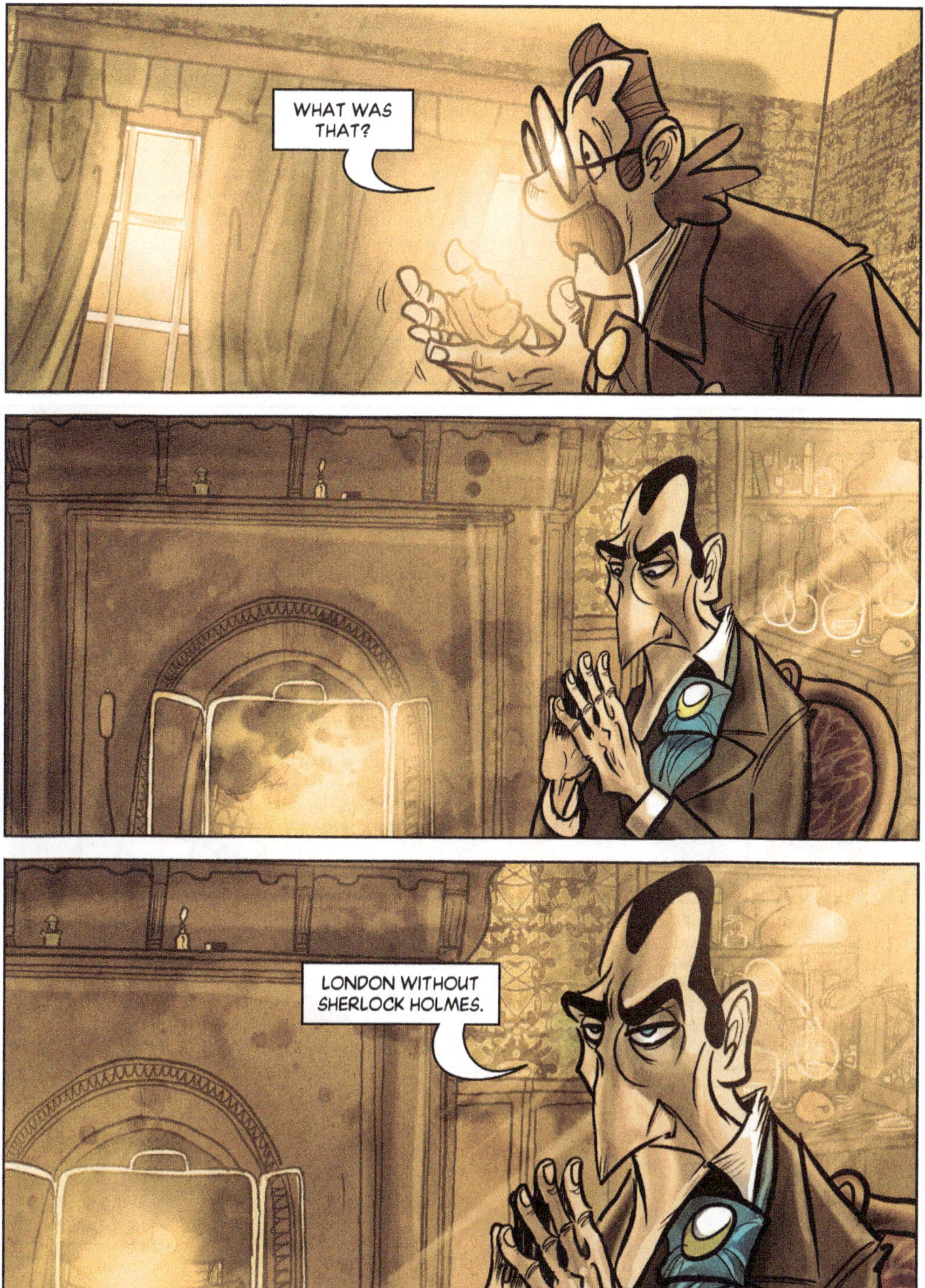
WHAT WAS THAT?
LONDON WITHOUT SHERLOCK HOLMES.

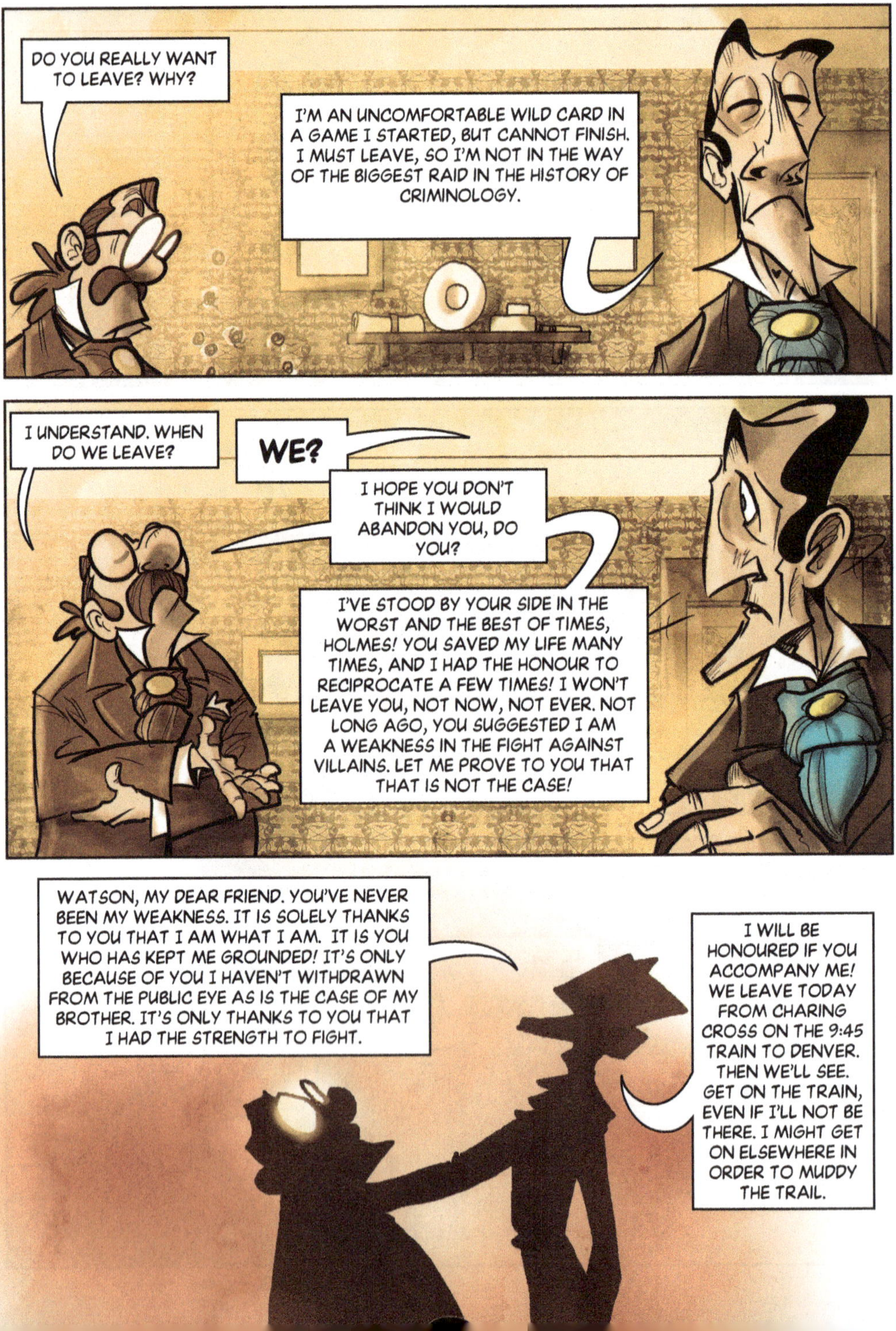
DO YOU REALLY WANT TO LEAVE? WHY?
I'M AN UNCOMFORTABLE WILD CARD IN A GAME I STARTED, BUT CANNOT FINISH. I MUST LEAVE, SO I'M NOT IN THE WAY OF THE BIGGEST RAID IN THE HISTORY OF CRIMINOLOGY.
I UNDERSTAND. WHEN DO WE LEAVE?
WE?
I HOPE YOU DON'T THINK I WOULD ABANDON YOU, DO YOU?
I'VE STOOD BY YOUR SIDE IN THE WORST AND THE BEST OF TIMES, HOLMES! YOU SAVED MY LIFE MANY TIMES, AND I HAD THE HONOUR TO RECIPROCATE A FEW TIMES! I WON'T LEAVE YOU, NOT NOW, NOT EVER. NOT LONG AGO, YOU SUGGESTED I AM A WEAKNESS IN THE FIGHT AGAINST VILLAINS. LET ME PROVE TO YOU THAT THAT IS NOT THE CASE!
WATSON, MY DEAR FRIEND. YOU'VE NEVER BEEN MY WEAKNESS. IT IS SOLELY THANKS TO YOU THAT I AM WHAT I AM. IT IS YOU WHO HAS KEPT ME GROUNDED! IT'S ONLY BECAUSE OF YOU I HAVEN'T WITHDRAWN FROM THE PUBLIC EYE AS IS THE CASE OF MY BROTHER. IT'S ONLY THANKS TO YOU THAT I HAD THE STRENGTH TO FIGHT.
I WILL BE HONOURED IF YOU ACCOMPANY ME! WE LEAVE TODAY FROM CHARING CROSS ON THE 9:45 TRAIN TO DENVER. THEN WE'LL SEE. GET ON THE TRAIN, EVEN IF I'LL NOT BE THERE. I MIGHT GET ON ELSEWHERE IN ORDER TO MUDDY THE TRAIL.

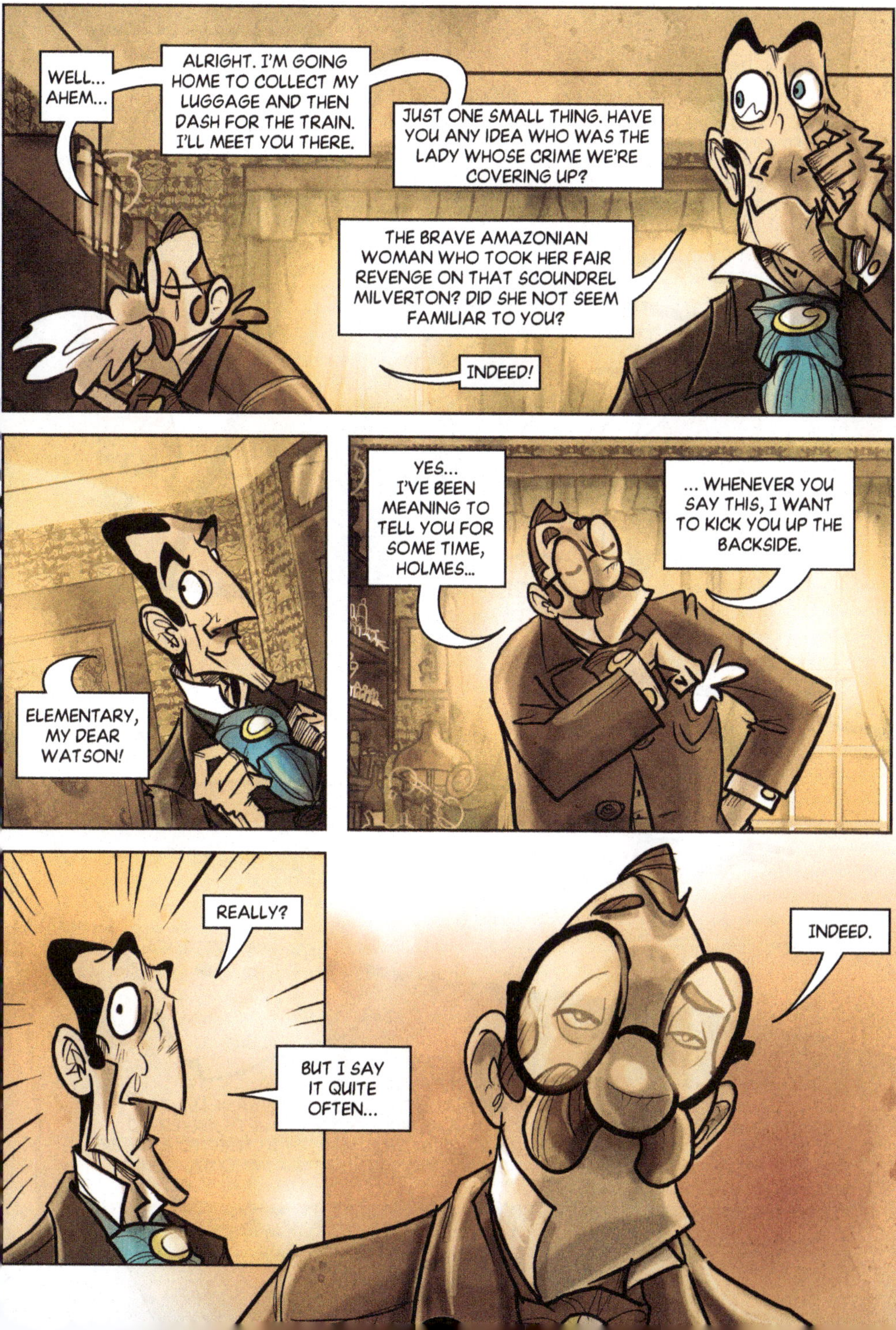
WELL... AHEM...
ALRIGHT. I'M GOING HOME TO COLLECT MY LUGGAGE AND THEN DASH FOR THE TRAIN. I'LL MEET YOU THERE.
JUST ONE SMALL THING. HAVE YOU ANY IDEA WHO WAS THE LADY WHOSE CRIME WE'RE COVERING UP?
THE BRAVE AMAZONIAN WOMAN WHO TOOK HER FAIR REVENGE ON THAT SCOUNDREL MILVERTON? DID SHE NOT SEEM FAMILIAR TO YOU?
INDEED!
ELEMENTARY, MY DEAR WATSON!
YES... I'VE BEEN MEANING TO TELL YOU FOR SOME TIME, HOLMES...
... WHENEVER YOU SAY THIS, I WANT TO KICK YOU UP THE BACKSIDE.
REALLY?
BUT I SAY IT QUITE OFTEN...
INDEED.

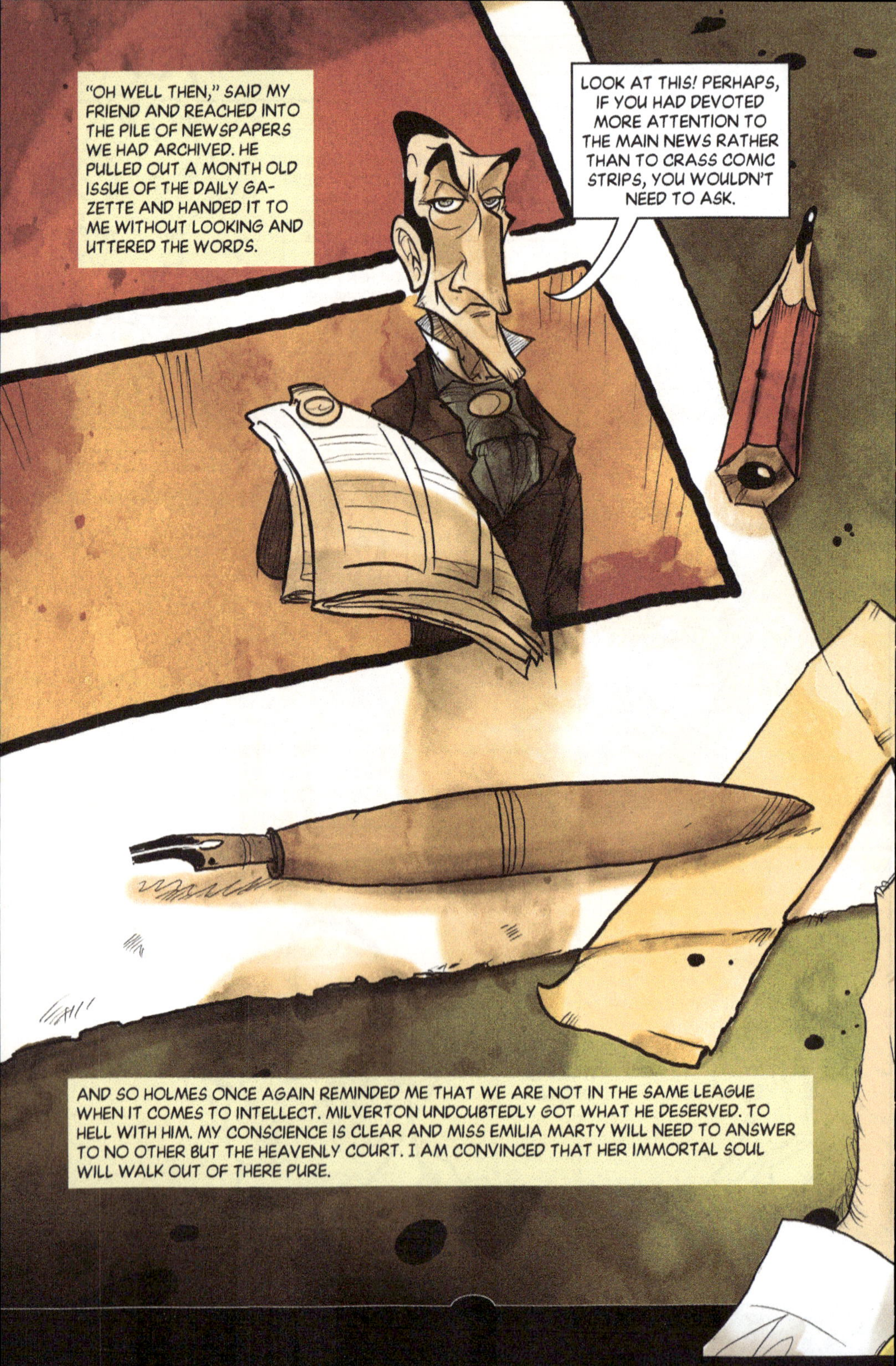
"OH WELL THEN," SAID MY FRIEND AND REACHED INTO THE PILE OF NEWSPAPERS WE HAD ARCHIVED. HE PULLED OUT A MONTH OLD ISSUE OF THE DAILY GAZETTE AND HANDED IT TO ME WITHOUT LOOKING AND UTTERED THE WORDS.
LOOK AT THIS! PERHAPS, IF YOU HAD DEVOTED MORE ATTENTION TO THE MAIN NEWS RATHER THAN TO CRASS COMIC STRIPS, YOU WOULDN'T NEED TO ASK.
AND SO HOLMES ONCE AGAIN REMINDED ME THAT WE ARE NOT IN THE SAME LEAGUE WHEN IT COMES TO INTELLECT. MILVERTON UNDOUBTEDLY GOT WHAT HE DESERVED. TO HELL WITH HIM. MY CONSCIENCE IS CLEAR AND MISS EMILIA MARTY WILL NEED TO ANSWER TO NO OTHER BUT THE HEAVENLY COURT. I AM CONVINCED THAT HER IMMORTAL SOUL WILL WALK OUT OF THERE PURE.

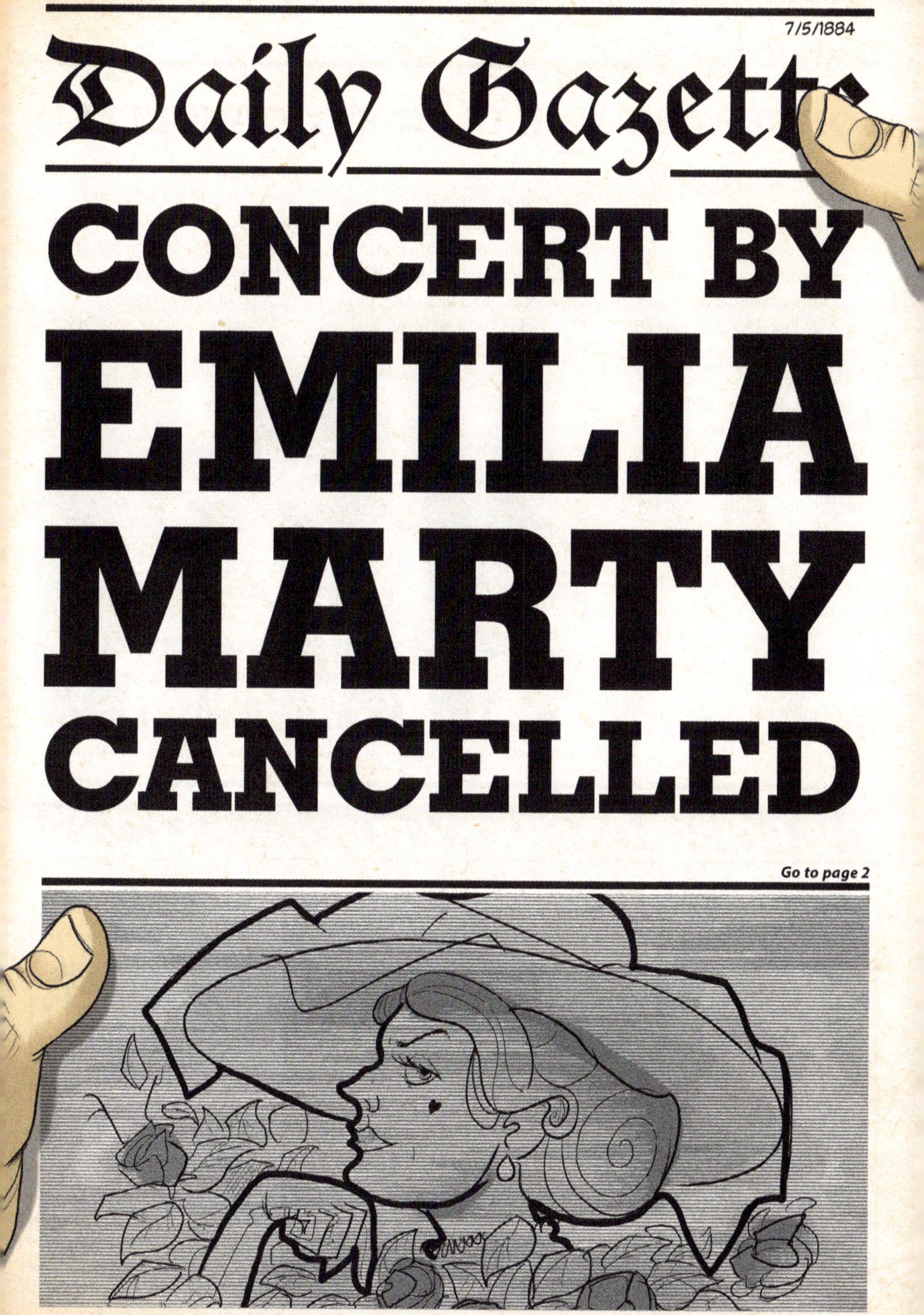
7/5/1884
Daily Gazette
CONCERT BY EMILIA MARTY CANCELLED
Go to page 2

Daily Gazette

CONCERT BY EMILIA MARTY CANCELLED

Continued from page 1

Exactly a week to the day, the Royal Opera was to host a concert by the celebrated European singer Emilia Marty. We regret to inform all ticket holders and fans of the international star that the diva has been forced to cancel the concert due to a sudden indisposition and is now in seclusion. It is an open secret that the reason for the unexpected change is the demise of Miss Marty's fiancé, whose name we will not mention out of respect for the deceased. As our competitors have triggered a whirlwind of gossip and misinformation around the singer, we have decided to simply inform our readers of the event, which has saddened London for various reasons. We do not wish to exacerbate the grief of a woman admired throughout the whole of Europe. The Opera Director has refused to comment on whether the concert will be rescheduled to a later date, or if the tickets will be refunded. We do however believe, that Londoners will eventually be allowed to hear the voice of Emilia Marty, known for her confidence and poise. The Queen has also sent condolences and a message of support to the singer.

E. D. M.

The Royal Opera. Unfortunately, the Opera Director, Lord Stockhart, refused to pose for an engraving.

THE BARKS OF MUCKY PUP

Panel 1: "I HEARD YOU'RE TELLING EVERYONE THAT I'M STUPID! WILL YOU STOP GOSSIPING ABOUT ME?" "I PROMISE!"

Panel 2: "THAT'S BETTER!"

Panel 3: "JUST A MOMENT!"

Panel 4: "YOU DIDN'T ANSWER ME!" "THAT'S TRUE."

Panel 5: "SO YOU BETTER BE CAREFUL!"

Panel 6: "JUST A MOMENT!" "YOU STILL DIDN'T ANSWER ME!" "JESUS, I'M SORRY!"

Panel 7: "GOOD!" "I'LL NEVER GET BORED OF THIS!"

Panel 8: "JUST A MOMENT!"

7/5/1884

CASTLE COLLAPSES IN THE CARPATHIAN VILLAGE OF VERST

Yesterday's report on the collapse of the castle in the Carpathian Verst remains unconfirmed. This castle fortress is not recorded on any maps, and the information we received from this region is incomplete, and we cannot vouch for its veracity. It is for this reason we are sending our number one journalist to the Carpathians to set the record straight.

So far we can only report with certainty that the castle stood on a high rocky needle in the rugged valley near the village of Verst. Informed readers will certainly recall the mysterious plague, which swept this region in the second half of the 18th century. The disease was also known as the red death and infected not only humans, but also the vegetation and fauna in the area. It spread exponentially, however at some point it stopped and gradually disappeared. What was the cause of the disease and ultimately its undoing is only guesswork, which we will not get involved in, due to the lack of information. We can safely say that it is incredibly difficult to obtain reliable information from the pile of superstitious tales and legends originating from a region where people still believe in vampires and werewolves.

The castle itself was nicknamed Devil's Castle by the locals, which is because of an object that fell from the sky prior to the epidemic outbreak. However, the castle belongs to the only remaining descendant of the Teleke family from Gortz. Count Teleke, however, is missing so cannot be questioned on the details. It is believed that his forgotten residence has now been abandoned for several decades. It is therefore unlikely that Count Teleke would be inside the castle at the time of the misfortune. On the contrary, his habit of travelling the world incognito supports the theory that he is currently away on one of his journeys.

Nevertheless, we were lucky enough to discover a man who visited the sites in question and who provided us with the above description of the castle and its surrounding area as well as the drawing printed below. Professor Van Helsing arrived in London to attend the autopsy of Joseph Merrik, the deceased elephant man. He was kind enough to share his impressions of the place with us.

"The Carpathians are a hotbed of strange legends and dark secrets. The people there live a hundred years behind civilization, and remain very close to nature, much closer than we do today. We live with a false sense of security and conveniently forget our place in the food chain. There is nothing in Count Teleke's castle. It has been abandoned for a long time and the terrain prevents anyone from reaching it. I think that there were no mysterious forces contributing to its collapse, perhaps with the exception of gravity."

There is still much we do not yet know. True and reliable information will be published in several weeks, as our newspaper can make do without the nonsense and fairytales brought to you by our competitors. Our reporter is on his way.

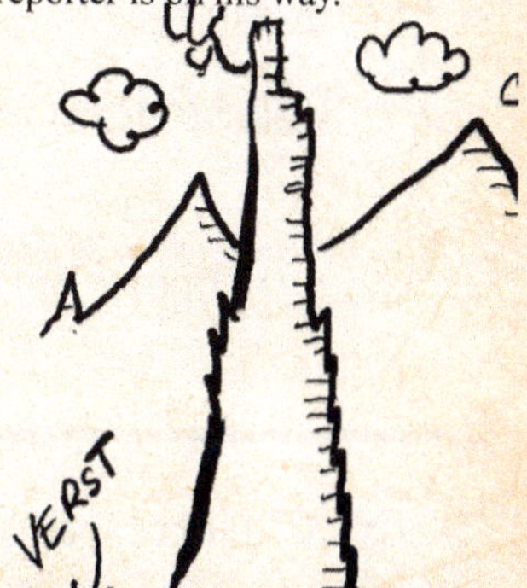
VERST

Drawing by Prof. Van Helsing

Daily Gazette

Advertisement

R.U.R.
ROSSUM'S UNIVERSAL ROBOTS

A GREAT AMENITY OF MODERN TIMES — ROSSUM'S IMPROVED SEMI-MECHANICAL ASSISTANT — KNOWN AS THE ROBOT — HAS LEFT THE PRODUCTION LINE ON ROSSUM'S ISLAND. THE PRICE OF THIS UNIVERSAL HELPER IS ONLY 2000 T.*

THEREFORE, PLEASE DO NOT HESITATE AND QUICKLY ORDER THIS IRREPLACEABLE WORKFORCE OF THE FUTURE! WE WILL ADJUST YOUR ROBOT FOR FREE DEPENDING ON THE TYPE OF WORKPLACE. NEW ROBOTS CONTAIN A BUILT-IN FUSE TO PREVENT THE GNASHING OF TEETH, THUS MAKING ACCIDENTS IMPOSSIBLE!**

Labels on robot diagram: IMPROVED LEGS, FUSE TO PREVENT GNASHING OF TEETH, DOUBLE SHOULDER STRENGTH, POSITIONING HANDLES, ADJUSTABLE HEIGHT, SILENT SPRING-LOADED FEET

✂ CUT HERE

ORDER VOUCHER
ADDRESS OF ORDERING PARTY

TITLE

NAME

ADDRESS

QUANTITY

WORK PLACE FOR ROBOT

* DISCOUNT AVAILABLE ON ALL ORDERS OF 10 ROBOTS OR MORE
** THE MANUFACTURER IS NOT LIABLE FOR ROBOTS WITH BROKEN SEALS OR FOR ROBOTS WORKING IN A MAGNETIC ENVIRONMENT.

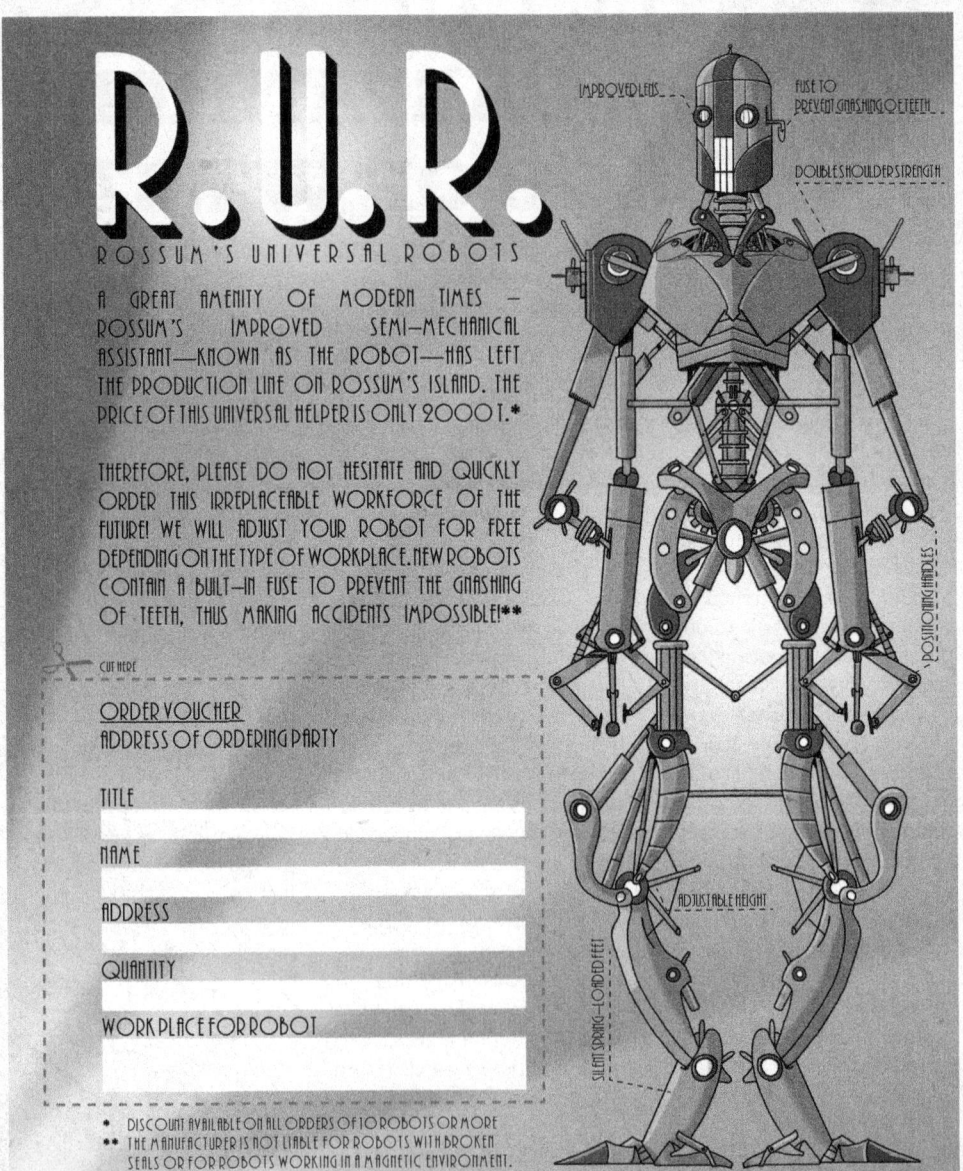

Daily Gazette published by the Daily Gazette since 1805. Chief Editor T. M. Rockfort, editorial office: 108 Lisson Grove, London, advertising department: 5 Glentworth Street, London. Daily circulation of 800,000. Printshop: Kopls company, 84/225 Brok-Schmutzig Street, London.

THE FINAL PROBLEM

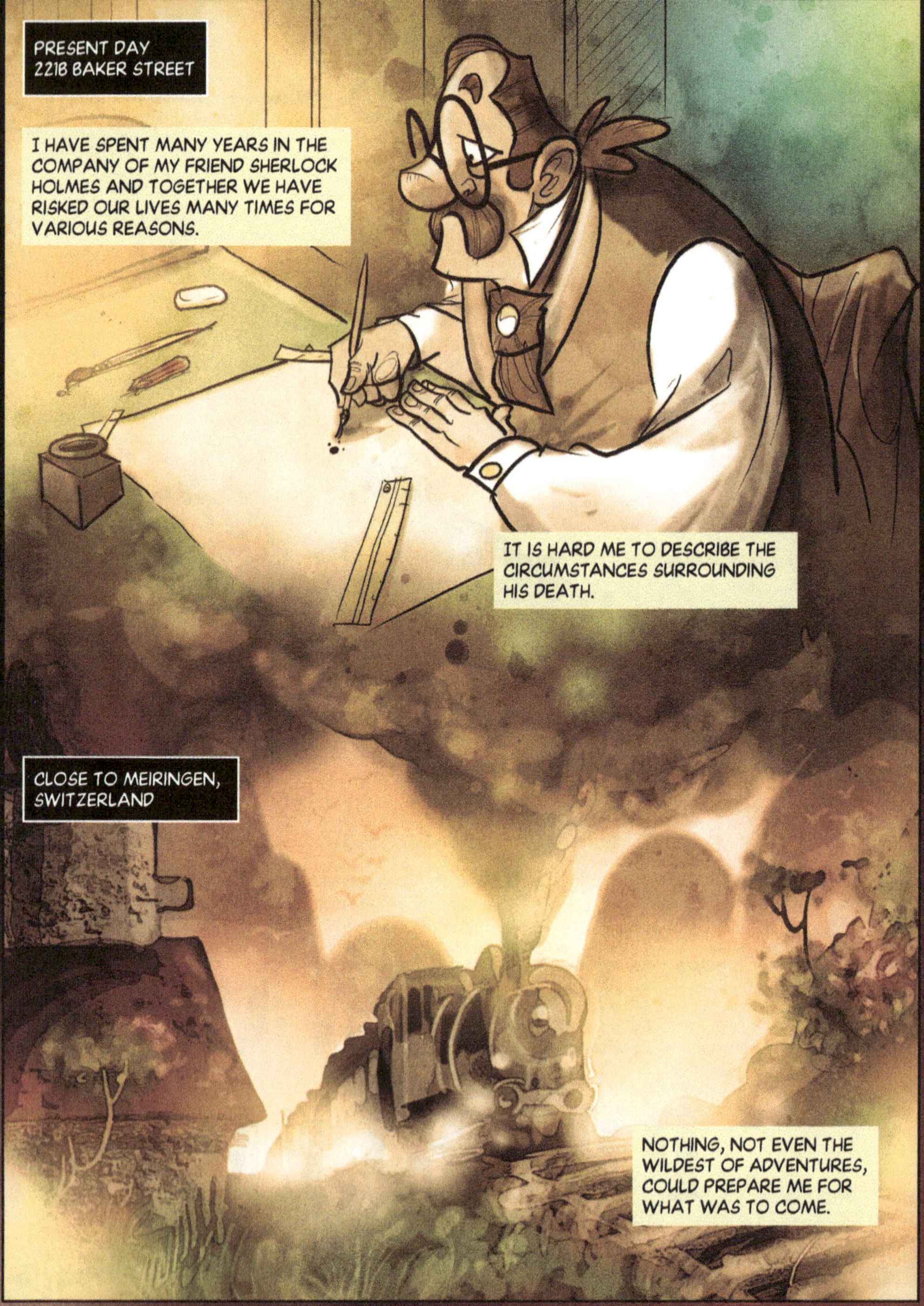
PRESENT DAY
221B BAKER STREET
I HAVE SPENT MANY YEARS IN THE COMPANY OF MY FRIEND SHERLOCK HOLMES AND TOGETHER WE HAVE RISKED OUR LIVES MANY TIMES FOR VARIOUS REASONS.
IT IS HARD ME TO DESCRIBE THE CIRCUMSTANCES SURROUNDING HIS DEATH.
CLOSE TO MEIRINGEN, SWITZERLAND
NOTHING, NOT EVEN THE WILDEST OF ADVENTURES, COULD PREPARE ME FOR WHAT WAS TO COME.

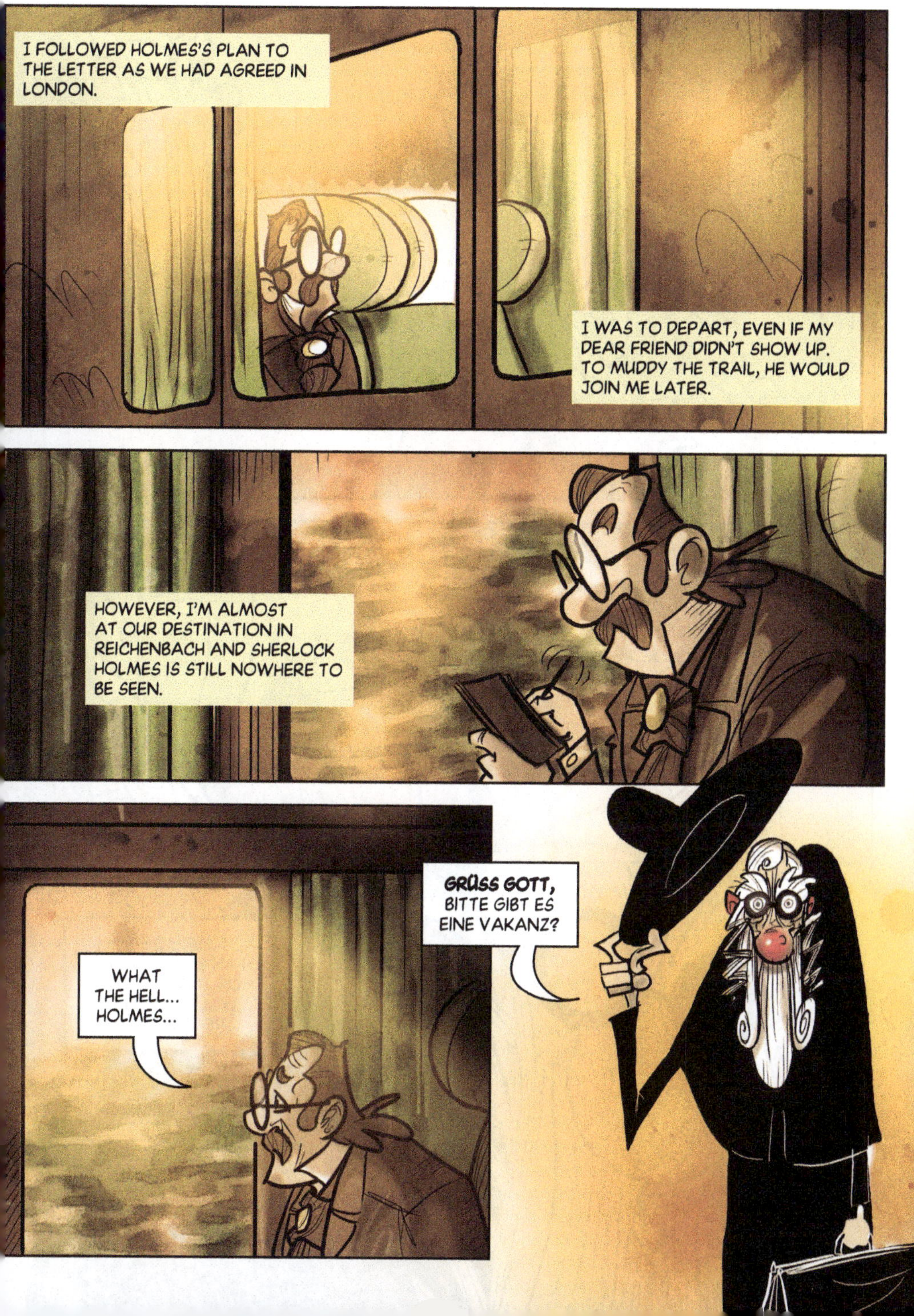
I FOLLOWED HOLMES'S PLAN TO THE LETTER AS WE HAD AGREED IN LONDON.
I WAS TO DEPART, EVEN IF MY DEAR FRIEND DIDN'T SHOW UP. TO MUDDY THE TRAIL, HE WOULD JOIN ME LATER.
HOWEVER, I'M ALMOST AT OUR DESTINATION IN REICHENBACH AND SHERLOCK HOLMES IS STILL NOWHERE TO BE SEEN.
GRÜSS GOTT, BITTE GIBT ES EINE VAKANZ?
WHAT THE HELL... HOLMES...

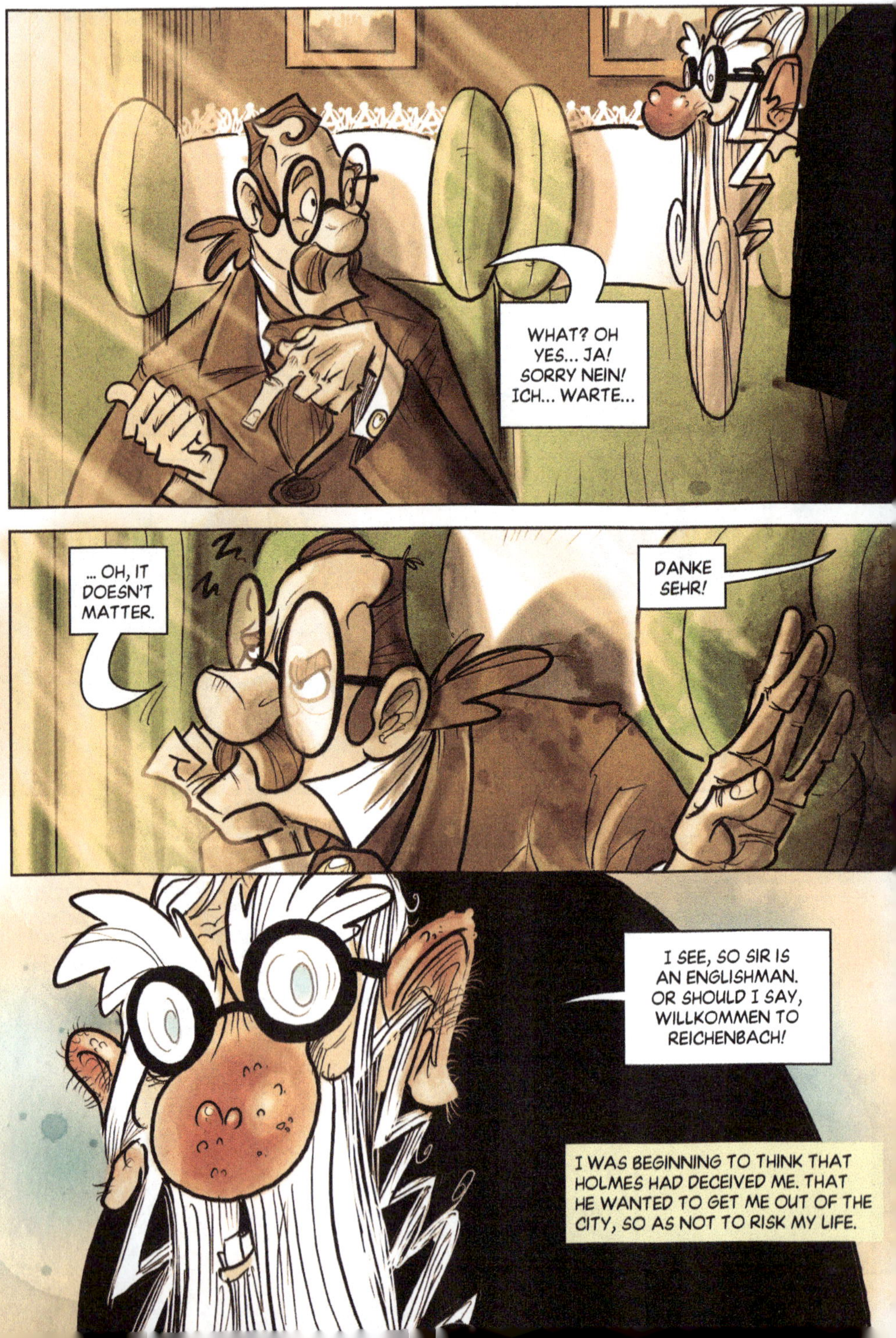
WHAT? OH YES... JA! SORRY NEIN! ICH... WARTE...
... OH, IT DOESN'T MATTER.
DANKE SEHR!
I SEE, SO SIR IS AN ENGLISHMAN. OR SHOULD I SAY, WILLKOMMEN TO REICHENBACH!
I WAS BEGINNING TO THINK THAT HOLMES HAD DECEIVED ME. THAT HE WANTED TO GET ME OUT OF THE CITY, SO AS NOT TO RISK MY LIFE.

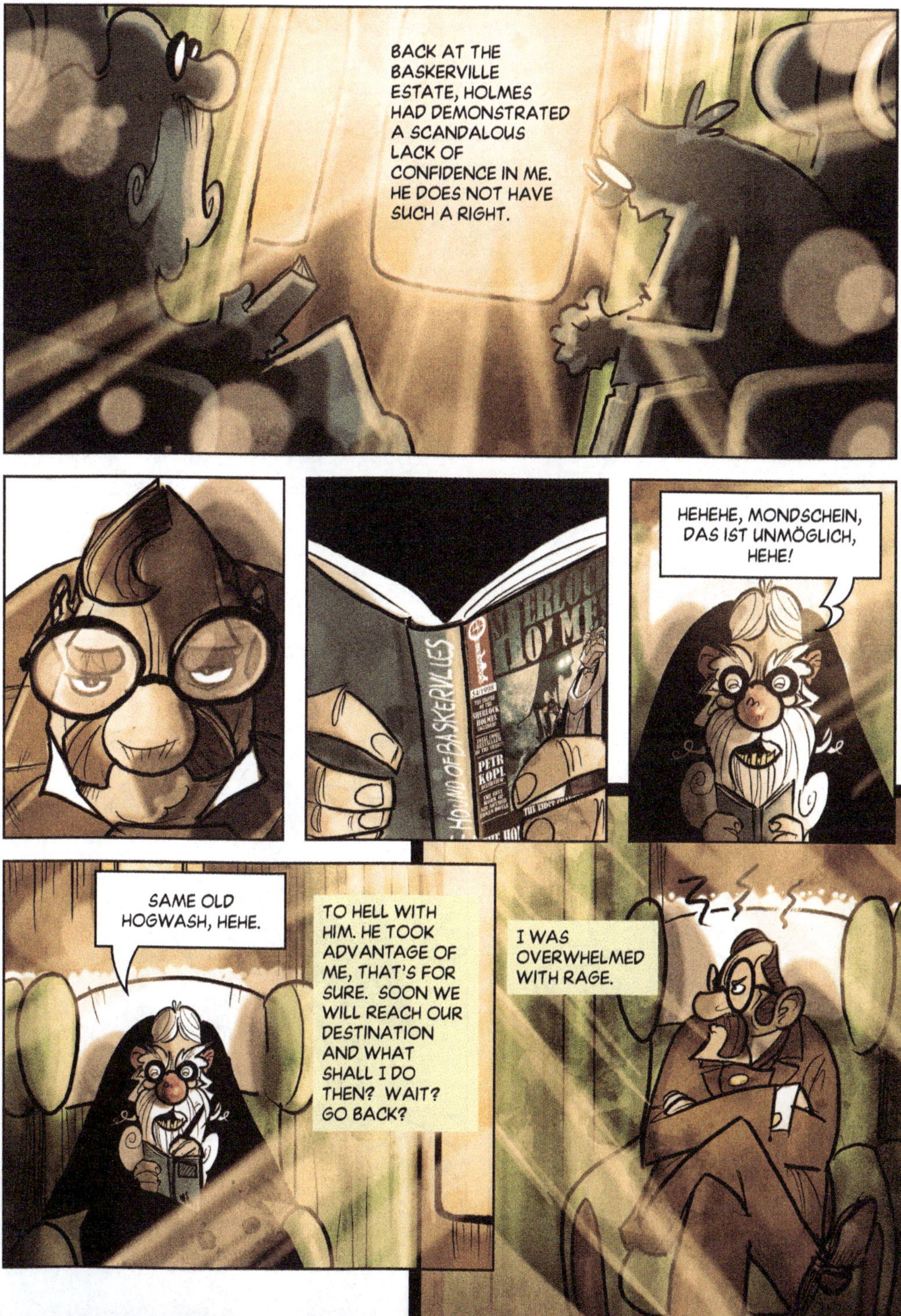

BACK AT THE BASKERVILLE ESTATE, HOLMES HAD DEMONSTRATED A SCANDALOUS LACK OF CONFIDENCE IN ME. HE DOES NOT HAVE SUCH A RIGHT.
HEHEHE, MONDSCHEIN, DAS IST UNMÖGLICH, HEHE!
SAME OLD HOGWASH, HEHE.
TO HELL WITH HIM. HE TOOK ADVANTAGE OF ME, THAT'S FOR SURE. SOON WE WILL REACH OUR DESTINATION AND WHAT SHALL I DO THEN? WAIT? GO BACK?
I WAS OVERWHELMED WITH RAGE.

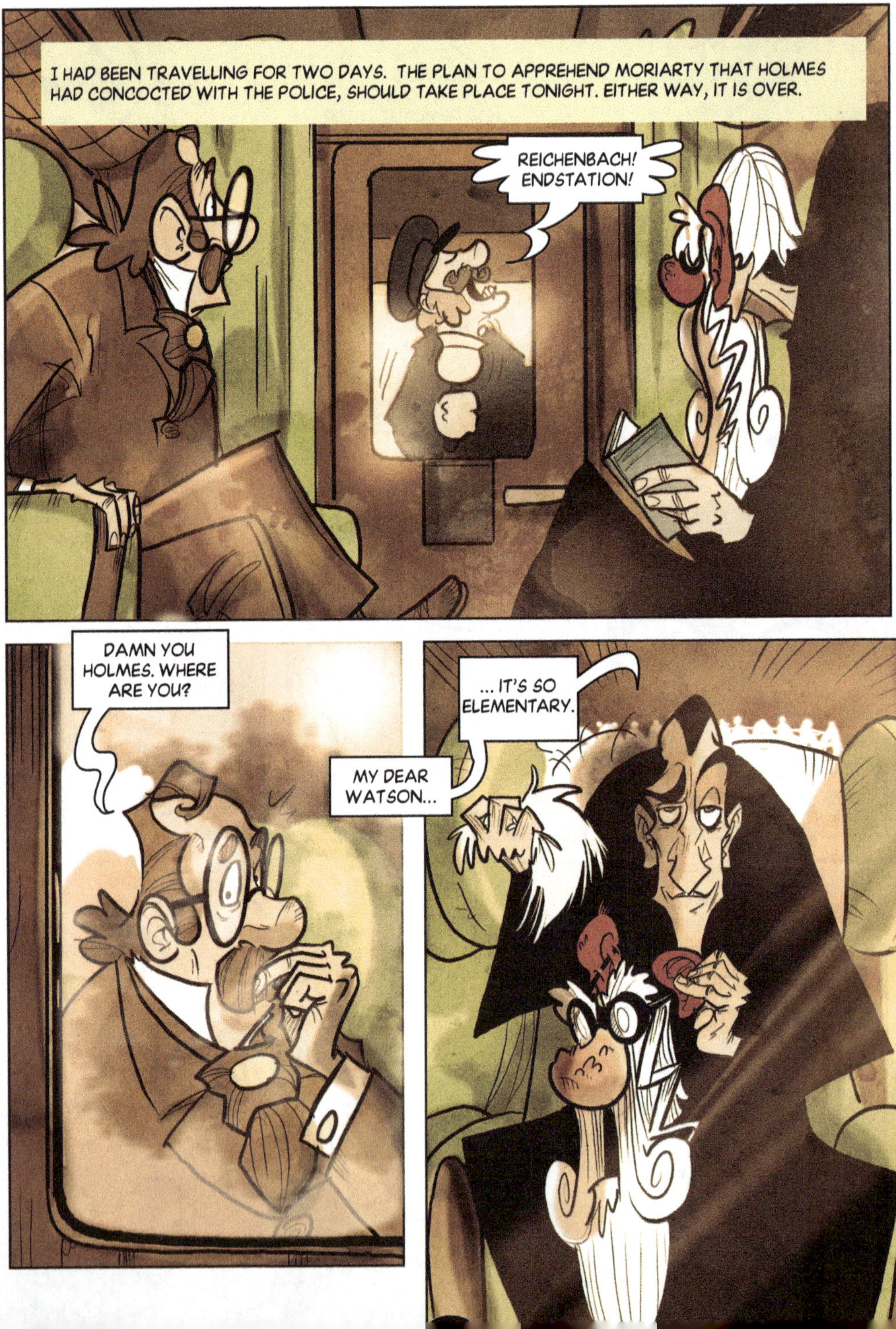
I HAD BEEN TRAVELLING FOR TWO DAYS. THE PLAN TO APPREHEND MORIARTY THAT HOLMES HAD CONCOCTED WITH THE POLICE, SHOULD TAKE PLACE TONIGHT. EITHER WAY, IT IS OVER.
REICHENBACH! ENDSTATION!
DAMN YOU HOLMES. WHERE ARE YOU?
MY DEAR WATSON...
... IT'S SO ELEMENTARY.

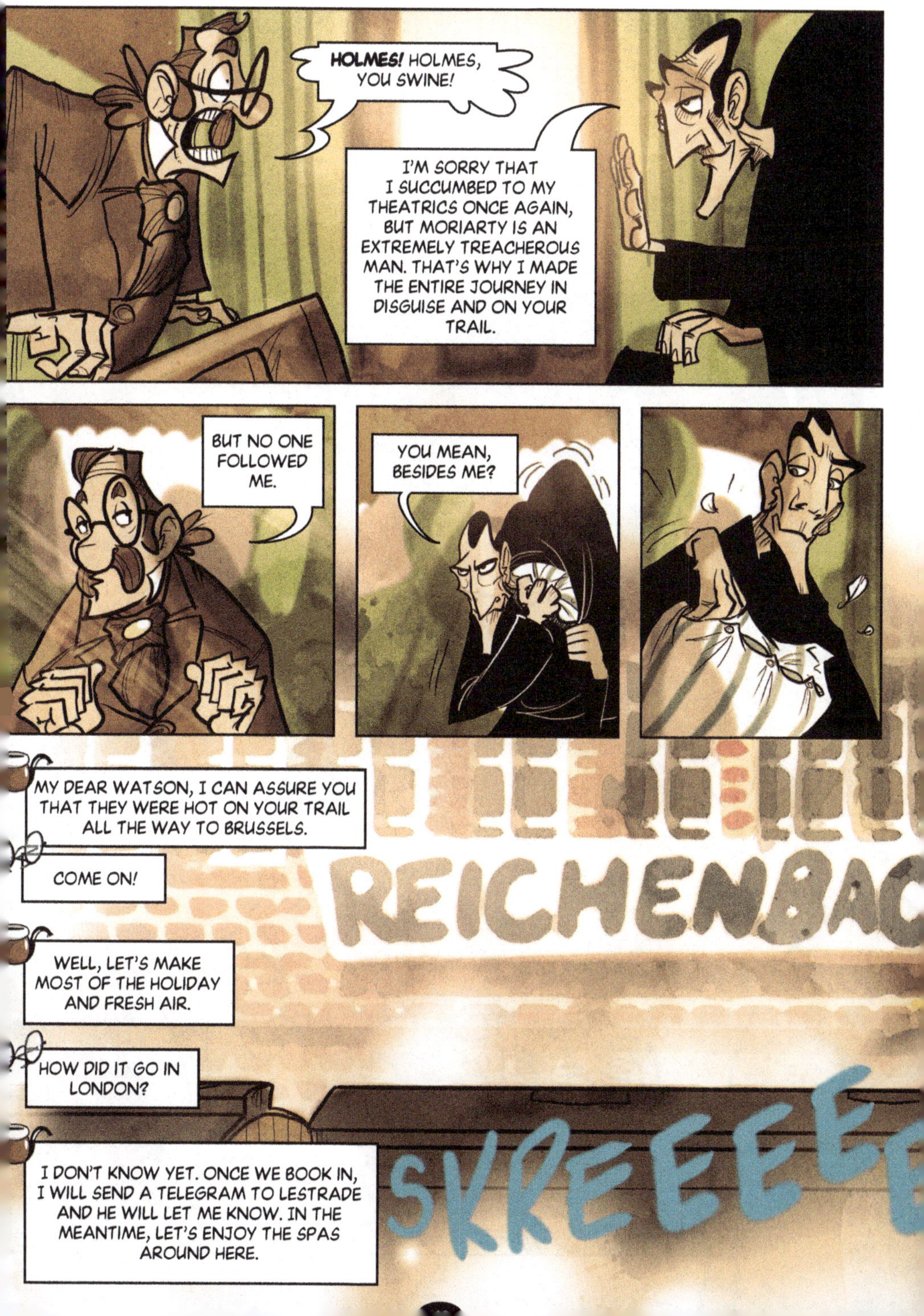
HOLMES! HOLMES, YOU SWINE!
I'M SORRY THAT I SUCCUMBED TO MY THEATRICS ONCE AGAIN, BUT MORIARTY IS AN EXTREMELY TREACHEROUS MAN. THAT'S WHY I MADE THE ENTIRE JOURNEY IN DISGUISE AND ON YOUR TRAIL.
BUT NO ONE FOLLOWED ME.
YOU MEAN, BESIDES ME?
MY DEAR WATSON, I CAN ASSURE YOU THAT THEY WERE HOT ON YOUR TRAIL ALL THE WAY TO BRUSSELS.
COME ON!
REICHENBAC
WELL, LET'S MAKE MOST OF THE HOLIDAY AND FRESH AIR.
HOW DID IT GO IN LONDON?
I DON'T KNOW YET. ONCE WE BOOK IN, I WILL SEND A TELEGRAM TO LESTRADE AND HE WILL LET ME KNOW. IN THE MEANTIME, LET'S ENJOY THE SPAS AROUND HERE.
SKREEEEE

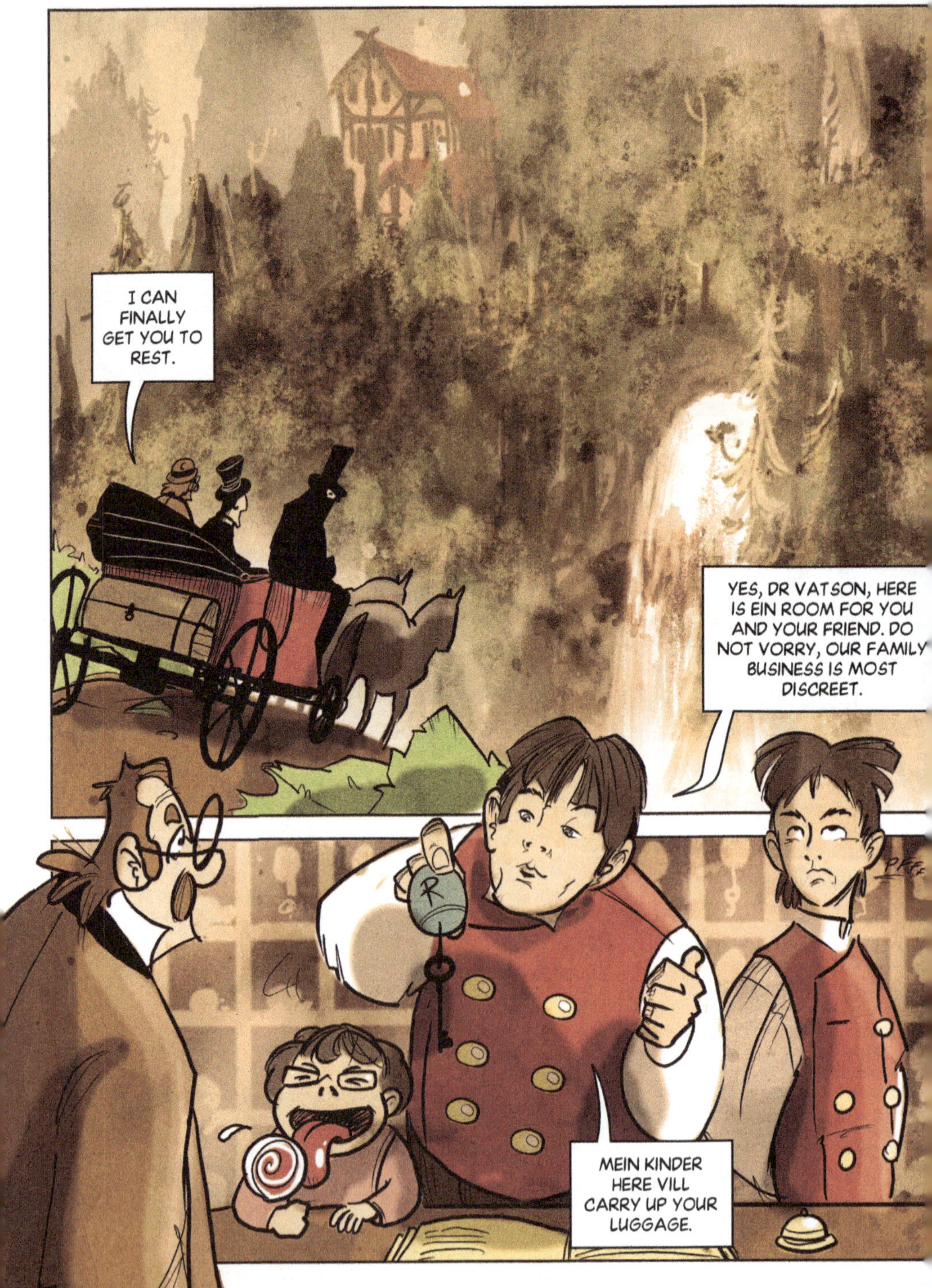

I CAN FINALLY GET YOU TO REST.
YES, DR VATSON, HERE IS EIN ROOM FOR YOU AND YOUR FRIEND. DO NOT VORRY, OUR FAMILY BUSINESS IS MOST DISCREET.
MEIN KINDER HERE VILL CARRY UP YOUR LUGGAGE.

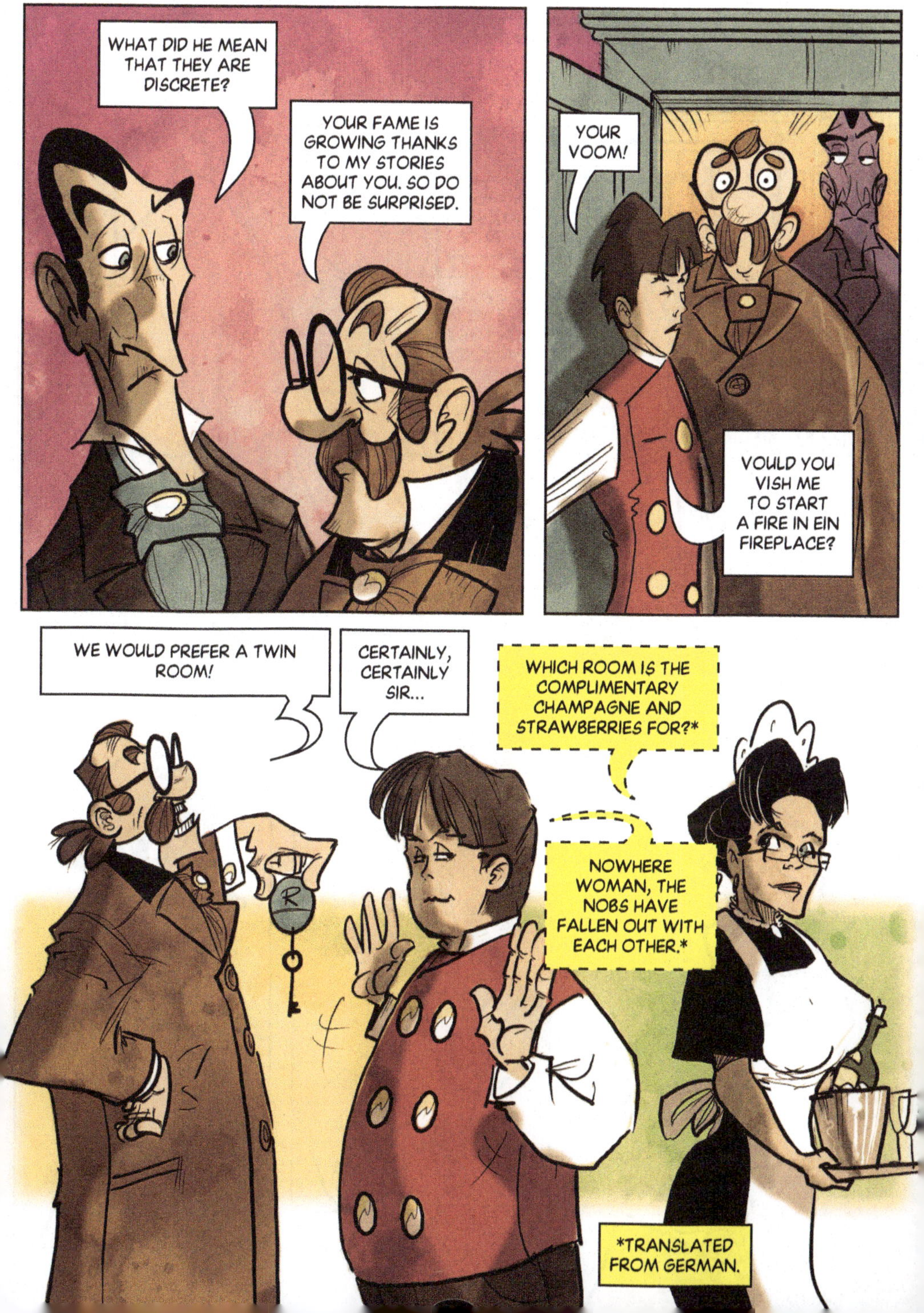
WHAT DID HE MEAN THAT THEY ARE DISCRETE?
YOUR FAME IS GROWING THANKS TO MY STORIES ABOUT YOU. SO DO NOT BE SURPRISED.
YOUR VOOM!
VOULD YOU VISH ME TO START A FIRE IN EIN FIREPLACE?
WE WOULD PREFER A TWIN ROOM!
CERTAINLY, CERTAINLY SIR...
WHICH ROOM IS THE COMPLIMENTARY CHAMPAGNE AND STRAWBERRIES FOR?*
NOWHERE WOMAN, THE NOBS HAVE FALLEN OUT WITH EACH OTHER.*
*TRANSLATED FROM GERMAN.

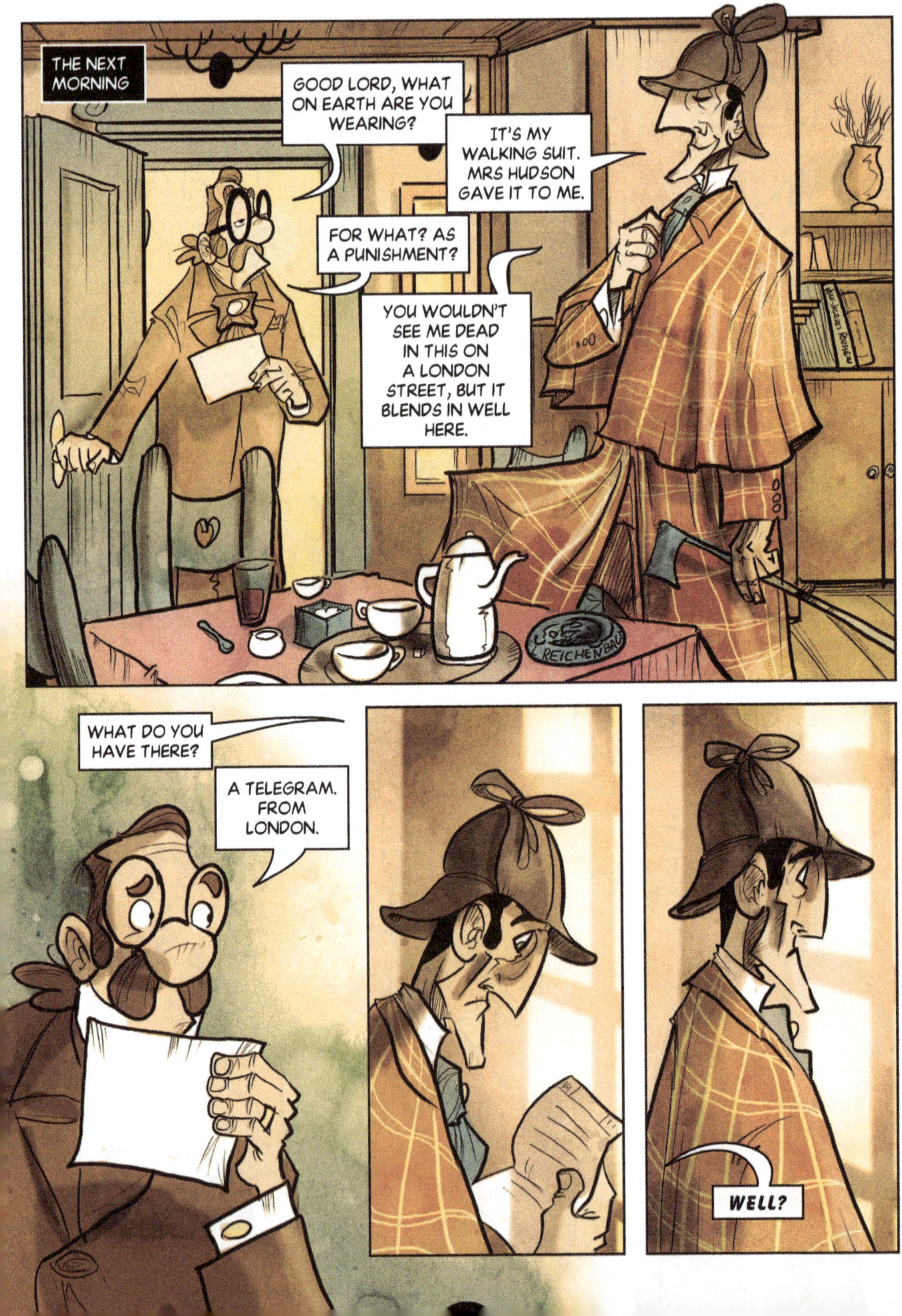
THE NEXT MORNING
GOOD LORD, WHAT ON EARTH ARE YOU WEARING?
IT'S MY WALKING SUIT. MRS HUDSON GAVE IT TO ME.
FOR WHAT? AS A PUNISHMENT?
YOU WOULDN'T SEE ME DEAD IN THIS ON A LONDON STREET, BUT IT BLENDS IN WELL HERE.
REICHENBACH
WHAT DO YOU HAVE THERE?
A TELEGRAM. FROM LONDON.
WELL?

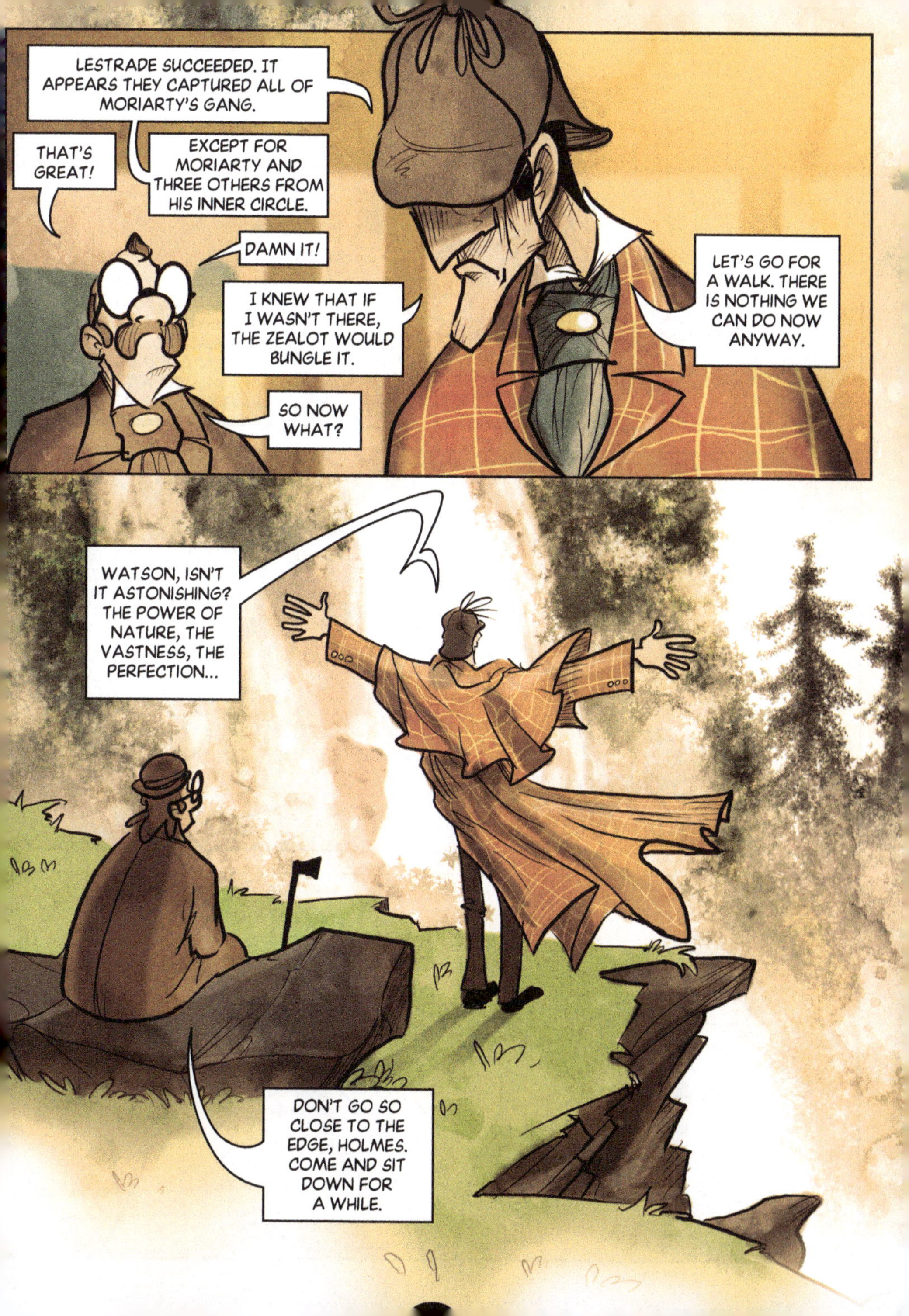
LESTRADE SUCCEEDED. IT APPEARS THEY CAPTURED ALL OF MORIARTY'S GANG.
THAT'S GREAT!
EXCEPT FOR MORIARTY AND THREE OTHERS FROM HIS INNER CIRCLE.
DAMN IT!
I KNEW THAT IF I WASN'T THERE, THE ZEALOT WOULD BUNGLE IT.
SO NOW WHAT?
LET'S GO FOR A WALK. THERE IS NOTHING WE CAN DO NOW ANYWAY.
WATSON, ISN'T IT ASTONISHING? THE POWER OF NATURE, THE VASTNESS, THE PERFECTION...
DON'T GO SO CLOSE TO THE EDGE, HOLMES. COME AND SIT DOWN FOR A WHILE.

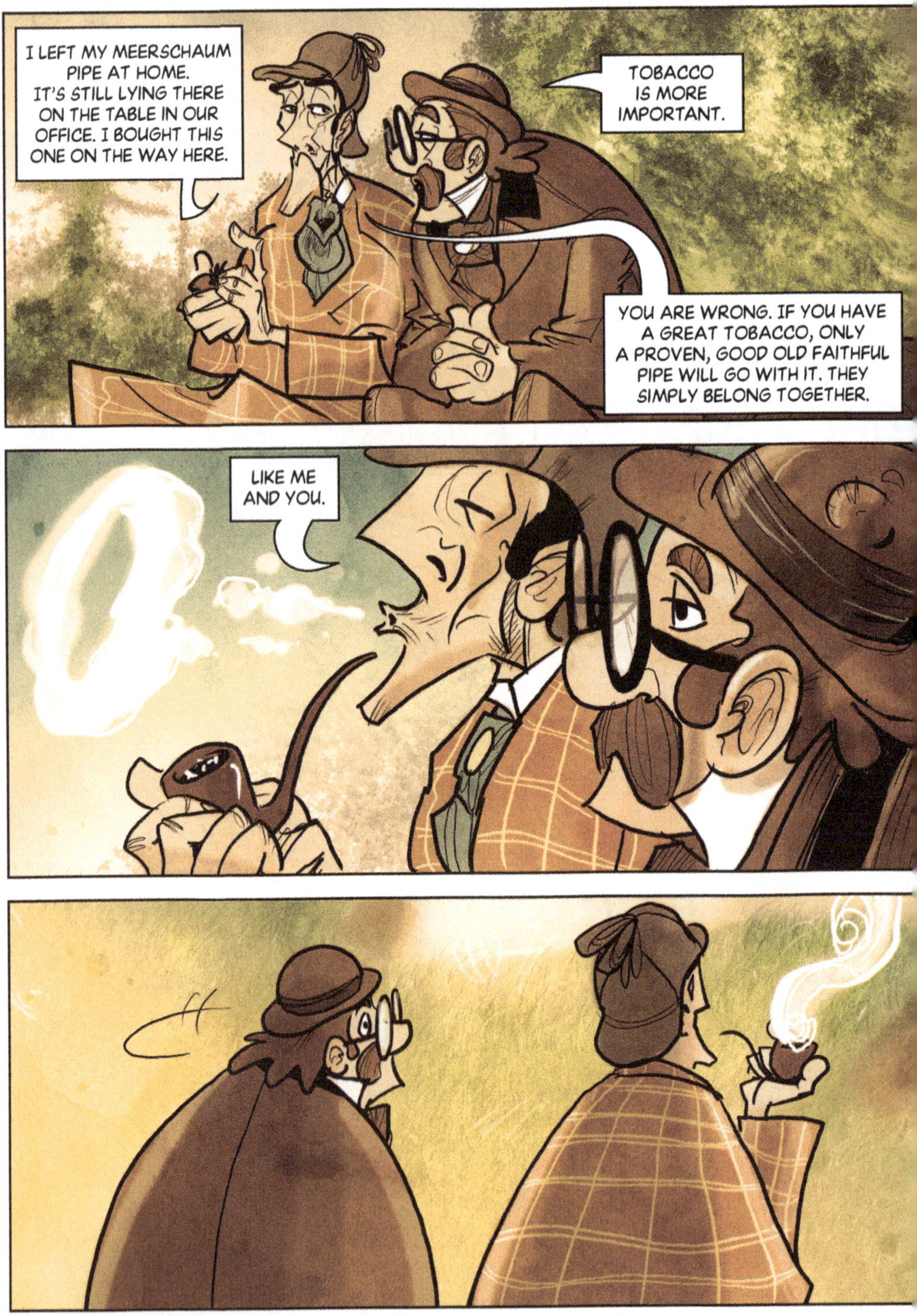
I LEFT MY MEERSCHAUM PIPE AT HOME. IT'S STILL LYING THERE ON THE TABLE IN OUR OFFICE. I BOUGHT THIS ONE ON THE WAY HERE.
TOBACCO IS MORE IMPORTANT.
YOU ARE WRONG. IF YOU HAVE A GREAT TOBACCO, ONLY A PROVEN, GOOD OLD FAITHFUL PIPE WILL GO WITH IT. THEY SIMPLY BELONG TOGETHER.
LIKE ME AND YOU.

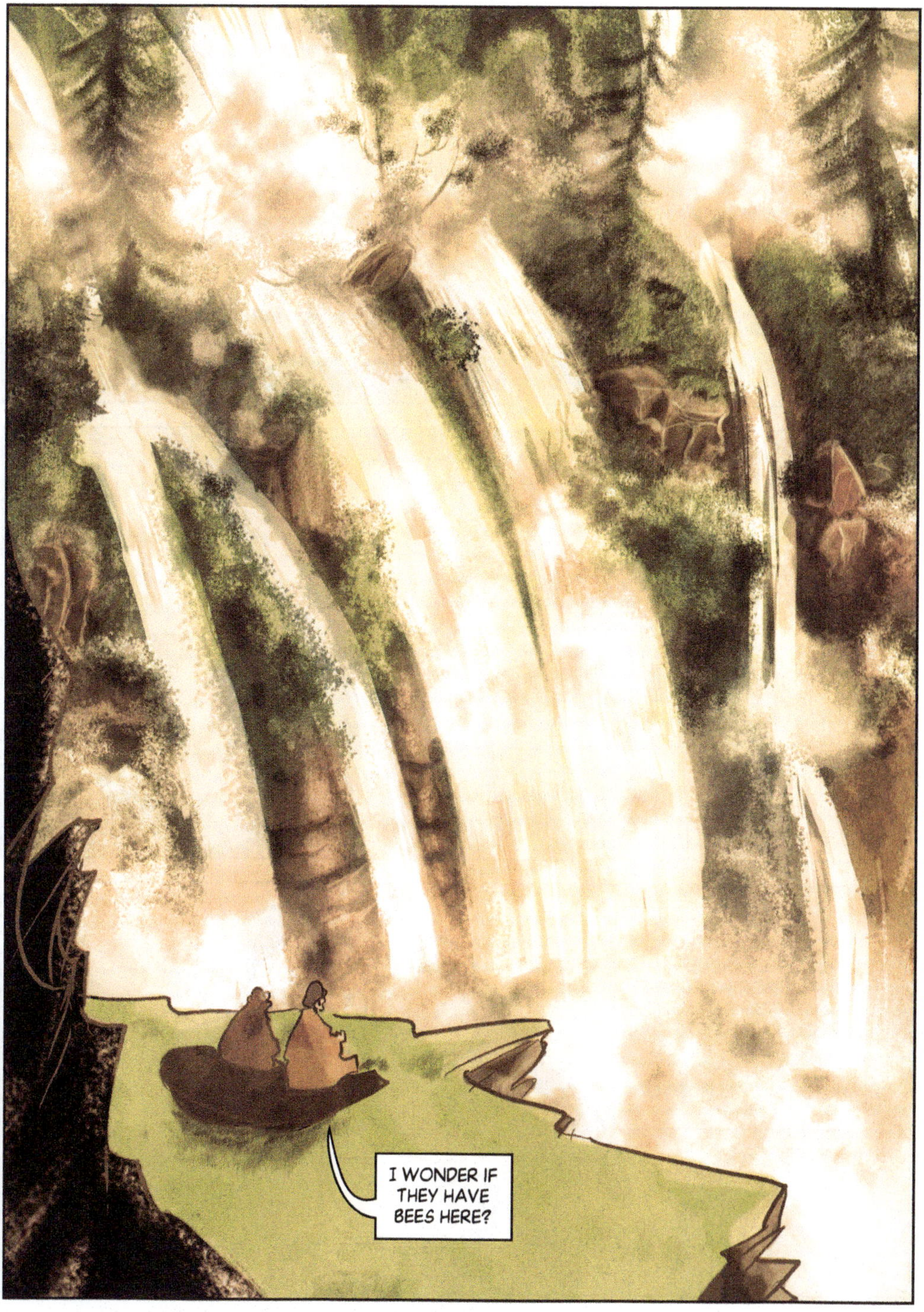
I WONDER IF THEY HAVE BEES HERE?

DR WATSON! DR WATSON!

WHAT'S GOING ON?

IN THE HOTEL... PHEW...

AN ELDERLY ENGLISH LADY ARRIVED WHEN SUDDENLY SHE BEGAN TO HAEMORRHAGE! SHE INSISTED ON AN ENGLISH DOCTOR! THE DIRECTOR SENT ME TO GET YOU. PLEASE HURRY UP. HOPEFULLY IT'S NOT TOO LATE!

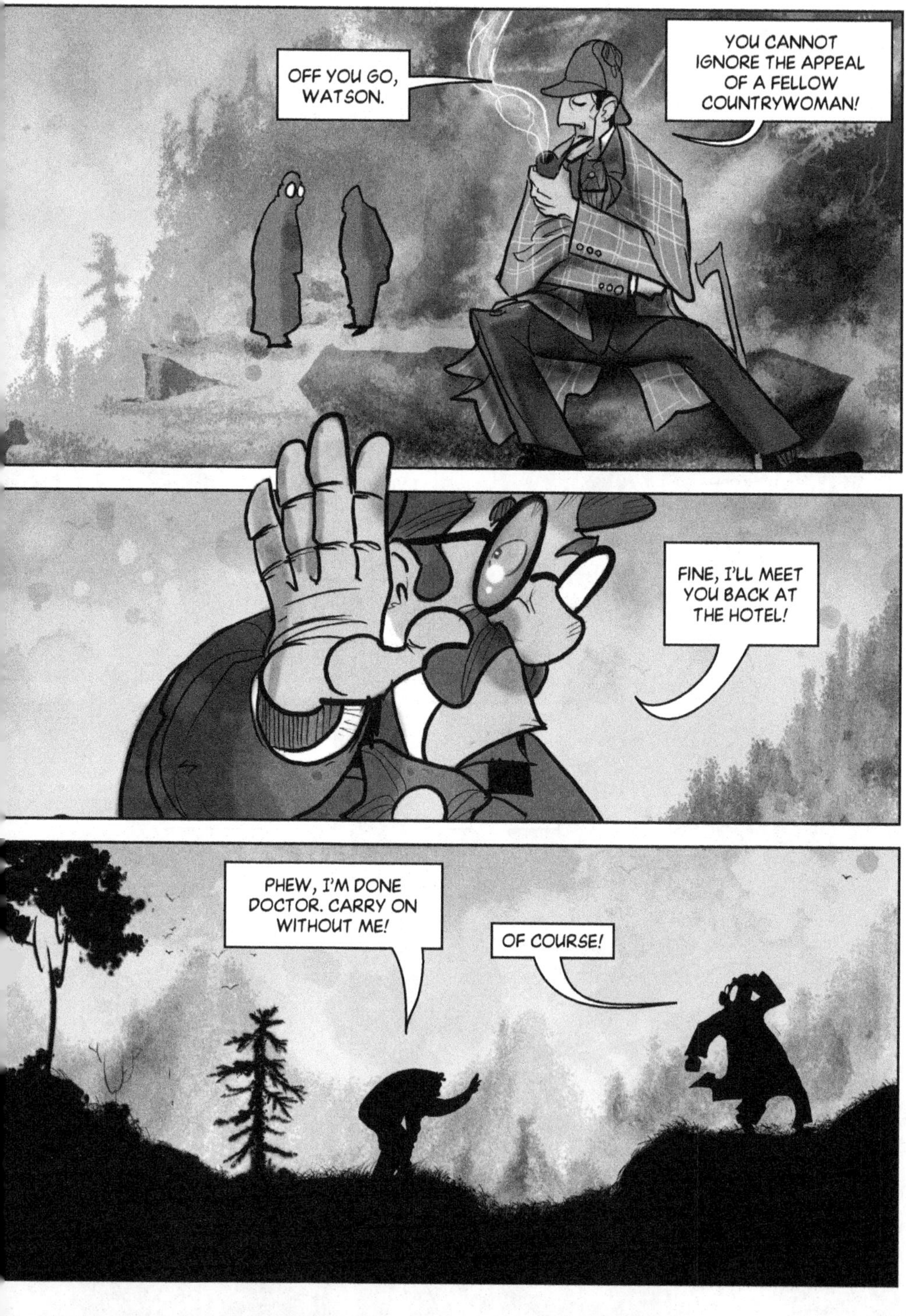
OFF YOU GO, WATSON.
YOU CANNOT IGNORE THE APPEAL OF A FELLOW COUNTRYWOMAN!
FINE, I'LL MEET YOU BACK AT THE HOTEL!
PHEW, I'M DONE DOCTOR. CARRY ON WITHOUT ME!
OF COURSE!

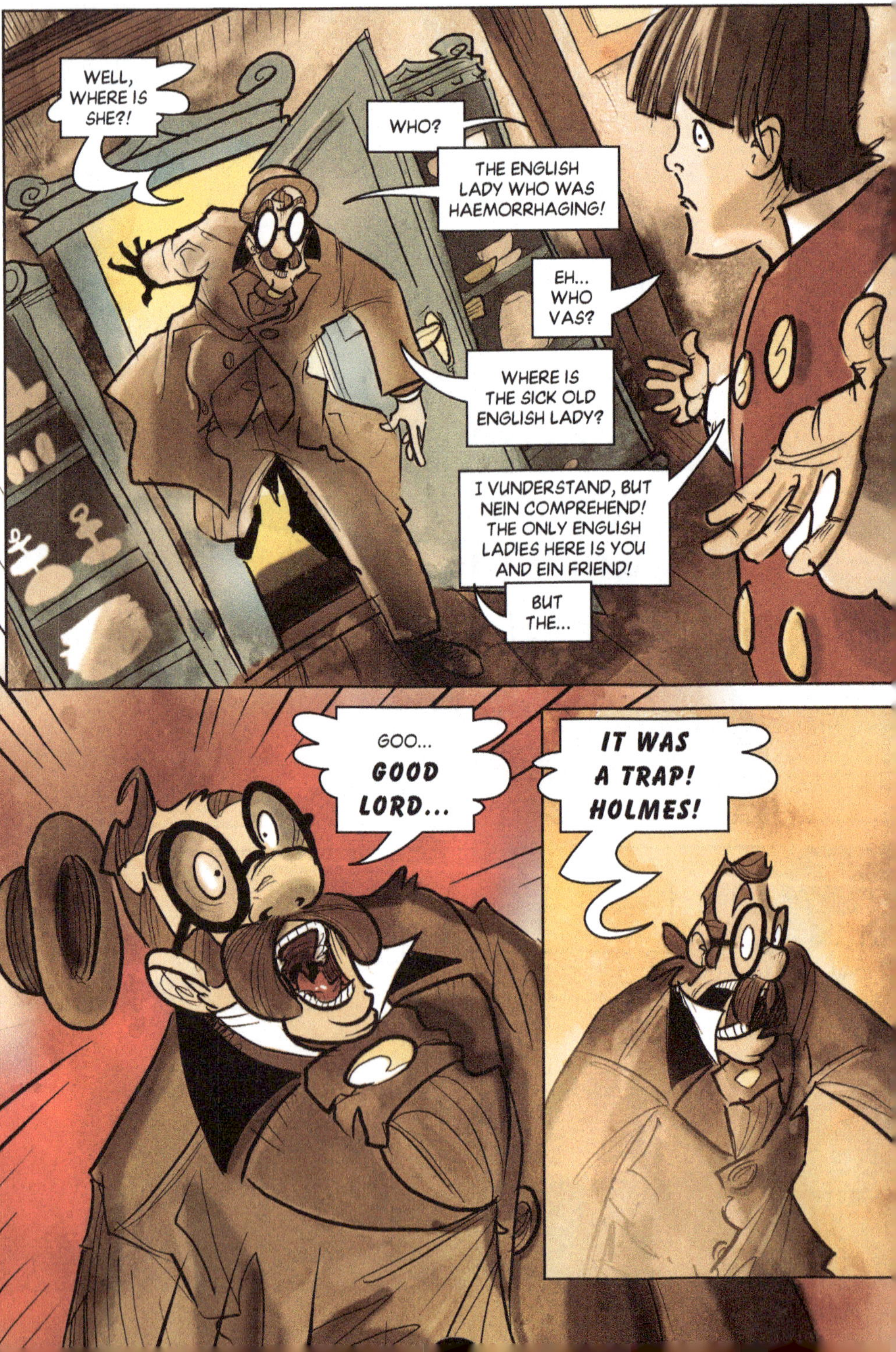
WELL, WHERE IS SHE?!
WHO?
THE ENGLISH LADY WHO WAS HAEMORRHAGING!
EH... WHO VAS?
WHERE IS THE SICK OLD ENGLISH LADY?
I VUNDERSTAND, BUT NEIN COMPREHEND! THE ONLY ENGLISH LADIES HERE IS YOU AND EIN FRIEND!
BUT THE...
GOO... GOOD LORD...
IT WAS A TRAP! HOLMES!

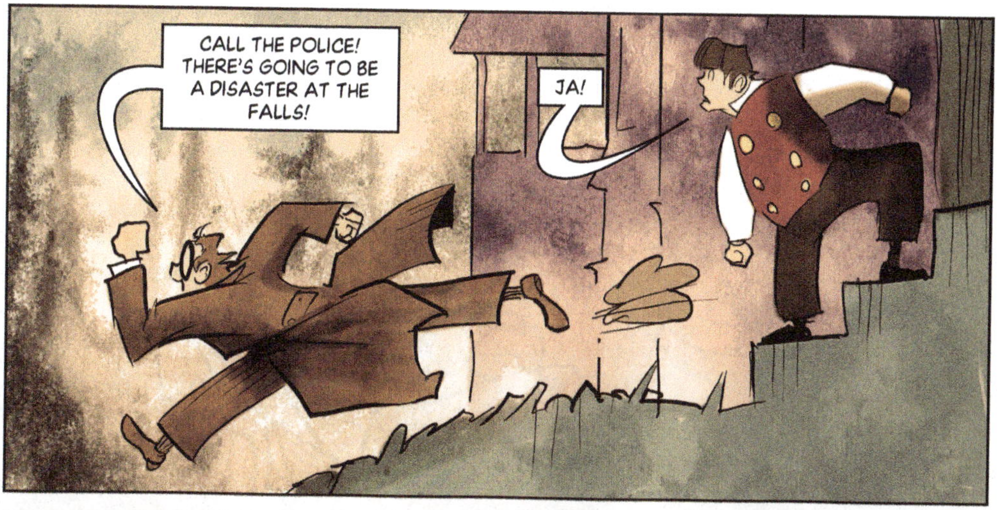
CALL THE POLICE! THERE'S GOING TO BE A DISASTER AT THE FALLS!
JA!

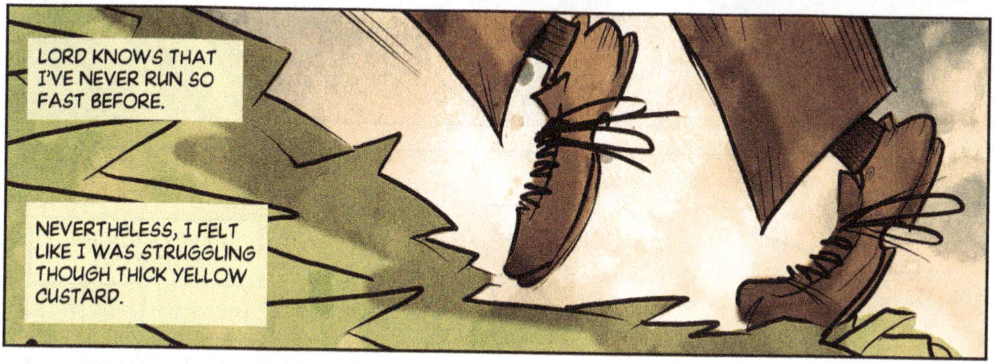
LORD KNOWS THAT I'VE NEVER RUN SO FAST BEFORE.
NEVERTHELESS, I FELT LIKE I WAS STRUGGLING THOUGH THICK YELLOW CUSTARD.

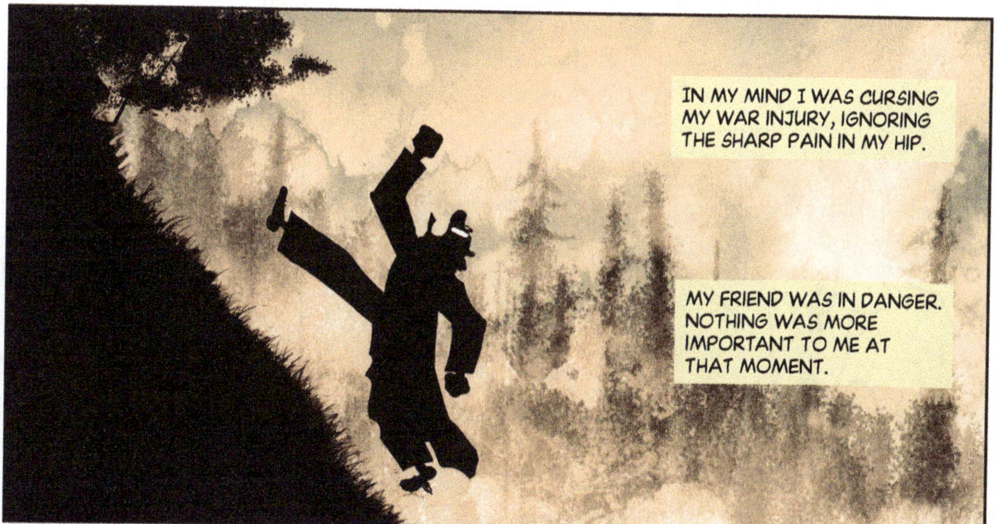
IN MY MIND I WAS CURSING MY WAR INJURY, IGNORING THE SHARP PAIN IN MY HIP.
MY FRIEND WAS IN DANGER. NOTHING WAS MORE IMPORTANT TO ME AT THAT MOMENT.

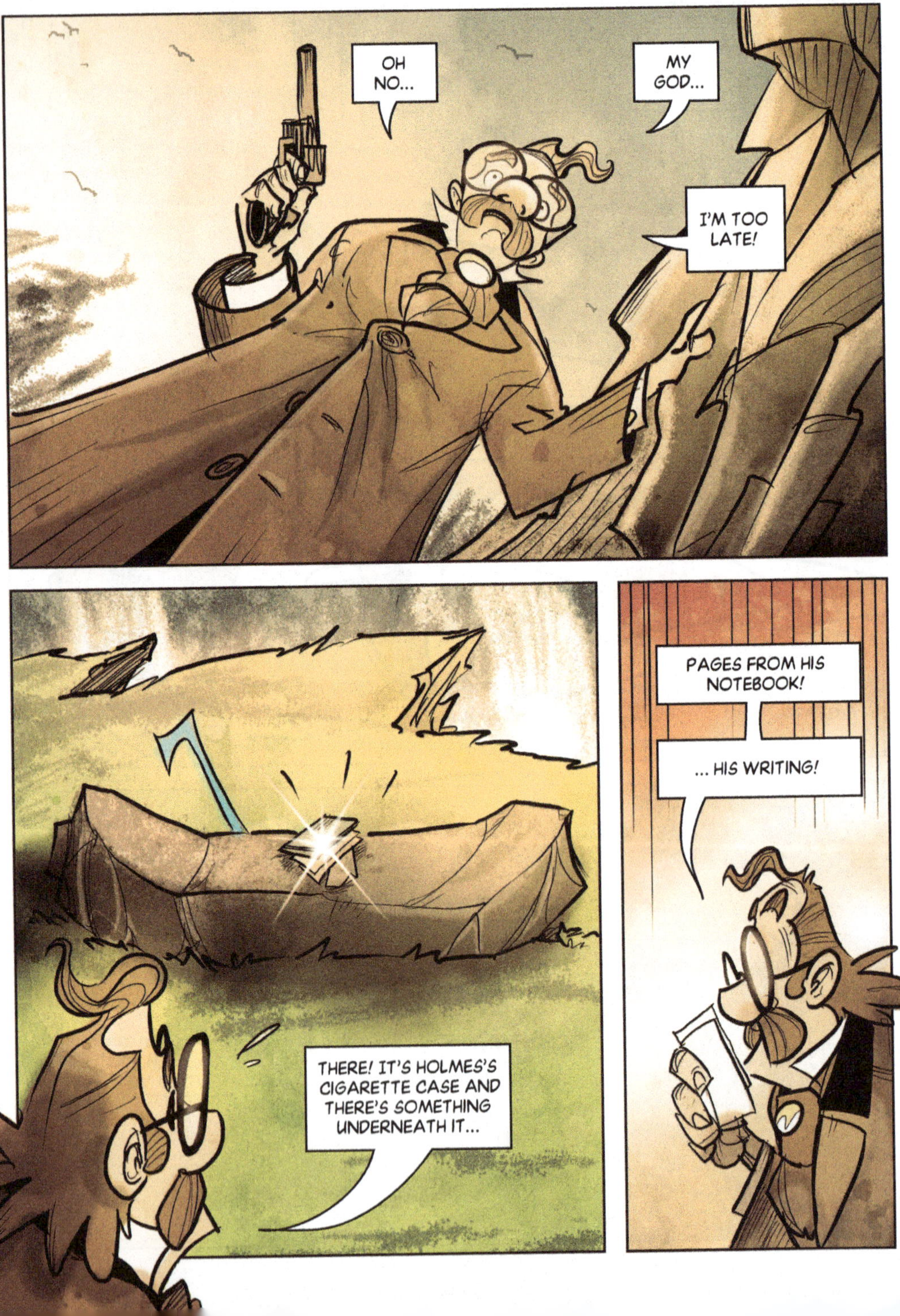
OH NO...
MY GOD...
I'M TOO LATE!
THERE! IT'S HOLMES'S CIGARETTE CASE AND THERE'S SOMETHING UNDERNEATH IT...
PAGES FROM HIS NOTEBOOK!
... HIS WRITING!

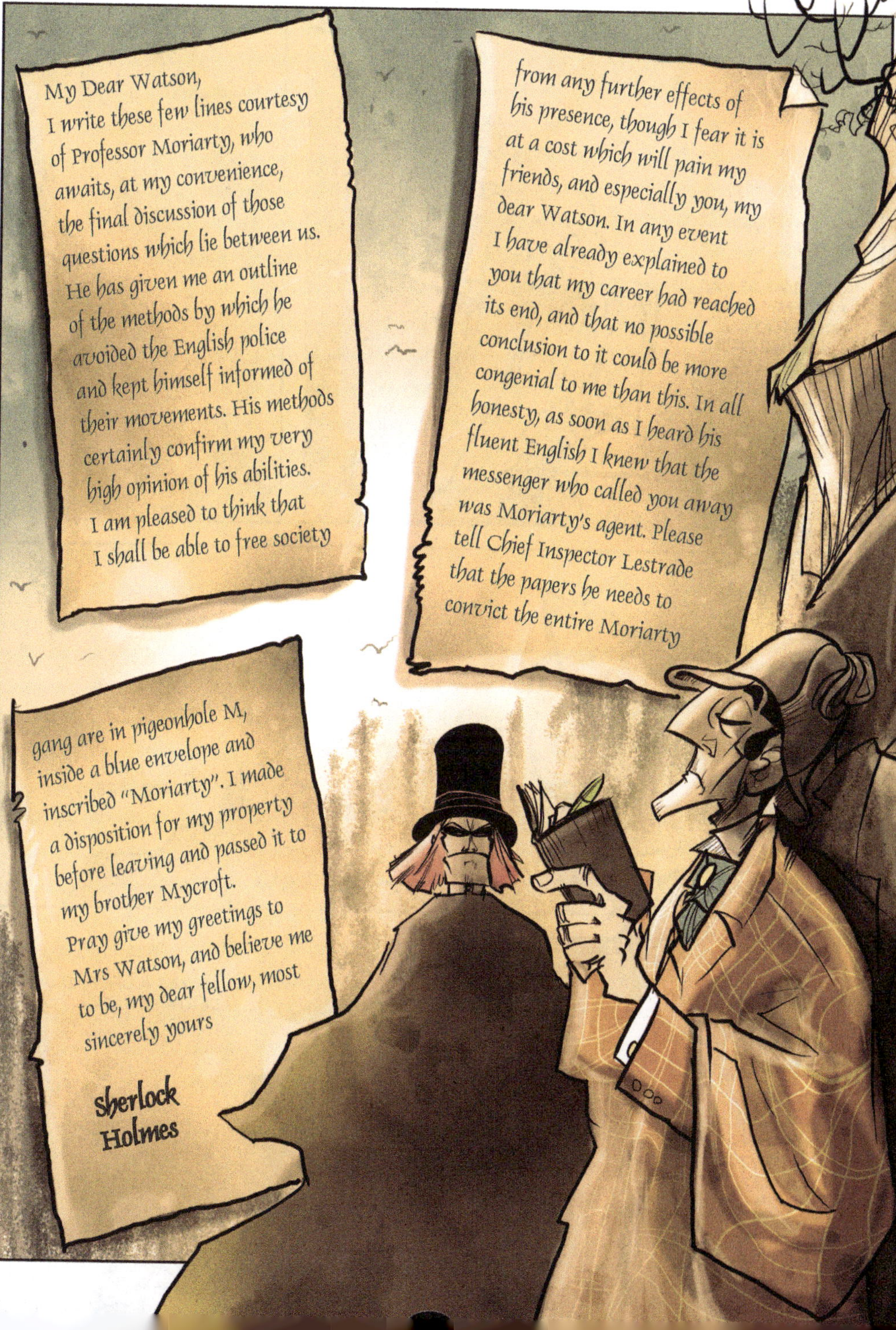
My Dear Watson,
I write these few lines courtesy of Professor Moriarty, who awaits, at my convenience, the final discussion of those questions which lie between us. He has given me an outline of the methods by which he avoided the English police and kept himself informed of their movements. His methods certainly confirm my very high opinion of his abilities. I am pleased to think that I shall be able to free society
from any further effects of his presence, though I fear it is at a cost which will pain my friends, and especially you, my dear Watson. In any event I have already explained to you that my career had reached its end, and that no possible conclusion to it could be more congenial to me than this. In all honesty, as soon as I heard his fluent English I knew that the messenger who called you away was Moriarty's agent. Please tell Chief Inspector Lestrade that the papers he needs to convict the entire Moriarty
gang are in pigeonhole M, inside a blue envelope and inscribed "Moriarty". I made a disposition for my property before leaving and passed it to my brother Mycroft.
Pray give my greetings to Mrs Watson, and believe me to be, my dear fellow, most sincerely yours
Sherlock Holmes

BY FOLLOWING THE TRACKS I WAS EASILY ABLE TO GUESS WHAT HAD HAPPENED. THE PROFESSIONAL EXPERTISE OF THE LOCAL POLICE LATER CONFIRMED MY FINDINGS.

HOLMES FOLLOWED MORIARTY ONTO A NARROW ROCKY LEDGE. THE FOOTPRINTS LED AWAY FROM ME. THEY DIDN'T RETURN.

A FIGHT HAD TAKEN PLACE HERE.

BLOOD.

IT WAS A LIFE AND DEATH SITUATION.

AND THEY FELL OVER THE EDGE HERE.

HOLMES WAS RIGHT. IT COULD NOT REALLY HAVE ANY OTHER POSSIBLE CONCLUSION.
HE KNEW IT AND LESTRADE KNEW IT TOO. ONLY I DIDN'T WANT TO SEE IT.

THERE, IN THE CAULDRON OF SWIRLING WATER, LIES THE BODY OF THE MOST DANGEROUS CRIMINAL...

... AND THE FOREMOST CHAMPION OF LAW AND ORDER OF A GENERATION.

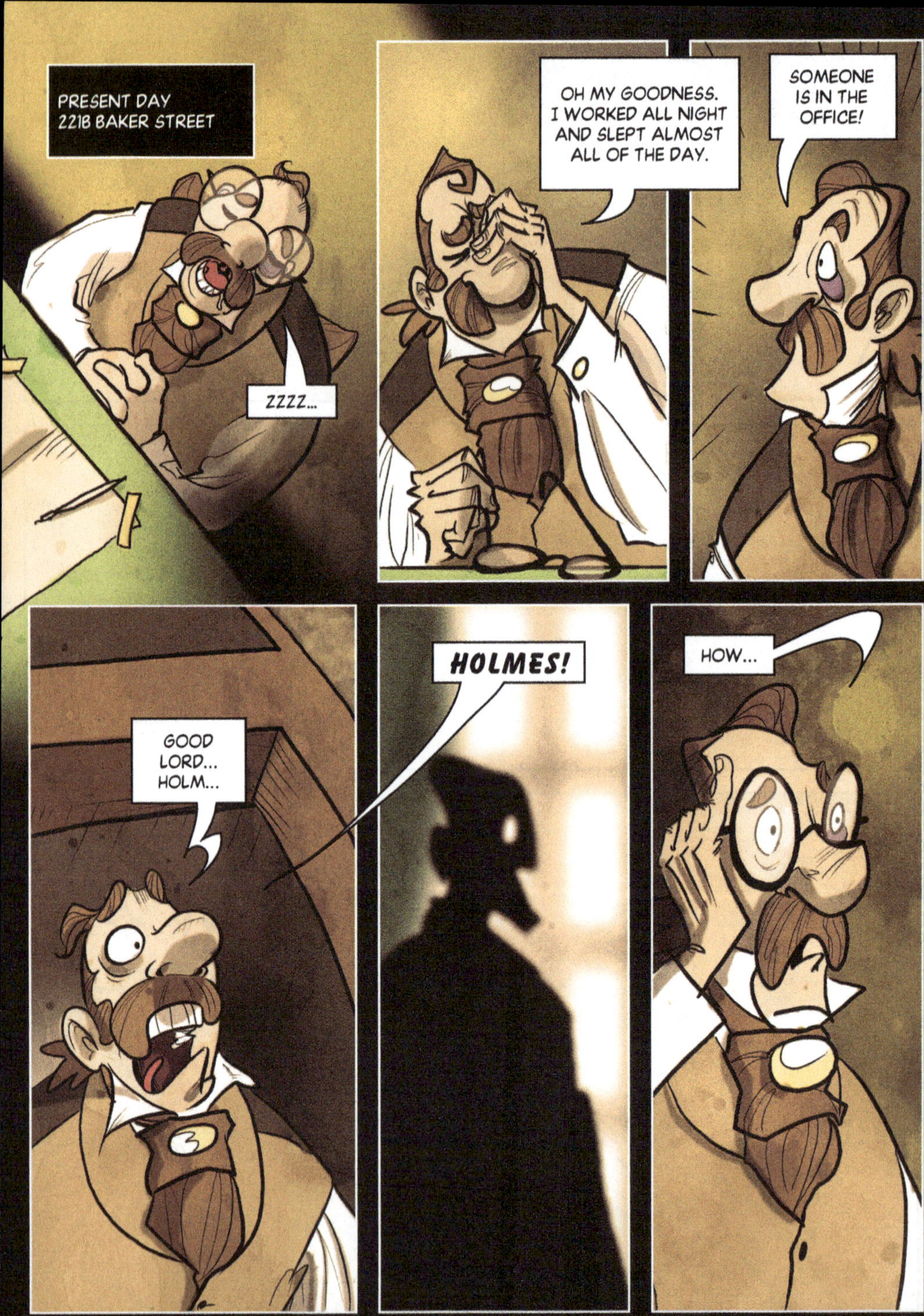
PRESENT DAY
221B BAKER STREET
ZZZZ...
OH MY GOODNESS. I WORKED ALL NIGHT AND SLEPT ALMOST ALL OF THE DAY.
SOMEONE IS IN THE OFFICE!
GOOD LORD... HOLM...
HOLMES!
HOW...

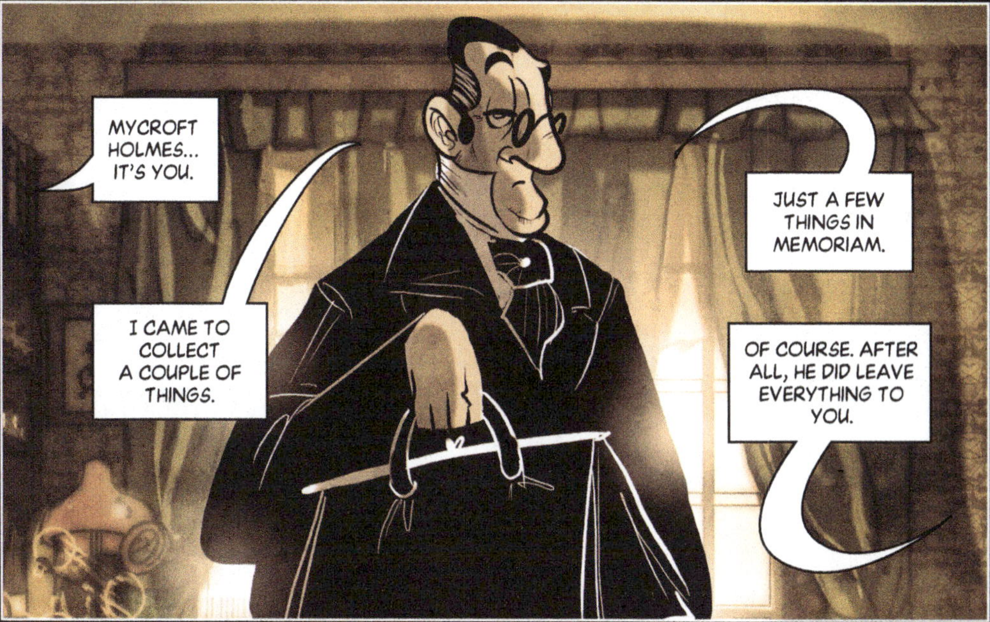
MYCROFT HOLMES... IT'S YOU.
I CAME TO COLLECT A COUPLE OF THINGS.
JUST A FEW THINGS IN MEMORIAM.
OF COURSE. AFTER ALL, HE DID LEAVE EVERYTHING TO YOU.

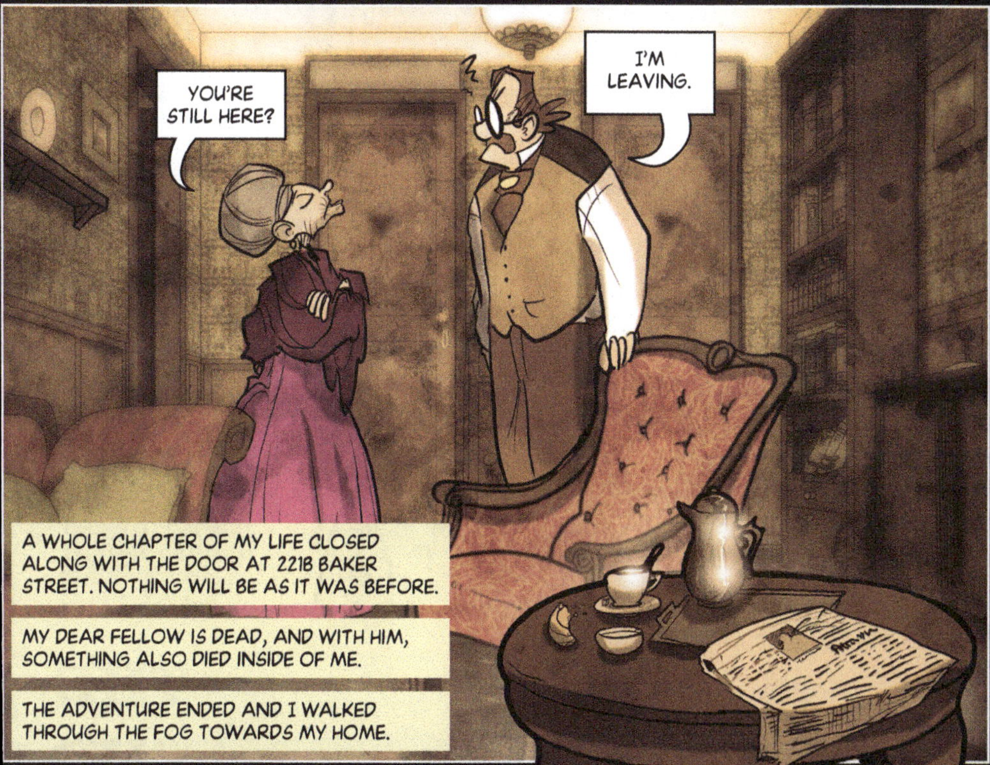
YOU'RE STILL HERE?
I'M LEAVING.
A WHOLE CHAPTER OF MY LIFE CLOSED ALONG WITH THE DOOR AT 221B BAKER STREET. NOTHING WILL BE AS IT WAS BEFORE.
MY DEAR FELLOW IS DEAD, AND WITH HIM, SOMETHING ALSO DIED INSIDE OF ME.
THE ADVENTURE ENDED AND I WALKED THROUGH THE FOG TOWARDS MY HOME.

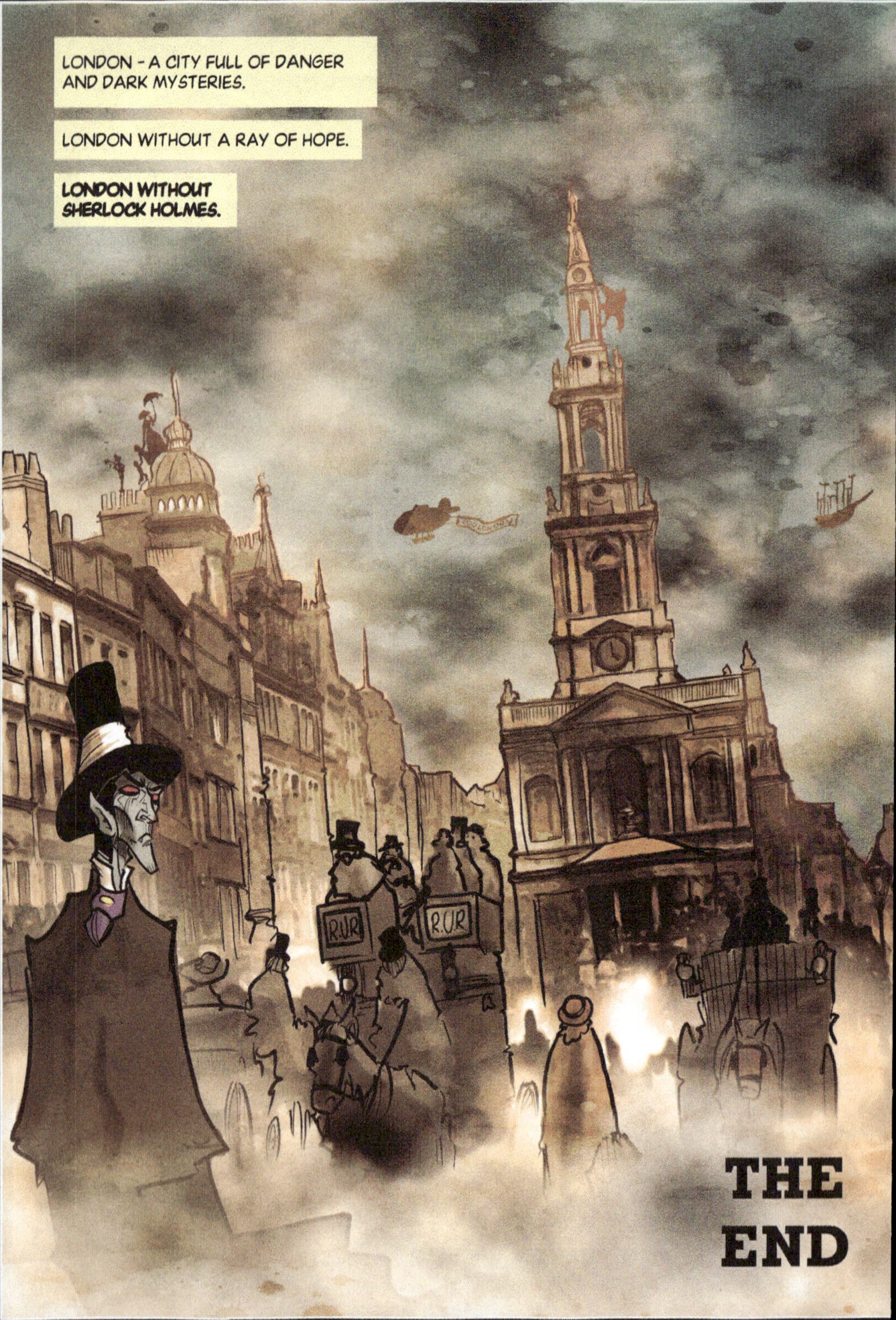
LONDON - A CITY FULL OF DANGER AND DARK MYSTERIES.
LONDON WITHOUT A RAY OF HOPE.
LONDON WITHOUT SHERLOCK HOLMES.
R.U.R
R.U.R
THE END

WHOSE WAS IT?

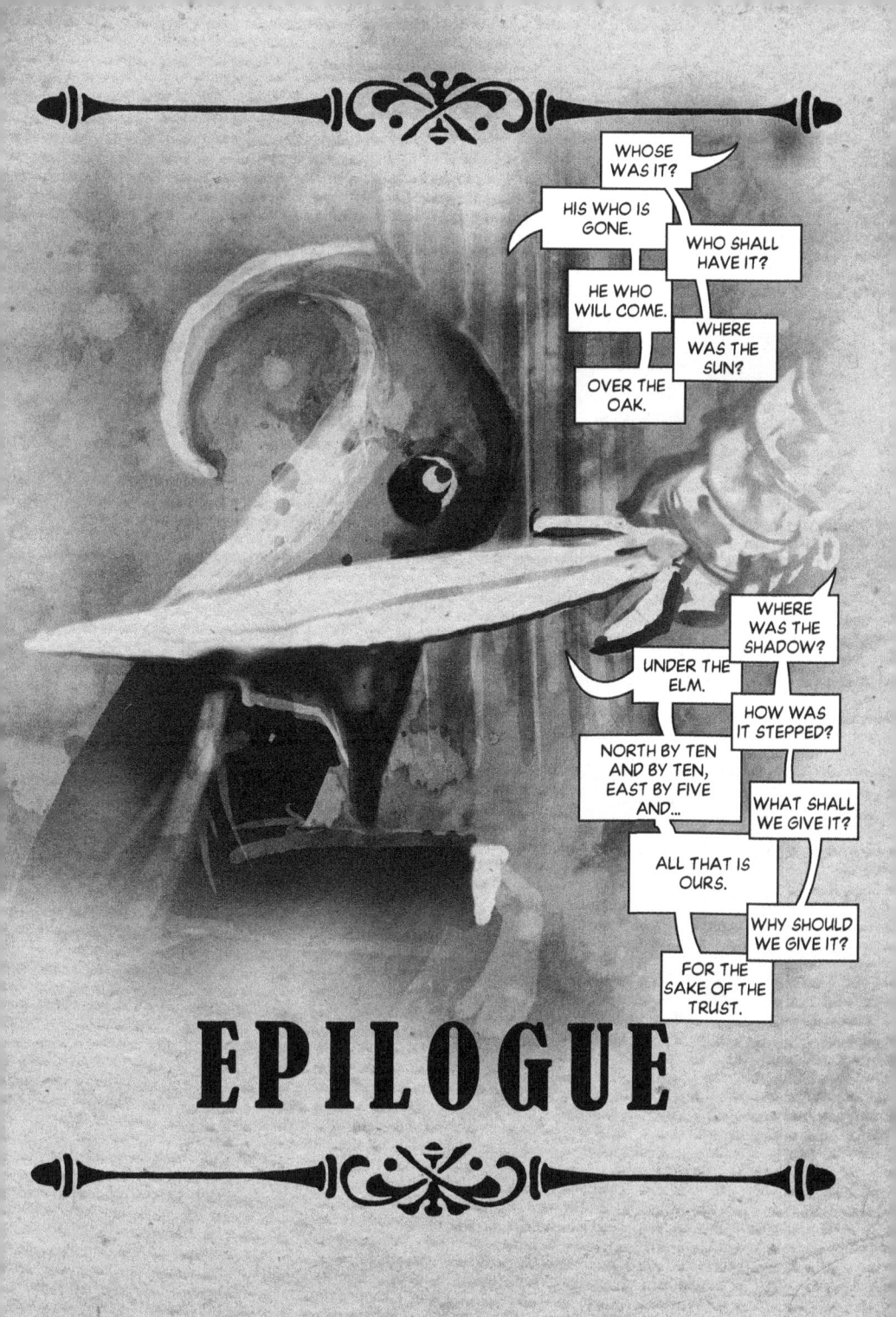

HIS WHO IS GONE.

WHO SHALL HAVE IT?

HE WHO WILL COME.

WHERE WAS THE SUN?

OVER THE OAK.

WHERE WAS THE SHADOW?

UNDER THE ELM.

HOW WAS IT STEPPED?

NORTH BY TEN AND BY TEN, EAST BY FIVE AND...

WHAT SHALL WE GIVE IT?

ALL THAT IS OURS.

WHY SHOULD WE GIVE IT?

FOR THE SAKE OF THE TRUST.

EPILOGUE

Comic page transcription

Panel 1:

"WITH THIS RITUAL, YOU ARE NOW THE NEW GRAND MASTER OF THE LONDON BRANCH OF THE SOCIETY OF THE NAMELESS."

"ALLOW ME TO BE THE FIRST TO CONGRATULATE YOU. PROFESSOR MORIARTY WAS A TRUE GREAT, BUT I BELIEVE THAT YOU, DESPITE NOT BEING AN ENGLISHMAN, WILL PUT OUR SOCIETY BACK ON ITS FEET."

"THE KING IS DEAD, LONG LIVE THE KING. THAT'S RIGHT, ISN'T IT?"

"ALTHOUGH..."

Panel 2:

"AS MORIARTY PREFERRED TO BE CALLED THE NAPOLEON OF CRIME, IT MAY BE MORE APPROPRIATE TO PROCLAIM: **THE EMPEROR IS DEAD...**"

Panel 3:

"...LONG LIVE THE COUNT!*"

HA HA

Panel 4:

HA HA HA HA HA HA HA HA

* Who is this new villain? You can find out in The Mysterious Castle in the Carpathians!

1/8/1884

Daily Gazette

THE DETECTIVE IS DEAD

We sincerely regret to inform the citizens of London that the unfortunate demise of the greatest detective of all time has now been confirmed. There is no other event (except perhaps the mystery of the Demeter shipwreck and the publication of the ship's logbook), that would more agitate the residents of our royal city.

We have only a few snippets of information available to us at this time. What is certain is that Sherlock Holmes died a violent death in the Swiss Reichenbach, where he was holidaying with his inseparable companion, Dr Watson.

The police report clearly implies that Sherlock Holmes was the victim of revenge by Professor Moriarty, the leader of the gang that London Scotland Yard successfully raided, which we informed our readers of yesterday. However, while the new Chief Inspector Lestrade, caught the body of the beast by its neck, the head was one step ahead and launched a terrible counterattack on the very person we should be grateful to for the incredibly complex raid.

Chief Inspector Lestrade told us after the event: "London is

Continues on page 2

Daily Gazette

DEMISE OF SHERLOCK HOLMES

Continued from page 1

now a safer place.

While I'm in charge of the famous Scotland Yard, I will not cease my efforts to make the citizens of London feel safe in their own city."

Chief Inspector Lestrade is famed for his Bulldog-like temperament. Let's hope that the swoop on Moriarty's gang is the first sign that Scotland Yard will be back on its feet soon, after former Chief Inspector Fix brought it to the lamentable state it is in today.

However, the long arm of the law failed to stretch to the Reichenbach falls, on whose riverbed now rests the body of the famous detective. Although the hero criminal investigator assisted justice on countless occasions, even she failed to help him when it really mattered.

A memorial service for, and we are not afraid to say this, our national hero will be held this Saturday at two o'clock at the London cemetery. Many prominent names have vowed to attend the memorial service. Although Her Majesty the Queen has already expressed deep sympathy and grief over the loss of such an outstanding man, she will not attend the memorial service.

Finally, we should add that our editorial staff decided to organize a benefit concert on behalf of Sherlock Holmes. The cast is still to be confirmed but once in place, we will immediately inform our readers. Meanwhile, you can pick up a free black ribbon as a sign of mourning in our newsroom or from our newspaper vendors.

Reichenbach falls – the final resting place of Sherlock Holmes. Source: Archive

P. K.

1/8/1884

THE CONSECRATION OF THE CHURCH OF THE HOLY MOTHER OF GOD IN VERST

We recently informed you of the collapse of the castle near Carpathian Verst. We still have no new information and the analysis of strange artefacts found by our reporter on the site has not yielded any answers so far. It is surprising how sluggishly the government there has handled the matter so far—not to mention the town hall members in Verst. Although Mayor Kolc refused to comment on the collapse of the fortress, the local Catholic priest was in a much more communicative mood.

"You see," said Father Jerome Kopls after a few shots of good whiskey, donated by our thoughtful reporter, "the local region is most strange and mysterious. You must not be surprised that the locals do not want to have anything to do with the townsfolk and refuse to be closer. I can reassure you however, that these people are inherently good and pious. Almost all the inhabitants of Verst contributed towards the repair and consecration of our church, if not with money then work."

At that moment, the priest paused and put his hand to his mouth, as if he had said something he shouldn't have. When questioned on why the church needed repairs and to be newly consecrated, the priest fell silent and took to his heels with a whisky in his hand, under the pretext of administering the last rites. Our reporter, the brave E. Malone, was made to feel unwelcome that day so not knowing what to do left Verst and headed towards Budapest.

Therefore, if we want to learn anything new about Devils Castle, we will have to rely on the artefacts that were found at the foot of the collapsed mountain. Hopefully, the answers will soon arrive.

F. K.

Sketch of the interior of the Church of the Holy Mother of God in Carpathian Verst.

THE BARKS OF MUCKY PUP

Panel 1: WHEN TWO DOGS MEET UP, THEY SNIFF EACH OTHER NOSES AND THEN THEIR BACKSIDES. / I WONDER WHAT THAT MEANS IN DOG LANGUAGE.

Panel 2: I THINK IT MUST BE SOMETHING ROMANTIC. / SOMETHING LIKE I SEE YOU OR SENSE YOUR PERSONALITY.

Panel 3: WHAT WAS YOUR LAST MEAL?

Panel 4: ARE YOU HIDING SOMETHING FROM ME?

Daily Gazette

Advertisements

KOPL'S FAT PILLS

BEFORE   **AFTER**

Are you tired of being ridiculed by your friends? Are you unhappy with your skinny and bony body? Is your weight the same, despite trying out countless recipes to gain more weight? In that case, we have just the solution for you! We don't promise miracles, but a scientifically proven method of gaining weight. Take

KOPL'S FAT PILLS

and we can guarantee that providing you keep to the prescribed diet, you will gain your dream curves, as desired by every modern woman. The best medical brains, such as Dr Moreau and many more of his calibre have developed this revolutionary food supplement. Kopl's fat pills can be purchased from every good chemist. Before taking the pills, consult your doctor regarding dosage and any potential side effects.

TESTED ON SALAMANDERS

- People with the name of Garrideb wanted. If you know of anyone of that name, or you yourself bear the said name, please leave a message in the newspaper's editorial room. Ref. Large reward guaranteed
- Selling a preserved Mummy's hand. Guaranteed authenticity, protected in a case with a glass lid. Ref. Urgent
- M., it's over! No more waiting for clarification, a successor must be elected. Do not try to find a way back. Ref. Unlisted
- Looking for a white bunny rabbit. Special features: Dressed in a clingy red outfit, nervously taps its paw and checks a gold pocket watch. Ref. He's a scatterbrain, don't hurt him please!
- We would like to announce that on 18.8.1884, the Auction Hall on Oxford Street will be auctioning the estate of the deceased Mr Milverton. This means that the pendants of Queen Anne, wife of the French King Louis XIII, will once again be back in circulation, as well as other highly valuable items from his collection. Due to a missing will and non-existent descendants, the proceeds from the auction will be forfeited to the English Crown. Ref. Quality service guaranteed.

Daily Gazette published by the Daily Gazette since 1805. Chief Editor T. M. Rockfort, editorial office: 108 Lisson Grove, London, advertising department: 5 Glentworth Street, London. Daily circulation of 800,000. Printshop: Kopls company, 84/225 Brok-Schmutzig Street, London.

KOPL

Petr Kopl presents
a comic book adaptation
of short stories by
Sir Arthur Conan Doyle

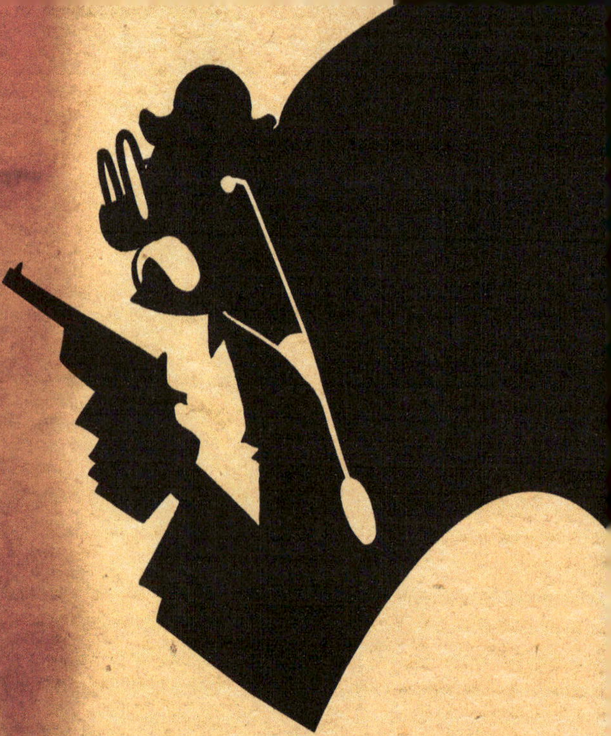

DR. WATSON

THE ADVENTURE OF

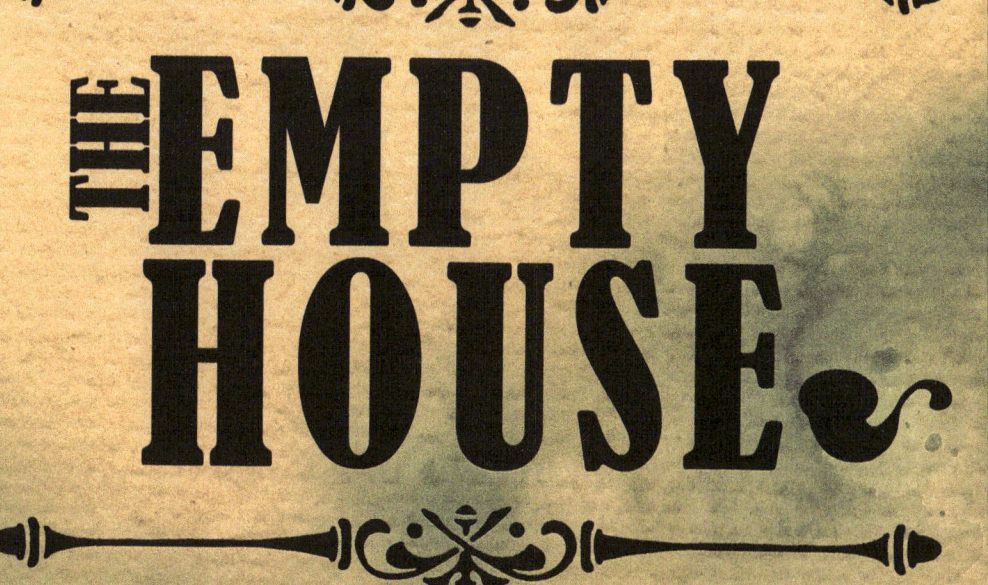

THE EMPTY HOUSE

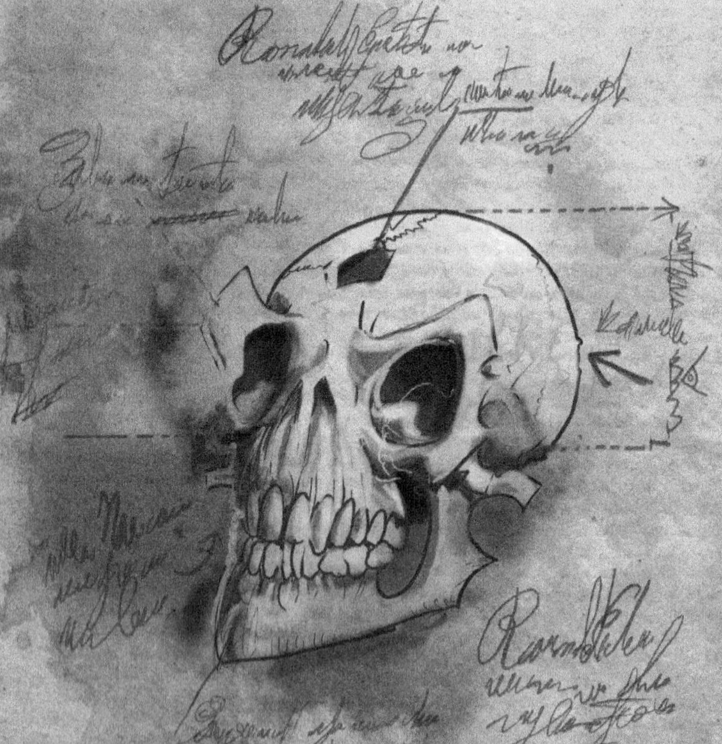

Preface

The fall of Sherlock Holmes meant a complete turnaround in my life. However, destiny had prepared an even a bigger shock for me than that at the Reichenbach falls. The adventure, which I am about to describe, happened two years ago, after the tragedy that saddened the whole of London, from the last messenger boy to the Queen.

I hope that my readers will forgive that I have kept the facts of the case secret up to now and publish them only in this year of 1892, when the dark clouds have hidden the whole world and heaven itself is in danger of collapse after HE lifted his ban on the third day of the previous month.

The two years since the involuntarily departure of my dear friend have not been easy. I openly admit that I failed myself. Depression and constant mood swings caused the departure of my wife and her decision to live in seclusion. It was at that point I should have got back on my feet. Instead I did the worst thing I could—drown my sorrows in alcohol.

I cannot say why I let it go so far, but I gradually lost nearly all of my already poor clientele, and was therefore shipwrecked alone in the field of medicine. I tried a few times, but with no great success, to apply the investigative methods of my dear friend in well-known cases. One such bright moment in those two years has been my adventure with Jonathan Harker, who asked me to help in the search for nightmares so horrific, that I will hardly ever be able to capture them on paper.* But I will have to. London was on the verge of total destruction and I was one of those to confront it. The world must know of it.

Holmes once compared the two of us to a pipe and tobacco. During such moments I was painfully reminded of how pertinent was this comparison. If in this case, Holmes is the tobacco, and with a bit of skill can get by without his pipe. However, the pipe, or shall we say in this case me, is both empty and useless when without tobacco.

"Beware the ides of March," Caesar was warned. And the middle of March 1886 was marked by major changes. Winter that year lasted an unusually long time. Some claimed that the meteor shower that struck Mars caused it, although I couldn't imagine that something like that could affect the weather in London. However, the flashes on the surface of the red planet, which were visible to the naked eye were a fact, just as was the two feet of snow in front of my surgery. Both can be easily ignored with a bottle of whisky.

Dr John H. Watson

*see Dracula - comic book adaptation by Petr Kopl

BANG!
BANG!
BANG!
MR ADAIR!
FOR THE LOVE OF GOD, MR ADAIR, OPEN THE DOOR!

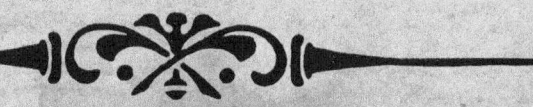

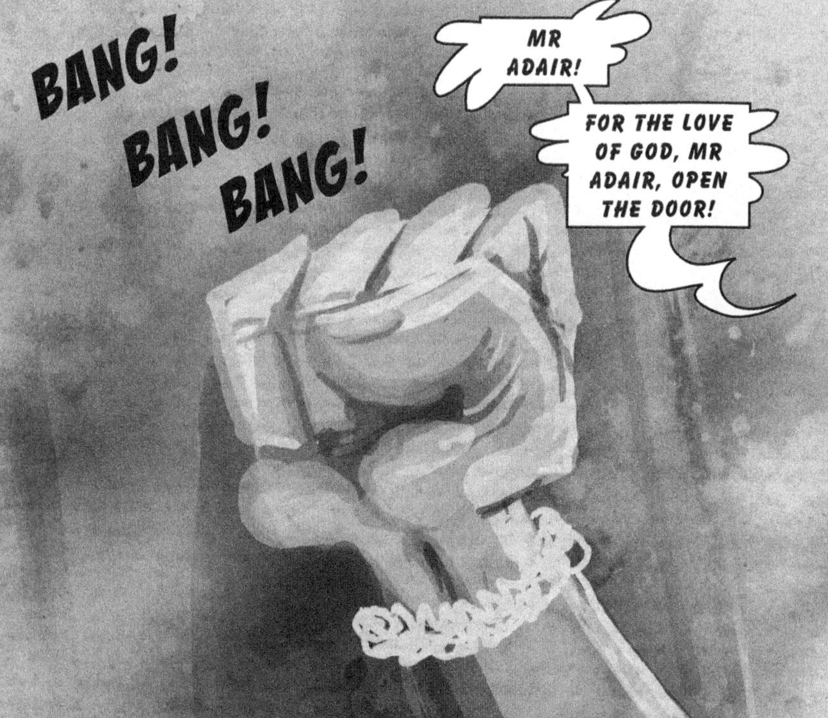

THE MYSTERY OF THE LOCKED ROOM

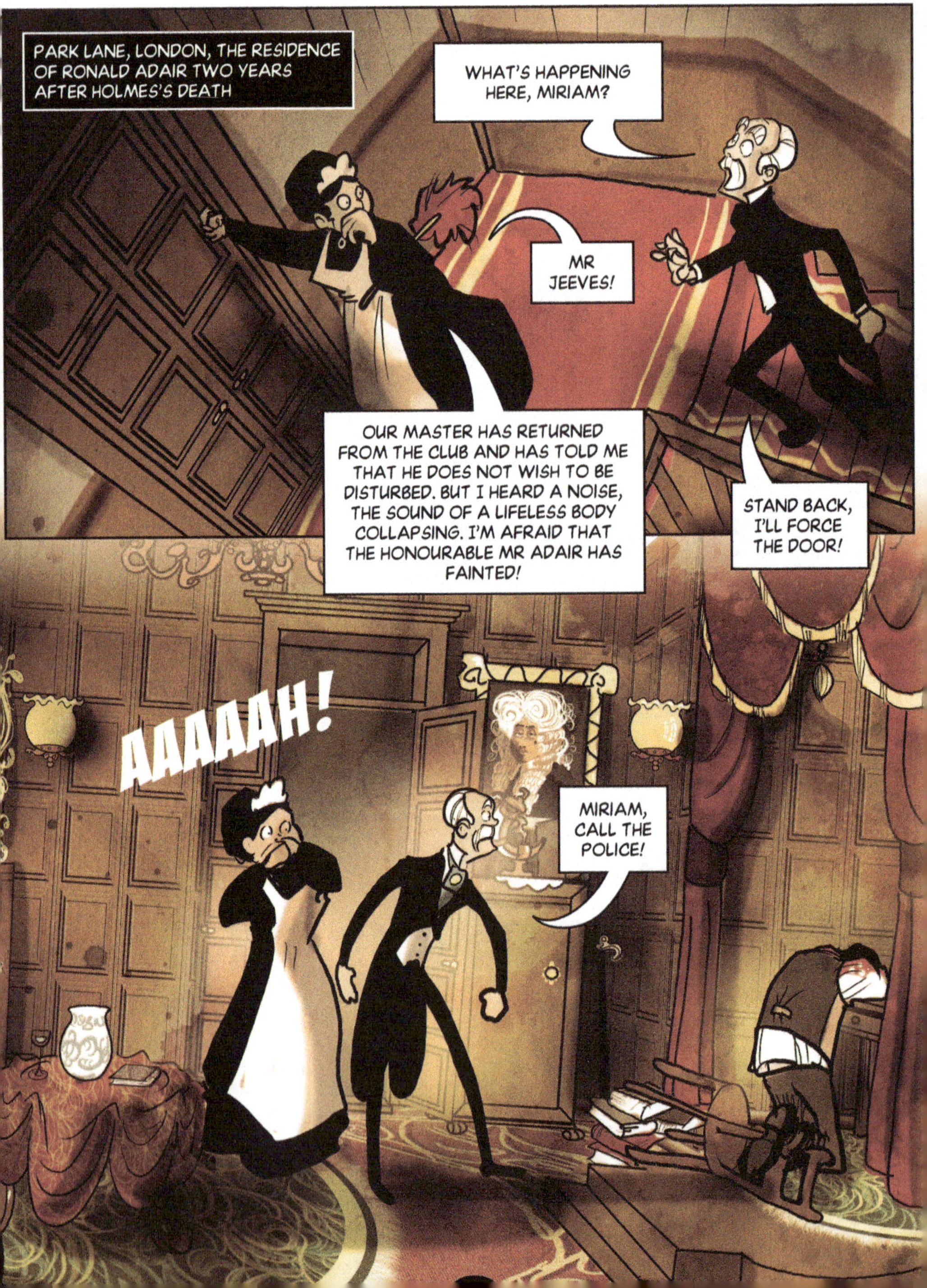
PARK LANE, LONDON, THE RESIDENCE OF RONALD ADAIR TWO YEARS AFTER HOLMES'S DEATH
WHAT'S HAPPENING HERE, MIRIAM?
MR JEEVES!
OUR MASTER HAS RETURNED FROM THE CLUB AND HAS TOLD ME THAT HE DOES NOT WISH TO BE DISTURBED. BUT I HEARD A NOISE, THE SOUND OF A LIFELESS BODY COLLAPSING. I'M AFRAID THAT THE HONOURABLE MR ADAIR HAS FAINTED!
STAND BACK, I'LL FORCE THE DOOR!
AAAAAH!
MIRIAM, CALL THE POLICE!

16/3/1886

Daily Gazette

THE HONOURABLE RONALD ADAIR MURDERED

"Miriam, call the police," shouted Jeeves, the brave butler to the deceased Ronald Adair.

Continued on page 2

Daily Gazette

THE MYSTERY OF THE LOCKED ROOM

Continued from page 1

Yesterday's murder of the Honourable Ronald Adair, committed under truly curious and mysterious circumstances, has shaken the aristocratic world and gripped the whole of London. The Honourable Ronald Adair was the second son of the Earl of Maynooth, now the governor of an Australian colony. The Honourable Ronald Adair moved in the best society and as far as we know, had no particular vices. Two years ago, he became engaged to Miss Edith Woodley of Carstairs, although this was quietly broken off after several months for reasons unknown. The youth's nature was unemotional and he moved in the narrow aristocratic circle of London. Therefore, the circumstances of his murder are highly surprising.

Ronald Adair was fond of playing cards and was a member of several card clubs. He was a cautious player and never lost any amounts that would significantly affect him, much less ruin him. On the night of March 30, 1884 he returned from one such party. He had played in the Bagatelle card club and those who played with him gave evidence that he left for home before 10 p.m. His fellow players – Mr Murray, Sir John Hardy, and Colonel Moran confirmed to us that he left with little money but in good spirits.

The maid testified that her master arrived home as usual and did not wish to be disturbed in the smoking room. Shortly afterwards the maid, Miriam

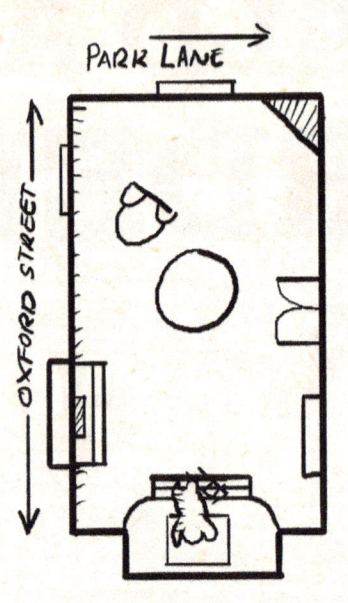

A rough sketch of Mr Adair's room

Erdber, heard a strange noise from the room and went to check that all was in order. The door was locked on the inside for reasons unknown, and there was no answer from Mr Adair. Therefore she and the butler Jeeves forced the door open.

They found a horrifying discovery inside the room. Mr Adair was found lying against the card table, his head horribly mutilated by an expanding bullet that had ripped through his skull.

The mystery lies in the fact that the weapon, which had caused the horrific wound, was not found and that all the windows and doors were locked on the inside. If a man had fired at Mr Adair through the window, he would indeed need to be a remarkable marksman to inflict such a deadly wound by using a revolver from across Park Lane. Nevertheless, this option is out of the question, because the window was intact and closed on the inside by a small handle.

There was a speculation that the killer climbed into the window and somehow closed it when escaping outside. However, this hypothesis is completely wrong, because it was snowing heavily the day before and the uninvited guest would have left some footprints.

So we are left with the true mystery of the locked room. We shall see how the renowned Scotland Yard will deal with this case. We will inform you once Chief Inspector Lestrade, who has an excellent track record so far, will give us his views.

P. K.

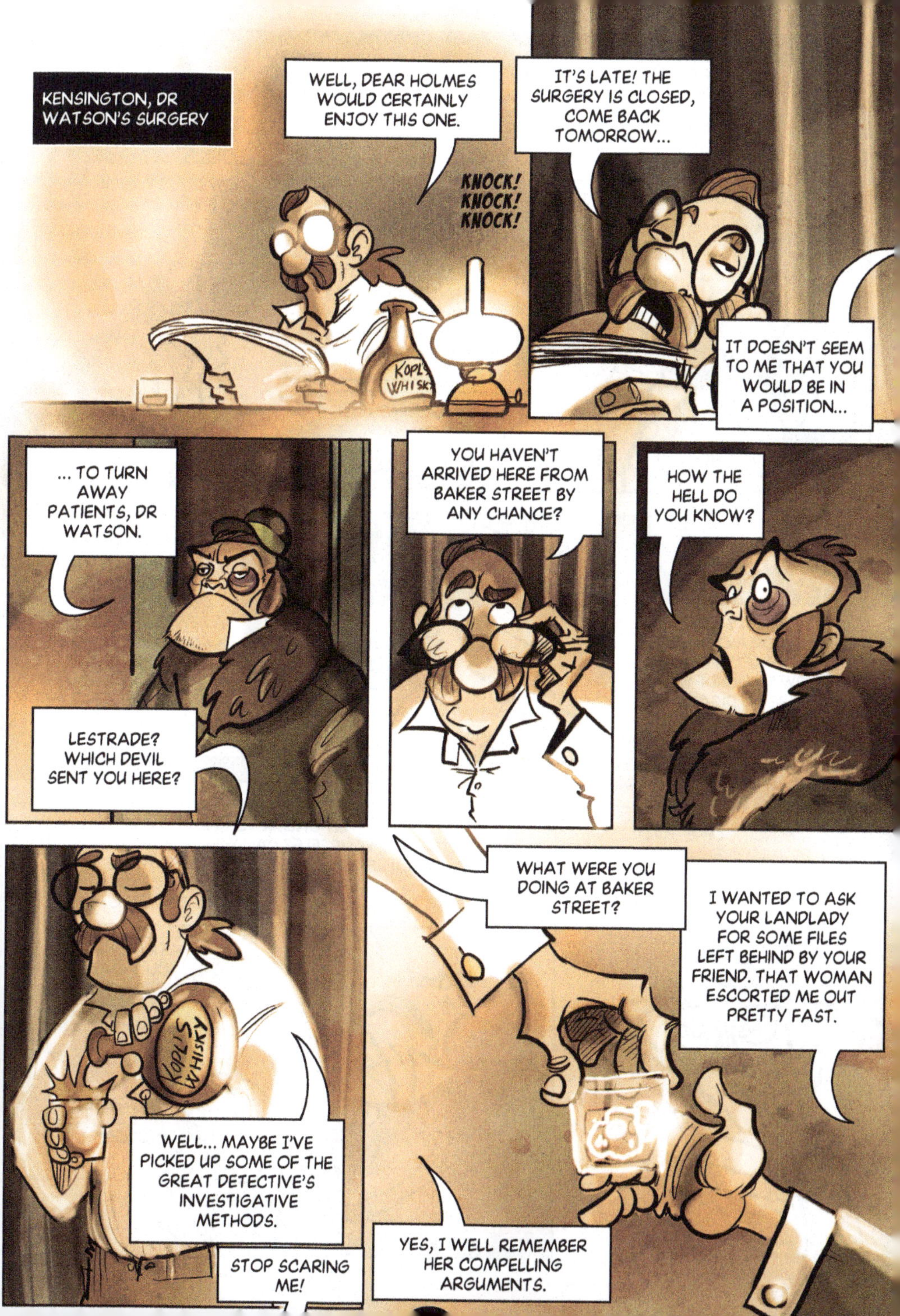
KENSINGTON, DR WATSON'S SURGERY
WELL, DEAR HOLMES WOULD CERTAINLY ENJOY THIS ONE.
KNOCK! KNOCK! KNOCK!
IT'S LATE! THE SURGERY IS CLOSED, COME BACK TOMORROW...
IT DOESN'T SEEM TO ME THAT YOU WOULD BE IN A POSITION...
... TO TURN AWAY PATIENTS, DR WATSON.
LESTRADE? WHICH DEVIL SENT YOU HERE?
YOU HAVEN'T ARRIVED HERE FROM BAKER STREET BY ANY CHANCE?
HOW THE HELL DO YOU KNOW?
WELL... MAYBE I'VE PICKED UP SOME OF THE GREAT DETECTIVE'S INVESTIGATIVE METHODS.
STOP SCARING ME!
WHAT WERE YOU DOING AT BAKER STREET?
I WANTED TO ASK YOUR LANDLADY FOR SOME FILES LEFT BEHIND BY YOUR FRIEND. THAT WOMAN ESCORTED ME OUT PRETTY FAST.
YES, I WELL REMEMBER HER COMPELLING ARGUMENTS.

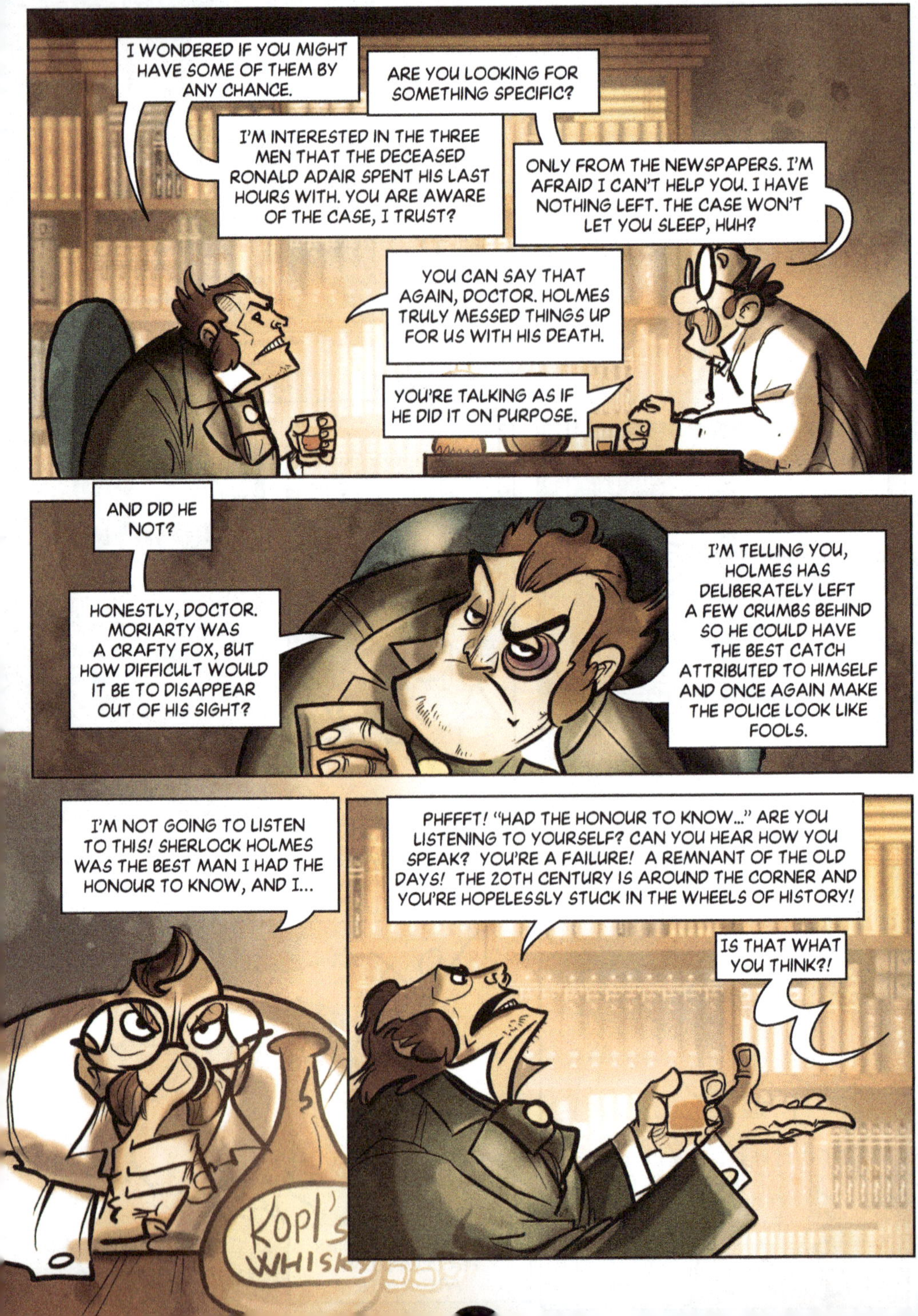
I WONDERED IF YOU MIGHT HAVE SOME OF THEM BY ANY CHANCE.
ARE YOU LOOKING FOR SOMETHING SPECIFIC?
I'M INTERESTED IN THE THREE MEN THAT THE DECEASED RONALD ADAIR SPENT HIS LAST HOURS WITH. YOU ARE AWARE OF THE CASE, I TRUST?
ONLY FROM THE NEWSPAPERS. I'M AFRAID I CAN'T HELP YOU. I HAVE NOTHING LEFT. THE CASE WON'T LET YOU SLEEP, HUH?
YOU CAN SAY THAT AGAIN, DOCTOR. HOLMES TRULY MESSED THINGS UP FOR US WITH HIS DEATH.
YOU'RE TALKING AS IF HE DID IT ON PURPOSE.
AND DID HE NOT?
HONESTLY, DOCTOR. MORIARTY WAS A CRAFTY FOX, BUT HOW DIFFICULT WOULD IT BE TO DISAPPEAR OUT OF HIS SIGHT?
I'M TELLING YOU, HOLMES HAS DELIBERATELY LEFT A FEW CRUMBS BEHIND SO HE COULD HAVE THE BEST CATCH ATTRIBUTED TO HIMSELF AND ONCE AGAIN MAKE THE POLICE LOOK LIKE FOOLS.
I'M NOT GOING TO LISTEN TO THIS! SHERLOCK HOLMES WAS THE BEST MAN I HAD THE HONOUR TO KNOW, AND I...
PHFFFT! "HAD THE HONOUR TO KNOW..." ARE YOU LISTENING TO YOURSELF? CAN YOU HEAR HOW YOU SPEAK? YOU'RE A FAILURE! A REMNANT OF THE OLD DAYS! THE 20TH CENTURY IS AROUND THE CORNER AND YOU'RE HOPELESSLY STUCK IN THE WHEELS OF HISTORY!
IS THAT WHAT YOU THINK?!
KOPL'S
WHISKY

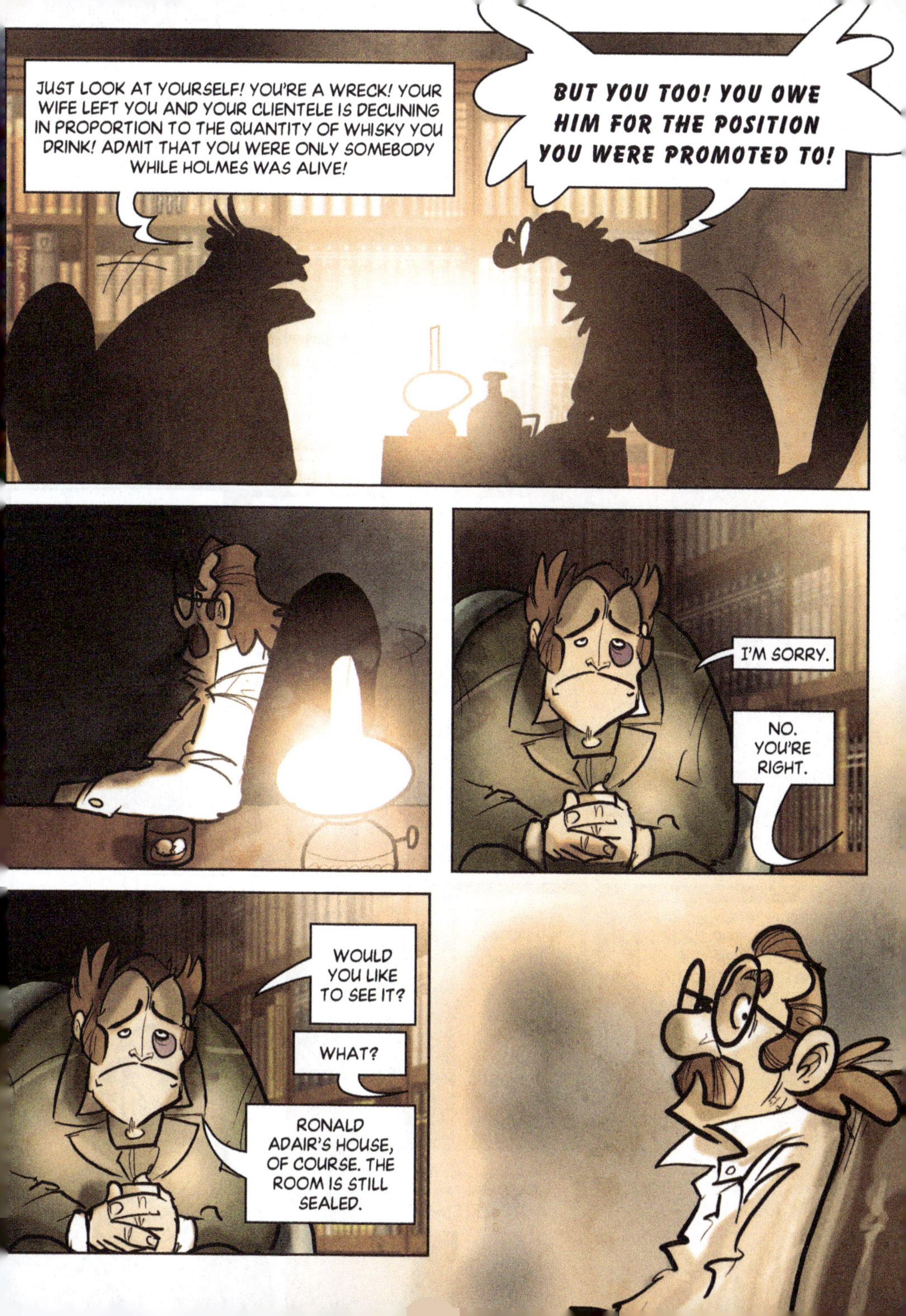
JUST LOOK AT YOURSELF! YOU'RE A WRECK! YOUR WIFE LEFT YOU AND YOUR CLIENTELE IS DECLINING IN PROPORTION TO THE QUANTITY OF WHISKY YOU DRINK! ADMIT THAT YOU WERE ONLY SOMEBODY WHILE HOLMES WAS ALIVE!
BUT YOU TOO! YOU OWE HIM FOR THE POSITION YOU WERE PROMOTED TO!
I'M SORRY.
NO. YOU'RE RIGHT.
WOULD YOU LIKE TO SEE IT?
WHAT?
RONALD ADAIR'S HOUSE, OF COURSE. THE ROOM IS STILL SEALED.

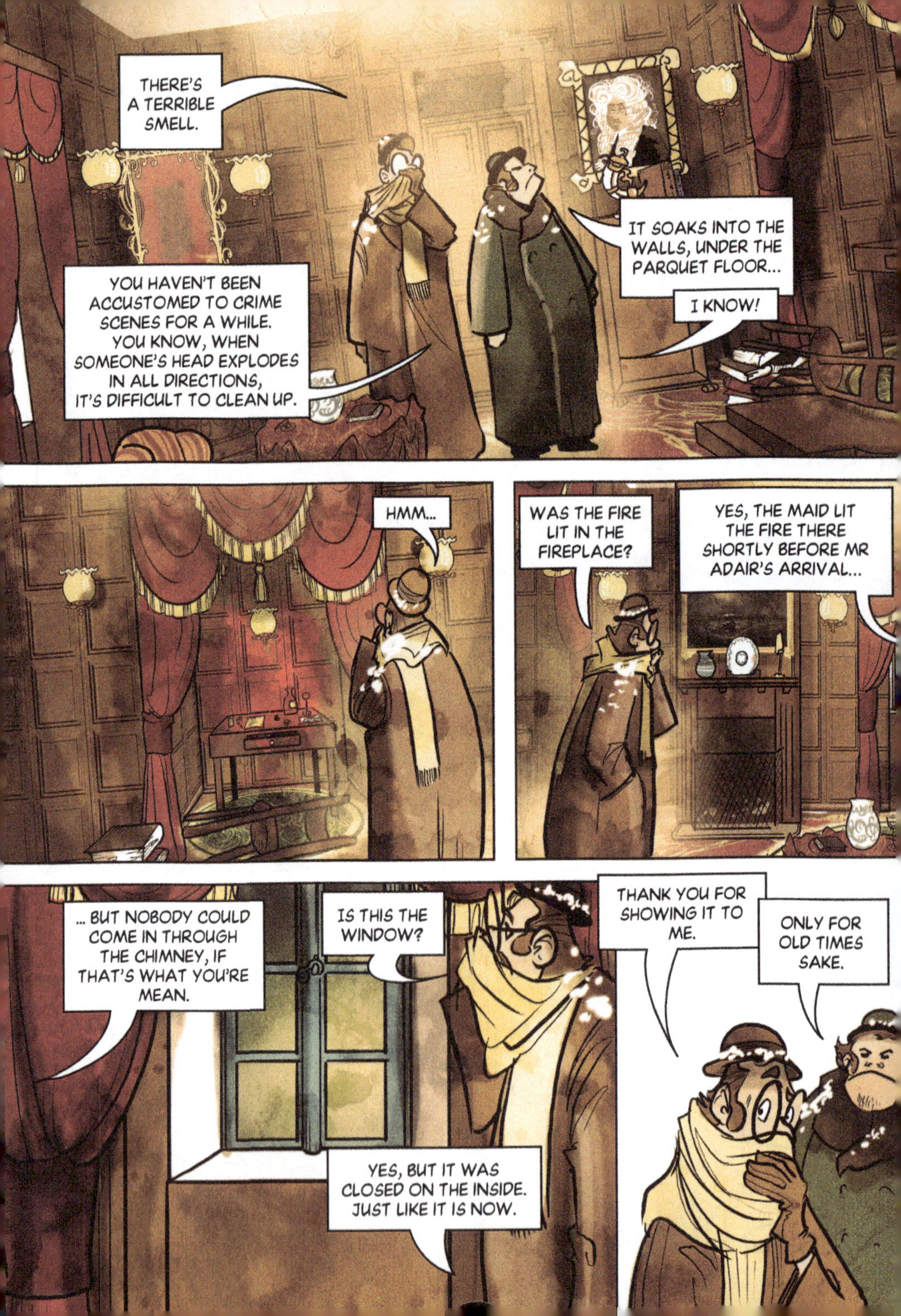
THERE'S A TERRIBLE SMELL.
YOU HAVEN'T BEEN ACCUSTOMED TO CRIME SCENES FOR A WHILE. YOU KNOW, WHEN SOMEONE'S HEAD EXPLODES IN ALL DIRECTIONS, IT'S DIFFICULT TO CLEAN UP.
IT SOAKS INTO THE WALLS, UNDER THE PARQUET FLOOR...
I KNOW!
HMM...
WAS THE FIRE LIT IN THE FIREPLACE?
YES, THE MAID LIT THE FIRE THERE SHORTLY BEFORE MR ADAIR'S ARRIVAL...
... BUT NOBODY COULD COME IN THROUGH THE CHIMNEY, IF THAT'S WHAT YOU'RE MEAN.
IS THIS THE WINDOW?
YES, BUT IT WAS CLOSED ON THE INSIDE. JUST LIKE IT IS NOW.
THANK YOU FOR SHOWING IT TO ME.
ONLY FOR OLD TIMES SAKE.

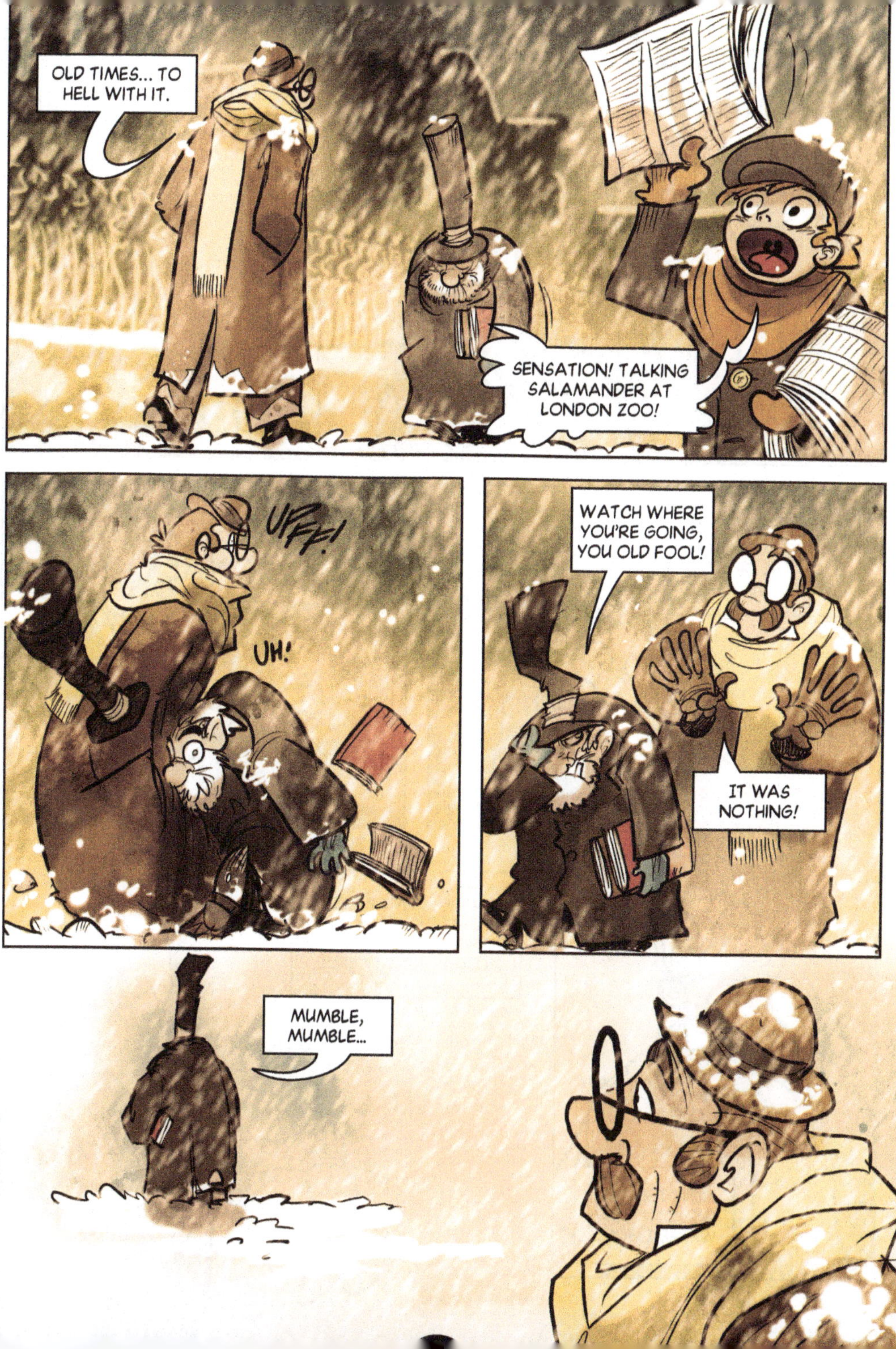
OLD TIMES... TO HELL WITH IT.
SENSATION! TALKING SALAMANDER AT LONDON ZOO!
UFF!
UH!
WATCH WHERE YOU'RE GOING, YOU OLD FOOL!
IT WAS NOTHING!
MUMBLE, MUMBLE...

KENSINGTON, DR WATSON'S SURGERY.

HOW DID YOU GET IN HERE? DID YOU FOLLOW ME?

I THWANTED TO APOLOTHIZE FOR MY BEHAVIOUR. I'M THVERY CAREFUL WHEN IT COMES TO MY THOOKS, YOU KNOW?

APOLOGY ACCEPTED, NOW GO!

NOT THO FAST. LOOK, I HAVE A BEAUTIFUL BOOK: THE ORIGINS OF TREE WORSHIP!

YOU COULD USE IT TO FILL THAT GAP WHERE YOU HIDE YOUR WHISKEY.

THERE....

YOU WOULDN'T BELIEVE, MY DEAR WATSON, HOW DIFFICULT IT IS TO WALK ALL DAY BENT-DOUBLE.

HOW THE HELL DO YOU KNOW WHERE I HIDE...

CRACK!

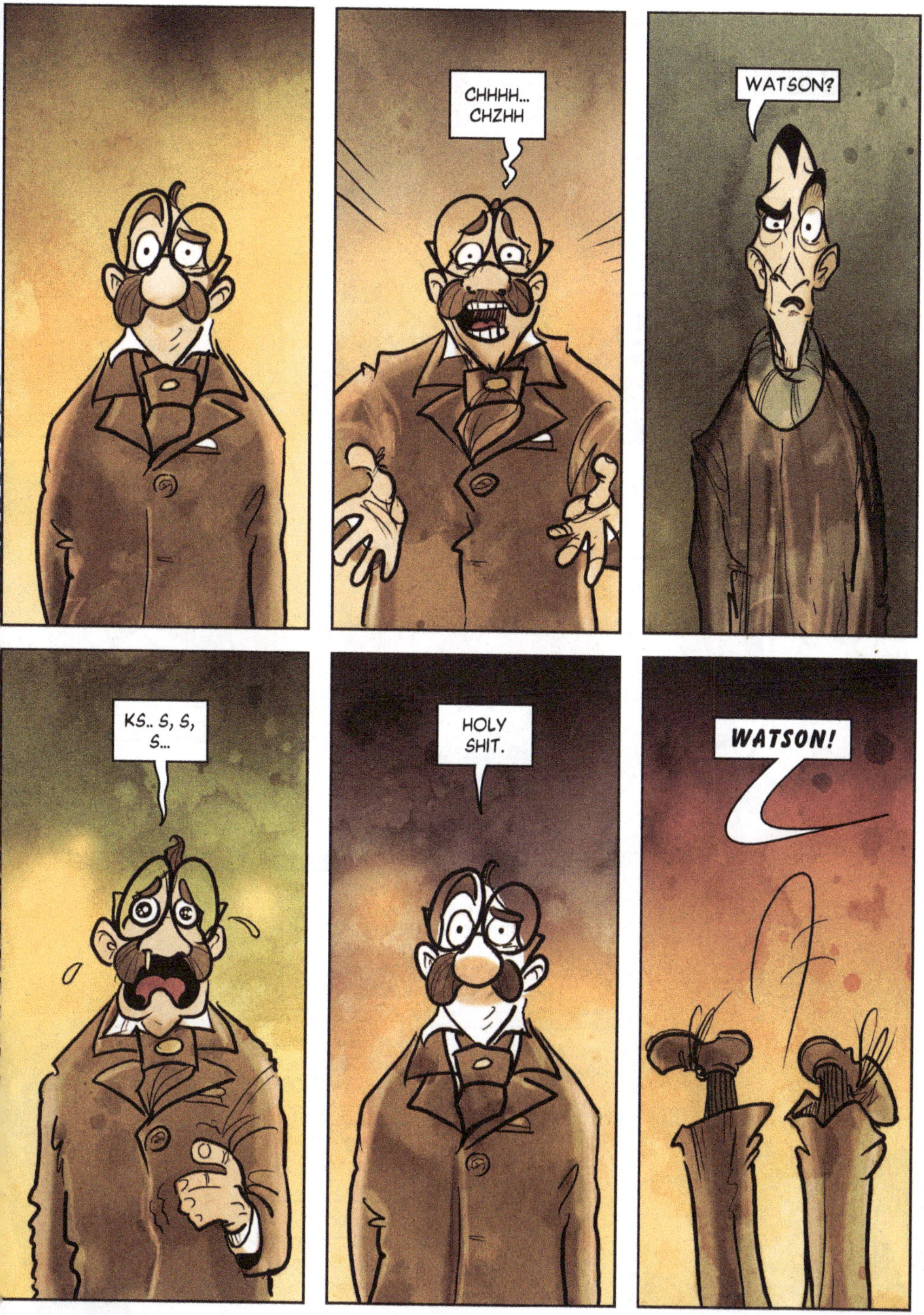
CHHHH...
CHZHH
WATSON?
KS.. S, S,
S...
HOLY
SHIT.
WATSON!

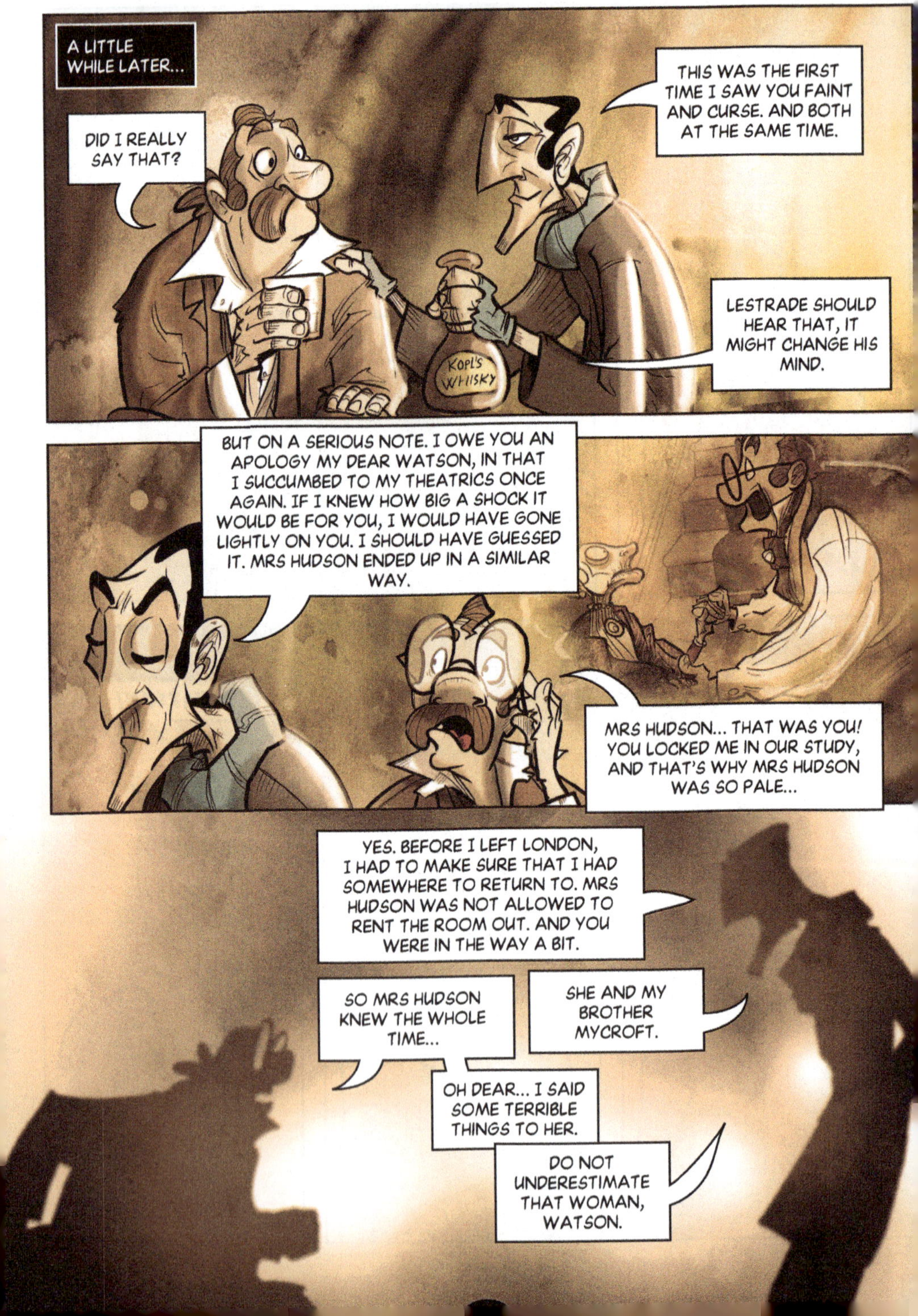
A LITTLE WHILE LATER...
THIS WAS THE FIRST TIME I SAW YOU FAINT AND CURSE. AND BOTH AT THE SAME TIME.
DID I REALLY SAY THAT?
KOPL'S WHISKY
LESTRADE SHOULD HEAR THAT, IT MIGHT CHANGE HIS MIND.
BUT ON A SERIOUS NOTE. I OWE YOU AN APOLOGY MY DEAR WATSON, IN THAT I SUCCUMBED TO MY THEATRICS ONCE AGAIN. IF I KNEW HOW BIG A SHOCK IT WOULD BE FOR YOU, I WOULD HAVE GONE LIGHTLY ON YOU. I SHOULD HAVE GUESSED IT. MRS HUDSON ENDED UP IN A SIMILAR WAY.
MRS HUDSON... THAT WAS YOU! YOU LOCKED ME IN OUR STUDY, AND THAT'S WHY MRS HUDSON WAS SO PALE...
YES. BEFORE I LEFT LONDON, I HAD TO MAKE SURE THAT I HAD SOMEWHERE TO RETURN TO. MRS HUDSON WAS NOT ALLOWED TO RENT THE ROOM OUT. AND YOU WERE IN THE WAY A BIT.
SO MRS HUDSON KNEW THE WHOLE TIME...
SHE AND MY BROTHER MYCROFT.
OH DEAR... I SAID SOME TERRIBLE THINGS TO HER.
DO NOT UNDERESTIMATE THAT WOMAN, WATSON.

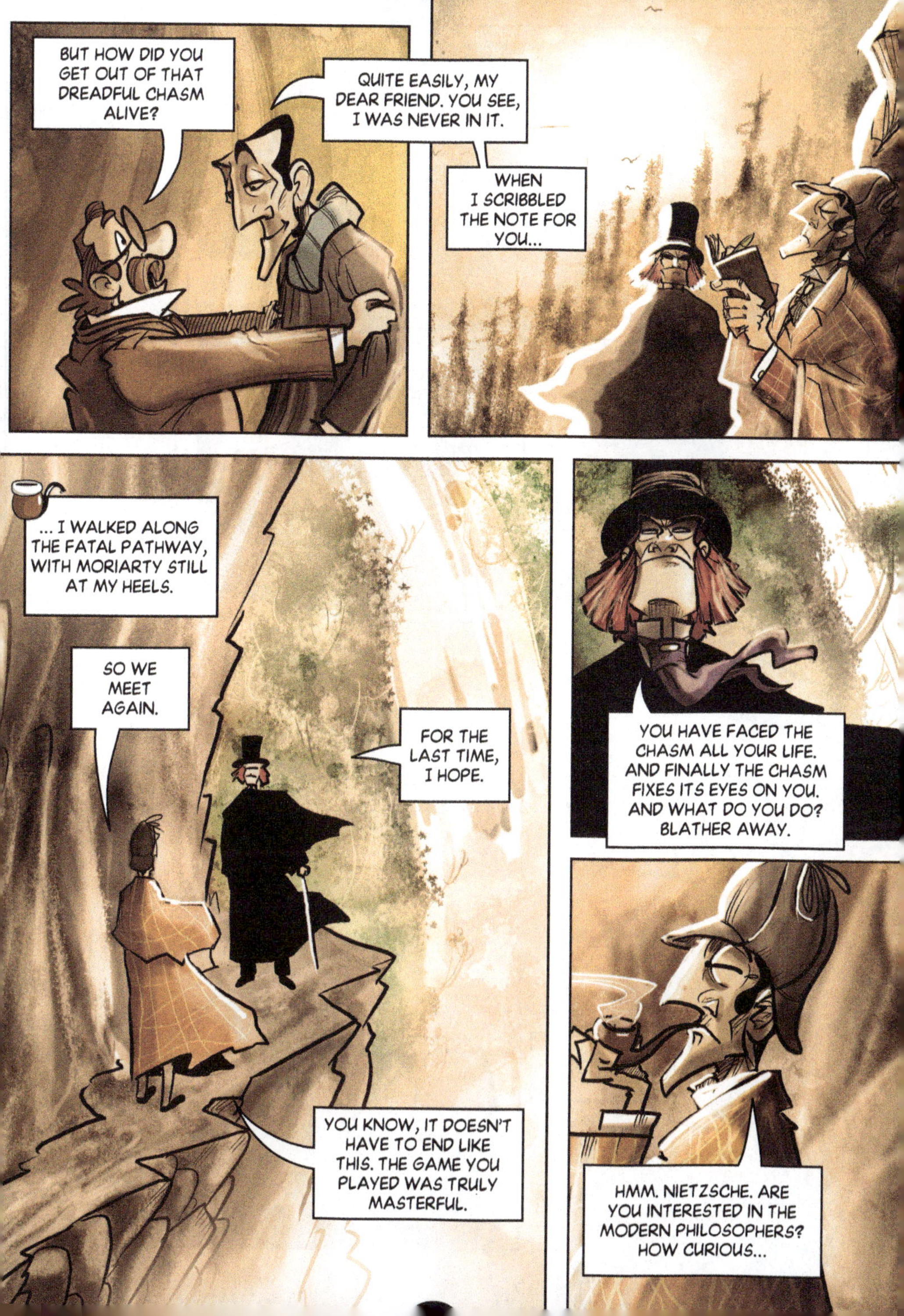
BUT HOW DID YOU GET OUT OF THAT DREADFUL CHASM ALIVE?
QUITE EASILY, MY DEAR FRIEND. YOU SEE, I WAS NEVER IN IT.
WHEN I SCRIBBLED THE NOTE FOR YOU...
... I WALKED ALONG THE FATAL PATHWAY, WITH MORIARTY STILL AT MY HEELS.
SO WE MEET AGAIN.
FOR THE LAST TIME, I HOPE.
YOU KNOW, IT DOESN'T HAVE TO END LIKE THIS. THE GAME YOU PLAYED WAS TRULY MASTERFUL.
YOU HAVE FACED THE CHASM ALL YOUR LIFE. AND FINALLY THE CHASM FIXES ITS EYES ON YOU. AND WHAT DO YOU DO? BLATHER AWAY.
HMM. NIETZSCHE. ARE YOU INTERESTED IN THE MODERN PHILOSOPHERS? HOW CURIOUS...

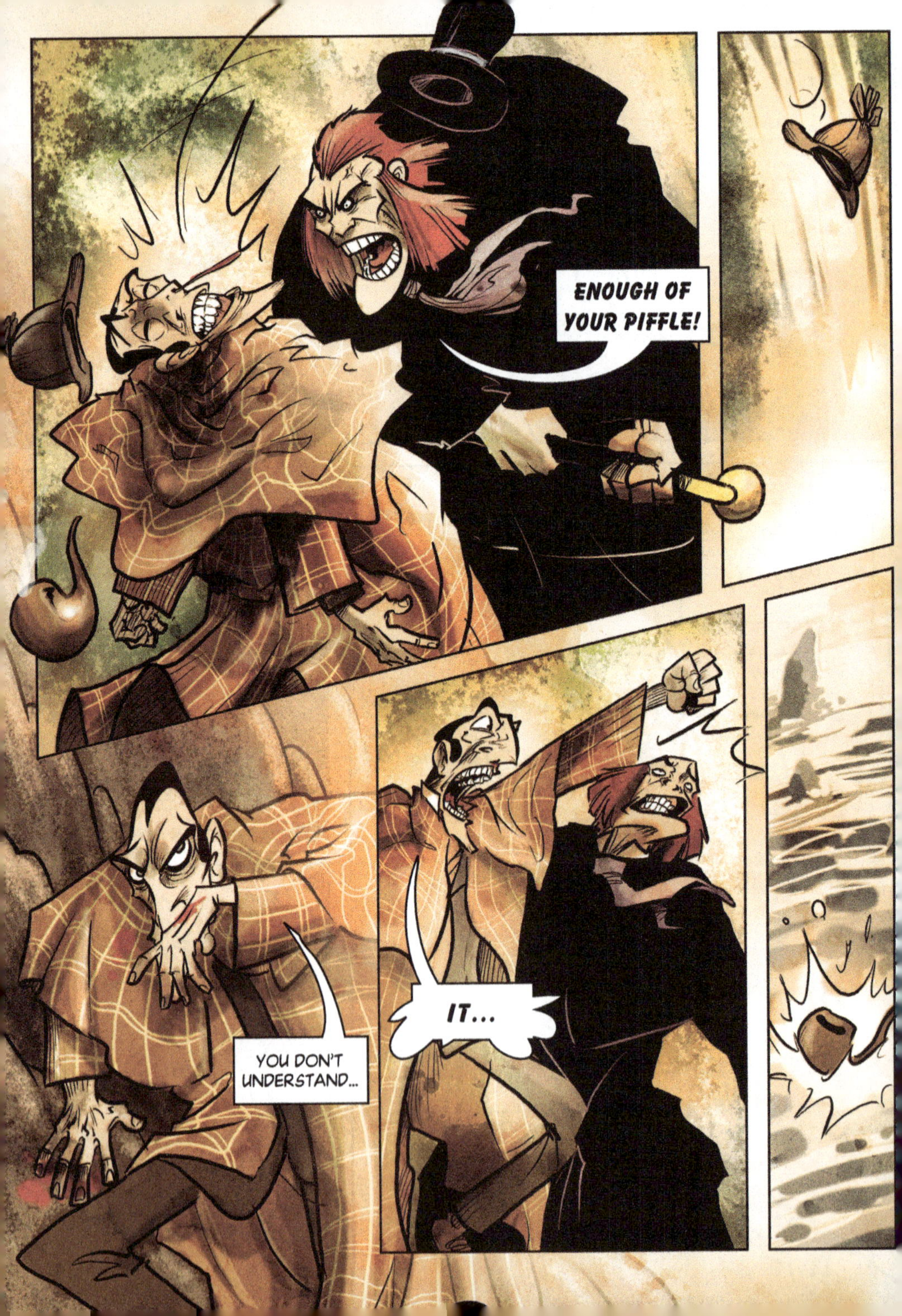
ENOUGH OF YOUR PIFFLE!
YOU DON'T UNDERSTAND...
IT...

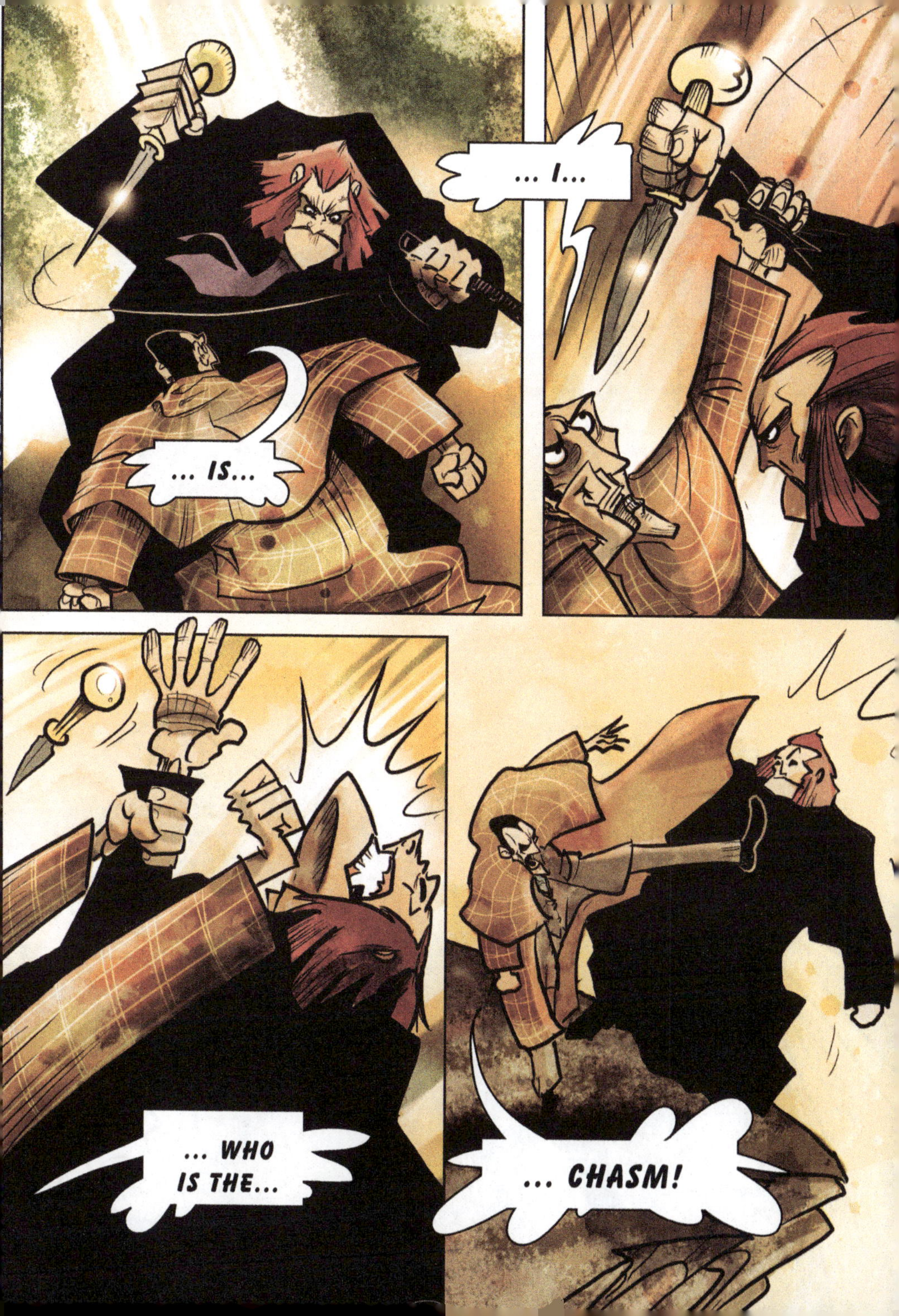
... IS...
... I...
... WHO IS THE...
... CHASM!

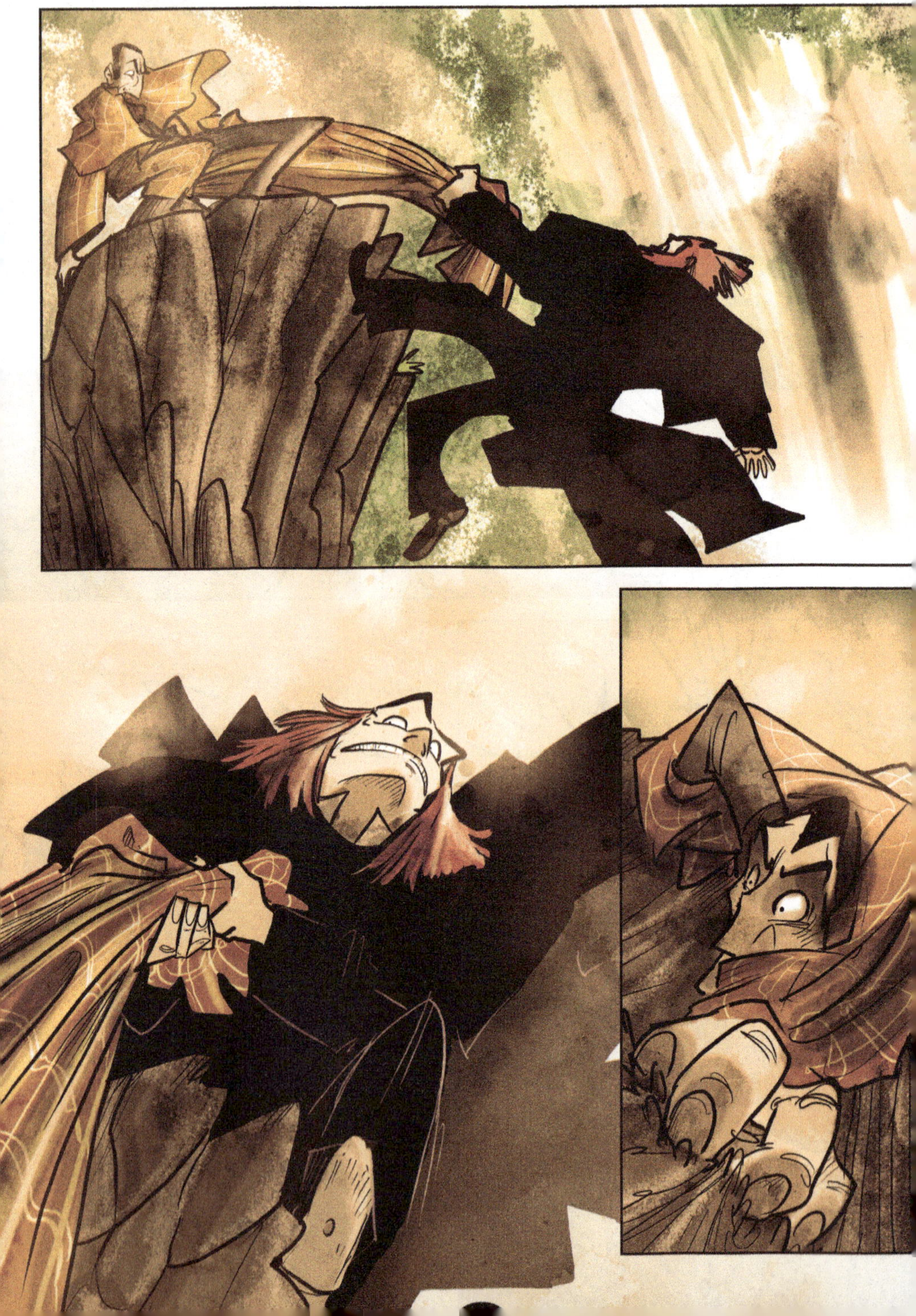

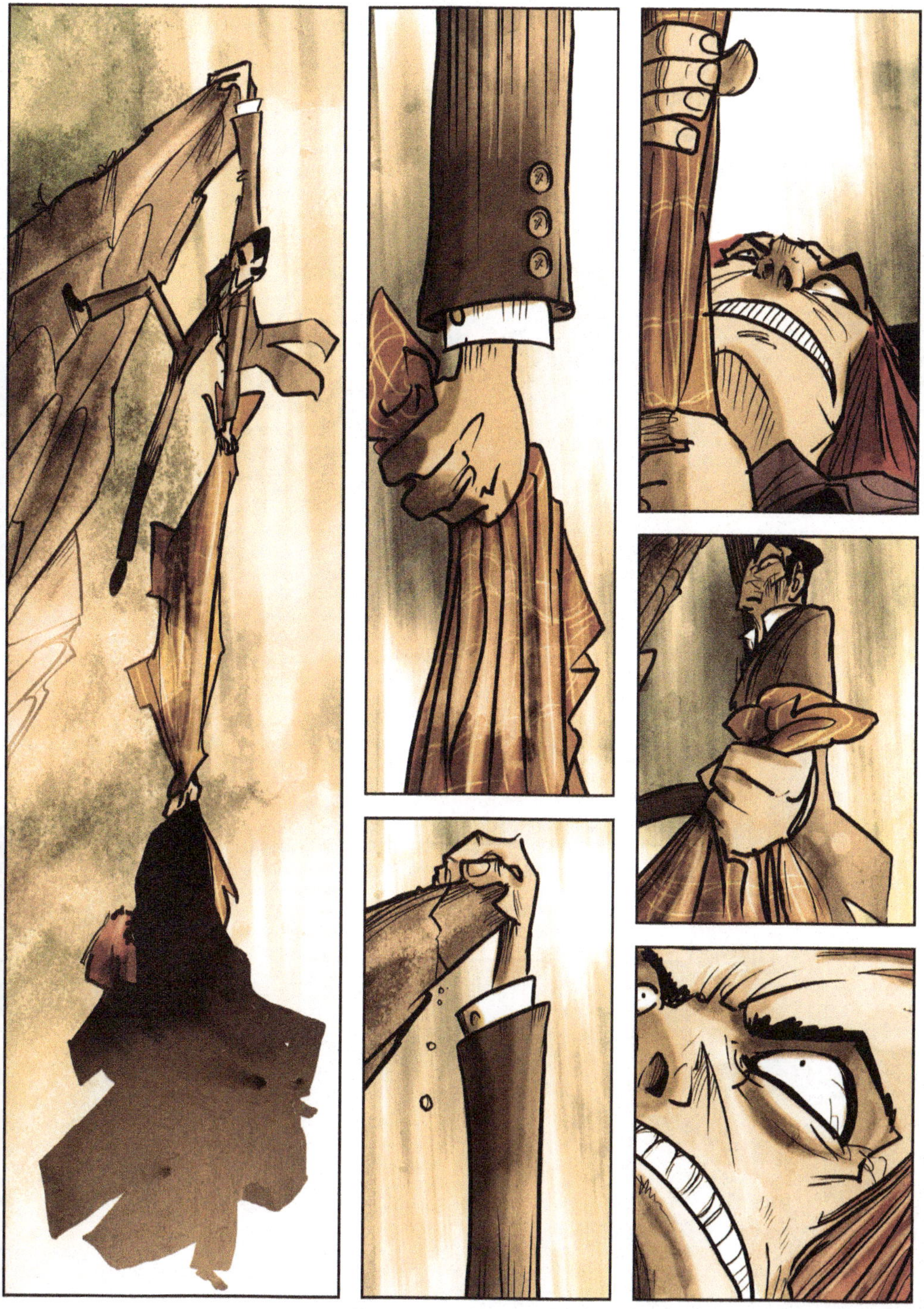

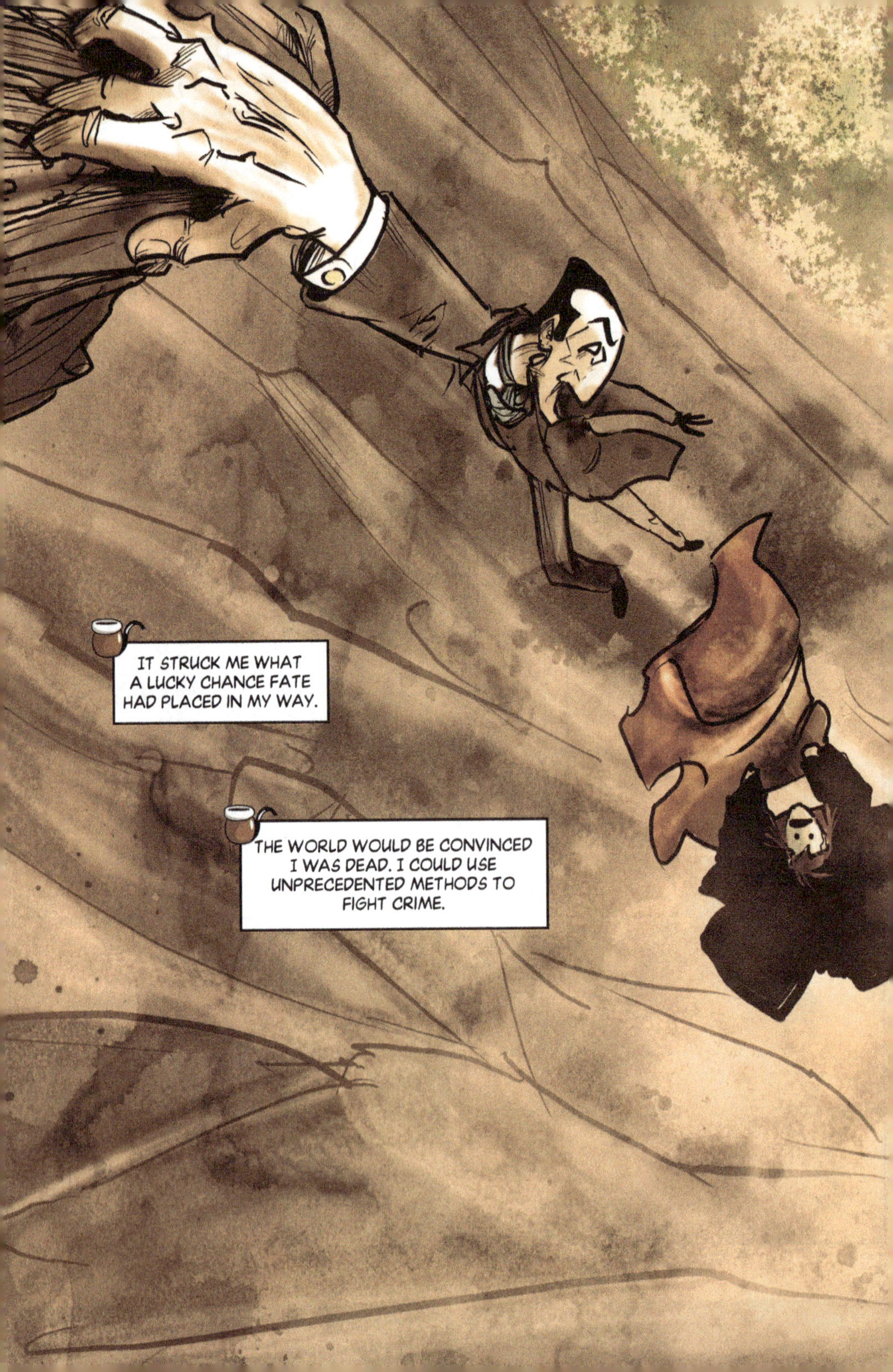
IT STRUCK ME WHAT A LUCKY CHANCE FATE HAD PLACED IN MY WAY.
THE WORLD WOULD BE CONVINCED I WAS DEAD. I COULD USE UNPRECEDENTED METHODS TO FIGHT CRIME.

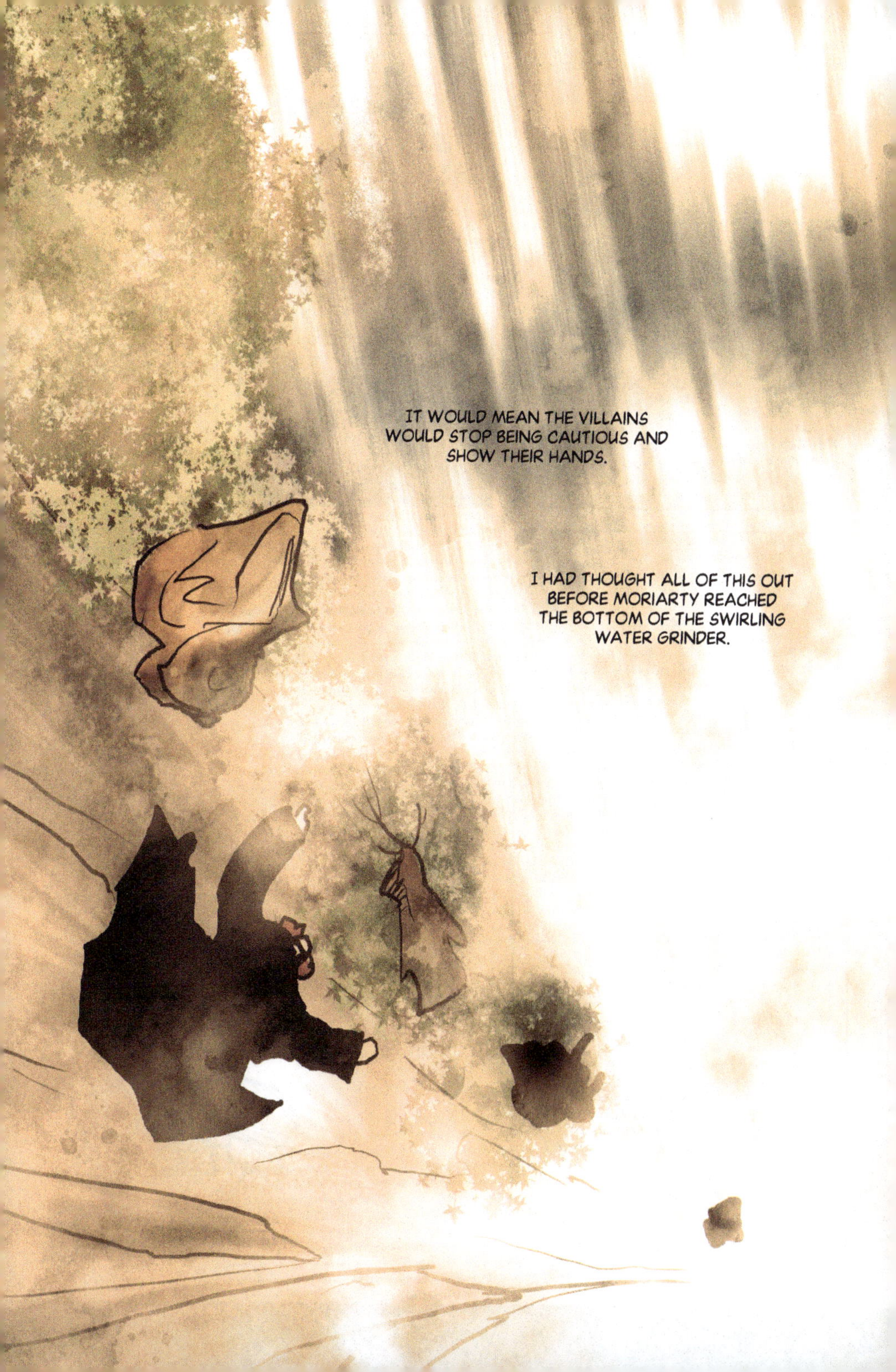
IT WOULD MEAN THE VILLAINS WOULD STOP BEING CAUTIOUS AND SHOW THEIR HANDS.
I HAD THOUGHT ALL OF THIS OUT BEFORE MORIARTY REACHED THE BOTTOM OF THE SWIRLING WATER GRINDER.

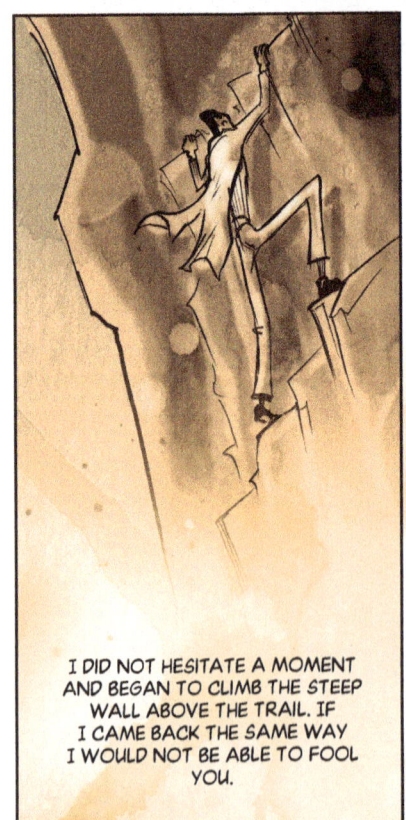

FROM THE POSITION ABOVE YOUR HEAD, MY DEAR WATSON, I WATCHED YOUR REACTION.

I DID NOT HESITATE A MOMENT AND BEGAN TO CLIMB THE STEEP WALL ABOVE THE TRAIL. IF I CAME BACK THE SAME WAY I WOULD NOT BE ABLE TO FOOL YOU.

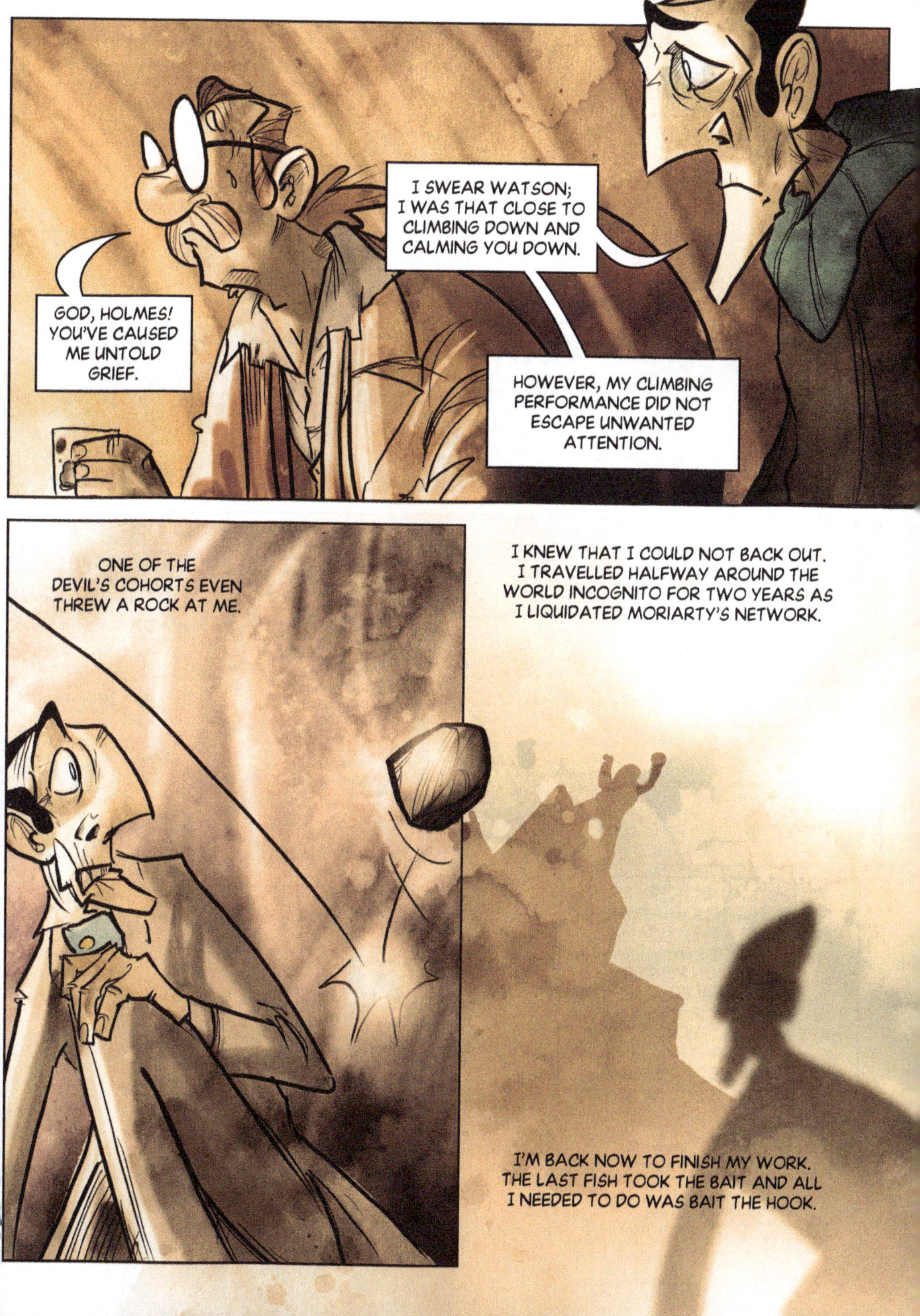

GOD, HOLMES! YOU'VE CAUSED ME UNTOLD GRIEF.
I SWEAR WATSON; I WAS THAT CLOSE TO CLIMBING DOWN AND CALMING YOU DOWN.
HOWEVER, MY CLIMBING PERFORMANCE DID NOT ESCAPE UNWANTED ATTENTION.
ONE OF THE DEVIL'S COHORTS EVEN THREW A ROCK AT ME.
I KNEW THAT I COULD NOT BACK OUT. I TRAVELLED HALFWAY AROUND THE WORLD INCOGNITO FOR TWO YEARS AS I LIQUIDATED MORIARTY'S NETWORK.
I'M BACK NOW TO FINISH MY WORK. THE LAST FISH TOOK THE BAIT AND ALL I NEEDED TO DO WAS BAIT THE HOOK.

THAT'S WHY I SHOWED UP AT BAKER STREET THIS MORNING AND WITH A LITTLE HELP FROM CARTWRIGHT'S DETECTIVES, I LET THE WORLD KNOW I'M BACK.

THE UNDERWORLD WILL NOT BELIEVE THIS NEWS FOR A WHILE, BUT ONE OF THEM KNOWS THAT IT IS TRUE, AND HE WILL TRY TO MURDER ME TONIGHT. THEREFORE, I HAVE NOW SENT A MESSAGE TO LESTRADE. IF HE IS SAVVY ENOUGH, HE WILL GO ALONG WITH IT.

HOLMES, ARE YOU SAYING THAT THE WHOLE OF LONDON IS ALREADY TALKING ABOUT YOUR RETURN, AND I'M THE LAST ONE TO KNOW?!? IS THAT HOW LITTLE YOU TRUST ME?

ON THE CONTRARY, MY DEAR FRIEND. IT'S TRUE THAT MANY TIMES, I'VE SAVED YOU FROM THE ROUTINES, WHICH MY INVESTIGATION RENDERED, ALTHOUGH I NEVER DEPRIVED YOU OF THE FINALE. IF YOU DIDN'T HAVE MY TRUST, YOU WOULDN'T BE AWARDED THIS PRIVILEGE AS THE ONLY ONE IN THE WORLD.

"ON THE CONTRARY, MY DEAR FRIEND. IT'S TRUE THAT MANY TIMES, I'VE SAVED YOU FROM THE ROUTINES, WHICH MY INVESTIGATION RENDERED, ALTHOUGH I NEVER DEPRIVED YOU OF THE FINALE. IF YOU DIDN'T HAVE MY TRUST, YOU WOULDN'T BE AWARDED THIS PRIVILEGE AS THE ONLY ONE IN THE WORLD."

"EH... WATSON?"

"WELL, WHERE ARE YOU? ARE WE GOING, OR NOT? LEAD THE WAY!"

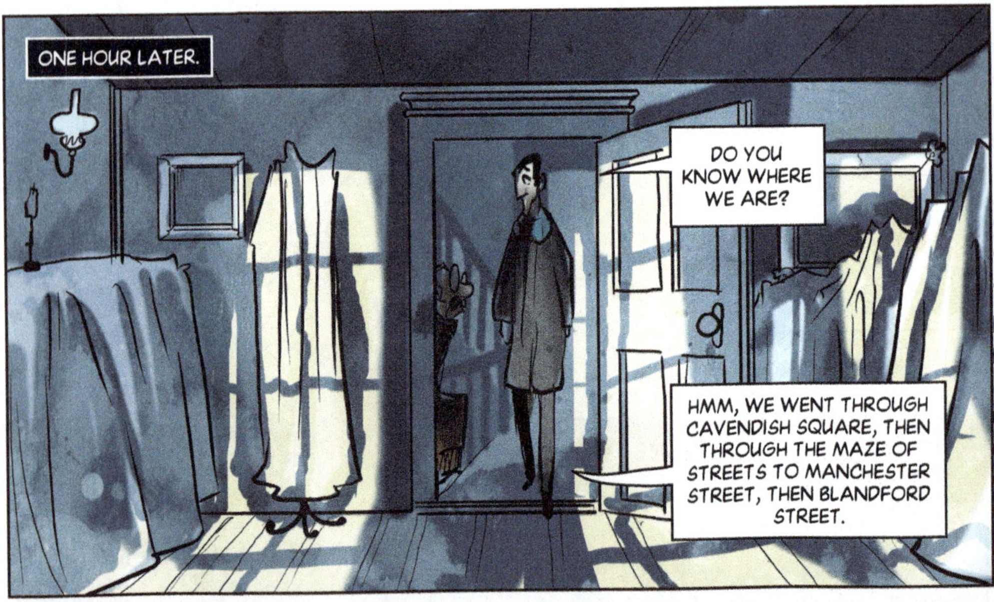
ONE HOUR LATER.
DO YOU KNOW WHERE WE ARE?
HMM, WE WENT THROUGH CAVENDISH SQUARE, THEN THROUGH THE MAZE OF STREETS TO MANCHESTER STREET, THEN BLANDFORD STREET.

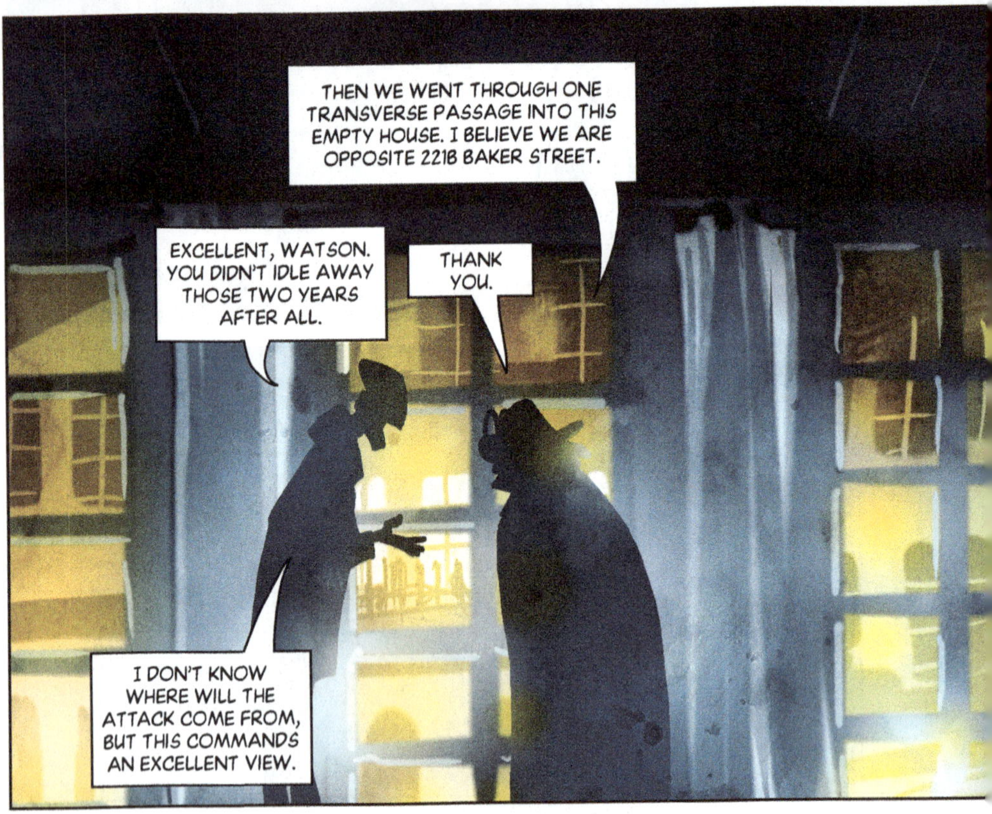
THEN WE WENT THROUGH ONE TRANSVERSE PASSAGE INTO THIS EMPTY HOUSE. I BELIEVE WE ARE OPPOSITE 221B BAKER STREET.
EXCELLENT, WATSON. YOU DIDN'T IDLE AWAY THOSE TWO YEARS AFTER ALL.
THANK YOU.
I DON'T KNOW WHERE WILL THE ATTACK COME FROM, BUT THIS COMMANDS AN EXCELLENT VIEW.

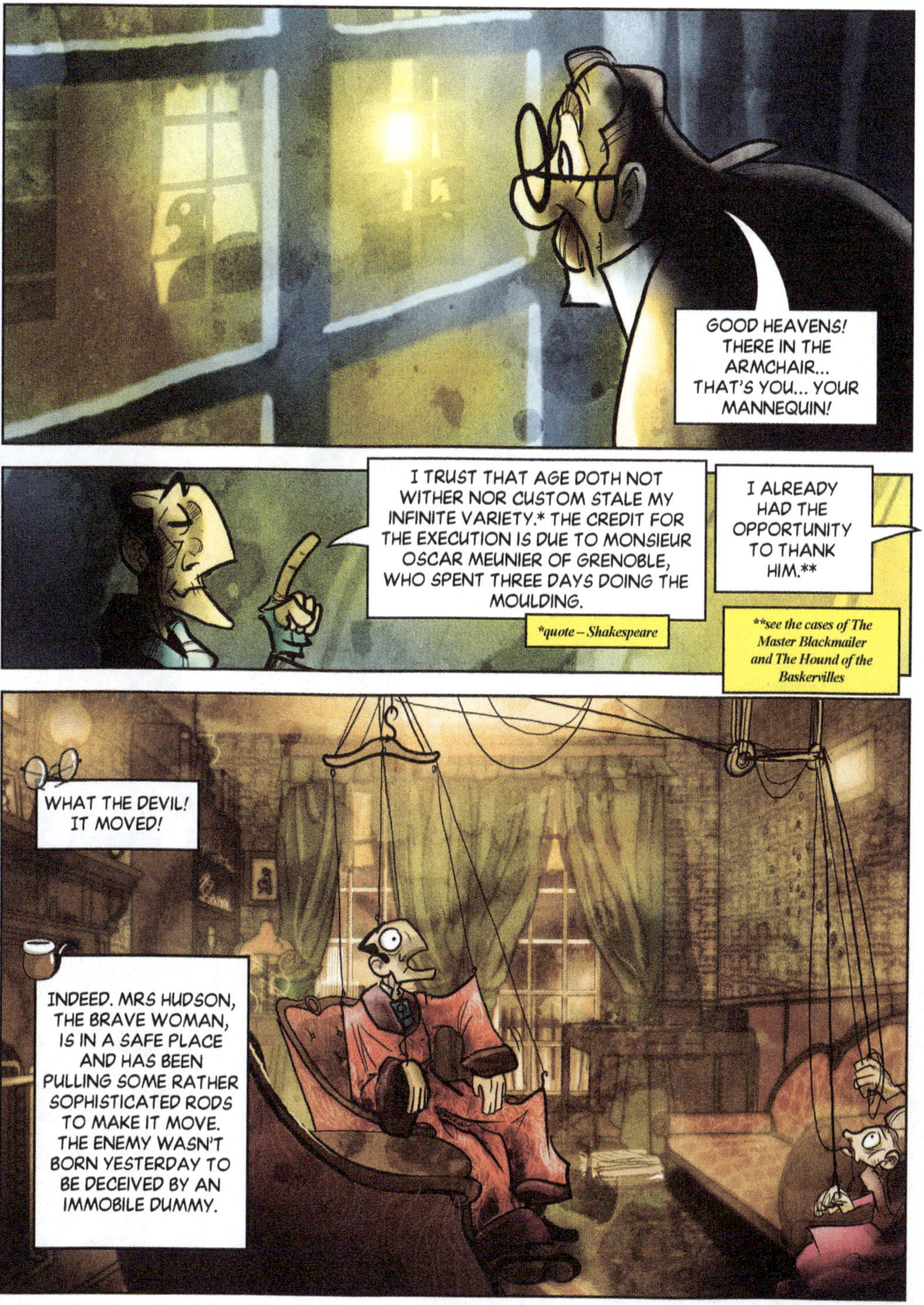
GOOD HEAVENS! THERE IN THE ARMCHAIR... THAT'S YOU... YOUR MANNEQUIN!
I TRUST THAT AGE DOTH NOT WITHER NOR CUSTOM STALE MY INFINITE VARIETY.* THE CREDIT FOR THE EXECUTION IS DUE TO MONSIEUR OSCAR MEUNIER OF GRENOBLE, WHO SPENT THREE DAYS DOING THE MOULDING.
*quote – Shakespeare
I ALREADY HAD THE OPPORTUNITY TO THANK HIM.**
**see the cases of The Master Blackmailer and The Hound of the Baskervilles
WHAT THE DEVIL! IT MOVED!
INDEED. MRS HUDSON, THE BRAVE WOMAN, IS IN A SAFE PLACE AND HAS BEEN PULLING SOME RATHER SOPHISTICATED RODS TO MAKE IT MOVE. THE ENEMY WASN'T BORN YESTERDAY TO BE DECEIVED BY AN IMMOBILE DUMMY.

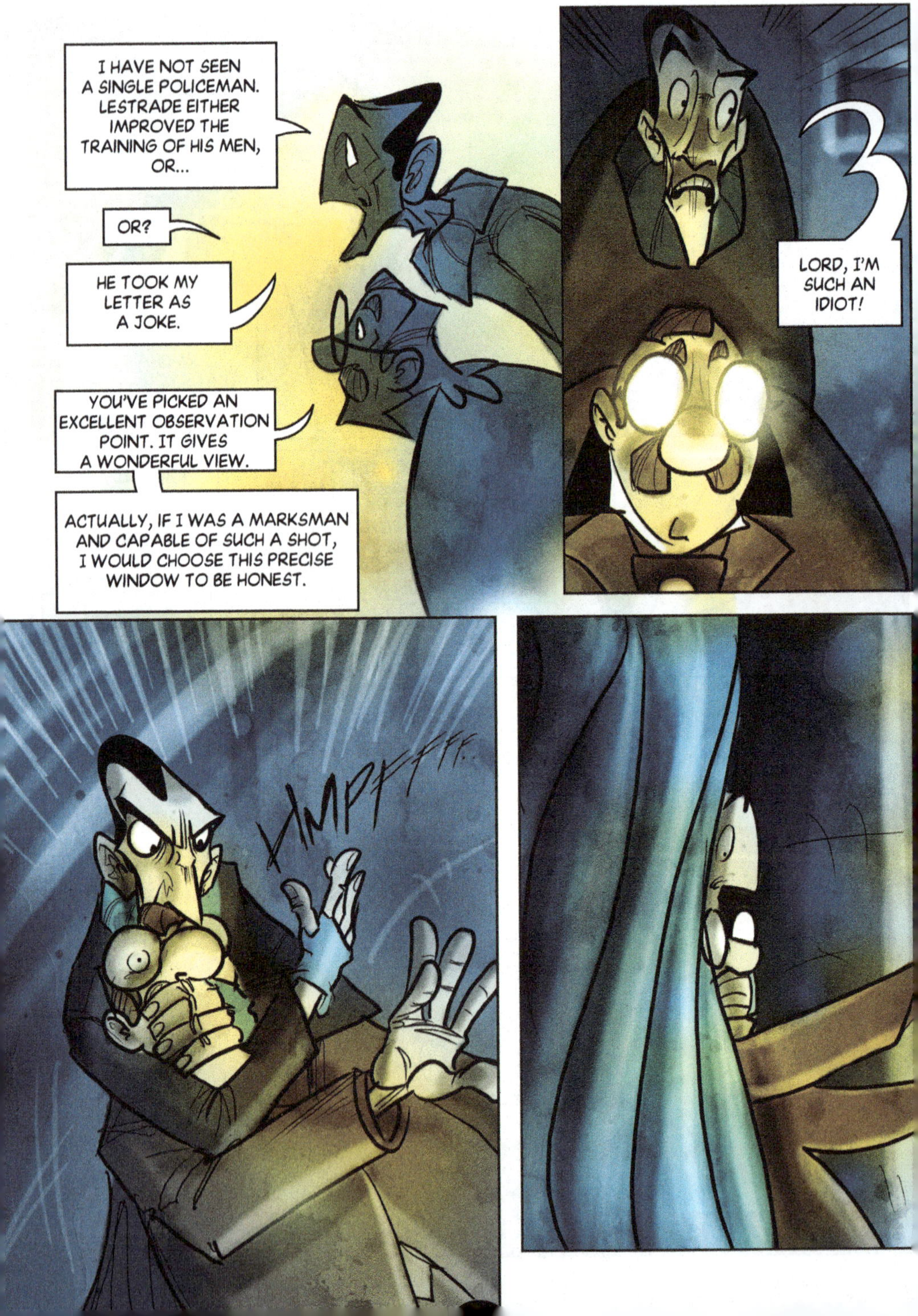
I HAVE NOT SEEN A SINGLE POLICEMAN. LESTRADE EITHER IMPROVED THE TRAINING OF HIS MEN, OR...
OR?
HE TOOK MY LETTER AS A JOKE.
YOU'VE PICKED AN EXCELLENT OBSERVATION POINT. IT GIVES A WONDERFUL VIEW.
ACTUALLY, IF I WAS A MARKSMAN AND CAPABLE OF SUCH A SHOT, I WOULD CHOOSE THIS PRECISE WINDOW TO BE HONEST.
LORD, I'M SUCH AN IDIOT!
HMPFFFF...

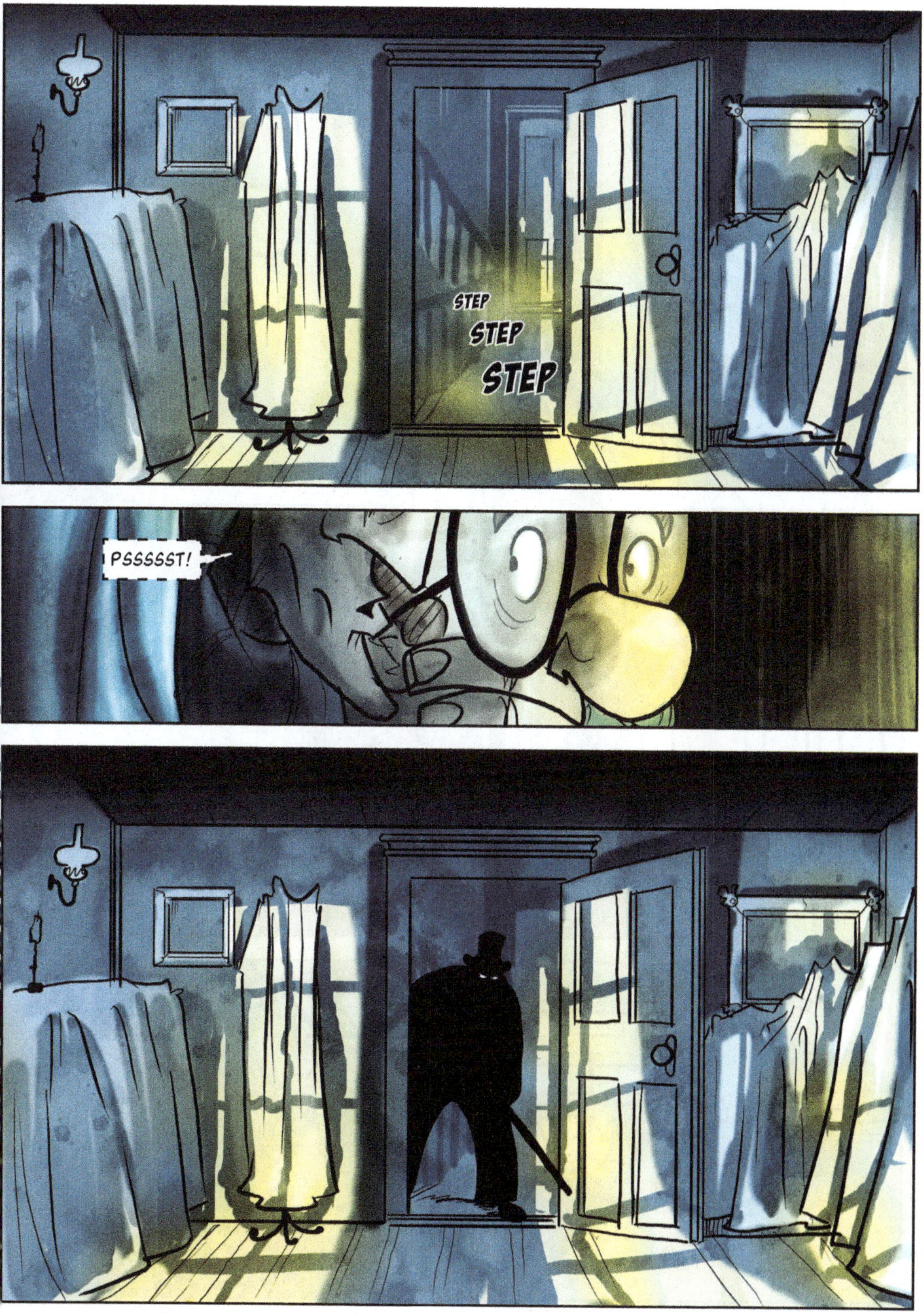
STEP
STEP
STEP
PSSSSST!

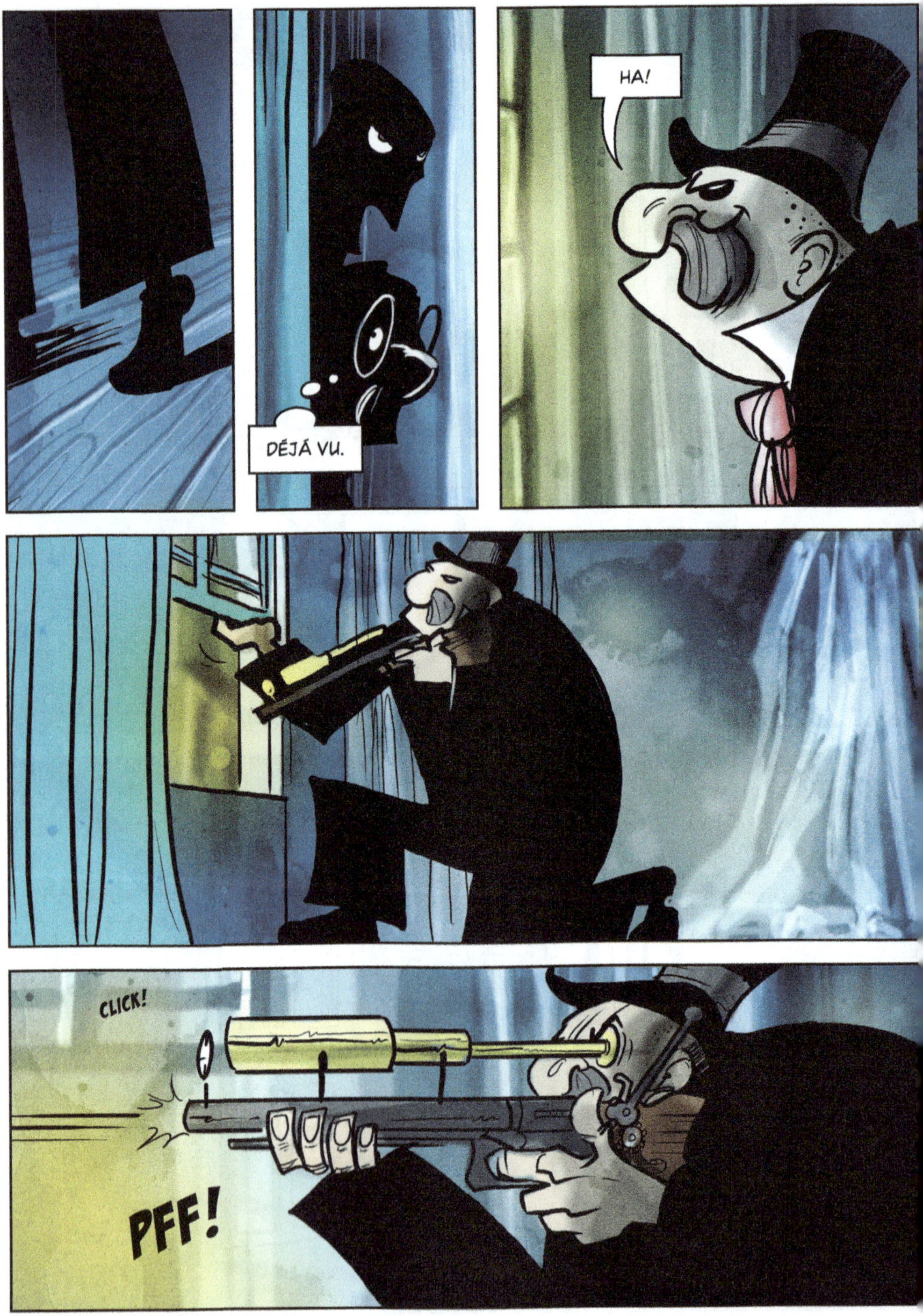
DÉJÀ VU.
HA!
CLICK!
PFF!

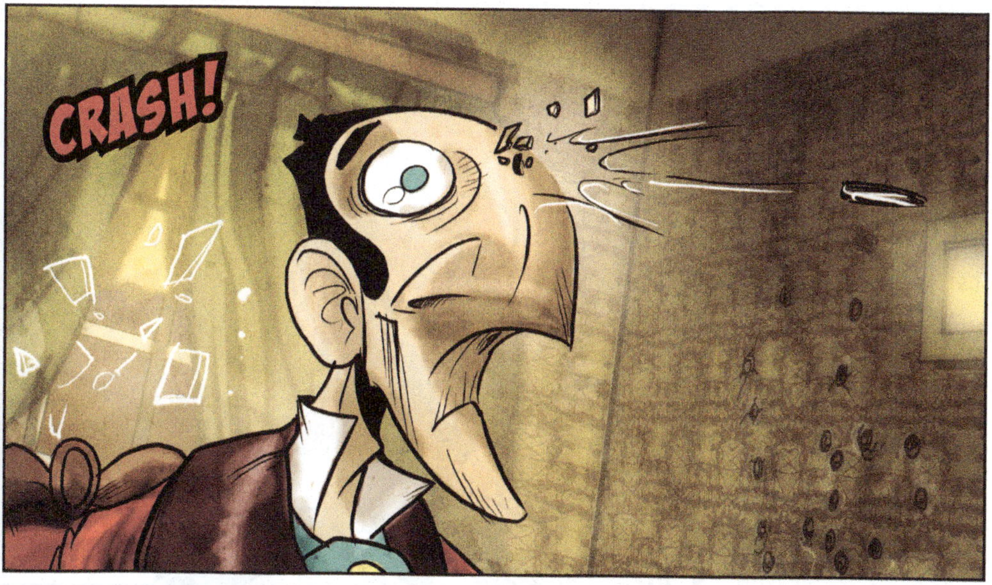
CRASH!

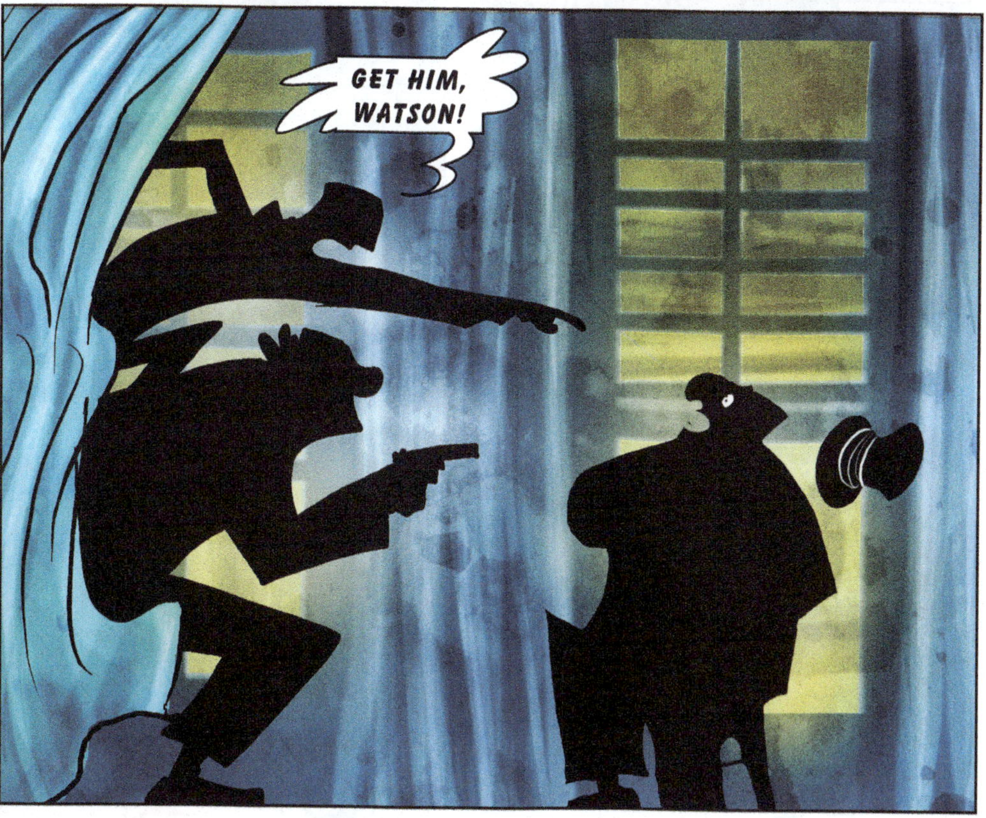
GET HIM, WATSON!

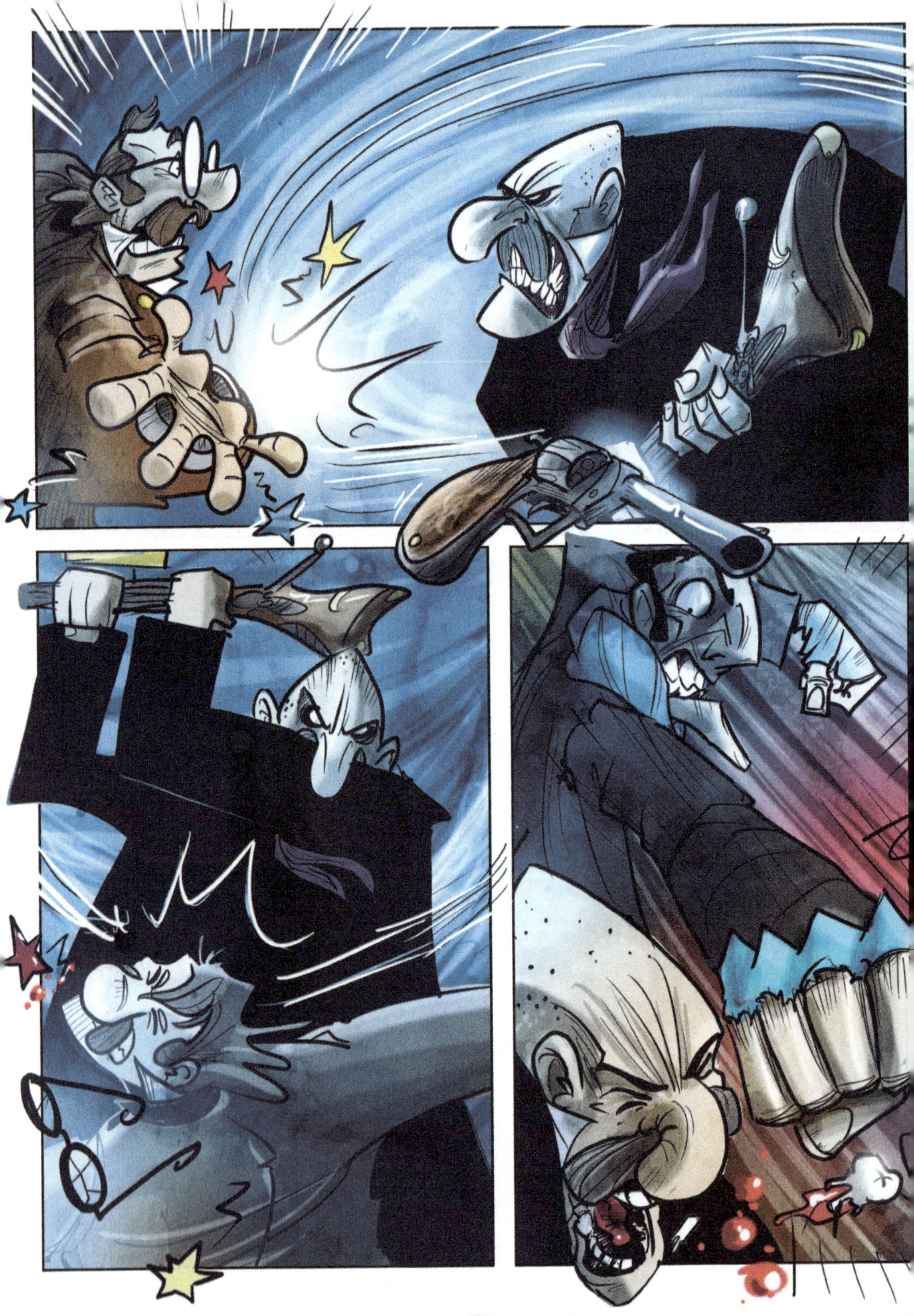

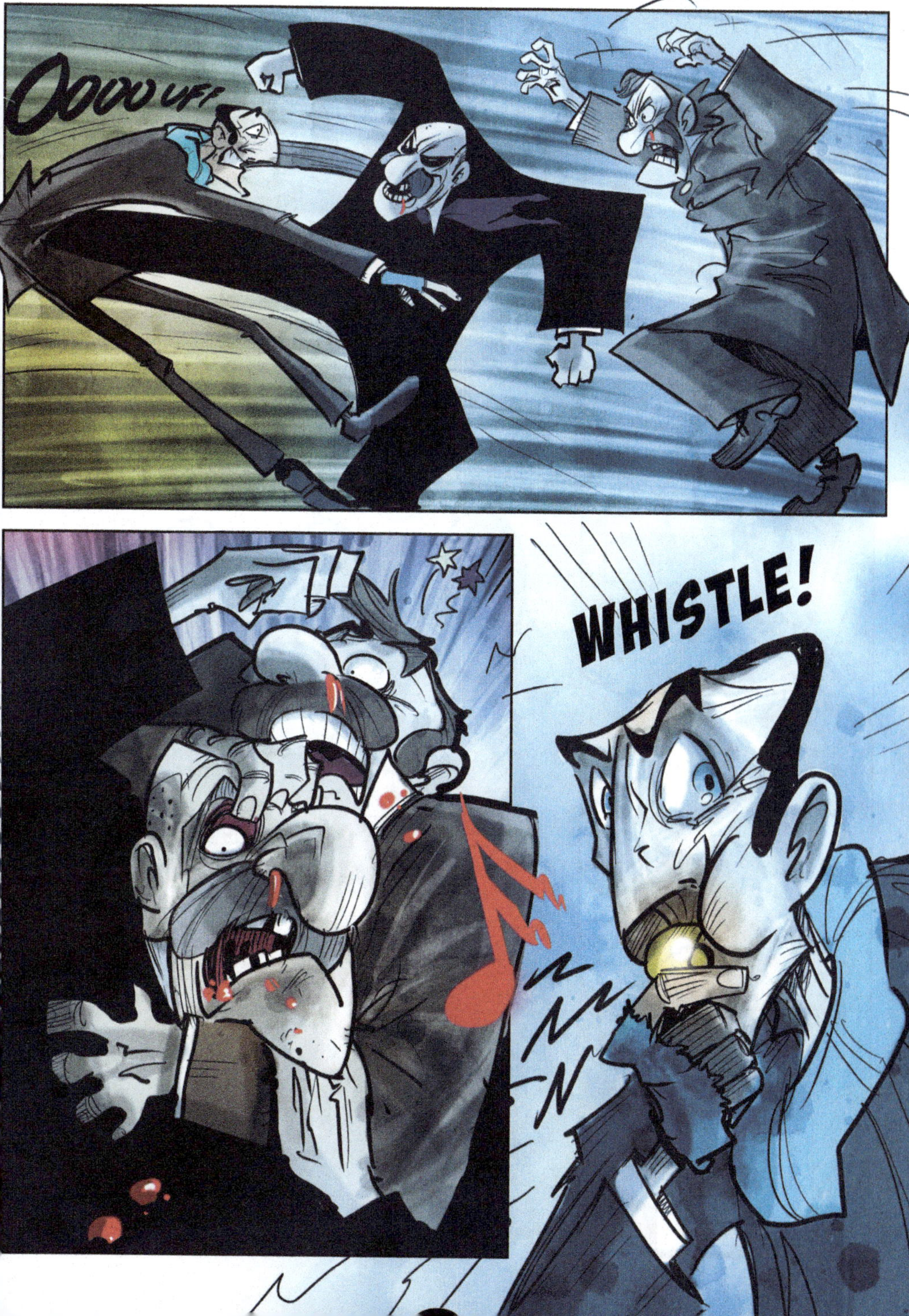
Ooooo uf!
WHISTLE!

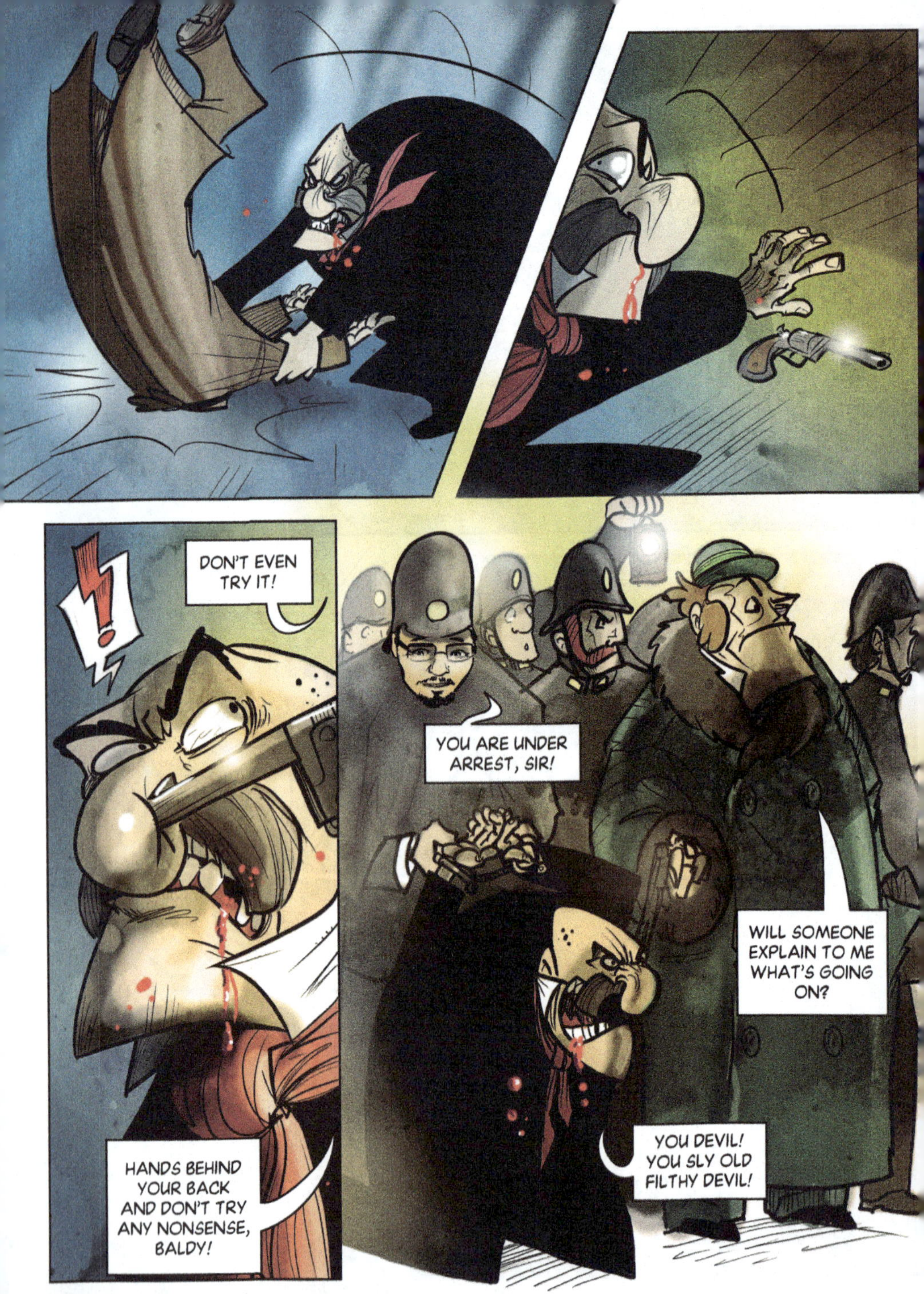
DON'T EVEN TRY IT!
YOU ARE UNDER ARREST, SIR!
WILL SOMEONE EXPLAIN TO ME WHAT'S GOING ON?
HANDS BEHIND YOUR BACK AND DON'T TRY ANY NONSENSE, BALDY!
YOU DEVIL! YOU SLY OLD FILTHY DEVIL!

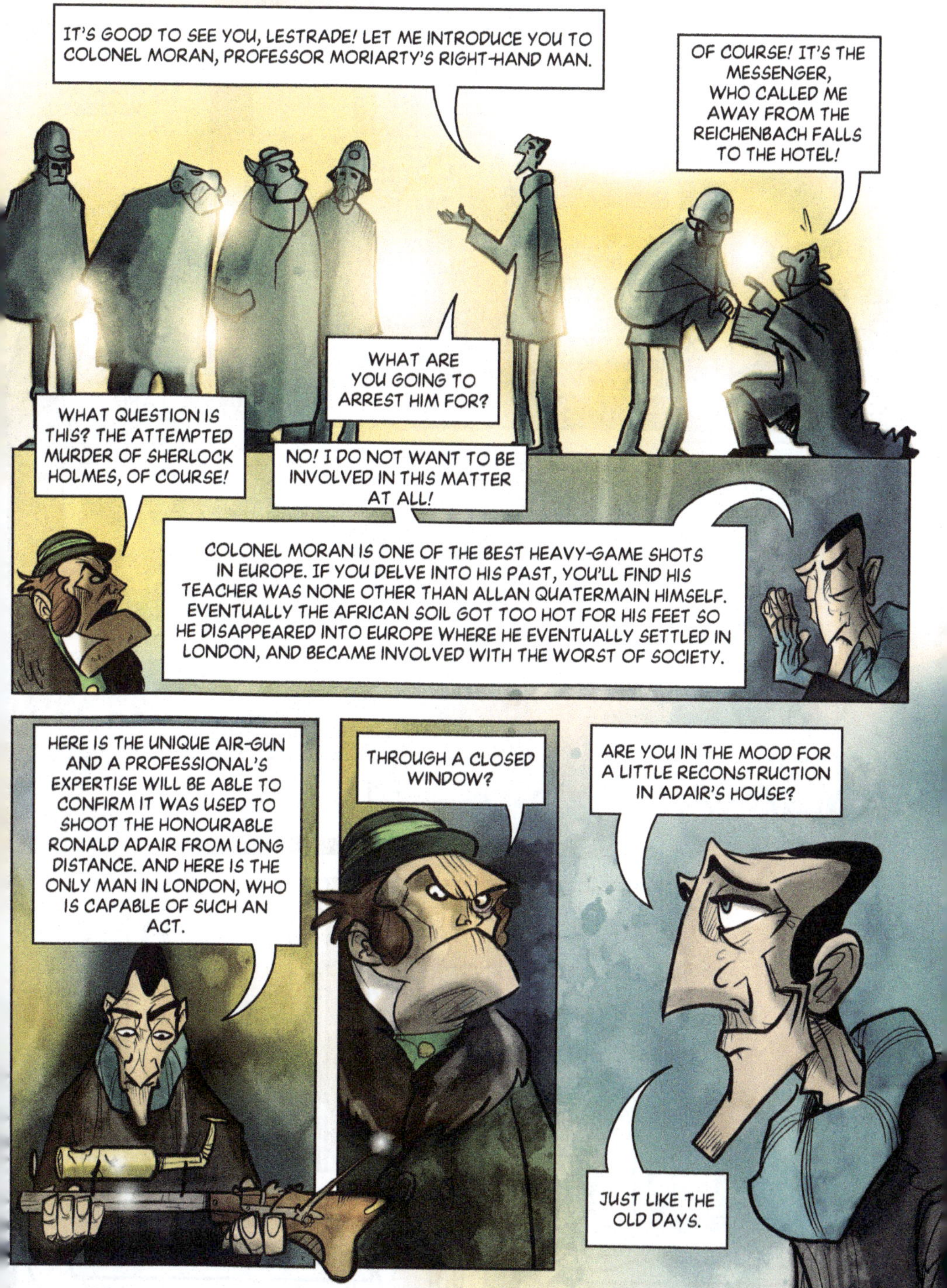
IT'S GOOD TO SEE YOU, LESTRADE! LET ME INTRODUCE YOU TO COLONEL MORAN, PROFESSOR MORIARTY'S RIGHT-HAND MAN.
OF COURSE! IT'S THE MESSENGER, WHO CALLED ME AWAY FROM THE REICHENBACH FALLS TO THE HOTEL!
WHAT ARE YOU GOING TO ARREST HIM FOR?
WHAT QUESTION IS THIS? THE ATTEMPTED MURDER OF SHERLOCK HOLMES, OF COURSE!
NO! I DO NOT WANT TO BE INVOLVED IN THIS MATTER AT ALL!
COLONEL MORAN IS ONE OF THE BEST HEAVY-GAME SHOTS IN EUROPE. IF YOU DELVE INTO HIS PAST, YOU'LL FIND HIS TEACHER WAS NONE OTHER THAN ALLAN QUATERMAIN HIMSELF. EVENTUALLY THE AFRICAN SOIL GOT TOO HOT FOR HIS FEET SO HE DISAPPEARED INTO EUROPE WHERE HE EVENTUALLY SETTLED IN LONDON, AND BECAME INVOLVED WITH THE WORST OF SOCIETY.
HERE IS THE UNIQUE AIR-GUN AND A PROFESSIONAL'S EXPERTISE WILL BE ABLE TO CONFIRM IT WAS USED TO SHOOT THE HONOURABLE RONALD ADAIR FROM LONG DISTANCE. AND HERE IS THE ONLY MAN IN LONDON, WHO IS CAPABLE OF SUCH AN ACT.
THROUGH A CLOSED WINDOW?
ARE YOU IN THE MOOD FOR A LITTLE RECONSTRUCTION IN ADAIR'S HOUSE?
JUST LIKE THE OLD DAYS.

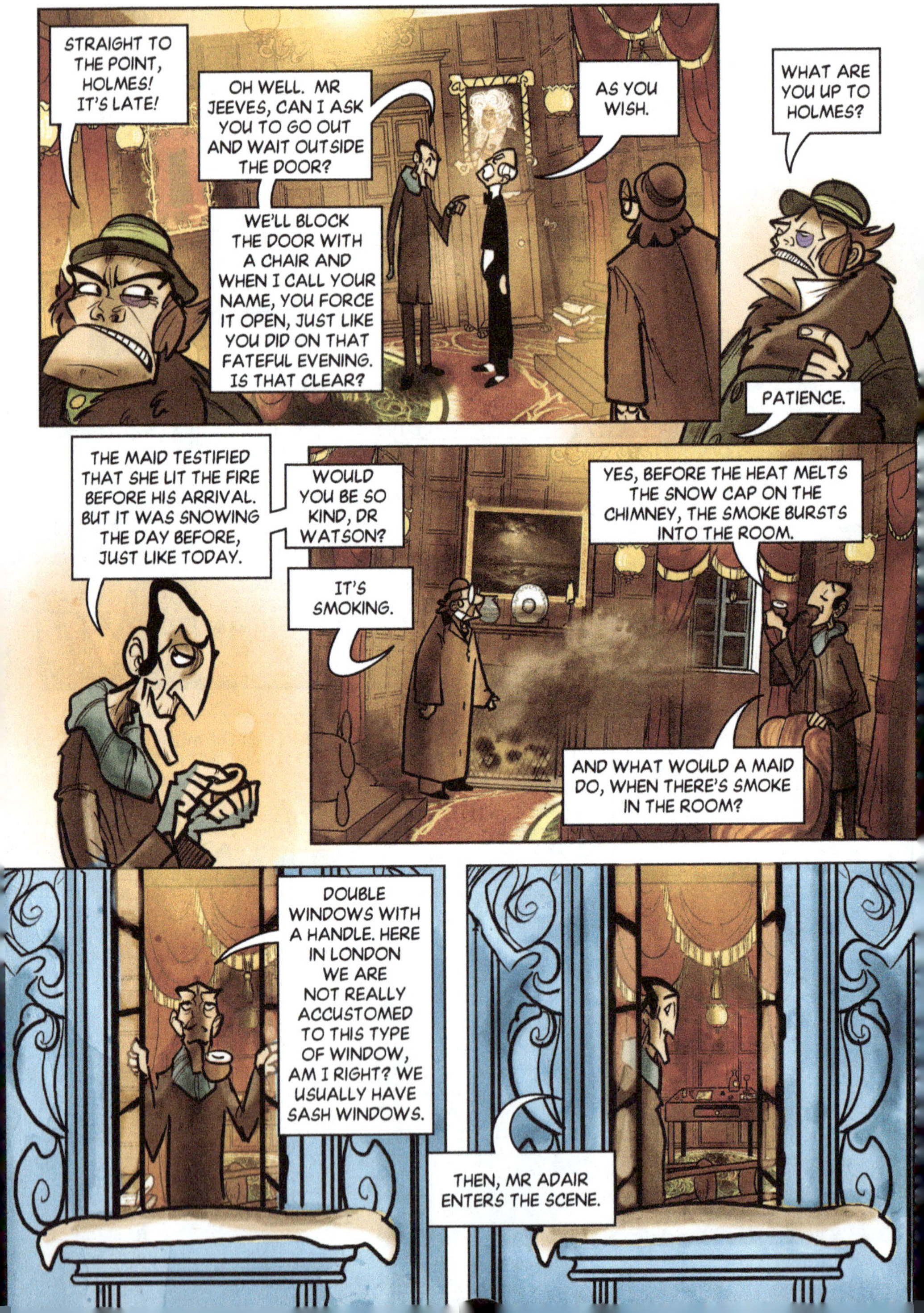

STRAIGHT TO THE POINT, HOLMES! IT'S LATE!
OH WELL. MR JEEVES, CAN I ASK YOU TO GO OUT AND WAIT OUTSIDE THE DOOR?
WE'LL BLOCK THE DOOR WITH A CHAIR AND WHEN I CALL YOUR NAME, YOU FORCE IT OPEN, JUST LIKE YOU DID ON THAT FATEFUL EVENING. IS THAT CLEAR?
AS YOU WISH.
WHAT ARE YOU UP TO HOLMES?
PATIENCE.
THE MAID TESTIFIED THAT SHE LIT THE FIRE BEFORE HIS ARRIVAL. BUT IT WAS SNOWING THE DAY BEFORE, JUST LIKE TODAY.
WOULD YOU BE SO KIND, DR WATSON?
IT'S SMOKING.
YES, BEFORE THE HEAT MELTS THE SNOW CAP ON THE CHIMNEY, THE SMOKE BURSTS INTO THE ROOM.
AND WHAT WOULD A MAID DO, WHEN THERE'S SMOKE IN THE ROOM?
DOUBLE WINDOWS WITH A HANDLE. HERE IN LONDON WE ARE NOT REALLY ACCUSTOMED TO THIS TYPE OF WINDOW, AM I RIGHT? WE USUALLY HAVE SASH WINDOWS.
THEN, MR ADAIR ENTERS THE SCENE.

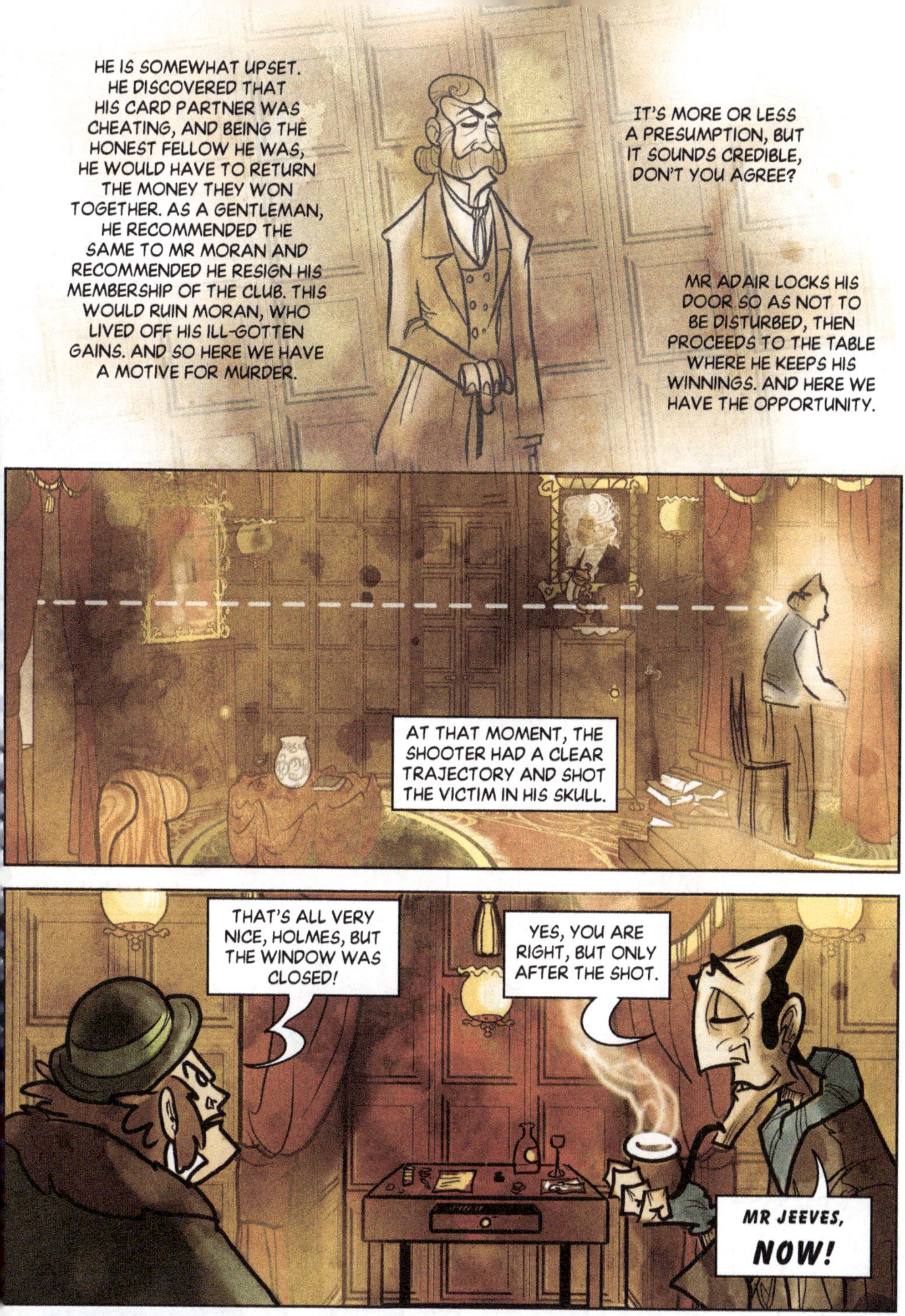
HE IS SOMEWHAT UPSET. HE DISCOVERED THAT HIS CARD PARTNER WAS CHEATING, AND BEING THE HONEST FELLOW HE WAS, HE WOULD HAVE TO RETURN THE MONEY THEY WON TOGETHER. AS A GENTLEMAN, HE RECOMMENDED THE SAME TO MR MORAN AND RECOMMENDED HE RESIGN HIS MEMBERSHIP OF THE CLUB. THIS WOULD RUIN MORAN, WHO LIVED OFF HIS ILL-GOTTEN GAINS. AND SO HERE WE HAVE A MOTIVE FOR MURDER.
IT'S MORE OR LESS A PRESUMPTION, BUT IT SOUNDS CREDIBLE, DON'T YOU AGREE?
MR ADAIR LOCKS HIS DOOR SO AS NOT TO BE DISTURBED, THEN PROCEEDS TO THE TABLE WHERE HE KEEPS HIS WINNINGS. AND HERE WE HAVE THE OPPORTUNITY.
AT THAT MOMENT, THE SHOOTER HAD A CLEAR TRAJECTORY AND SHOT THE VICTIM IN HIS SKULL.
THAT'S ALL VERY NICE, HOLMES, BUT THE WINDOW WAS CLOSED!
YES, YOU ARE RIGHT, BUT ONLY AFTER THE SHOT.
MR JEEVES, NOW!

CRASH!

BANG!

CLICK!

DRAUGHT!?

BUT THAT WAS SO ELEMENTARY!

YES. IT'S OFTEN THE CASE. FANCIFUL THEORIES ALWAYS LOOK MORE ATTRACTIVE THAN THE SIMPLE TRUTH.

IF YOU'VE NEVER BEEN HERE BEFORE, HOW DID YOU FIGURE IT OUT?

WHEN YOU ELIMINATE THE IMPOSSIBLE, WHATEVER REMAINS AND HOWEVER IMPROBABLE, IS PROBABLY TRUE.

TO BE CLEAR, THE CAPTURE OF COLONEL MORAN IS **YOUR** CLAIM TO FAME. I DO NOT WISH TO HAVE MY NAME ASSOCIATED WITH THIS CASE.

IN THAT CASE: WELCOME BACK, HOLMES.

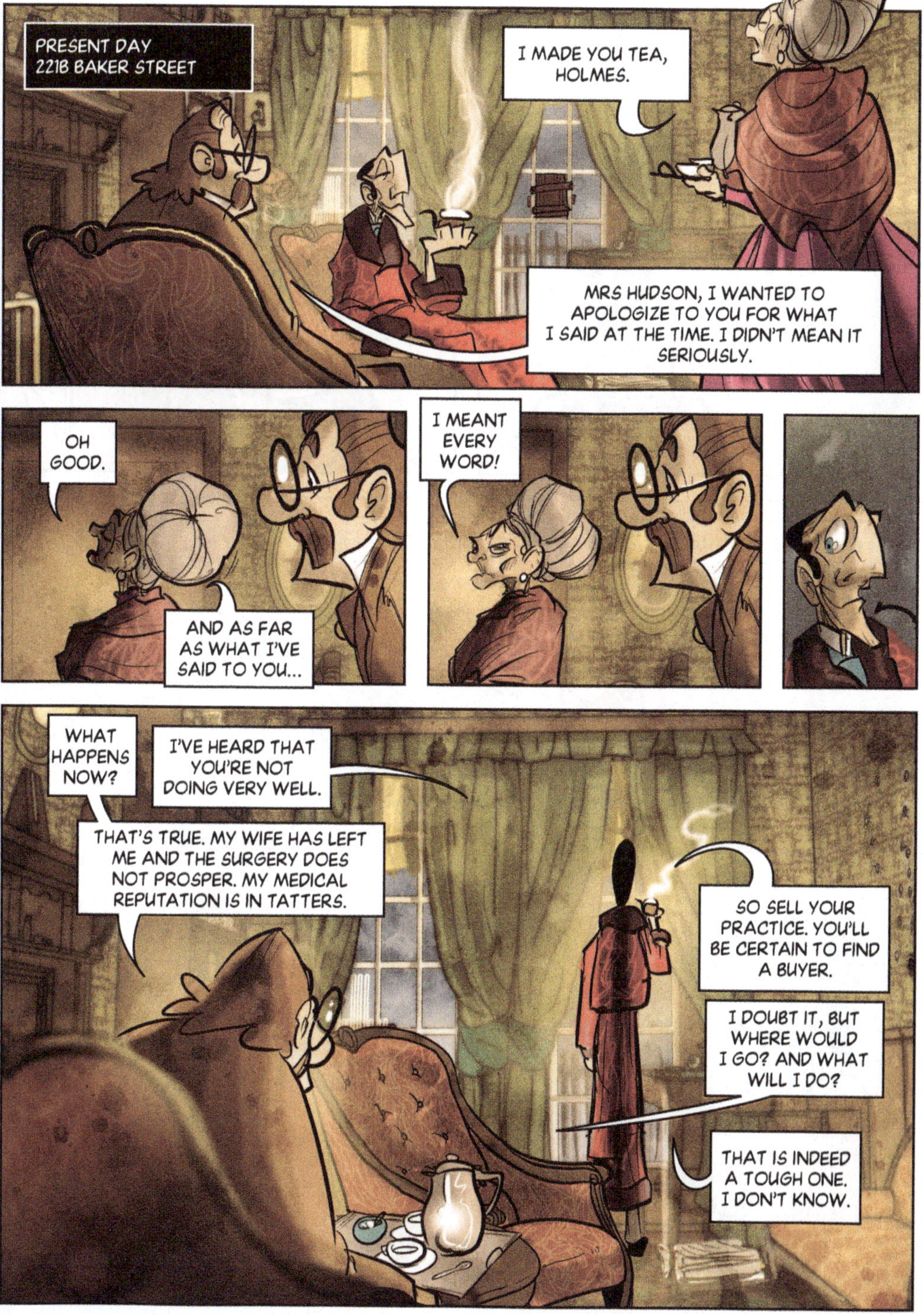
PRESENT DAY
221B BAKER STREET
I MADE YOU TEA, HOLMES.
MRS HUDSON, I WANTED TO APOLOGIZE TO YOU FOR WHAT I SAID AT THE TIME. I DIDN'T MEAN IT SERIOUSLY.
OH GOOD.
AND AS FAR AS WHAT I'VE SAID TO YOU...
I MEANT EVERY WORD!
WHAT HAPPENS NOW?
I'VE HEARD THAT YOU'RE NOT DOING VERY WELL.
THAT'S TRUE. MY WIFE HAS LEFT ME AND THE SURGERY DOES NOT PROSPER. MY MEDICAL REPUTATION IS IN TATTERS.
SO SELL YOUR PRACTICE. YOU'LL BE CERTAIN TO FIND A BUYER.
I DOUBT IT, BUT WHERE WOULD I GO? AND WHAT WILL I DO?
THAT IS INDEED A TOUGH ONE. I DON'T KNOW.

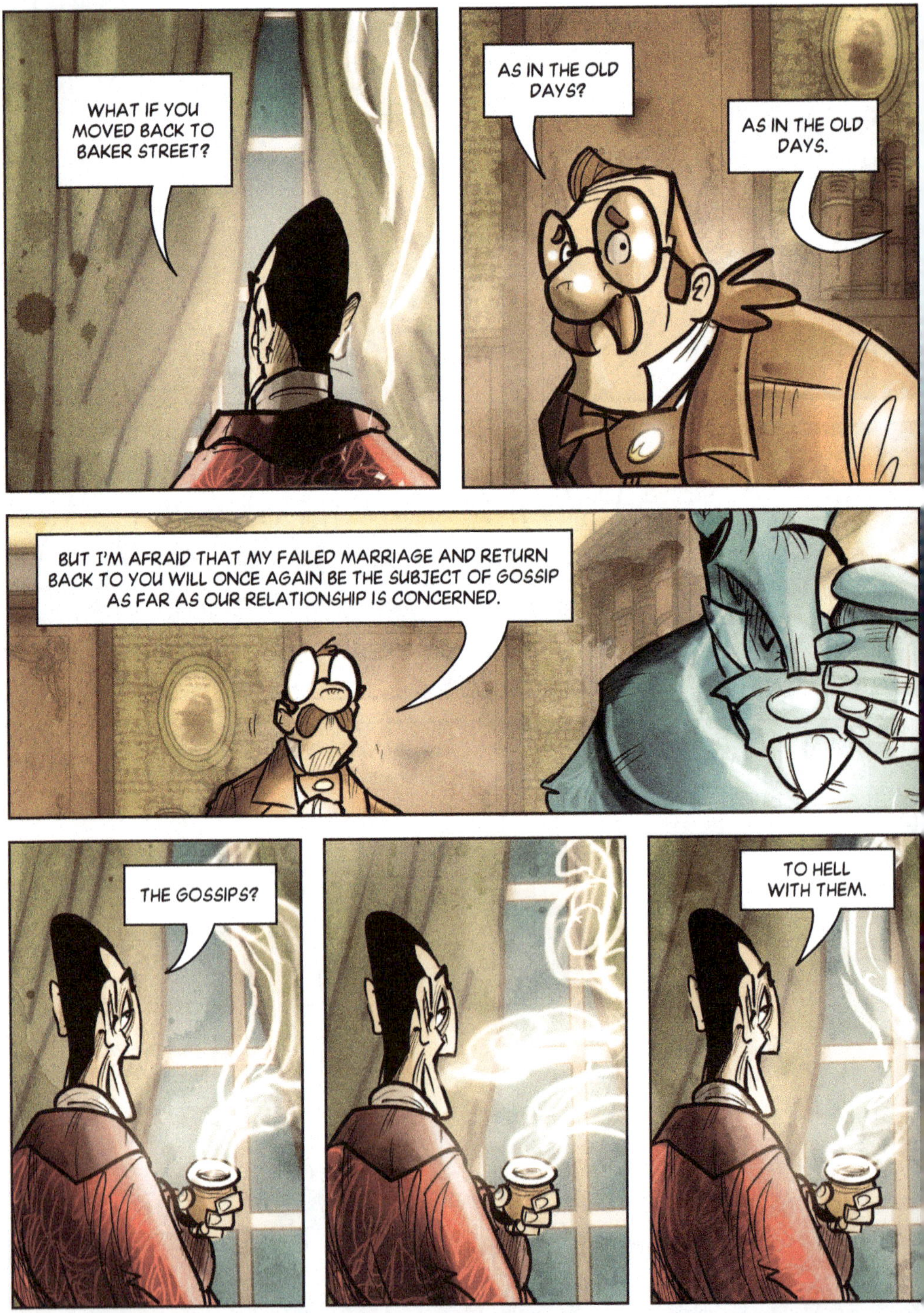
WHAT IF YOU MOVED BACK TO BAKER STREET?
AS IN THE OLD DAYS?
AS IN THE OLD DAYS.
BUT I'M AFRAID THAT MY FAILED MARRIAGE AND RETURN BACK TO YOU WILL ONCE AGAIN BE THE SUBJECT OF GOSSIP AS FAR AS OUR RELATIONSHIP IS CONCERNED.
THE GOSSIPS?
TO HELL WITH THEM.

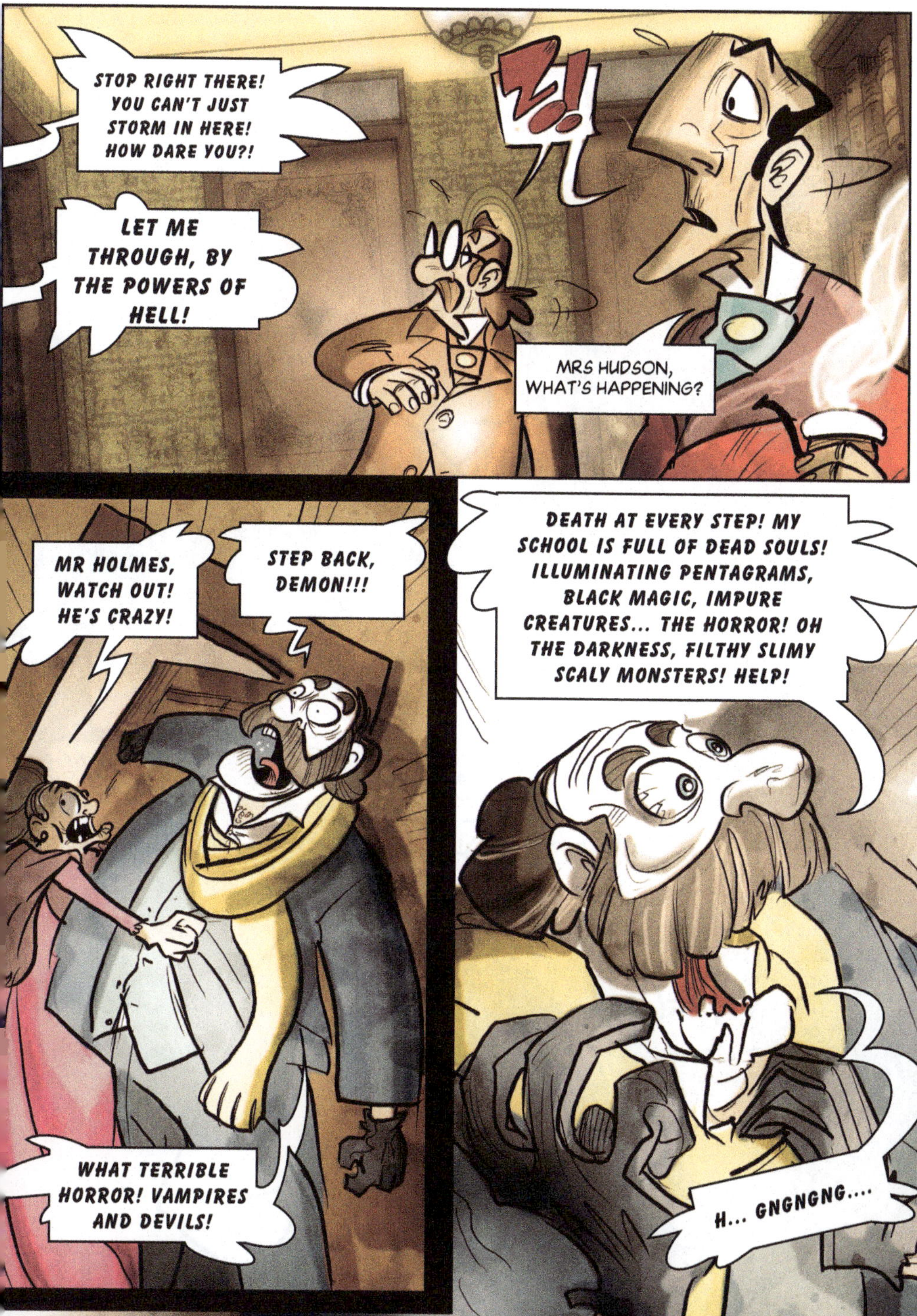
STOP RIGHT THERE! YOU CAN'T JUST STORM IN HERE! HOW DARE YOU?!
Z!
LET ME THROUGH, BY THE POWERS OF HELL!
MRS HUDSON, WHAT'S HAPPENING?
MR HOLMES, WATCH OUT! HE'S CRAZY!
STEP BACK, DEMON!!!
WHAT TERRIBLE HORROR! VAMPIRES AND DEVILS!
DEATH AT EVERY STEP! MY SCHOOL IS FULL OF DEAD SOULS! ILLUMINATING PENTAGRAMS, BLACK MAGIC, IMPURE CREATURES... THE HORROR! OH THE DARKNESS, FILTHY SLIMY SCALY MONSTERS! HELP!
H... GNGNGNG....

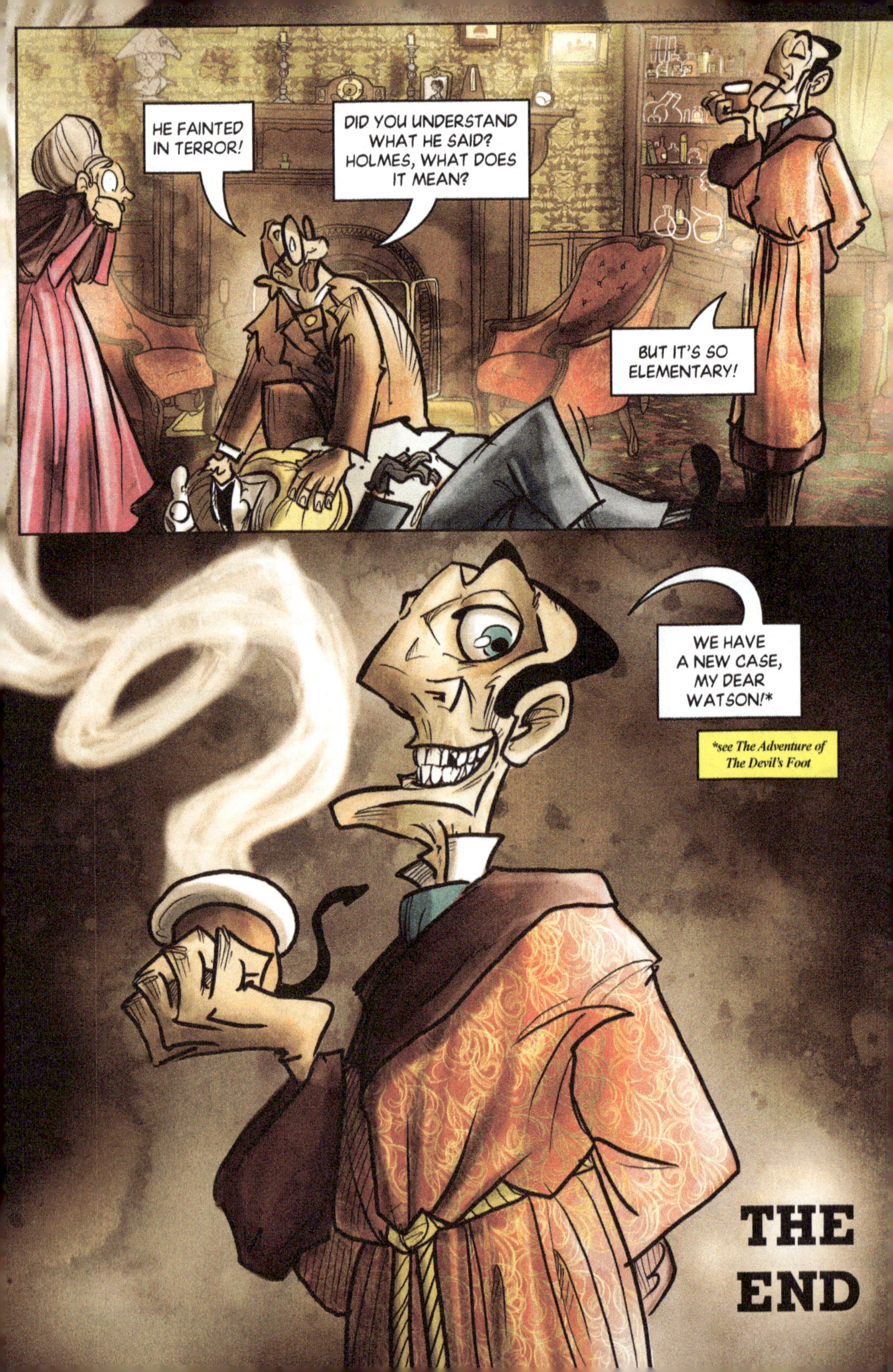
HE FAINTED IN TERROR!
DID YOU UNDERSTAND WHAT HE SAID? HOLMES, WHAT DOES IT MEAN?
BUT IT'S SO ELEMENTARY!
WE HAVE A NEW CASE, MY DEAR WATSON!*
*see The Adventure of The Devil's Foot
THE END

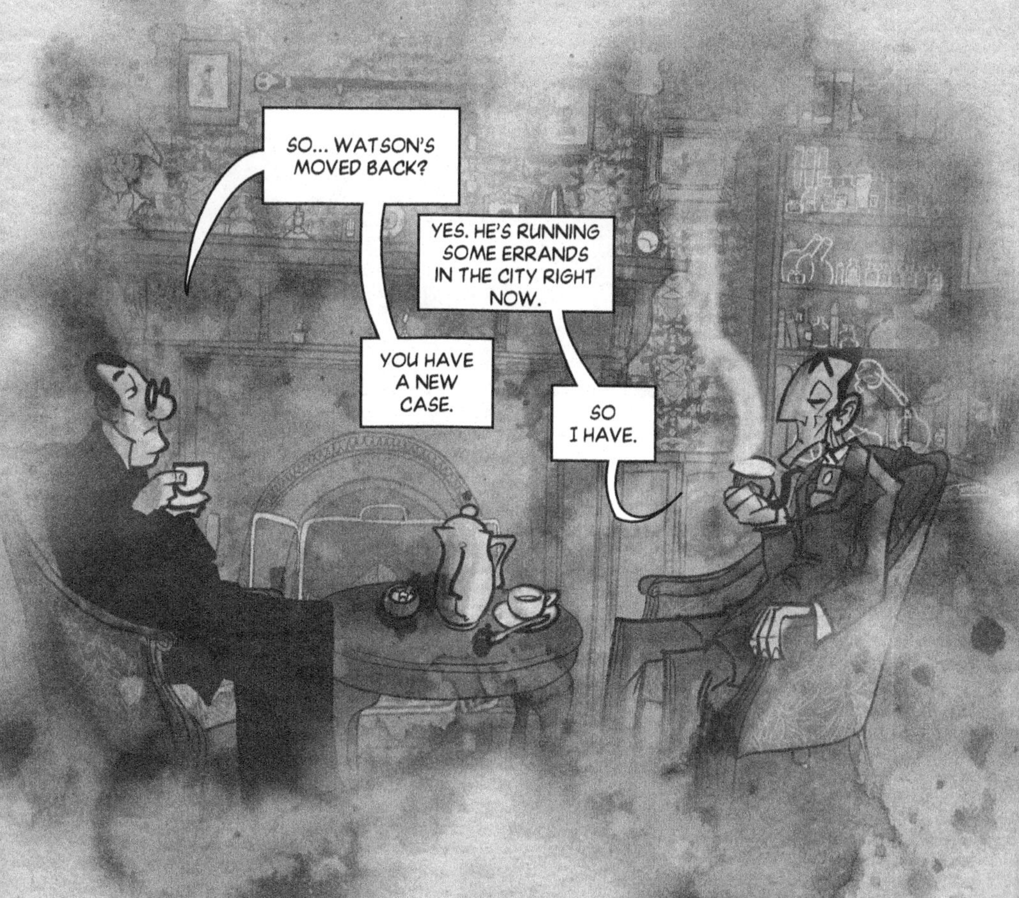
SO... WATSON'S MOVED BACK?
YES. HE'S RUNNING SOME ERRANDS IN THE CITY RIGHT NOW.
YOU HAVE A NEW CASE.
SO I HAVE.

EPILOGUE

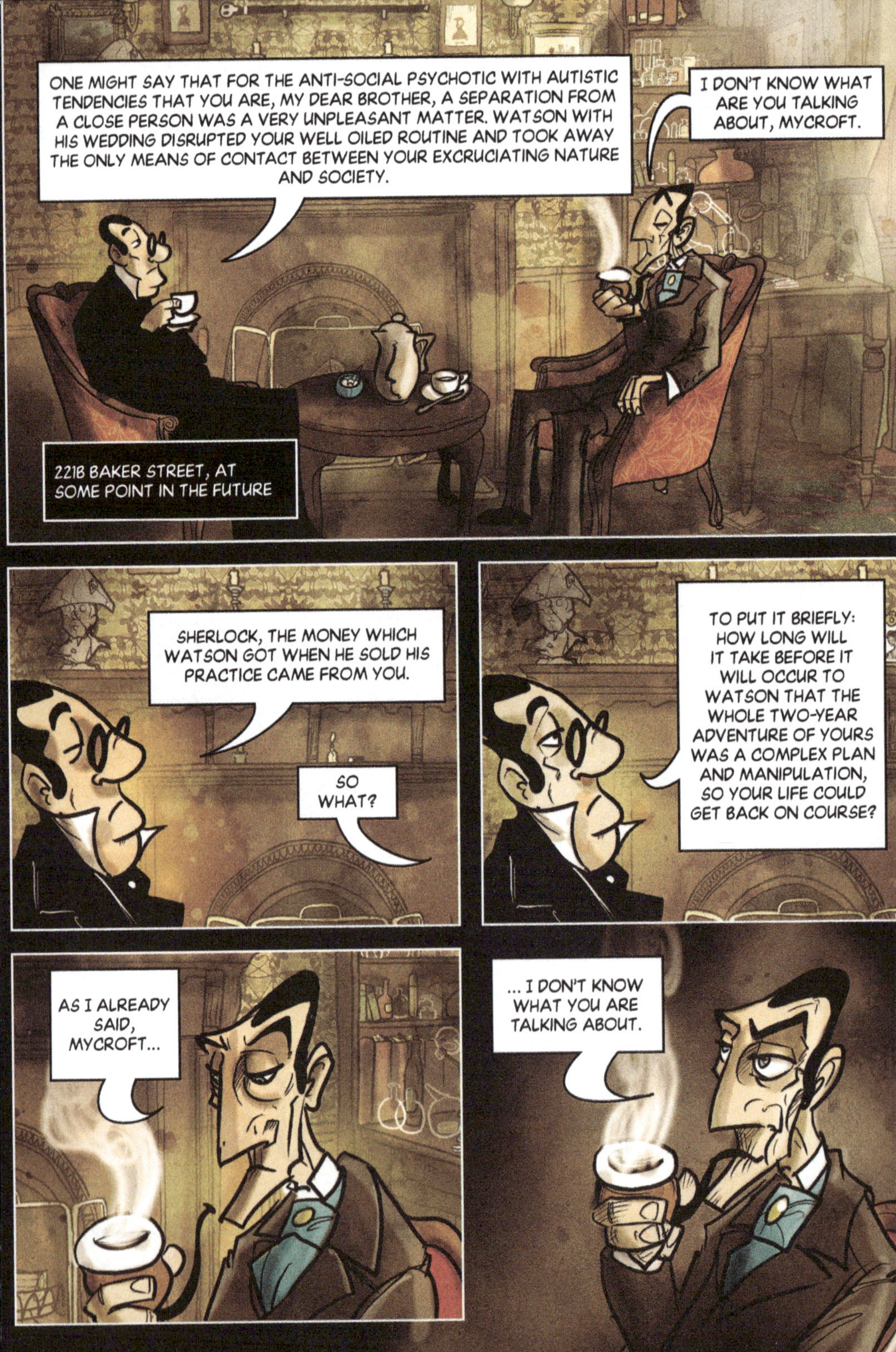
ONE MIGHT SAY THAT FOR THE ANTI-SOCIAL PSYCHOTIC WITH AUTISTIC TENDENCIES THAT YOU ARE, MY DEAR BROTHER, A SEPARATION FROM A CLOSE PERSON WAS A VERY UNPLEASANT MATTER. WATSON WITH HIS WEDDING DISRUPTED YOUR WELL OILED ROUTINE AND TOOK AWAY THE ONLY MEANS OF CONTACT BETWEEN YOUR EXCRUCIATING NATURE AND SOCIETY.
I DON'T KNOW WHAT ARE YOU TALKING ABOUT, MYCROFT.
221B BAKER STREET, AT SOME POINT IN THE FUTURE
SHERLOCK, THE MONEY WHICH WATSON GOT WHEN HE SOLD HIS PRACTICE CAME FROM YOU.
SO WHAT?
TO PUT IT BRIEFLY: HOW LONG WILL IT TAKE BEFORE IT WILL OCCUR TO WATSON THAT THE WHOLE TWO-YEAR ADVENTURE OF YOURS WAS A COMPLEX PLAN AND MANIPULATION, SO YOUR LIFE COULD GET BACK ON COURSE?
AS I ALREADY SAID, MYCROFT...
... I DON'T KNOW WHAT YOU ARE TALKING ABOUT.

Gallery of covers

SIR ARTHUR CONAN DOYLE
SHERLOCK HOLMES
POSLEDNÍ PŘÍPAD

Alternative cover to this book

SHERLOCK HOLMES
COMICS
58/1999
THE HAND GLASS OF SHERLOCK HOLMES INCLUDED!
"COMIC I HAVE NEVER SEEN!!"
PETR BIRIAN DIRECTOR OF VASHICA STUDIO
VERONIKA VALKOVA INTERVIEW
80 PAGES!!!
THE BEST WORK OF SIR ARTHUR CONAN DOYLE
BLACKMAILER
PRELUDE OF THE FINAL PROBLEM!

SHERLOCK HOLMES
COMICS
59/2000
THE FIGURE OF MORI-ARTY INCLUDED!
ING. KOLO-DRUBEC THE PRESIDENT OF CSSH
"STIRRING AND IMPRESSIVE!"
100 PAGES!
THE BEST WORK OF SIR ARTHUR CONAN DOYLE
THE FINAL PROBLEM
THE DEATH OF SHERLOCK HOLMES!

COMPE-TITION!
DR. WATSON
COMICS
60/2000
THE FIGURE OF ROBOT INCLUDED!
80 PAGES!
THE BEST WORK OF SIR ARTHUR CONAN DOYLE
THE ADVENTURE OF THE EMPTY HOUSE

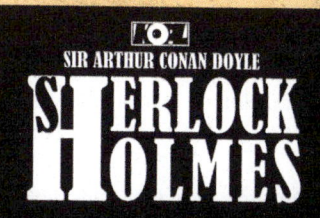

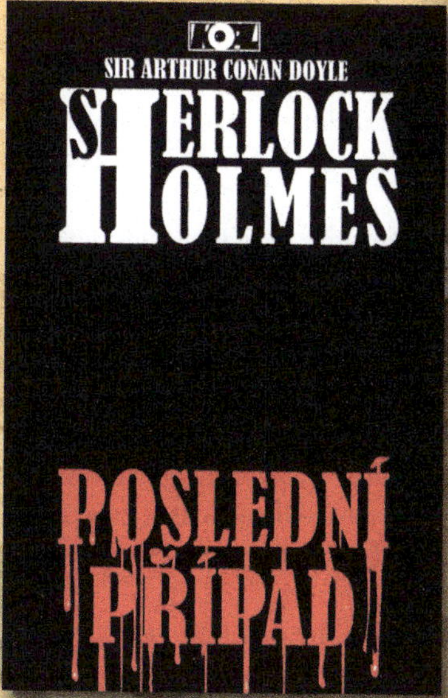

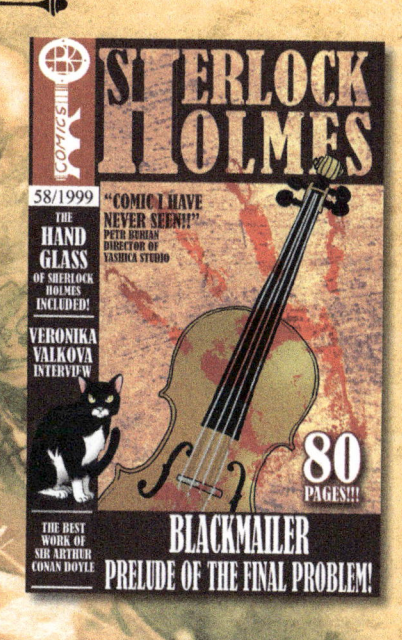

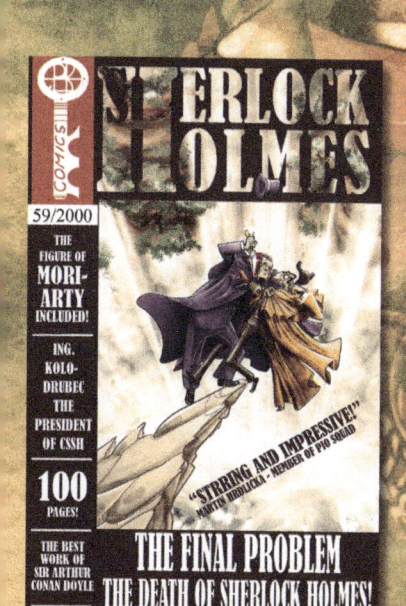

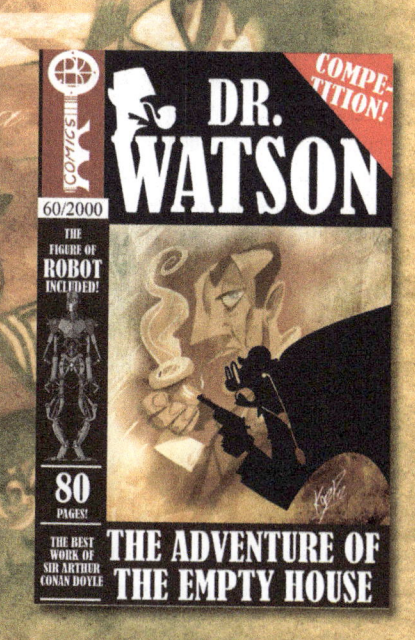

Afterword

So, it's now done. And I just fulfilled a childhood dream. From the first encounter with the king of all detectives I yearned to create a comic book based on this excellent work, despite it being rejected in terms of artistic value. In fact, Sir Arthur succeeded (and let's believe that he did so unintentionally) in doing something unprecedented at that time. He created the epitome of a genius detective, who was not the first in a series of criminologists and adventurers of that time, but in many respects was distinguished by his very nature and completely devoted to his interest. Readers fell in love with him and demanded more and more adventures, until Sir Arthur became fed up with his hero. Holmes completely ruthlessly and selfishly eclipsed all other literary works of that time, many of which were of a higher quality than the pulp fiction, and let's face it, even somewhat infantile and naive stories of the famous detective. So, what to do about it? There was only one option: Holmes dies.

If however, Sir Arthur intended to get rid of his hero, he made a considerable mistake. He let him die a hero's death. When the Final Problem was published, the readers got a hell of a shock. This is how it is with the death of your favourite heroes: Every reader wants to know what it would be like, if... their hero had to encounter someone equal to their own shadow or even someone who is more capable and stronger. And yes, we want to know what it would be like if the hero died. But in reality, we don't really want it to happen. It is therefore not surprising that people expressed real grief over the death of the detective and wore black arm bands in memoriam. Even the Queen herself reportedly expressed her indignation over the loss of a favourite literary character. This only proves (as someone once said before me) that people should not break their toys, no matter how much they desire to find out what it would be like without them.

Public pressure grew to an intolerable level and Sir Arthur was eventually forced to resurrect his hero. Maybe it's just my gut feeling, but if we look closely at the story of The Empty House, we can but note that the story is somewhat ill-conceived and as if it was written against the will of the author. Minor inconsistencies, however, will not prevent the die-hard fan that I am from becoming emotional upon reacquainting myself with my favourite hero.

Sherlock Holmes demonstrates an extraordinary toughness in our minds when it comes to survival and for a literary figure, perhaps way too much. It seems to me that Sir Arthur tried to get rid of him once more when he attributed so many negative qualities to him, beginning with his excruciating nature and ending with his cocaine addiction. One would have assumed that the readers would have quickly grown tired of this man. Wrong again. In this way, the author fills the almost empty shell of a character that was partly occupied by honour and partly by the genius of an investigator while giving the character a human dimension. With this, he breathed life into his character and sealed Holmes's almost immortal destiny. The character survived its author, and although more than one hundred years have passed since his first adventure, his supporters are unwilling to believe in his death.

And this is the reason why the next time a Sherlockian asks you if Sherlock Holmes is still alive, the only possible and correct answer is: "Of course!"

Holmes got into my head too. If the same happened to you with a literary character, then you know how easy it is to come to believe that you know the answers that character would give and how they would react to certain situations. Therefore, be it forgiven that I have amended Sherlock a little, not only to fit him into my Victoria Regina series, but so he met my expectations. I have broached some of the questions that had troubled Sherlockians for a long time, but I do not have the answers, since only Sir Arthur Conan Doyle holds that right. I could have prepared some puzzles that you could solve yourself, but you would probably choose to ignore them because they are not important to the story. Once again the storyline introduces characters from my other Victorian comic books that are already published or are in the pipeline. They are discreetly hidden, and can be found if you make the effort, so as not to interfere with the plot. This book in the Victoria Regina series, more than the others, has touched on the Czech literary scene. Good luck in your search.

Here are my three outstanding questions for those die-hard readers that enjoy such mysteries:

1. After the disappearance of his brother, Mycroft Holmes took three things from the study. Those of you who noticed what they were, probably realized that Holmes is alive and that he sent his brother for the items. Therefore, Mycroft knew that Sherlock's death was staged. But what were the items? It's easy, just look at what has gone from the study. Nevertheless, while two of those items can be easily identified, the third will require investigative work involving the previous book, The Hound of the Baskervilles.

2. Yet, it will be much harder to figure out what weighs on the conscience of Dr Watson. What was in the documents they took from Milverton's safe? What was in the red folder bearing the doctor's name? I am afraid that Sir Arthur did not write about this and I admit that I added this purely to offset Holmes's negative characteristics and deepen the friendship of the two men to an even more intense level. Clue: Look for an answer in the actual history of the First Boer War.

3. This is actually two questions. There are two incognito characters in the blackmailer's story. However, you can find out what was the secret of the singer Emilia Marty, and you can also find out the full name of Lady Eva, whose honour was so valiantly defended by Holmes and Watson, and also what happened to her engagement.

Good luck with your investigation!

Acknowledgement

To my parents who have never hesitated to support me and encourage me in everything I have ever done. I realize more and more that this cannot be taken for granted and that it is one hundred times more valuable than all the money in the world.

To Bohouš Dvořák, without whom I would not be who I am, but possibly I would not be at all. We must value friends that will make us realize who we are.

To Yashica Studio for their continual support and patience.

Finally, to Aleš Kolodrubec, Jayantika Ganguly, Miroslav Balabán and Jan Anděl and his family for much kind advice, help and support.

OTHER BOOKS
BY PETR KOPL IN ENGLISH

Sir Arthur Conan Doyle
Petr Kopl
SHERLOCK HOLMES
A SCANDAL IN BOHEMIA

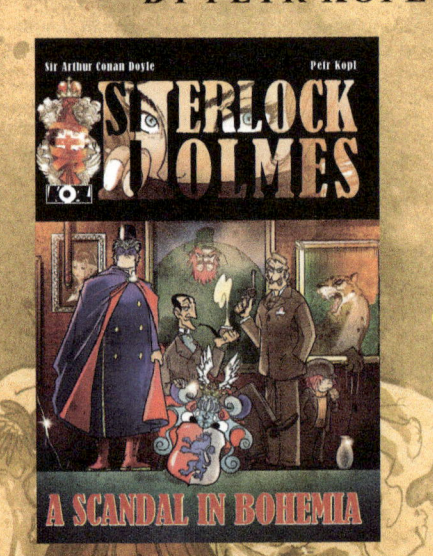

FABULA RASA
Czech Award
for the best screenplay,
the best artwork
and the best
comic book
of 2013

VICTORIA REGINA
THE LOST WORLD
BASED ON SIR ARTHUR CONAN DOYLE
CREATED BY PETR KOPL

Sir Arthur Conan Doyle
Petr Kopl
SHERLOCK HOLMES
THE HOUND OF THE BASKERVILLES

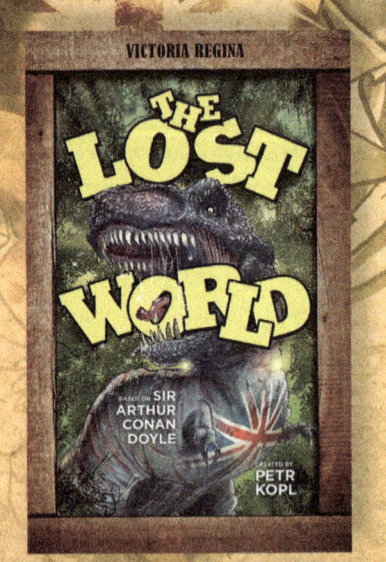

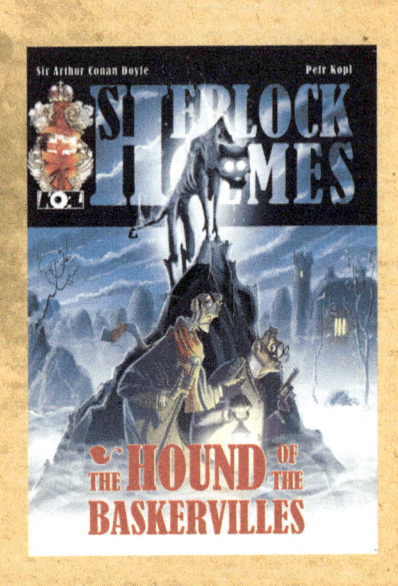

BECOME A COMIC BOOK HERO!

This comic book was created as a result of the support from backers at Kickstarter. One of the prizes was the chance to play a supporting role in the comic book. Oh yes, even you can play alongside the immortal Sherlock Holmes and take part in his story. All you need to do is to follow the future activities of MX Publishing in order to have this opportunity.

Mr Joe Lee, pictured right took his chance and now plays the role of the policeman on page 180. He says: "You are under arrest, sir!"

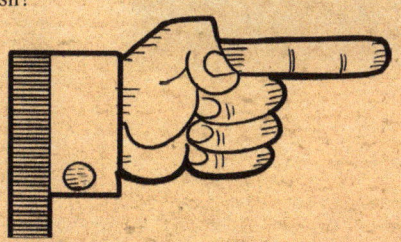

OTHER
MX GRAPHIC NOVELS

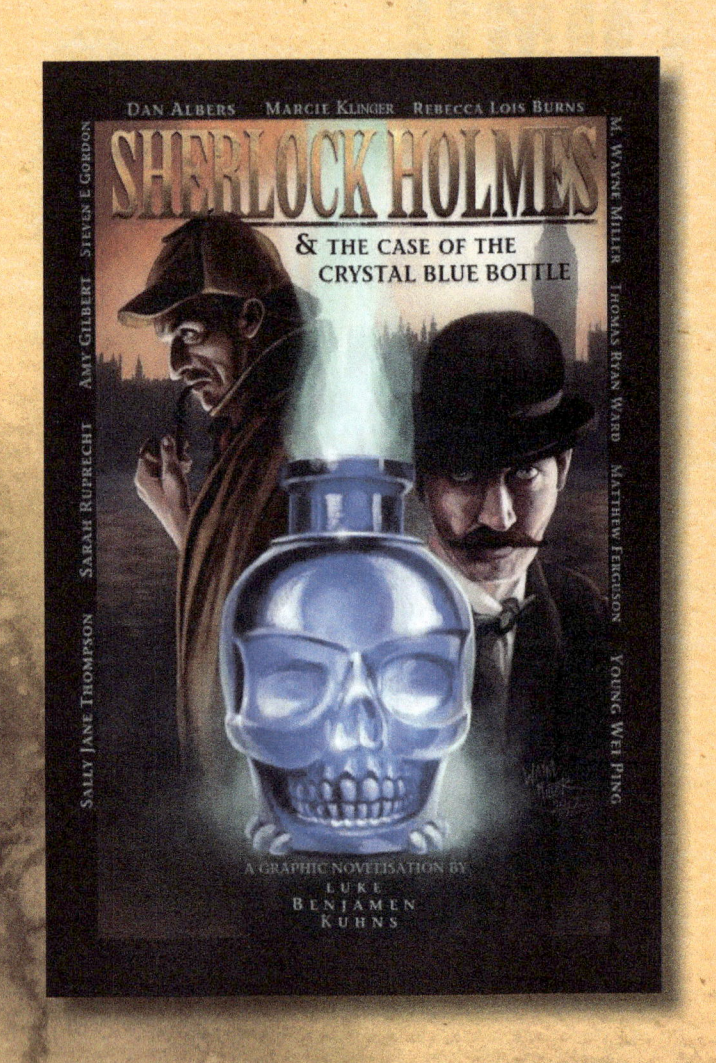

OTHER
MX GRAPHIC NOVELS

SHERLOCK HOLMES AND THE HORROR OF FRANKENSTEIN

Luke Benjamen Kuhns
Marcie Klinger

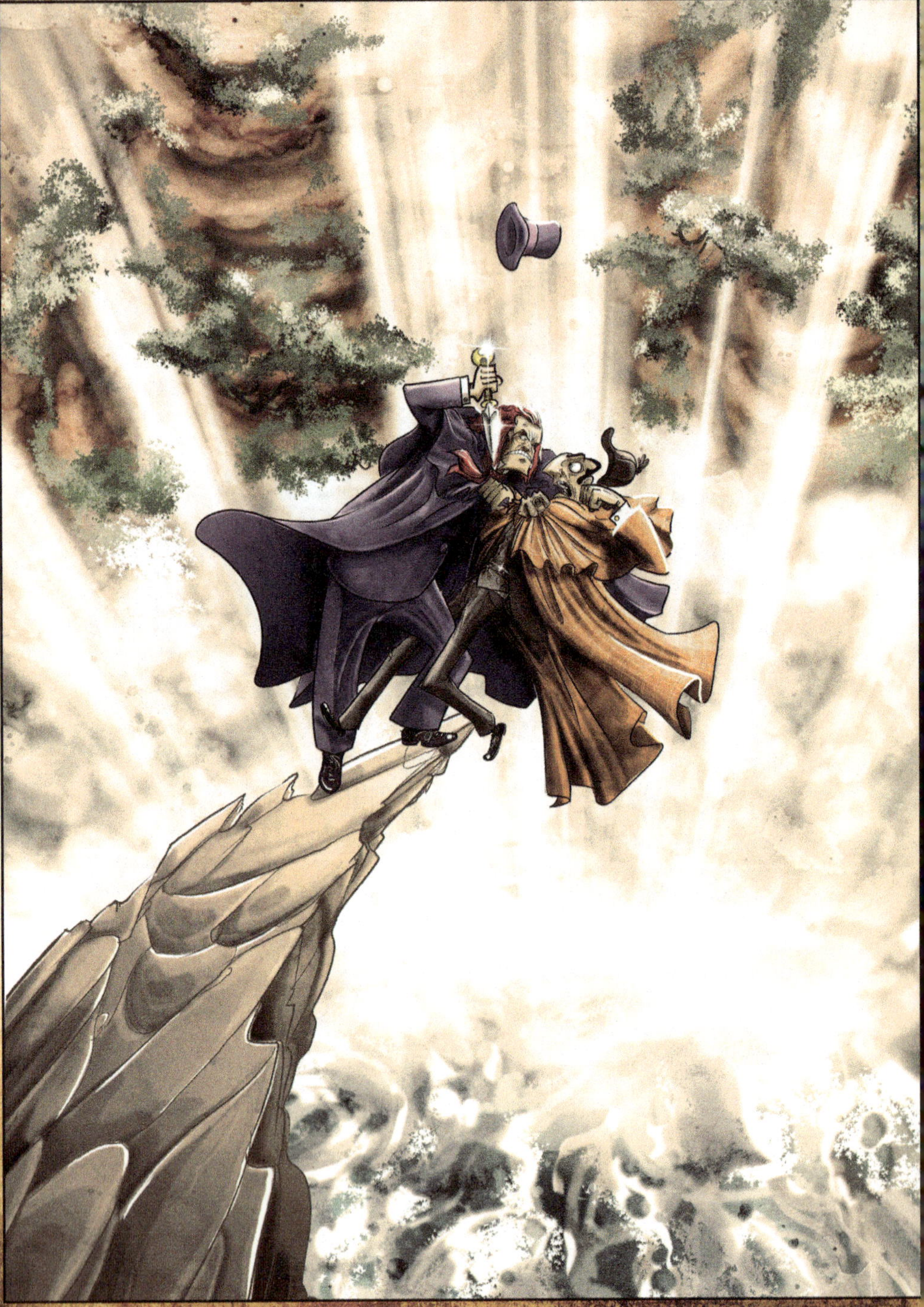

MANY BONUS FEATURES CAN BE FOUND AT
WWW.PETRKOPL.CZ

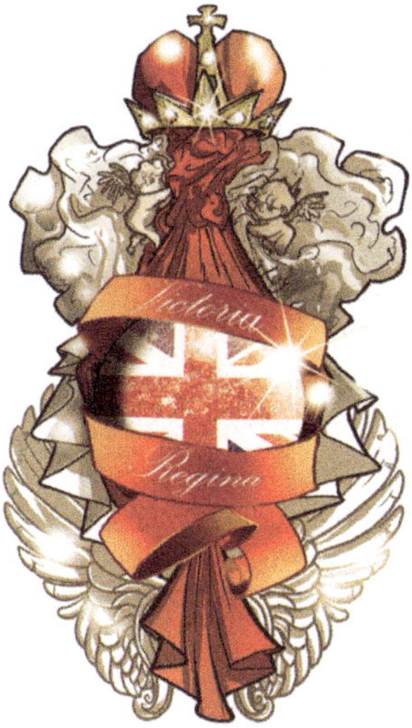
Victoria
Regina

Lightning Source UK Ltd.
Milton Keynes UK
UKOW07f1220071116
287013UK00005B/13/P

9 781780 928357